Sarah Shatz

Hyatt Bass wrote, directed, and produced the film *75 Degrees in July,* which was released in 2006. *The Embers* is her first novel.

The
Embers

The Embers

A NOVEL

Hyatt Bass

PICADOR

Henry Holt and Company

New York

www.picadorusa.com

Picador® is a U.S. registered trademark and is used by Henry Holt and Company under license from Pan Books Limited.

For information on Picador Reading Group Guides, please contact Picador. E-mail: readinggroupguides@picadorusa.com

Designed by Meryl Sussman Levavi

The Library of Congress has cataloged the Henry Holt edition as follows:

Bass, Hyatt.
    The Embers : a novel / Hyatt Bass.—1st ed.
        p. cm.
    ISBN 978-0-8050-8994-3
    1. Upper East Side (New York, N.Y.)—Fiction.   2. Upper-class families—Fiction.   3. Domestic fiction.   4. Psychological fiction.   I. Title.
    PS3602.A847515E63   2009
    813'.6—dc22

                                                        200804336

Picador ISBN 978-0-312-42971-3

First published in the United States by Henry Holt and Company

First Picador Edition: June 2010

10 9 8 7 6 5 4 3 2 1

For Josh,

my blazing hearth

The Embers

Fall

2007

IT WAS ODD HOW QUICKLY NATURE RECLAIMED the land. Emily stepped out of the car and headed into the grass. Where the house used to be, there was only meadow now—her family's own piece of rolling Berkshire hills.

Ahead, the trees stretched black and bare against the sky. Though it was the end of October, she'd hoped to catch at least a few scarlet maple leaves and pick the last apples of the season. She glanced at Clay, wandering aimlessly with his hands in his coat pockets. There was something about the way he looked, angled against the wind in his wool jacket, that reminded her of an old Bob Dylan album her dad used to have. Dylan if he were half-Korean and had come to New York for a finance job instead of rock and roll. Her hair blowing across her face, she started toward him, then stopped as her eyes fell on a rusted metal rod sticking up out of a block of cement.

Trying to orient herself, she began slowly mapping out the first floor: were the walls still standing, she'd be in the kitchen right now. She could see the whole room in her head—the big wooden table, the fireplace, the old fridge—could practically even see her brother, Thomas, slicing mushrooms at the counter. What would he think of that guy over there? She saw herself leading Clay into the room. *Hey,* her brother would say, wiping his hands on his pants before reaching out to shake, *really great to meet you.* Thomas would set Clay at ease immediately, and before she knew it the two of them, her brother and her boyfriend, would be cooking together, experimenting and laughing at the stove. At some point, her mother would come in all aflutter, carrying a basket of herbs and flowers from the garden. *My God! When did you get here? I never heard you pull in*—trying to mask her surprise as she registered Clay's Asian-American features. *Your father's upstairs, of course, working. Don't bother him just yet.*

According to the laws of science, neither mass nor energy is created or destroyed; the total amount in the universe always remains constant. And fundamentally, Emily understood this. But, as she moved through the knee-high grass, which used to be the kitchen and used to be animated by four lives—one of which was no longer being lived—she could not fathom where it had all gone. Was the energy still there? And what of Thomas? How did the laws of conservation apply to him?

Following the pattern of cement blocks, she circled the periphery of the house, mentally rebuilding and refurnishing each room. There was the bathroom with the pedestal sink, where she'd fallen and chipped a tooth while she and Thomas were horsing around; her bedroom where she retreated to write poetry and listen to music, but mostly to get away from her mother; and the living room with the couch in front of the fire.

For the first time, the actual destruction of the house didn't have the feeling of something that had happened to her personally. It felt instead like an epic or a myth. And it *was* mythic, really, the way her father had destroyed everything: his house, his family, and of course most tragically, his son. In retrospect, it all seemed inevitable, as if fate had destined things to be so and had never offered the possibility of them happening any other way.

"So, I guess we'll put the reception tent here. Right?" Clay was standing several yards away, sweeping his arm to include the relatively flat area where they were both standing.

She looked at him blankly. There was something incongruous about the sight of him on this property. He didn't seem to belong here, and that concerned her.

"Em?"

"Sure. That makes sense."

He watched her for a moment before coming over. "What's up? Do you want to wait for your mom?"

"I don't know." She gazed up the road and shivered.

He wrapped his arms around her, rubbing his hands up and down her back to generate warmth. She looked into his face. She loved that face, she knew she did—the soft curves of the nose and chin, those beautiful eyes rimmed with thick black lashes. *This is an amazing person,* she told herself, *a unique and amazing person.*

They'd come here the first time a few years ago, after they'd been together about a year. She'd brought other boyfriends before Clay, and something about being on this property with them had forced her to stop lying to herself about them. But with Clay, it was the opposite—a sure sign that what they had was real. He hadn't felt the need to act formal and somber as they walked up the hill and through the woods, nor had he felt a compulsive need to lighten things and make her laugh. He'd simply been himself, which meant what it always meant: letting her be without leaving her alone.

She watched him walk away and lower himself to the ground. Exactly a week ago, she and Clay had been strolling through Central Park. It was a perfect fall day, crisp and bright, and the entire city was reveling in it. But when the two of them arrived at the Alice in Wonderland sculpture, they found themselves alone. Clay suggested they climb up on the mushroom as they often saw children do, and laughing, she agreed. As she began to pull herself up, however, she noticed that he hung behind, jangling his keys in his pocket.

"Don't worry," she told him, "nobody's going to see you."

He looked at her with a funny smile. "I'm not afraid of looking dumb. It was my idea in the first place."

Once they were both up there, lying back on the bronze surface, they stripped off their jackets and used them as pillows. After a couple of minutes, he took her hand and slipped a delicate pearl ring onto her finger. He watched her face with anticipation.

"Emily, will you marry me? I would kneel, but . . ." Indicating the absurdity of their location, he gave her a quick apologetic smile.

"What?" she said, still stunned. "No way."

"I hope that's not your answer."

She laughed. "Yes!" she said, kissing him. "Of course I'll marry you. Definitely yes."

They had spoken about marriage many times, and for a while now, whenever they spoke of the future, they spoke of their being together as a given. But still, this was a surprise.

"Oh my God," she said, admiring the ring. "How long have you been planning this?"

"I didn't plan to do it here. I've been carrying the ring around for a week, trying to figure out something really imaginative. And then this just seemed better somehow."

"It's perfect."

"If the ring isn't right, there are lots of others. I talked to the woman at the store—"

"Clay, stop," she said, grabbing his hand. "I love it. Really." She gazed up at the clouds moving slowly across the sky, thick and lumpy in their centers, thinning out and breaking up around the edges like flour sifted onto a blue counter. Right then, out of the corner of her eye, she saw something flapping—a plastic deli sack caught on a bush, *thank you* printed over and over in red down its wind-crinkled side.

Even now as she thought back on it, the ugliness of that sack dominated her memory of the day. She looked over at Clay, partially hidden among the weeds, contentedly fiddling with a piece of straw. Why had they talked so much about the ring? It was such a trivial detail. They'd clearly both been nervous. But why?

Car wheels scraped on gravel, and Clay stood up as the silver Mercedes pulled in next to their Honda. Her mother and Earl eventually got out of the car and made their way toward them. Earl, in a tweed cap, looked ready for a grouse shoot on the Scottish moors. Laura was carrying a shopping bag, which Earl took from her as they leaned on each other and carefully picked a path over the ever so slightly graded ground.

"Sorry we're late," Laura said, girlish as always with her un-styled hair and baggy sweater. She hugged Emily and then Clay.

"How was the drive?" he asked.

"Oh." Earl stopped for a moment, panting a bit. "It was all right." He hugged them both, surveying the property through squinted eyes. "Nice to be here, though."

"Mom, you might want a coat."

"I'll be fine."

"You sure? It's pretty cold. Look." Emily made a hushed *ho* sound, and a cloud of white vapor drifted out of her mouth.

"Boy, look at that," Earl said.

"I always forget how much cooler it is up here." Laura took the bag from him and handed it to Emily. "I got you this in Paris. A little engagement present."

"Thanks," Emily said, taking the bag. "That's so sweet."

"It's a little something I found for you at a lingerie store. I couldn't resist."

"Ooh." She raised her eyebrows at Clay. "Lucky you."

"Yeah." He laughed. "A present for me, I guess."

"I also have a bottle of Lafite for you at home."

"Mom . . ."

Laura gave a coy shrug. "Well, you can't drink it for some time anyway."

"Yes, but I don't drink at all."

"Come on. Don't you think it's fun to have a bottle of wine that was released the same month you got engaged?"

Emily looked at Clay, incredulous. There was an awkward pause.

"We were thinking we could put the reception tent over here," Clay said, motioning toward the area behind them.

Laura nodded. "Seems like a good place for it."

They all grew silent and business-like as they focused on the area.

"Have you decided where you want to do the ceremony?" Laura asked.

Clay shook his head. "Not yet."

"I know where we're going to do the ceremony," Emily told them.

Clay gave her an inquisitive look. They all waited in vain for her to take the next step.

"Do you want to show us?" he asked. "Or are we supposed to guess?"

"I'll show you," she said, starting out across the grass. The straw-like strands grew taller and thicker as they moved up the hill so that her shins were eventually plowing through waves of vegetation, the shopping bag making a swishing sound as it skimmed along the top.

Halfway up the hill, the land leveled off as if to serve the cluster of apple trees that dominated the even plane. She stopped in the center of the orchard and turned to wait for the others. Clay was patiently making his way up the hill in a pair of slippery-soled loafers. Her mother and Earl followed slowly, her mother's hand grasping onto his elbow.

In the far distance, a few developments had sprung up over the years, but for the most part, everything within twenty miles remained unspoiled. Her parents had been lucky—they hadn't realized how lucky at the time—to find a property that was virtually surrounded by state-owned nature reserves, protected from the encroachment of real estate developers and urban sprawl.

Clay smiled up at her. "I can't believe I didn't think of this. Of course it's the perfect spot." As he arrived beside her, he added, "For so many reasons."

She took his hand. "I'm glad you think so."

Her mother sighed, suddenly looking much more tired than the climb justified. "You want to get married *here*?"

"Yes."

"Well . . ." She put her hands on her hips and gazed off into the distance. "How do you think you're going to fit all those chairs up here?"

"I was thinking people could stand."

"*Stand?*" She said this as if there had never been an occasion on which people had stood for a good thirty minutes beneath these very trees.

"Yeah."

Her mom was looking everywhere but at her. After a while, she gave a tight, forced smile, and Emily could see that there were tears in her eyes.

"Oh, Mom," she said, putting her arm around her. "It's not a sad thing."

"Yes, it is," her mother shot back. "It's a *very* sad thing."

Emily dropped her arm. "What I meant was . . . I wish you wouldn't see it as a sad thing to be having the ceremony here. I like the idea that he'll be here for it. You know?"

Her mother's lips began to tremble, and she brought a fist to her mouth.

Emily put her arm around her again.

Clay cast a glance at Earl, then said, "Maybe the two of you would like a few minutes up here alone."

Emily nodded.

As the men started to walk away, her mother pulled herself together. "We won't be long," she called after them.

She gave Emily's hand a couple of friendly pats to signal that she could remove the arm from her shoulder. "Have you told your father?"

It took a moment to adjust to this new line of conversation. "Um . . . No. I mean I haven't had the chance to speak to him yet." She didn't feel like mentioning the appointment tomorrow in Dr. Shepherd's office. If all went well, she'd probably tell him there.

"Oh," her mom said, reaching over to a nearby branch and twisting at the stem of a lone brown apple until it released into her palm. She examined it and then tossed it down the hill.

They both watched it roll and hop and roll again until it eventually disappeared into a tall mound of grass.

"How was Scotland?" Emily asked.

"You know . . . It was okay. Of course, shooting isn't really my thing. But it was very pretty, and Paris was fun."

Emily nodded, and they stood there quietly for a moment.

"What are we going to do about bathrooms?" Laura asked.

Emily's face fell. "I hadn't thought about that."

"I still don't see why you refuse to get married in the city."

"I want to do it here."

Laura rubbed her hands up and down her arms. "I should have worn a coat. Are you ready to go back?"

"You go ahead. I'm going to stay a little longer."

Her mother peered at her apprehensively. "I hope you're not upset with me."

"No. Not at all."

"I was only trying to be realistic about the problems you're facing here."

"I know."

"Don't worry. We'll make it work."

She smiled to let her mom know she appreciated the sentiment. Then, as Laura started down the hill, treading carefully on the path the four of them had cleared on the way up, Emily sat down and stared up through the bare apple branches at the sky. There was no symphony of insects, no rustle of leaves—just the sound of the wind blowing cold upon the wood and stroking the tops of the grass, a white noise interrupted by nothing but the occasional squawk of a crow.

One clenched, brown fist of fruit hung directly overhead. The wind moved the twigs around it. The branch itself even swayed a little. But the apple did not budge. It held strong and willfully still. She thought of how her brother had become a part of these trees, every rainfall and every snowmelt encouraging his ashes to be drunk up by the trees' roots, climbing from there high into the trunk and out through each limb to the buds, flowers, fruits, and leaves.

She wished that her brother would descend from the branches and come and sit beside her for a few minutes. He had always been the one to provide her with a sense of perspective, to let her know when she was being unreasonable, and to nudge her gently back toward her own version of equilibrium. She had never been able, and would never be able, to achieve that extraordinary level of balance which, for Thomas, was simply status quo.

Lying back on the grass, she closed her eyes. In the blackness, she could feel her brother stretched out beside her, propped up on an elbow, his head resting in his hand. It was as if they were lounging on a picnic blanket as they had done so many times over the years no matter whether it was sunny and warm or drizzling and cold.

I think you'd like Clay.

Even Mom likes him, miracle of miracles—crazy about him, in fact.

She imagined Thomas listening as he had always done, waiting until she'd said everything she needed to say before giving any sort of response. He remained still, expecting her to proceed.

He's such a good person. Really nice, solid . . .

Goddammit, the wind was relentless. Wiping a bit of moisture from her cheek, she shut her eyes more tightly. She wanted to keep talking so that the conversation would not end, but she couldn't think of anything else to say. The only response she got was from a crow way off in the distance. She lay there for a little while longer, trying to hold on to the image of Thomas lying beside her. But he was back up in the trees, out of reach.

1992

RAIN HAD FALLEN STEADILY THROUGHOUT THE night, intermittently rousing the four weekend inhabitants of 42 Chatham Lane from their slumber and sending them shuffling across the chilly pine floorboards to the even chillier ceramic tile of their bathrooms, then back to their beds where they kicked their legs and tossed restlessly, unable to warm up again. Finally, around six, a dim glow began to chase the night from the three bedrooms, and there was a collective, defeated migration toward the kitchen. Joe, who had sprained his left ankle on stage two days before and had been subsequently ordered by the doctor to remain on crutches for a solid seven more, hobbled from refrigerator to sink to stove, making omelets for his wife, daughter, and son, now gathered on stools around the crackling kitchen fireplace.

Thomas was watching his mother's cigarette, which she held between her fingers, but seemed to have forgotten. He was curious to see how long the ash would grow before dropping into the lap of her silk kimono. She scratched absentmindedly at her elbow, pulling a flock of pale beige birds this way and that as she stared past the drizzly windowpane at the flooded vegetable garden.

Emily was flexing and pointing her feet so that her elephant slippers seemed to be having a chat down near the lower rungs of her stool. One foot nodded while the other emphatically shook his head, his trunk flapping and occasionally hitting Thomas in the leg. Laura finally tapped her ash into the fire, freeing Thomas to wander off in search of yesterday's newspaper.

Already, the kitchen had filled with the welcoming smells of browning butter and fresh coffee. "This is kind of nice, isn't it?" Joe asked. "All of us up to watch the sunrise together?"

Nobody answered.

He began to whistle "Here Comes the Sun," prodding the eggs with a spatula. The light from the oven's exhaust hood caught the curve of his bicep, and he thought with satisfaction that the crutches were probably building up the muscles in his arms. A longtime beneficiary of the genetic luck of the draw, he'd rarely had to expend much effort on his physique beyond the occasional jog. Even now that he was edging close to sixty, his body remained firm enough to elicit envious remarks from his wife—although, fifteen years his junior and even younger in appearance, she hardly had cause for envy. But he was convinced that the combination of his laziness and his love of food would eventually catch up with him, and he would wake up one day to find that he had ballooned into a male version of his father's sister, Leba. As a child, he had found Aunt Leba's rolls of doughy skin so terrifyingly grotesque that nightmares of suffocating to death in one of her hugs had plagued him nearly as frequently as the recurring dream in which all of the Jewish kids in his Bronx elementary school, including the half-Jews like himself, were rounded up and sent back to whichever European country, now under Nazi control, their own parents or grandparents had once left. Currently deprived of the physical benefits provided by routine activities—like his thirty-odd-block walk through Central Park to the theater every day or the hauling of firewood from the shed into the house on weekends—he was relieved to realize that there might be some positive effect on his body from the crutches themselves.

Though, of course, the real benefit provided by his accident was the time it allowed him to take off from the play and spend with his family. He looked over at his son, who had set down the paper to return a fallen whisk to him and was now making his way back to the center island. Thomas's heels no longer touched the ground when he walked, so he bounced along on his tiptoes. According to the doctor, this was a temporary phenomenon caused by the inability of his Achilles tendons to catch up with his latest growth spurt. Joe wondered how much more the boy would grow. At five foot ten, he had only three inches to go before catching up to his father.

Emily was tall for her age, too. Her coloring, like his own and her brother's, was dark, and she shared their wide, intense eyes and gently sloping noses. But she had inherited her mother's exceptionally high forehead and her elegance, which somehow shone through even now, in Emily's current stage of adolescent awkwardness. It made the sight of a girl donning floppy elephant slippers at the end of long, slender, not-yet-womanly legs a simultaneously comical and beautiful thing to behold.

Joe noted the contrast between the frenetic energy of his daughter and the stillness that surrounded her mother. Even from this vantage point, he could make out the fine webbing of blue veins beneath the surface of his wife's paper-thin skin. The vein beside her right eye was often mistaken for a smudge of makeup, and every now and then someone might subtly indicate to her from across a table that she should wipe the mark off her face. He called it the Blue Nile because, like the river, it ran west and then north before disappearing into a larger tributary, and next to her pale eyes, it looked startlingly blue.

Thomas was now circling the rectangular pine table, setting a fork and a knife and a folded paper towel in front of each of the four wooden chairs. In the city, they never ate anything but snacks in the kitchen. But up here, things were more casual, and Thomas liked it that way. A draft blew steadily in around the frame of each window, competing with the heat from the fire, and the boy thought about how much it felt like swimming in the ocean in Hawaii, where the geothermal activity beneath the ocean floor made it so you could drift from a warm spot to a cold and into another warm without moving so much as thirty inches.

"Dad, did you really eat octopus once?" he asked, thinking back to the various sea creatures he'd seen on his first magical deep-sea dive.

No response.

After a couple of minutes, Emily rested her chin on her hand and began to recite.

"*Lugubrious, saturnine, atrabilious, dolorous, mournful . . .*" The words tumbled quietly into the room.

Their mom looked at her. "What are you saying?"

"I'm going over my list of favorite words."

"Really cheerful," said Thomas.

"I don't understand how somebody with a vocabulary like that can do so poorly in English class." Their mother kept her eyes on Emily, waiting for an answer.

Moving closer to the fire, Thomas grabbed the trunk of his sister's slipper and shook it. "Hey, guess what?" he said. "Next time we go to Hawaii, we'll both be old enough to scuba."

"That's cool," she said, brightening.

The logs sighed and changed position in the fireplace.

"What?" Emily sneered at their mother. "Would you please stop staring at me."

Their mom looked away.

Oblivious to this exchange, their dad prodded the darkening, yellow edges of the second omelet from the pan.

"Yes, I did," he finally said, turning to look at Thomas. "In Greece. More than once, as a matter of fact."

Thomas was starting to get used to his dad chiming in a little late. Ever since his one-man show had moved to Broadway, he'd simply had too much going on in his head to be able to register what other people said at the time they actually said it.

"What was it like?" Thomas asked him.

"Well, it was a little hard to eat because it kept wrapping its tentacles around my fork."

He was also always making things up. That was nothing new. Thomas rolled his eyes at Emily, and she laughed.

"Daddy, that's gross."

"Anyway, darling," their mother said, putting a hand on Emily's knee to draw her attention back to her.

Emily yanked her knee away. "English is boring."

"I'll tell you what's going to be a lot more boring. Not being able to get a decent job because you can't get into college."

"Dad doesn't have a college degree."

"That's true," Thomas agreed, impressed by how easily she always stood up for herself.

His mom exhaled smoke through her nose, and he hoped she wasn't mad at him.

"Well," she said to no one in particular. "I suppose you don't *have* to get a college degree if you want to be an actor or something like that."

His dad divided the omelet between the last two plates. "Or, you might go to college for two years and drop out because you're a big jerk and think you know everything. But then you'd better get lucky like I did and fall in love with someone smart enough to keep you from making a total fool of yourself all the time."

Thomas looked at his mother, who was smiling the way she did when she had a headache.

"Don't be silly," she said.

She put a plate of eggs at every place, and Thomas brought over the toast. Then she got the mugs and a carton of milk while his dad wiped down the stove and loaded the dirty things into the sink.

Once they were all seated at the table, everybody was quiet for a bit as they ate their breakfast. After a while, his dad looked at his watch.

"Guess what time it is?" He grinned, shoveling the last bit of egg onto a piece of toast. "Only 6:45."

"Jesus," his mom said with a sigh.

Licking butter off a thumb, his dad sat back in his chair, chewing. "So, what are we going to do with this long day ahead of us? If it's only 6:45, I'm going to be totally sick of you people by lunch."

"Daddy!" Emily giggled.

He smiled and winked at her, then brought both fists down enthusiastically on the table. "Let's go to the beach!"

"Yeah, right," said Thomas.

"Come on!" his dad groaned. "Where's this family's sense of adventure? Let's go on an outing."

His mom put down her coffee and let out an exhausted sigh.

"I wish we had a space heater at least," said Thomas.

"Well," his dad replied, "we can pick one up on our way to the beach."

Thomas gave a thumbs-up. "Yeah. Okay, Dad. Meetcha there."

"I'll go get a space heater with you, Dad," Emily offered.

"Great. Anyone else? Laura? You sure you don't want to come?"

His mom was standing up now, and Thomas watched his dad reach over and caress the end of the silk tie hanging from her waist. As she started to stack the dirty plates, she turned slightly, and his dad's hand fell away.

"I'm sure," she said briskly.

"Mom, I'll do that," Thomas told her, rising from his place and taking a plate from her hand. "It's my turn."

Minutes later, Emily and her dad were off, mud balls spewing from the station wagon's accelerating tires. Emily pulled her coat sleeves over her hands to keep them warm until the heater began to work. He had cranked the temperature-control knob all the way to the right, but the air coming out of the vents remained arctic.

"Where are we going?" she asked.

"To the beach for ice cream cones."

She knew this to be untrue because for one thing, the closest beach was two hours away, and for another, it was too cold—for the beach or ice cream. But she decided to humor him. She wouldn't have been able to get a straight answer anyway. He tended to stick to his guns until the truth finally revealed itself. She expected to soon see the white plastic sign with the green tractor and an arrow directing them to Ace Hardware, where she knew there were space heaters for sale. Until then, it was nice to pretend that it was a sweltering afternoon and that she and her father were driving under the lacy, emerald branches of trees, the windows open to the sweet smells of honeysuckle and fresh-cut hay. Closing her eyes, she imagined that the air coming from the vents was wind whipping at her hair. They were on their way to the pebbled shore of the ice-cold Atlantic, where they could *at last* cool off.

She looked over at her father in his fedora and smiled. In that hat, with the collar of his coat turned up, he looked pretty cool. Most of her friends' fathers were losing their hair or had jowly necks that hung over their tight shirt collars. And most of them would never attempt a look that their daughters would consider cool. Emily's friends sometimes found her father aloof and a little intimidating, but they all agreed he was positively unembarrassing.

She looked out the window. The sky hung low over the asphalt, and the mountains that usually showed in the distance were just barely visible over the treetops lining the other side of the road.

The sky was an atrabilious shade of gray.

She tried this out in her head and was disappointed by the way it sounded. *The sky was an atrabilious gray on the day her lover left town.* She didn't like that either.

"Hey, Dad?"

He gave a slight nod of acknowledgment.

"When you sit down to write a play, how do you figure out what you're going to write about?"

"You got me," he said, still staring out the windshield.

"Dad, come on. I'm serious."

"So am I," he said, finally glancing in her direction. "Sometimes I can see what made me write something once it's done. But, other times, I never know."

"But if you're the one that makes the play, how can you not understand how you're doing it?"

He was silent for a moment. "It wasn't until man figured out how to build a pump that he was able to understand how the heart works. And yet, what compelled him to build a pump in the first place? Perhaps it was the very fact he had one working inside of him. But nobody could have told you that at the time because they didn't know."

She sighed heavily. "Whatever. I just don't know how I'm supposed to write a decent poem when nothing interesting has ever happened to me."

He smiled.

"I'm *serious*," she said.

"Oh, come on, Emmy. Lots of interesting things have happened to you."

"Name one."

"Didn't you go to a roller-skating party last weekend?"

She flashed him an annoyed look. "Roller-*blade*. Anyway, I'm talking about major, dramatic things—death or heartbreak."

"Ah." Joe tried not to smile. "I don't think you have to experience all that in order to write good poetry. The important thing is to put down the things you *do* experience. Whatever bothers you or excites you, use that. And don't worry whether or not it's interesting. Chances are, if it's honest, it will strike a chord in someone else."

He watched his daughter turn back to the window and wondered if there was any need to worry. He'd recently noticed an edge of pessimism creeping into her conversation. It was only puberty, Laura said—a stage all girls went through. And given Emily's flair for the dramatic, he wouldn't be surprised if she were simply mimicking something she'd picked up on in other girls, trying it on like a pair of falsies to see what it felt like and what sort of effect it had.

The truth was that both of his children were much easier than he felt that he, as a parent, deserved. The other day, he'd returned home from the Sunday matinee only to discover that he'd left his cigarettes at the theater, and both kids had jumped at the chance to accompany him to the corner deli for another pack. They walked with him down the sidewalk, taking turns being the one at his side and the one following behind, speaking excitedly and rapidly and making him feel that he'd been sincerely missed. And while they'd stood at a crosswalk waiting for the light to change, Thomas asked him what sort of gift he thought would be appropriate to give to the nanny of his closest friend. Apparently, she was headed back to England, and Thomas had been invited to her going-away party.

"You'd better ask your mom," he told him. "She's more well versed in those matters than I am. I didn't grow up with any of that stuff."

"I don't care," Thomas said. "I respect your opinion, and I'd like to know what you think."

Emotions welled up, catching him by surprise, and he quickly urged the kids into the crosswalk before they could notice.

Respect—the kind of respect Thomas alluded to—was not a term he would use to describe any of the myriad feelings he'd held for his own parents. He had always respected their authority, but he did not recall ever—even as a young boy—respecting their opinions.

After straightening up the house a little, Laura stretched out on the couch to take a nap. As she lay there, her eyes wandered around the room, landing first on the simple new Danish TV cabinet before continuing on to the bookcase, where, over time, an eclectic mix of ceramic pots, lacquer boxes, and various, odd little objects had gathered among the hundreds of leather-bound and dust-jacketed volumes. She'd always liked the haphazard feel of this living room. Here, the decorating—if it could even be called that—had a much more organic feeling than could ever be achieved at their apartment in the city. She had grown up in that apartment, and now, after years of making one change after another to its original, immaculate design, she had resigned herself to its rigid, slightly stifling aura.

She gazed at the photograph hanging on the wall: Thomas and Emily, ages six and four, grinning happily on the steps of a white stucco church, a row of cypress trees beside them, the Aegean Sea behind. They had passed the church several times a day that summer, on their way in or out of town, to or from the market, the beach, the little pastry shop. She thought about the group of local fishermen that used to hang out near the church—enjoying the sun, the view, the shade of an olive tree while breaking bread with the same friends, not seeming to need anything beyond that. She still wondered what it was precisely that accounted for the men's contentment. Was it only a fantasy she had created, or did they have fewer needs? Was there such a thing as contentment? A life without wanting, wanting, wanting. Wanting what? That was the real question. People rarely wanted what they thought they did.

She remembered how her parents used to tell her she wasn't hungry enough to succeed as an actor. *You don't know what it feels like to want something that badly,* they'd say. They also thought it was an unattractive pursuit to begin with. *Show trash* was what her parents called all performers. But the truth of the matter was, she'd been *too* hungry. Her desire ran so deep it had scared her. She recalled the exhilaration of playing Hedda in college. And Stella in New York—it was only one night, but she'd blasted the roof right off the theater. Joe's words. He'd said after that, the role was rightfully hers, that the director should fire the other actress straightaway. She smiled ironically at the memory of it. She had no doubt he'd meant it, but Joe was all talk. At the time, she'd been doing quite well—he was the one who was struggling to get noticed. But even now, with all his success and the power to get her back on stage if he wanted, he never offered anything beyond flattering remarks about her "vast talent."

Laura looked at the photograph of Thomas and Emily again. *What if they'd all stayed in Greece?* she wondered. For a while they had thought they would. If her parents hadn't died that summer in the car accident, would they still be living there instead of splitting their time between here and their Park Avenue apartment? How different their lives would be. But it was inevitable. Joe was too ambitious. She knew that. And frankly she was glad. She wouldn't have really wanted to go on living in Greece either. By their second month there, Joe was already restless. She could see that plainly. For a while, he had calmed down. Having one of his plays produced had finally sated him and stopped the constant talk of being a kept man, of needing to earn some money and forge a name for himself. Though the play was all about New York, it was oddly enough first mounted in London. And both there, and after, in Greece, where nobody knew them, they were free from the constraining labels put on them back home: the guy from the Bronx, and the rich banker's daughter. In Greece especially, they both lost some of their desperation—that ravenousness which felt so exciting in the beginning, but which had driven them each half-mad after a few years of marriage. She was happy there just being a wife and a mother, glad to part with the agonies of stage fright and bad auditions and nasty critiques. Toward the end of their stay, however, she sensed that Joe's ambition was returning, and she had to admit she felt relieved. Her own ambition was returning, too. And then her parents died.

Leaving Greece was only hard because of the kids. She and Joe had joked about wanting to raise them on Aeschylus and ouzo. But there really was something intriguing about the idea of letting them grow up there. She knew from her own experience how New York tended to plant in the minds of its children a daunting perception of the world; to be surrounded by the best of everything was both a privilege and a curse.

They had gotten the place up here as a compromise. And it seemed to have worked. Either that, or her kids were special, but neither of them was daunted by much of anything. And they both liked spending time in the country. Emily sometimes complained about having to leave her friends on weekends, but Thomas had turned into quite the naturalist. He was sitting across the room at the moment, pouring over seed catalogs in an effort to replace the young plants that had been washed out of the garden by last night's rain.

"Find anything good?" she asked.

He didn't look up. "Yeah. Some cool-looking artichokes." Pushing the soles of his sneakers into the table, he tilted back in the chair.

"Christ, Thomas, I wish you wouldn't do that."

Smiling devilishly, he tipped his chair back even farther, then let it come forward, then tipped it back farther still.

Laura covered her eyes with both hands. "Please, sweetie. You're giving me a heart attack."

"Sorry," he said, letting the front legs of the chair bang down on the floor. "We certainly wouldn't want that to happen."

It was nice to have Emily and Joe gone for a while. In Emily's eyes, her mother could do nothing right, but her father—who was finally gracing them with his undivided attention for the first time in months—was a veritable magician, able to turn any dull moment into an exciting adventure and transform his sulky adolescent daughter into a giggly, charming girl.

When Emily woke, she found that the car was parked and her father had disappeared. Startled, she looked out the window and, as she wiped the drool from her chin, saw a seagull hovering over the choppy waters of the Massachusetts shore. She hardly recognized the beach at this time of year. The sea looked angry and uninviting, the sand rough and wet.

Groggily, she chewed on the collar of her jacket.

The sky was kissed by the atrabilious sea.

"Garbage," she said out loud. And as she said it, she caught a glimpse of her face in the sunshade mirror. Her brown bangs hung limply over what she'd recently decided were pathetically unglamorous eyes. With the palm of her hand, she swept the hair up off her forehead and folded it back, trying to imitate Ingrid Bergman's style from the old black-and-white movie she and Thomas had watched last week. In it, Bergman and Cary Grant played spies who fell hopelessly in love and spent endless amounts of time kissing and staring passionately into each other's eyes.

Her father came out of Dippin' Don's negotiating his crutch with one hand and an ice cream cone with the other. Angled against the wind so that he wouldn't lose his hat, he hobbled across the parking lot, grimacing at each blustery squall. Emily leaned across and opened the door for him.

"I got you chocolate. I hope that's all right."

He handed her the cone, then crammed himself and his crutch back into the car along with a pungent blast of salt and rotting seaweed.

Her eyelids fluttered lazily as she let the first creamy bite dissolve on her tongue.

"Thanks. It's yummy."

He picked up his hat and smoothed his hair. Then, replacing the hat on his head, he reached into the backseat and pulled a can of beer off a plastic-bound six-pack.

"Where'd you get that?"

"Down the street."

She couldn't believe she'd slept through an entire stop. The can sighed as he cracked the tab. He took a sip and settled contentedly into his seat. The toasty car air was rapidly transforming Emily's chocolaty solid into a liquid, and she lapped it up as fast as possible from the paper-wrapped cone.

"Daddy?"

"Mmm?"

"I just wanted to let you know that I've started dating."

He raised his eyebrows in mild surprise.

"Oh?"

"Yeah," she said, "I have a boyfriend."

"Is that so?"

"Mm-hmm."

"Well, that's something interesting that's happened to you lately."

She shrugged. "Yeah, I guess."

Ripping into the paper that encased her cone, she nibbled away at the waffle. Except for the hum of the motor and the loud crunching going on inside her own mouth, everything was silent for a little while as she and her father took in the bleak scenery beyond the windshield. The same seagull still hovered over the water, dancing through the mist like a kite at the end of an invisible string. Emily reached the bottom of the cone and popped its pointed tip into her mouth. Licking a sticky finger, she looked over at her father.

"I think I maybe exaggerated a little. I mean I did start going with this one guy last week. But he's the only guy I've dated. And I guess I've only been going with him for two days, since he only asked me to go on Thursday."

Her father nodded. "Uh-huh."

"The thing is," she continued, "I think I liked him a lot better before he asked me to go with him."

He smiled.

"What's so funny?"

"Nothing," he said. "I'm having a nice time. That's all."

On the way home, Joe asked his daughter whether she'd enjoyed the drive. And though she told him she'd had a blast, he suspected that the kid in the passenger seat, currently tracing either an uppercase *E* or an *F* in the condensation on her window, was wondering why on earth her dad had made her sit in the car for four hours to eat some mediocre chocolate ice cream and stare at an ugly seascape. Admittedly, his vision of the outing had been a lot different earlier in the week. By Thursday night, as a matter of fact, the vision had become so vivid and alluring that while he sat in his dressing room with an ice pack on his ankle, all he could think about was the feel of his wife's bare thigh beneath his hand as they drove, with the kids in the back, on their way to the shore. Later, his producer, Gina Dole, had jokingly accused him of spraining his ankle on purpose. And he'd had to wonder if there wasn't some truth in that. *E* for *Emily, F* for? She had already wiped out whatever it was she'd been writing.

That night, after the kids went upstairs, Joe and Laura lingered at the table, finishing the bottle of wine they'd opened for dinner. As they sat there in the dim glow of the candles and the fire, talking about nothing at all—how they missed playing tennis and why it might be time for them to consider a new car—Laura felt herself being drawn in by the gorgeous low rattle of her husband's voice. He had a way of focusing his attention on her when they were alone that was so intense, it could make her uncomfortable. When they were with others, she often craved this consuming gaze; but when they were left to themselves, and all of that energy was pointed toward her, there was a voraciousness that seduced and frightened her. Her impulse was often to turn away or to say something trite or even demeaning to cut the tension. But for now, she was enjoying it. He was hers again, and she drank him in.

As he finished the last bit of wine, she climbed onto his lap. "Listen," she said, sliding her hands up under his shirt onto the warm smooth skin of his back. "Why don't we leave this stuff till the morning."

He pulled her into him, and she could feel him getting hard. "Mmm. Fine with me."

She unbuttoned his jeans, but as she started to pull them off, his ankle buckled under him. He cried out, and she jumped up to free him from her weight.

"I'm sorry. Are you hurt?"

"No." He stood up carefully and embraced her, then lowered her body slowly with his, down to the ground.

"Goddamned show," he said, lying down beside her.

She rolled her eyes. "Oh, yeah—I feel so sorry for you. My poor Tony nominee."

He laughed. "Not yet."

Feverishly, she pulled his shirt off, and they started to kiss.

"It's going to happen," she told him.

"You really think so?"

"I do."

He kissed her again and unhooked her bra.

"The kids," she breathed.

"Don't worry."

He got the rest of her clothes off and soon was inside of her. She closed her eyes, everything working together so perfectly: the wine, their bodies, the way he always knew exactly what to do. She loved this closeness, what it made her remember and made her forget. *This*, she thought, completely absorbed, but also observing from a delightful height, *this is a wonderful time in our life*. Then, as she opened her eyes again and looked up at Joe's neck and chin moving back and forth above, while her head bumped over the recessed border between two tiles, the thought began to change. For him, this most likely wasn't about her. For him, it was about a body, a distraction, something to quell his anxiety about his work and to satisfy a male hormonal need.

She tried to concentrate on the sensation in her groin. She was being crazy, she told herself, crazy. But it was too late. Her head had laid siege to her senses and was denying her access to any point of pleasure. She waited patiently until his body tensed and collapsed like a parachute, on top of her. She ran her fingernails lightly down his arm, and he shivered. After a while, he lifted himself up slightly, away from her, so that he could see her face. Her breasts, wet from his sweat, felt cold in the absence of contact. Tiny beads of sweat clung to the dark hairs on his chest.

"Was that okay?" he asked, hopefully and maybe a little guiltily.

"Yes," she said, "wonderful," her smile genuinely tender.

He lay down again, and they stayed there for a few minutes. When he rolled off of her, he said, "I forgot to tell you Ella called. They want us to come for dinner next Monday."

She sighed.

"Come on," he said. "It'll be fun."

"Sure."

He stared up at the ceiling, then looked at her again, furrowing his brow. "You know, I think if it were up to you, we'd disappear off the map altogether. You never want to do anything, meet anyone . . ."

She propped herself up on her elbow. "That's not true. It's just that I'm sick of all those people—who are all your friends, by the way, and who we're with *all the time*—"

"I'm happy to spend time with your friends," he interjected.

"That's not the point. Would you let me finish, please? I'm sick of all those people looking at me and wondering what kinds of things are going on behind my back."

He ran his hand over her rib cage.

"Laura," he said softly. "For the *last* time, *nobody* thinks that stuff is about us."

She sat up and pulled her sweater on over her head. "It's not just that anyway. I mean the way they all talk to me about the theater as if I'm some little housewife who—I don't know—as if they have to *educate* me or something . . . Ugh, it's maddening."

"Why don't you tell them you're an actor?"

"Because I'm not."

She picked up her pants and underwear, stood up, and started off toward the bedroom.

He got up and grabbed his crutch, following her.

"Hey," he said, when she finally stopped in the doorway to their bathroom. "Why don't you start going to auditions again? Or at least take a class?"

"Because. I don't want to. All right? I don't want to be an actor."

He waited for a moment, then shrugged. "Fine."

"Excuse me," she said, and closed the bathroom door.

BACK HOME IN THEIR OWN APARTMENT, LAURA changed into a robe and got bottled waters from the fridge while Earl put some music on.

"This is that CD I got in Paris," he said, joining her on the couch, where she'd already curled up in her favorite spot.

"I can't believe I drank so much," she said.

He leaned in and kissed her. "I know. But it was fun, wasn't it?"

"Yeah."

Following their return from the Berkshires that afternoon, they had attended a jazz concert at Lincoln Center with some of Earl's business associates—a mix of New York and Texas finance guys—and their wives. They'd all had dinner together after the concert and had then gone on to one couple's apartment for a nightcap. She'd downed several glasses of wine at dinner, but everyone had had a lot to drink. At one point late in the evening, one of the men had taken off his tie and thrown it out the window of their limo. The group was a little raucous for her taste, but it was also fun to get swept up in their revelry for the night. Ever since she'd gotten the news in

Paris that her daughter—*their* daughter, hers and Joe's—would be getting married this coming May, the past had begun to loom a little too large. And then being back on the property today had been harder than she'd anticipated, especially with Emily insisting on that particular site, and going on about how her brother would be there for the ceremony.

In the limo, shortly after the man relieved himself of his necktie, Laura withdrew her hand from Earl's and stood up through the limo's open sunroof. The wind whipped through her hair and blouse, making her feel like a teenager in a speeding convertible. Hoping that nobody below was taking note of the varicose veins in her legs, she called out "whoooooo!" into the rushing air, letting the folds of her silk top shift so that they exposed a piece of lace bra. Her hair tossed wildly around her head, and when they finally pulled up in front of the apartment building and she rejoined the others down below, she feigned ignorance of her loosened top and unruly coif and adjusted nothing. Everyone was laughing as they piled out of the limo. Vivian Miller, the vibrant wife of one of Earl's Houston-based colleagues, gushed in her heavy accent about how wonderful Laura had looked up there, *FAN-tastic! Like one of those women carved into the bow of a ship! You know what I mean? Sooo powerful!* They all filed through the lobby and into the elevator, which carried them up to the penthouse. Right before the doors opened, Laura—still brimming with reckless energy, her top still hanging askew—slapped two of the men on the back and announced, "I've got to piss," pleased by how brazen it sounded.

Her bravado imploded the second she caught a glimpse of herself in the bathroom mirror. Under the glaring overhead lights, she saw no wildness, no unbridled, youthful sexuality. Her stormy mess of hair and the open blouse merely made her look drunk and foolish. She leaned in and examined herself. Lipstick-stained rivulets branched off of her thin lips. She did not yet have an old woman's face, but there were signs that she soon would. She smoothed the brittle mass of blond-rinsed hair back into a presentable shape, reapplied lipstick and powder, straightened her silk top. For a moment, she wondered what the others had thought, then quickly decided it didn't matter. Fifteen years ago, if she had walked into the bathroom and discovered that she looked like an absolute mess and then re-called with a wince that she had drunkenly told some men that she "had to piss," she would have been mortified. But now it didn't faze her. It had taken the extreme shock and sorrow of true loss to make her realize the insignificance of those tiny losses of face that used to consume her. She used to replay over and over every embarrassing thing she'd done or said. Like her other old habit of digging her fingernails into the soft, inner part of her wrists, it had had a sooth-ing effect. A cat dangling from a ledge, she'd needed to feel her claws at work in order to feel secure. But now that she had survived a fall, she no longer needed that.

When she came out of the bathroom, everyone was gathered around the piano, singing and laughing, doing their best to keep up with their host's bawdy rendition of "Thank Heaven for Little Girls." Earl, who was standing at the periphery of the group, took her in his arms and whispered that he was ready to go home. Re-lieved, she nodded in agreement.

Smiling at the recollection of their adventurous evening, Laura sank back into the couch, listening to the music Earl had put on. It was heavy on piano, which wasn't ordinarily her favorite jazz instru-ment. But the way this person played gave it a sexy, old-fashioned bluesy sound that appealed to her. She'd always liked jazz but had never listened to it at home prior to meeting Earl. The few times she'd ventured into the jazz section of a record store, she'd ended up with a mix of cutesy marching band music and some jarringly unharmonious, modern-sounding stuff that she thought was called fusion, though she wasn't sure. She was still relatively ignorant on the subject. But now that she had at her disposal Earl's vast col-lection of jazz that suited her taste, she could select virtually any album from the CD cabinet and appreciate the sultry, slightly iniq-uitous feel it lent to whatever she happened to be doing around the apartment.

"Who is this?" she asked, handing him a water.

He set it down on the coffee table and picked up his pipe.

"This is Oscar Peterson. Well, to be precise, it's the Oscar Peter-son Trio, which is Oscar Peterson—on piano, of course, along with

Ray Brown on bass and Ed Thigpen on drums. They're all geniuses, but together—man, it doesn't get any better. Listen to how they dig down into those deep bass notes."

He stopped and listened, grinning blissfully as he plunked out a few imaginary keys on his thigh. Then, leaning forward, he took up a pouch of tobacco, and she watched him go through the ritual of packing and lighting his pipe. As she breathed in the deliciously sweet smell of his smoke, her mind wandered back to the conversation she'd had with Clay earlier that afternoon, while Emily was still up on the hill. She and Earl had been talking about the house they were thinking about building where the old one once stood, and she had gotten a panicky feeling that when they died, Clay and Emily would move into it. "Please promise me something," she'd said to Clay. "Promise me that you'll sell this place after I die."

Earl put his feet up on the table and crossed his ankles.

"You like it?" he asked, referring to the music.

She nodded. "It's great." She reached over and smoothed the skin between his temple and his eye. "That was a stupid thing I said to Clay about the house. Darling, I wish you wouldn't squint so much. It's giving you such deep wrinkles here."

He had no response to this.

"I worry that he's going to tell Emily and that she's going to think I have some strange ulterior motive."

"Well," he replied, the pipe between his teeth, "I imagine that he will tell her."

They were silent for a moment, and then Earl said, "If you don't mind my asking, why were you so adamant that they sell it?"

She sighed. "I wasn't thinking. I mean, of course there's no way that Emily's going to part with that land. But it seems unfair to saddle her with all of that history. You know, it's one thing for you and me to decide to be there. But . . ."

Her voice trailed off.

She gave him a repentant look. "I'm sorry. I know we should be looking for a villa on Lake Como or the Côte d'Azur or something like that instead."

"What makes you think I'd prefer that?"

"I don't know." She examined her nails, which were overdue for a trim. She liked to keep them short enough that only the smallest sliver of white showed at the tips.

"It always frustrated Joe that I had such simple taste," she said.

"I hate to tell you this, my dear," Earl said with a wink. "But your taste is not quite as simple as you would like everyone to believe."

She laughed, embarrassed. "You're probably right."

Her bare feet had drifted away from the warmth of her robe, and she tucked them back under her rear.

"I really wish I hadn't said anything to Clay." She sighed. "I know I'm going to get an earful about it from Emily. And I'm sure she'll have some issue with the lingerie I got her, too—'Why would you spend hundreds of dollars on silk underwear for me when the countries that export the silk are guilty of such egregious human rights abuses? And do you have any idea how many silkworms died to make that underwear?'"

Earl smiled. "Come on now. I'm sure she won't give it that much thought. She's so nervous about being the lead defense counsel on this murder case, and now there's the excitement of the engagement, too."

"You're right. I shouldn't make fun of her anyway. I really do admire her, but sometimes I think she should take some of that compassion and apply it to the people in her life."

"You don't think Emily's compassionate?"

She pressed her finger into the skin beneath her nose and began to chew at her upper lip.

"I guess so," she answered finally, letting her hand drop into her lap. "It's just that she holds people to such ludicrously high standards. I remember the first time when she and Thomas went off to Joe's parents' house for the weekend, and Joe and I were all worried that they wouldn't get along with the neighborhood kids or that they would make some hurtful observation to one of their grandparents about the modesty of the house, which had happened before. But it turned out that when we called the first night, they were absolutely on cloud nine about everything. Except for right when we were about to hang up the phone, Emily lowered her voice so that her grandmother couldn't hear and told us in this sort of disdainful way that her grandmother had made them chocolate chip cookies *from a mix*."

Earl smiled.

"No." Laura gave him a bemused look and shook her head. "No. Wait a minute. I got that wrong. It wasn't Emily who said that. It was Thomas."

Her eyes softened. "I'd forgotten that. It was definitely Thomas."

Her mouth spread into a melancholy smile. "He was such a purist," she said lovingly.

"A purist? What happened to Emily's *ludicrously high standards*?"

"Well," she said, dismissing the question, "I'm sure he was really very disappointed with his grandmother. Because, of course, I would have never dreamed of making cookies from a mix."

"Anyway," she continued after a moment, "I'm sure I did plenty of other things wrong. There's undoubtedly a long list of gripes Emily has against me. But, let's face it, if we're going to talk about who's responsible for screwing the girl up, Joe definitely wins the grand prize." She took the cap off her water and drank until she'd gulped down half the bottle.

Earl raised his eyebrows in surprise. "You really think Emily's so screwed up?"

"That didn't come out the way I meant it. It's only that she's been through so much."

Laura turned to the window behind the couch. In an apartment across the way, someone was watching television in the dark. "It honestly broke my heart to see her under those trees today, talking about how she wanted her brother to be there for the ceremony."

On this last word her voice quavered, and Earl reached over and took her hand.

She bit her lip and smiled. "I'm okay," she said. "So, um . . ." She searched for a moment to regain her train of thought. She pressed her finger into her upper lip. "I'm just saying that it's made Emily kind of hard. I don't mean difficult. I mean hard in the sense of . . . stony." She took another sip of water. "I hope Clay's got it in him to work as much as he's going to need to in order to find her softer side."

"I'm not worried about them at all," said Earl.

She was stunned to hear him say this. He rarely voiced such strong opposition to her opinions, especially when they regarded her child.

"Of course you know her much better than I do," he conceded. "But I think that she and Clay are very open with each other."

"Really?"

"They're probably about as well equipped as any couple I know to handle whatever obstacles get thrown at them."

"I'm relieved to hear that," she said. "I suppose I just worry because I'm her mother."

He gave her hand a squeeze, and she smiled.

"I sort of envy all that they have ahead of them. Don't you?" he asked.

"No," she replied emphatically. "Don't you remember how when you were younger, you had to question everything all the time?"

He was obviously trying to remember if this was the case, but she didn't give him time to answer.

"Jesus," she said. "I certainly did anyway. It was torture."

There was a brief pause in the music as one track ended, and then another one began. She snuggled in under Earl's arm and closed her eyes. The piece was nice and slow, punctuated by the soft percussive *tchiss, tchiss* sound of a brush on cymbals. And when her mind started to slip back to the chocolate chip cookies and thoughts of her son—and then of her ex-husband—she was glad to have something to listen to.

Emily looked at her watch. Her father was five minutes late. She couldn't believe she had to be in court in a couple of hours. It was an important day, and her nerves were already a bit rattled, which wasn't good. She'd known this was a risk when she'd scheduled the appointment here, but it was the only time in the foreseeable future that worked with all of their calendars.

Dr. Shepherd smiled across her desk. "How do you feel?"

"Good," she answered.

The room was very still, no noise from the street, just the electric drone of an air filter in the corner. Photogravures of alien-looking plants in thick, black frames adorned what little wall space wasn't taken up by bookcases.

She liked it in here. The room reflected Dr. Shepherd's take-charge personality. With her stylish suits, athletic carriage, and serene power, her doctor had always seemed to her like the kind of woman who felt at home wherever she went—be it a library, a golf course, or a chic New York cocktail party.

There was a knock in the waiting room, and she heard her father's voice—*Hello?*

"Yes, come in," Dr. Shepherd called out. "We're in here."

After a moment, he appeared in the doorway, and Emily got up to greet him. As usual, he was impeccably dressed in a perfectly fitted blazer with a pocket handkerchief that matched his pale blue dress shirt.

"Hi, Dad."

Walking toward her, he smoothed down the scant wisps of white hair on his head, then opened his arms to give her a hug. She was surprised by how old he looked at the moment. His face was more bloated and reddened than she remembered, and there was a slight translucence to the soft folds of his cheeks.

He hugged her lightly, as he always did, with three soft pats on the back.

"Hi, Emmy," he said, stepping back again.

He hadn't called her that in years, and she felt an unexpected thrill, as if he had unveiled something precious and rare.

"This is Dr. Shepherd," she said.

"Hello, Joe," the doctor said, leaving her desk to shake his hand. "So nice to meet you."

"Thank you," her father said. "You as well."

He seemed a little stiff, a little awkward—not quite himself, she thought as she sat down. Dr. Shepherd motioned to the empty chair. "Please have a seat, Joe."

"I want to thank you for coming, Joe," the doctor said when they were all settled. "I think that your being here means a great deal to Emily."

Her father looked over at her, the corners of his mouth rising in an uncomfortable smile.

"It seems," Dr. Shepherd continued, "that there are many things that are difficult for the two of you to discuss. And Emily and I thought that being in this room with me to guide you might make it a little easier."

Her father tipped his head forward slightly to signal he understood.

"I'd like to think of this as the beginning of something new, and something quite separate from the work Emily and I have done up to this point."

"Emily," the doctor said, turning to her. "You and I have talked a lot about your relationship with your father, and I know there are some things you'd like to discuss with him. Why don't we begin with what you and I talked about last week, and I'll sort of paraphrase to get things started."

She nodded.

"And Joe, if you have any questions about the process or anything else before we begin, please feel free—" A loud buzz sounded from a box on the wall behind the desk.

The doctor cocked her head, confused.

Again, the buzz.

"I'm sorry. I have no idea who that could be. Just a minute."

She got up and walked briskly across the room, her heels making a muffled scraping sound on the beige carpet as they watched her disappear into the waiting room. After a moment, they could hear that she was talking to someone, but couldn't make out her words. They turned to face each other, and Emily shrugged and smiled.

"So, how are you, Emmy?"

For some reason, this time the familiarity annoyed her. "Good, Dad. How are you?"

She noticed that his hand trembled slightly on the arm of the chair. She wondered how long this had been going on, and thought it must be fairly new.

"Great," her father said. "How's Clay?"

He had met Clay for the first time in June. She and her father were having lunch together; something they did roughly three or four times a year, and Clay had come by at the end. They'd stuck to safe topics—movies, books, sports—and they'd gotten along fine. But she didn't feel ready yet to tell him that they were engaged.

"He's okay," she replied.

"Your mom?"

She stiffened slightly. "Good."

"She still with what's his name?"

"Earl. You know his name."

Her father raised his eyebrows contentiously.

"Dad, you ask me that every time we see each other. What do you expect the answer to be? They're *married*."

They stared down at their laps, waiting for the doctor to return. She was sure her father didn't understand why this woman suddenly had to be present for every word they spoke. He didn't seem to have a clue that there was anything wrong between them.

He cleared his throat with an air of importance. "They're doing a tribute to me at Williamstown next summer in honor of my seventy-fifth birthday."

"Yeah." She gave him a tight-lipped smile. "You told me."

And with that, thank God, Dr. Shepherd returned and took charge. She resituated herself in the armchair and joined her hands together on the desk.

"So. Let's see. I was going to sum up what Emily and I have been discussing recently, and then we were going to try to open up a dialogue. From what she's told me, the two of you have had a rather strained relationship for the last several years."

Her father glanced over and gave her an odd smirk.

"Now," Dr. Shepherd said, "as I understand it, things had already been difficult a year or so before Thomas's death, but it was really after that when the gap between you began to widen."

At this point, for her father's benefit, Dr. Shepherd began to outline the dynamics of their family and the unrecognized impact of loss—all the things she and her doctor had been over countless times in their weekly sessions. After a few minutes, the doctor asked her—again for her father's benefit—what she'd like to achieve in this meeting.

"I'd like to get to the point where we can *really* talk. Whenever we go to lunch, everything just feels so superficial, like we're having a business meeting or something—which is ridiculous."

Her father looked angry. He glared at her and then at Dr. Shepherd as if they'd both ambushed him. Finally, after a long and uncomfortable silence, he blurted out, "I didn't do anything!"

What an odd answer, Emily thought. But no sooner had she thought it than she lost her conviction. She folded her arms across her chest and held on to her elbows. "That's the whole problem, Dad. You never *do* anything."

He eyed her contemptuously. "I don't really know what you're trying to say."

Fighting to regain control of the situation, she leaned forward. "I'm trying to say that my problem isn't with anything you did. It's what you didn't do—what you continue to not do. You never call me—I'm the one who sets up our lunches. You never want to talk about anything very meaningful, and when I bring things up, you totally brush me off." Her voice was strong, forceful. "You never make any effort toward our relationship, Dad. You never have."

Her father stood up. And then, as if he was watching a rehearsal for one of his plays and the actors were distorting the meaning of his lines, he said, "I'm sorry. But this isn't working for me."

Emily was incredulous.

"We'll talk about all this over lunch sometime soon," he told her. "This doesn't feel right."

He turned back to Dr. Shepherd, and as though thanking his hostess for a lovely party, smiled politely. "It was nice to meet you. I'm sorry."

Emily and Dr. Shepherd both stared in stunned disbelief as he started for the door.

"Joe, just a minute," Dr. Shepherd called after him.

"Dad, come on," Emily pleaded.

He reached for the knob.

"I'm sorry," he repeated.

And with that, he walked out.

A tuxedoed waiter set down a champagne glass and poured first the elderflower syrup, then the champagne that made up the complimentary house cocktail the Jefferson Inn offered its guests every night. Joe thanked the man, and when he was alone again took a sip, enjoying the flavors. It was a little like drinking a flower, and it made him feel appropriately transported.

The dining room was almost full. The sun had set, and the darkness outside had transformed the dining room windows into reflective panes. Instead of grassy meadows and colorful autumn foliage, the glass gave a view, distorted and surreal, of the flickering light and moving bodies that animated the room.

He had sold his soul to get here, but it had been worth it. To get away from New York for a while was a tremendous relief—especially now that his friend at Williamstown was breathing down his neck for a new play. Aside from the occasional article for a travel or food magazine, he hadn't been able to write for the last twelve years. How the hell was he going to pull this off? And yet it was exactly what he needed. Twelve years seemed like more than enough time to spend wading through the aftermath of any personal crisis, and he finally felt ready to move on. He was optimistic, too, that the travel article he'd been sent here to write for *Contact* magazine might recharge his system by giving him something else to focus on. And of course it was always nice to get out of town without any of the usual problems of a vacation: the effortful planning, the expense, the unanchored feeling he always got when he wasn't working . . . Anyway, he liked writing travel pieces, even if he did have to answer to Rick Renzwig for the next few weeks.

He shuddered slightly as he remembered Rick leaning back in his chair, shaking his cherubic curls, and saying, *Hey, Joe, how are you doing? You look like you've got a new lease on life, buddy.* He'd known Rick (née Randy Greenberg Jr.) since he was born. Randy Senior had been one of his closest friends before he died, and he still held a measure of paternal fondness for Randy's slickly ambitious son. Only thirty years old, Rick was now editor in chief of *Contact* magazine, which boasted one of the widest and fastest-growing readerships in the United States. He had written for Rick before, but as Rick had pointed out the other day, "the magazine" wasn't very happy with the last piece he wrote. It incensed him that this kid whom he'd once held on his lap in teddy bear–printed pajamas had designated himself the arbiter of good and bad writing. He wanted desperately to tell him off, to pull back the curtain and expose him for the foolish impostor that he was. But instead, he bowed his head and said quietly, "I've stopped drinking." And after a while, Rick finally broke down and offered up a piece on a midwestern hotel that another writer had covered a few years ago in an article that never ran. Rick had heard reports that the hotel—a snazzy boutique-type thing surrounded by picturesque farms—had greatly improved, and the hotel was bugging the hell out of him to send somebody back out. He wanted to run the piece in the February issue, so it was going to have to be written right away. This special issue of *Contact* would focus on ordinary working-class people, rather than social-ites and celebrities. Of course, the majority of the magazine's read-ers did not want to live like real people. They wanted to observe them from a distance—preferably through the lens of a famous photographer. How fabulous in Rick's view that the Jefferson Inn should offer such luxury in the middle of the country's heartland, providing Joe with ample opportunity to find some working farms or other such quaint and real situations. Joe assured Rick that he would make "the magazine" proud, and swallowing his last ounce of pride, thanked him. The boy shook his curls and leaned back in his chair, apparently weighted down with love for his own magna-nimity—"Hey, don't worry about it, buddy."

Joe wished Randy Senior could have seen the arrogance with which Rick had treated him. It would have appalled him. Surrender-ing to the seductive clutch of self-pity, he mentally scrolled through the list of people in whom he used to seek solace when he'd been wronged. Every one of them either had died or had sided with Laura, or had somehow grown tired of him over the last few years. There were a number of people who'd called recently to say they were back in town for the fall and they'd love to get together for a play or a dinner, but none of them were particularly close friends. They were either old acquaintances in whom he'd lost interest or new acquaintances who had not yet inspired his interest and who he doubted ever would. In both cases, he knew exactly what the conversations would be like: everyone would chastise themselves for not getting together more often, then go on and on about the Vineyard or the Hamptons and what a wonderful summer they'd had. He knew which stories he'd tell, the responses they would get from his companions, the curious flip-flop of emotions he'd feel as he wavered between a sense of effortless superiority and a crippling, self-conscious inadequacy. He was much happier here, away from it all.

For a brief moment, he couldn't stop himself from thinking once again about Emily and the way she had spoken to him in Dr. Shepherd's office that morning: *You never* do *anything, Dad. You never make any effort.* But before he got worked up about it, he turned his attention to the neighboring table, where two couples appeared to be celebrating a special occasion. His attention was particularly drawn to one of the women. Her companions were all sunburned and jovial, like three plump red berries hanging from the same bush. But she seemed of another variety altogether. Her style conjured not country club tennis matches and poolside barbecues but long, lunchless days at the office and solitary nights spent at home.

The waiter—wholesome and farm-raised like all of the inn's staff—poured the wine for them, and as he left their table, one of the husbands said something that made everybody laugh. The woman Joe had been watching threw her arms around the man, but Joe detected a strained quality to her laughter and felt a compulsive urge to separate her from her friends. It simply didn't seem right for her life to be linked with those other three. Catching Joe's eye, she gave him the kind of smile one gives to someone eating alone who's overly interested in the goings-on at one's own table. Joe realized he was staring and looked away.

As he ate his dinner, he tried to be more discreet, but because they were speaking fairly loudly and because there was no noise at his own table or at the empty table on his other side, it was impossible for him to fully turn his attention elsewhere. The staff hovered about, executing their duties with admirable precision. He observed the balance they struck between attentiveness and respectful lack of intrusion, and concluded with a measure of disappointment that they were too professional and sophisticated to be farm-raised.

Probably all of them had spent years working in the chicest hotels and restaurants of Chicago or Minneapolis and had been imported to boost the inn's service ratings.

After polishing off a perfect tarte tatin with a scoop of cinnamon ice cream and downing a glass of the inn's homemade pear brandy, he took leave of his loud neighbors and their incongruous companion and headed back to his room. The staff member who'd checked him in that afternoon had explained that the inn had only twenty guest rooms, to make the place feel cozy rather than crowded. His room was decorated with comfortable furniture, and there were several handmade, nineteenth-century farm tools hung on the walls. Entering now, he reveled in the luxurious anonymity of his surroundings. Often, when he returned to his own apartment in the city, he experienced a slight pang of disappointment that everything was exactly as he'd left it, even though there was no reason to expect otherwise—for the last twelve years there had been nobody but himself to take a book off a shelf or to carelessly leave an orange peel out on the kitchen counter. Even the cleaning lady who came every Tuesday had learned to put everything back in its place.

Crossing the room to the foot of the bed, he opened his suitcase and began to unpack. He wished he hadn't let his mind wander during the appointment with Dr. Shepherd. It had gotten him into trouble and undoubtedly made him look foolish.

As he refolded his shirts and underwear and put them away in the antique dresser, he wondered how Laura was taking Emily's involvement with psychotherapy and whether she too had been confronted. Difficult as it had been to put up with the old Emily (especially when he and Laura were under the greatest strain, and the last thing they had time to worry about was the possibility of her flunking out of school or sneaking out of the apartment at night), he vastly preferred her to the one who seemed to materialize gradually after Thomas's death—who finished law school at the top of her class and took the high road to the public defender's office. Unfortunately, every one of Emily's accomplishments served only to undermine her tolerance for the frailties of others, and over the last several years, he'd found his daughter's pomposity increasingly insufferable. It was clear how she saw him: his son was gone; his wife would not speak to him; his career had gone down the tubes; she was all that remained of his former life. Even her affectation of forgiveness—dragging him into her shrink's office, then pretending all she wanted was to be pals again—reeked of superiority.

Having finished unloading his duffle, he moved on to the closet and began sorting through the various items in his hanging bag, transferring his jackets to the wonderfully sturdy wooden hangers that had been provided by the hotel. As he did so, he revisited this morning's abominable appointment. Emily's doctor—a handsome woman with a jaunty sort of femininity—had mentioned Thomas's death, then started in about the unrecognized impact of loss. *Christ almighty,* he had thought, *here we go* . . . He'd looked at Emily and marveled over how much she resembled Laura in her gestures and facial expressions, the tension in her jaw, the regal posture, the lovely high forehead. Then, glancing around Dr. Shepherd's office, his gaze had fallen upon a blue and white Delftware vase. It reminded him of one his mother used to have. It had been her prized possession. Throughout his childhood, it sat on a lace doily in the middle of their dining room table. After his mother died, he packed up her house and was shocked to find that upon closer inspection, the vase was only a cheap-looking reproduction. The disillusionment was not dissimilar from something he'd felt at fifteen when, sitting on the toilet one day in the family bathroom, he had come across a newspaper article on Errol Flynn. The article was part of the carpet of newspaper with which his mother daily covered the bathroom floor in order to catch the drops that he and his father occasionally cast short of the john. He had begun reading the article through the gap between his knees, then eventually picked it up in order to get a better look at the accompanying photographs of the Flynns' Hollywood home. A gigantic crystal chandelier hung in the entrance hall, and the master bedroom looked like an elaborate parlor rather than a place to sleep. But it was the Flynns' master bathroom that really struck him. As he sat gazing at what the article described as "imported emerald green marble" gleaming beneath the Flynns' bathtub, twin sinks, and toilet, it dawned on him for the first time that not everyone had newspapers spread out like diapers at the base of their commodes. Of course, he had long known that there were people who lived far better than he and his parents and their neighbors and friends. But the particular contrast between the newspaper-covered floor of his own bathroom and the virile sophistication of Errol Flynn's marble was too much to bear. He thought about the disdain with which Dr. Shepherd would regard his mother's cheap imitation of her Delftware vase, and it rankled him. Then, abruptly, he realized that Dr. Shepherd had stopped talking and that Emily had said something he hadn't heard. Both of them were staring at him, and he realized one of them must have asked a question or leveled an accusation. A bizarre sense of disfigurement came over him. He felt embarrassed, and his anger toward them grew.

Finally, he blurted out, "I didn't do anything!"

Emily folded her arms across her chest and sighed. She seemed calm—not too upset, just mildly irritated.

"That's the whole problem, Dad. You never *do* anything."

He had expected her to get angry, to light into him. From the moment she first asked him to meet her in her psychologist's office, he was sure she wanted to talk about his role in her brother's death. And if she'd done so, he could have defended himself. He'd prepared himself for that. But he had not expected this.

He wondered whether it was possible to be outgrown by one's child. *It's because she's a lawyer,* he thought. Lawyers and businessmen always had that air about them. It was easy to believe you had the answers when you could cite a rule or a number in response to any question you thought to ask. Artistic temperaments like his own worked differently. Curiosity was the point: there are questions upon questions, too many answers and no answers at all. He tried to meet Emily's gaze. "I don't really know what you're trying to say."

"I'm trying to say that my problem isn't with anything you did." *Another lie.* "It's what you didn't do," she went on. "What you continue to not do . . ." On and on until she finally said he had never—*never*—made any effort at all.

He took off his clothes and put on the terry cloth robe he found in the closet. *How about all of those theater outings?* he thought, tying the belt around his waist—*not only around the city but up to Hartford and*

New Haven and Williamstown . . . Between the summer of 1992 and fall of 1994, they must have seen almost every production in the Northeast. He'd enjoyed each minute of those outings, especially the road trips, when they'd talk about acting and writing and life. Those were some of his fondest memories. *How about that?* he wanted to ask her now. *That wasn't anything?*

There was some truth to what she'd said. He didn't make the effort to set up lunches with her. She was right. But he didn't get the feeling she enjoyed those lunches—or any other time she spent with him. He didn't know her anymore, didn't know how to make her laugh or what to say to hold her interest. When he finally met her boyfriend, sometime back at the beginning of the summer, he was surprised to find that he was Asian American. He'd heard about Clay of course for the last few years, and knew the boy was from Michigan and that he worked in finance. From Emily's description, he'd imagined someone who was a little conservative but had a quiet magnetism. And when he met him, he was pleased to find that this was pretty much the case: Clay was nice and polite, obviously full of integrity, and even seemed to have a decent sense of humor. But by associating his last name, Lee, with various other American Lees such as Robert E., Joe had failed to guess the surname's actual, Korean origin. It didn't bother him that his daughter's boyfriend was Asian American. But it wasn't what he had imagined for her. And this one missed detail pained him somehow.

⁓

Emily walked through the door of her apartment, dropped her purse and briefcase to the ground, and stepped out of her shoes. What a wretched day.

"Em?" Clay called out. She left her bags and shoes on the floor and made her way toward the study. He was sitting in front of the computer, checking his e-mail, still wearing his suit. His dark hair was sticking straight out over his right ear, where he'd been resting his head on his hand. Behind him, the bland voice of a news reporter streamed out of the television.

"How's it going?" he asked.

She shrugged. "I have a terrible headache."

He finished typing something, then swiveled his chair away from the computer to show her she had his full attention.

"No wonder," he said.

"No kidding." She reached up under her skirt and began to take off her stockings. "I realized on the way home I forgot to even tell you this thing Dr. Shepherd did."

"What?"

"Right after my dad storms out, she turns to me and goes, 'You know, it's incredible. Your dad still looks exactly the same.' Can you believe that?—I mean as if she used to go to the theater to see him all the time and was completely smitten. I didn't even know she had any idea who he was. She never mentioned it before."

He caught hold of her bare thighs and scooted her toward him.

"Are you listening?" she asked.

"Yes." He let go. "I'm sorry."

"It really bummed me out," she said. "Even if she thought he was a genius, it was a totally inappropriate thing to say."

"You're right."

She ran her fingers through his hair.

"Are you giving me a faux-hawk?"

She laughed. "What should we do about dinner?"

"You choose."

"Whatever you feel like. My head's killing me. Chinese?"

"Sure. Here." He turned her around and massaged her shoulders. "I thought Steve seemed like a pretty cool guy."

"What?"

He gestured to the computer. "Ellen just e-mailed us asking what we thought."

Ellen, one of her college roommates, had had them over the night before, along with a few other friends, in order to introduce everyone to her new boyfriend, a Brit with a pretty face and loads of charisma.

"Hmm."

"I thought he seemed great," said Clay. "We had a good talk—about Michigan and stuff. Did you know he lived there for a while?"

"No. That's funny."

"You didn't like him?"

"I did. I only wonder if it's such a smart thing for Ellen to be going out with him already—I mean, so soon after he got sober."

His hands dropped away.

"Okay," he said calmly. "What's she supposed to do? By the time another ten months or whatever goes by, one of them could be dating someone else, or could have moved out of the country or something, and then that's it."

"You're such a romantic."

Their eyes met briefly.

Irritated, she wandered over to her pile of mail. "I know you think it's bullshit. But what if he starts drinking again? That would suck for Ellen." She stopped flipping through the bills and looked at him. "Whatever." She waved her hand dismissively. "This is an area where we'll never see eye to eye."

"What's going on? For the last week, it seems like you're annoyed with everything I say."

"No, I'm not." She took a few envelopes and tossed them in the trash. "By the way, have you given any more thought to the whole checking account thing? Because I really don't care."

"I don't care either."

"All right. Then let's keep them separate for now." She started for the door. "I'm going to take a bath. Can you order?"

"Sure."

She took a bottle of Excedrin from her medicine chest and thought about Ellen's boyfriend. Last night, he'd had her laughing like mad throughout dinner. She could see how he could be exciting but also risky—and not only because of the newness of his sobriety. He was the kind of guy who made you feel great when you were with him, yet could easily be sleeping with everyone in town.

She sat down on the edge of the tub. Watching the water stream out of the faucet, she tried not to think about the pain in her head. It must be the stress—the pressure she was under from her current case.

Undressing, she climbed into the bath. A few minutes later, she heard Clay's footsteps in the hallway.

"I ordered the food," he said, pulling off his tie.

"Thanks."

He found her chapstick on the counter and in his usual, masculine way began to apply it to only the middle portion of his lower lip.

She sighed. "I really fucked up the hearing today. All my motions were denied."

"Oh, no. I'm sorry."

She wrung out the washcloth and draped it across her forehead.

"You'll still have no trouble getting the guy off."

"That's not true at all. Especially after today."

"Come on." He sat down on the counter. "You're just nervous. First chair jitters."

She shook her head. "I really don't know what I was thinking taking this guy on. Jesus."

"Well. Why did you?" he asked. "There must be a reason."

The question irritated her, but he was right. She tried to remember the answer. From the start, her client, Ramon Torres, had treated her with suspicion; he was hostile and reticent to speak. Compared to most of her other clients, she knew very little about him: He'd grown up in Red Hook, Brooklyn. His parents were divorced; and he had one sister who was twenty-one years old and lived with their mother. He'd been in and out of jail since he was fifteen—first on a minor drug charge, then later for involvement in a gang shoot-out, which as far as she could ascertain, amounted to simply being there when the shoot-out occurred, in the wrong place at the wrong time. He had been serving his last day of a two-year sentence at Rikers Island Prison when a fellow inmate, Angel Rojas, was found dead in a bathroom stall, with a number of stab wounds inflicted by something other than a knife. A corrections officer had provided the sole eyewitness testimony: roughly half an hour before Angel's body was found, the CO said he saw Ramon exit the bathroom. During the preliminary hearing, Emily had tried unsuccessfully to get the case thrown out based on insufficient evidence.

"I took the case because I'm an idiot," she said. "Because I was being arrogant."

"That's not true. You know you're incredibly smart and capable. And now they've finally let you take the wheel, so . . ."

"I don't know." She closed her eyes. "It would be such a coup to get this kid off. He's really tough, you know—doesn't have the best bedside manner. But . . ." She sighed. "Also, the inmate who was killed was definitely a Blood."

"Oh," He frowned.

"I know." She dropped the washcloth back in the water. "That's what sucks about it. If you look at it one way—from the prosecution's point of view—the pieces all fall into place."

"Are you sure the kid didn't do it?"

"Pretty sure."

She closed her eyes again. If only she were a better lawyer, she'd instinctively know how to vindicate Ramon. Wouldn't she? Plenty of lawyers seemed to have that kind of instinct. People in her office. People she'd known at law school. She was a dreamer, for God's sake—she'd spent her childhood writing poetry and dressing up in costumes to play different people on a stage.

She stood up, and Clay grabbed a towel, holding it open for her as she stepped out of the bath. She lowered the towel and un-buttoned his shirt. He watched her do it, waiting until she'd gotten all the buttons. She leaned her naked chest against his, and he held her. After a bit, with one hand, he caressed her waist, her rib cage, her breast. She tensed up. He gave her a questioning look.

"My head's killing me," she said.

He dropped his hand. "I'm sorry you're having such a rough time." He kissed her. "I wish there was something I could say."

"I know." She sighed.

"I'm sure things will improve soon."

She looked at him and nodded.

The buzzer sounded in the other room.

"That's the food."

"Yeah." She gave him another kiss.

He wrapped the towel around her and started toward the door, his shirt still flapping open. She bent over and pulled up the plug, watching the water spiral slowly down, then eventually began to dry herself off. She thought about Steve again and the way he and Ellen had exchanged those intense lustful looks last night. She wondered what it was like to be with Steve. He would have ignored her headache and the buzzer. Then stopping herself, she stood up. Tucking the end of the towel under her armpit, she went in search of Clay and found him in the living room, setting the table.

She leaned against the wall. "I'm sorry I've been so snippy."

"You've had a tough day," he said without looking up. "I understand."

She watched him unload the Chinese food onto the counter like a buffet. Couldn't they ever just kick back on the sofa and eat out of the cartons? God, she was irritable.

"I'll go get dressed," she said, starting back down the hall.

In the bedroom, she flicked on the closet light and once again ran through the mistakes she'd made today. The first was scheduling that appointment this morning with her dad. What a jerk. If he hadn't stormed out of there the way he had, she might have been able to focus better in court and win some of her motions. At one moment during the delivery of her argument, the judge shot her a stern look, and she was instantly reminded of the withering glance her father had given when she said she wished they could talk more openly. The recollection only lasted a second, but still, it threw her off, and she was sure she saw a shift in the judge. Perhaps he had been with her—at least, he'd seemed open to her argument. But then she lost him.

Afterward, she had gone up to Ramon, who sat slumped in his chair.

"How are you doing?" she asked.

"Fine," he said, his head bowed so that instead of his face, she was looking at the cornrows in his hair.

"I think it's going pretty well. That case I just mentioned is good for us."

Ramon smiled slightly, playing with his fingers. "That Moses thing?"

"Yeah. *New York versus Moses.* I guess that does sound kind of funny."

"That was my dog's name. Moses."

"Really? What kind of dog?"

"Mutt." Another smile flickered across his face. "Big ugly mutt.

Great dog, though. The people at the shelter promised to keep him for me as long as they could."

He fell silent, and she could see he didn't want to talk anymore. It dawned on her that Moses was possibly the one being Ramon imagined might be waiting for him if he ever got out. What would it feel like, she wondered, to be handed a life sentence at the age of nineteen? Your life not even really rolling yet, and already your number's up.

She pulled on a T-shirt and a pair of sweatpants and headed out, stopping before she passed the phone on the bedside table. For a moment, she considered calling her dad, then decided against it. It was pathetic, but despite everything, she still wanted him to walk her down the aisle.

Joe woke much earlier than he ever did in the city, not to the harsh crowing of a rooster, but to the gentle, rolling warble of flying geese. The first rays of the sun poured over the crest of a distant hill and fell in long, golden shafts across the landscape, sparkling on patches of dewy pasture.

Downstairs, the lobby was empty, and the lights at the front desk were off. Treading lightly across the stone floor, he slipped outside and was greeted by a considerably livelier world. Insects buzzed around the inn's garden, occasionally veering off-course and dive-bombing a fence post or the side of the building, hitting with a hard thwack. The sunflowers and morning glories were beginning to raise their heads. In the distance, cows grazed, and here and there, flocks of geese and ducks continued their noisy migration overhead.

He passed along the edge of the garden, then struck out across the meadow on a path that led to the woods. The grass on either side of him lay in soft, knee-high waves. Moisture seeped quickly through the thin leather of his black loafers and drenched his black cotton socks. He ignored the discomfort and upon reaching the forest, came to a cedar-chip trail.

Stepping into the shade of the towering pines, he felt the

warmth of the sun abandon the back of his balding head. Somewhere a woodpecker began to peck at a tree, and its staccato rap
echoed through the forest. There was something faintly ominous
about the sound, like a warning being issued in code. Other than
the woodpecker and the occasional snap of a twig under his foot,
things were utterly still. He continued on for a while until, finding
a large caramel-colored mushroom in his path, he stooped down to
take a closer look.

Thomas, the naturalist in the family, had tried to teach him to
identify the mushrooms of various shapes and sizes that had populated their property in the Berkshires. It had scared Laura out of
her wits to watch their son gather and cook these mushrooms. She
was constantly reminding him that one small bite of the wrong one
could paralyze his nervous system. But Joe trusted the boy's identi-
fication skills and frequently joined him for the foraging walks and
the delightful little repasts that followed. Not once did either of them
suffer even a mild stomachache, which Joe knew was not a matter
of luck. He would never dare try to pick a mushroom on his own.
He lacked Thomas's sensitivity to the minute distinctions nature
made between its edible and poisonous fungi. This one looked be-
nign enough, but Joe respectfully left it where it stood.

Now that he was still, what had only a moment before seemed
like silence revealed itself as a subtle cacophony of sound. He eased
himself onto the ground, tuning in to the wind rustling through
the pines, then to the chirping of the birds, realizing in the process
that this was the first time, in all the years since Thomas's death,
he'd set foot in a forest. He fiddled with his watch, a gift from his
son. It wasn't anything fancy—just a standard jogging watch with
a nylon Velcro band—but it was one of his most valued possessions. He remained that way for some time, sitting on the ground,
fiddling with the watch as he enjoyed the rat-tat-tat of the woodpecker and the smell of the earth. Slowly, he realized that his right
hand was trembling. He grabbed it to stop the fingers dancing in
the air, but he could see even as he held his hand, the wrist continued to flinch uncontrollably. He knew he should see a doctor, but
he couldn't bring himself to go. Best-case scenario, there was absolutely nothing wrong—which, in some way, was the outcome he

feared most. If he was going to bother with an appointment, he'd have to tell the doctor everything, including the fact that one morning last week he'd woken, like a toddler, in a soaked bed. To divulge this to some fit, young physician—who might then tell him reassuringly, with a pat on his trembling hand, that his health was A-OK and all he needed was a pack of adult diapers—was simply not an option. *No, thank you very much,* he thought, rising from the ground, *a man does not need to put himself through that.*

When he returned from the woods, he took the Dictaphone out to the garden with the hope of working on his own writing over breakfast. The patio was empty except for a fairly miserable looking, middle-aged couple who quietly perused the *Chicago Tribune* over their coffee. Joe chose a spot as far from them as possible at the edge of the patio, settling into a wicker chair. Vines dense with starry white flowers hung from an arch over a nearby gate, which served as the only connection to the landscape beyond. There was a distinct separation between the carefully trained, rarefied atmosphere of the inn and the earthy fecundity outside its bounds.

Soon, a waiter named Albert arrived, asking what Joe might like for breakfast. Albert looked to be about Joe's age, and the droopy folds of his cheeks and his kind, sorrowful eyes gave him something of a basset hound quality. But he carried himself with a proud elegance, bordering on snootiness, which Joe partly attributed to his natty hotel uniform.

"Some farm-fresh eggs perhaps?" Albert suggested. "Or a plate of freshly baked scones?"

Thanking him, Joe accepted the offer of eggs (two, over-easy), and Albert left with a short bow.

Joe relaxed into his chair and tried to focus his thoughts. Back in August, he had lied to his friend at Williamstown, pretending to be well into a new play. But he still hadn't begun one at all. To make matters worse, it was this lie which had generated the notion of the tribute in the first place. If he continued to find himself unable to write, what then? He looked around the patio, with an odd sense that he was being watched, but since there was nobody else there besides the one other couple, he brushed it off as another incidence of the self-consciousness that had been plaguing him lately.

Not for the first time, he wondered how the younger generation would respond to his work. Aside from the new play he'd promised to be sending in any day now, the festival would be putting on a couple of readings of his older stuff as well: *Before Swine*, his Tony winner and, for better or worse, his most popular play, and *The Morning Men*, which had been chosen because it wasn't a one-man show—despite that being the form he was best known for. The new play would also have parts for more than one actor (that much he knew), and the festival organizers had hinted he might want to come out of retirement to play one of them.

He was aware that his work had influenced other writers. Several currently popular writer-performers had credited him in interviews as the primary inspiration for their work. While he found this flattering and even fortifying, there was something about the experience of hearing or reading praise—or for that matter, being chosen as the honoree of a summer stock tribute—that made him extremely uncomfortable. He supposed he had a certain mistrust of it, especially when the praise came from younger people. He couldn't help feeling that buried in their compliments was a winking appreciation of something dated—the same sentiment that, say, caused *Contact* magazine to embrace a Vargas girl as its mascot. He recalled with irritation the tolerant smile Emily had given him yesterday as she reminded him that he'd already told her about the tribute at Williamstown. How typically arrogant it was of her to assume that his redundancy resulted from pride rather than simple forgetfulness.

Abruptly, he sat up. His eyes had been wandering along the evergreen hedge that enclosed the patio, and he now noticed two eyes peering at him through the branches only a few feet away. From what he could tell, they belonged to a girl of maybe thirteen or fourteen. And despite the fact that he was now staring back at her, she didn't budge—or even blink. At that moment, however, Albert returned, and spotting the girl immediately, took a few menacing steps in the direction of the hedge, at which point the girl ran away.

"Who was that?" Joe asked as Albert brought over a crisp white tablecloth and a tray of food.

"A local kid who's always snooping around. Comes here every now and then. Guess she doesn't have anything better to do. She's harmless, though—just curious. You know how kids are. But I apologize. She won't be back today, sir."

Joe nodded, then in order to busy himself while Albert was spreading out the tablecloth, he dug through his briefcase and pulled out his Dictaphone. Albert proceeded to lay the table in silent formality, setting down plates of toast, berries, and eggs, and a pot of coffee. Watching him, Joe was reminded of a Borges story in which a character sets out to "dream a man": to create from nothing a complete person with a beating heart and a soul, to somehow dream this person into existence. In order to accomplish this, he is guided—as if by fate—to the ruins of a temple. There, he is supplied with fruit and rice by the land's natives so all that's left for him to do is to sleep and dream.

Joe spent several hours at the table, moving from breakfast to lunch, and eventually tea. Nothing was coming to him, and after a while, hoping that some movement would help, he got up and set off on a tour of the garden. He crossed the flagstones and the green herbaceous tendrils that stretched out between them, and slowly made his way along a path, admiring the rose beds and the argyle-patterned squares of boxwood and lavender. Mindlessly leaning in to smell one of the climbing roses, he snagged his shirt on a thorn—and as he was struggling to free himself, was met with an amusing vision. Stretched out on the grass, on the other side of the garden wall, was the gangly adolescent girl he had glimpsed earlier. She lay facing the garden, with her head propped up on one hand. She was reading a book, which she held in the air at arm's length from her face, probably to block the sun from her eyes. She wore a black men's jacket several sizes too large for her, a problem she'd solved by rolling up the sleeves a couple of times, revealing the shiny, pink and white lining which hung in bulky cuffs over her slender wrists and dwarfed her childlike hands. Her thick brown hair kept falling into her face, and she would put her book down to pull the hair back and twist it into a knot. As soon as she had resituated herself, the knot would begin to slip again. Despite this, she seemed to be enjoying herself immensely. A pair of unlaced Doc Martens sat on the ground behind her, and she was continuously rubbing her dirty white sock–clad feet together.

The girl was visibly caught in that awkward stage between childhood and adulthood, and Joe continued to stand there for some time, watching with delight. She lowered the book and stared intensely at a patch of clover, picking out one stem at a time and plucking all three leaves off before moving on to the next. Unaware that she was being watched, she went dreamily on about her business, now and then waving insects away from her face.

Suddenly, the girl burst into laughter, throwing herself back on the ground and slapping her thigh.

Joe laughed, too, and the girl looked up, startled.

"Oh, I was about to go," she told him. "Really. Please don't say anything to me. I'll get my stuff together and leave. I promise."

"No, please stay. I'm sorry. I didn't mean to disturb you."

Looking first confused, and then relieved, she let her posture slacken.

"Never mind. I thought you worked at the hotel."

"No. I'm a guest here, actually. Do you live around here?"

"Kinda. I bike over from town."

Glancing at the bicycle lying in the grass beside her, he nodded. "Oh, I see."

"Where are you from?" she asked.

"New York."

"The city?"

"Yes."

"That's cool. I'm going to move there next year. Either there or London."

"Really? Does one of your parents have work there, or something?"

"No. I'm going by myself."

He raised his eyebrows in surprise. "How old are you?"

"Fourteen."

"Hmm. When I was growing up, I don't think people left home until they were sixteen or seventeen."

"Yeah, it's okay. You don't have to say it like that. I know it's weird, but I don't really like it around here. So I'm leaving."

He tried to keep from smiling. It was clear that she was serious about her plan.

"I'm not running away or anything," she assured him. "My parents know."

"That's good."

"My name's Ingrid by the way."

"Well, Ingrid, would you like to join me for a cup of tea?"

"Look, I'm not some poor, small-town kid who comes and sits out here to fantasize about what goes on inside some stupid, fancy hotel. I really couldn't care less about all that. If you must know, I come to the garden in order to live more deliberately . . . like Thoreau."

She said this with deep earnestness, and he struggled again not to smile.

"I certainly understand that. I didn't mean to infringe on your solitude."

Cocking her head to one side, she seemed to be debating whether or not to accept his apology.

"What's your name?" she asked.

"Joe."

"Well, Joe, it was nice to meet you."

"You, too."

As he turned to go, her voice caught him midstep.

"Do you think they'd mind? If I were to come in?"

"Frankly, I don't think they have any right to mind. You're my guest."

"Then maybe I'll come in for a little bit. I don't want to be rude or anything. You know, since you invited me."

"Come around over here. I'll let you in through the gate."

Once she'd gathered her things, she joined him inside the garden, leaving her bike where it was. "Isn't this garden the most beautiful place in the whole world?" she asked.

"It's very nice. I'm sure it's even more beautiful in the spring when these cherry trees are in bloom."

She followed his gaze to a cluster of nearby trees with shiny black bark. "Those aren't cherries. They're black birch. They do look kind of like cherry trees. In fact, I think they're also called cherry birch. But come here."

She reached over and grabbed a branch, scratched one of the

twigs with her fingernail, and then held her fingers out in front of his face. "Here, smell."

He looked at her fingers, which were round and childlike with stubby, gnawed nails. The jagged half-moon of her index nail had little bits of brown and green wedged under it from scraping the tree. He leaned down and sniffed. "Hmm. It smells like root beer."

"Yeah, or birch beer. It's basically the same thing. They make it from this tree."

"Do you know all the plants in this garden?"

"Just some. I have a friend who's really into identifying trees and stuff."

Joe smiled. "So do I."

After a moment, he realized she was waiting for him. "Should we sit down?"

"Sure."

He led her over to his table, and she moved shyly across the patio, holding on with both hands to the strap of a bunny rabbit backpack she'd slung over her right shoulder. The bag was essentially a fuzzy, gray stuffed animal whose abdomen acted as a repository for her book and other belongings while its long legs, arms, and ears flopped around uselessly. Once she was seated at the table, she held the bunny in her lap and stroked the faded pink strips on its inner ears. He asked her what she was reading.

"It's a book called *Walden*."

He raised his eyebrows. "That's pretty dry stuff. Don't tell me that's what had you in stitches over there."

Her cheeks flushed with embarrassment. "It's not very nice to spy on people."

"It seems that you were more in the position of spy, hiding in the shrubbery, looking in at all of us."

"I told you I couldn't care less about what goes on inside the hotel, Joe. I come here for the garden. To live more deliberately."

"Right. Like Thoreau."

"Exactly. I think he's a genius. He also happens to be very funny."

"Really?"

"Sure." She pulled the book out of her bag and opened it up to a page distinguished by a pink polka-dotted bookmark with a silver tassel.

"Listen to this." She read dramatically, "'This is a delicious evening, when the whole body is one sense, and imbibes delight through every pore.' Doesn't that kill you? Imbibes delight through every pore? Oh wait, here's a better part: 'The bullfrogs trump to usher in the night, and the note of the whippoorwill is borne on the rippling wind from over the water. Sympathy with the fluttering alder and poplar leaves almost takes away my breath; yet, like the lake, my serenity is rippled but not ruffled.' Rippled but not ruffled! I love that. And the bullfrogs *trump*! I mean, come on. It's kind of pretty, but it's so funny at the same time. Don't you think? Who talks like that?"

"Are you reading this for school?"

She rolled her eyes as if this were an absolutely preposterous question. "God, no. We would never read this at school. We only read the dumbest books ever there. I'm going through the school library alphabetically on my own. I'm only on *C* right now, but I decided to jump ahead because my friend told me that Thoreau has all the answers, and it's going to take me forever to get to the *T*'s."

"And does he have all the answers?"

She shrugged. "I don't know."

"Would you like some of this?" he asked, nodding toward the various tea things spread out on the table.

"Sure."

"Here." He pushed the cup and saucer over to her and picked up the teapot.

"Thank you," she said, watching him pour the tea. "Aren't you going to have some?"

"Not at the moment."

He set down the pot and offered her the plate of cookies. "Would you like a madeleine? They've apparently just been made."

Her eyes went wide. "*Real* madeleines? Like in Proust?"

"Proust?" he said, "that's *P*. Did you skip ahead to him, too?"

"No," she replied, "I haven't actually read Proust, but I read a book that made such a big deal about Proust's madeleines, that I feel like I have. I will someday—when I get to *P*."

"You certainly are well read."

"No." Her shoulders collapsed as she said this, and she looked utterly hopeless. "I'm really not. Considering how many books there are in the world and how many new ones are put out each year, I don't know how I'm ever going to come close to even half of them—and that's not counting all the stuff that's been written in other languages and hasn't been translated into English."

"Mmm. And may I ask, what are you planning to accomplish through all of this reading?"

"Scientia est potentia," she replied, then added, "That means 'knowledge is power.'"

"Yes," he said. "I know."

He noted a sense of futility in her tone and suspected the conversation was getting her down. He was about to change the subject when she said, "One day, I'm going to do something really great that nobody's ever done before. But, right now, I'm in the process of figuring out what that's going to be."

"I don't doubt you're capable of doing anything you want."

This seemed to cheer her up a bit. And as she picked up a madeleine and bit into it, her gloom evaporated entirely. He watched as she delightedly dipped one cookie after another into her tea (to which she had already added a substantial amount of milk and sugar). He could see that, enrapt as she was with her snack, she was also taking in the painted porcelain cups and the silver teapot, examining the ebony and silver acorn sitting on top of the lid and the hotel's insignia engraved on the side of the pot with the focus of someone trying to commit every detail to memory.

From across the fields came the chime of distant church bells. Ingrid explained that she didn't go to church because she didn't believe in organized religion. Besides, she said, the church was totally depressing and smelled like old ladies. He asked her what old ladies smelled like, and she closed her eyes and thought about it for a while. "If you know what a smell is like, you just know it. That's all. You can't really explain it." He told her he agreed with her about organized religion. The one time he had seen the appeal was on a trip to Europe. He'd visited several of the severe Gothic cathedrals in northern France and a Florentine basilica filled with precious fading frescoes and found the buildings themselves so magnificent—the soaring ceilings and the pale stone, so quiet and cool in contrast to the chaos and heat outside—that the experience of being inside them was deeply spiritual, much like being in a forest.

Ingrid gazed at him over the edge of her teacup, her eyes full of fascination. Very daintily, she set the cup down on its saucer. Then, as if she were conducting an interview, she folded her hands in her lap and narrowed her eyes inquisitively.

"What kind of work do you do, Joe?"

"I write travel articles for magazines."

"Wow. That must be cool."

"Well . . ."

"Are you going to write something about this place?"

"Yes. As a matter of fact, I am."

Her mouth hung open slightly, and a cluster of crumbs on her cheek echoed the pattern of tiny brown freckles on her nose.

"Why don't you take me on a tour of the hotel so that I have a better idea of the article?" she asked him. "Then maybe I can help you."

He laughed. "I thought you weren't interested in the hotel."

"Well, *yes*. Didn't I *say* I wasn't interested? I'm just trying to help you, Joe. Do you want my help or not?"

"I'd love it."

"Well . . ." With an official air, she glanced at her watch. "I can't do it right now. But how about I drop by another afternoon?"

"Sure," he said, trying to keep from smiling. "I'll be here for another couple of days. I spend as much time as I can out here in the garden, so it shouldn't be too hard to find me."

"Okay." She grabbed her backpack and her book and rose from the chair. "Thanks for the tea."

"My pleasure. I really enjoyed meeting you."

She shook his hand and slung the bag over her shoulder. "Yeah, you too."

He watched her walk back across the flagstones toward the

gate, loping along in her semigraceful, semi-awkward way. Then, letting herself out, she disappeared around the hedge.

I met someone today.

Seated at the desk in his hotel room after dinner, Joe was startled to hear this declaration emerge from his tiny tape recorder. It was his own voice, though a much younger version.

I was out buying diapers, and I stopped on the way home to fill up the car. When I headed inside to pay, I saw a woman getting off the pay phone. She was crying, so I stopped to ask if she was okay. She had broad, pretty shoulders and deep-set eyes, and she was wearing a floppy, purple hat with a daisy on it—a real one.

He smiled. He remembered the woman who had inspired this flight of fancy, who was in fact the inspiration for one of his most celebrated plays. He had always recorded his initial ideas on tape, sorting out the details later when he transcribed everything onto the page. But perhaps there was something here that could be reworked into a new play.

She said she'd broken up with her boyfriend, who was a mechanic at the gas station, and she'd been on the phone trying to find someone to come pick her up. She was a little younger than me—maybe early thirties. I offered her a ride. She lived way out on route 40, so we had a lot of time to talk. She was not particularly educated, but she had a beautiful way of putting words together. When we got to her house . . . It was small but very clean, and you could tell she'd put a lot of effort into decorating it. She'd hung a giant picture of a duck over the bed—which killed me. I told her about my wife. I don't know why. I suppose I needed to talk to someone. I said sometimes I didn't feel so much like we were sharing a life but simply inhabiting the same cage.

Jesus, he thought. *Inhabiting the same cage?* How trite.

At this point, Laura's voice broke in. It was far away; coming from somewhere in the distance—the hallway, maybe, or the stairwell—but he recognized it instantly.

Joe? she called.

Yeah.

There came the sound of footsteps, tap-tap-tap on the wooden floor, until they got right up close to the machine and then stopped.

Are you coming? she asked. *The kids are already in the car.*

No. I've got to finish this thing by the end of next week, and I've barely even started.

Long pause.

All right. She sounded disappointed. Annoyed.

What? He asked.

Another long pause.

Nothing.

Tap-tap-tap, the footsteps receded until they could no longer be heard.

Joe shut off the machine.

He got up slowly, went over to the minibar, and found a tiny bottle of vodka, then poured the liquor over a handful of ice cubes he took from a silver-plated bucket.

Everything about that time and place rushed back to him, every detail of their home in the Berkshires: the faint mildew smell, the kids playing down the hall, the vase of fresh-cut roses by his typewriter, Laura calling up every now and then from the kitchen or the living room, the humid air barely stirring on either side of the window screens despite the ceiling fan whipping around above.

Joe rubbed the back of his neck and felt that he was perspiring. He ejected the tape from the Dictaphone and set it on the desk, telling himself he'd listen to the rest of it later.

This was not the memory of Laura he carried around in his head. He carried her voice, her smile—the genuine one—and her laugh. He carried her generosity toward her family, the way she loved the kids, the way she loved him. As soon as he heard it, though, this came back to him, too. She was never openly hostile. But he'd found it difficult to please her, and she'd had no trouble letting him know when he'd failed.

Sitting back down, he found a tape he knew to be blank, pressed the RECORD button, and began to dictate.

"Dinner this evening: tomato and basil aspic with warm goat cheese croutons—the ideal way to celebrate the end of summer—followed by venison with lingonberry sauce and souffléed potatoes. Everything perfectly suited to the season, fresh and simple and skillfully prepared. For dessert, a poached pear with brown sugar ice cream."

He shut off the machine. He had only a few short days here, and he felt he should be taking advantage of every second. For the last several years, he had been consumed by a desire to create and equally consumed by his inability to do so. But today, at the entrance of Ingrid, something had changed. He had forgotten how wonderfully innocent and unguarded young people could be. He'd tired long ago of writing about cynical adults who deceived and betrayed, and ultimately broke one another. Instead of writing about the darker side of humanity, why not record a series of conversations between himself and this touchingly amusing teenage girl? The fact that Ingrid reminded him so strongly of his own daughter at that age had initially steered him away from her as a subject, but he now realized that there was something deeply inspiring for him here. His plays tended toward the self-referential anyway. He had always mined his own life for characters, story lines, and even dialogue, which he often reproduced verbatim. *This time,* he thought, *why not make the writer himself a character in the work and explore the process of the play's own creation?* There was something fascinating to him about the idea of a man's urge to give birth, in his own way, to another human—something that cut right to the core of what he was or wasn't and what he could or could not do.

"Joe. Rick Renzwig."

He held the barking receiver away from his ear.

"What in the hell are you still doing there?"

Joe rubbed his eyes and pushed himself up into a seated position on the quaintly upholstered loveseat, struggling to emerge from the fog of his postprandial (and post–delightful Bordeaux) nap. He had been dreaming about the considerably attractive woman who was seated directly across from him at lunch. As she was alone and he was alone, the fact that they had only to raise their eyes from their plates to stare straight at each other made for a bit of an uncomfortable situation. The woman dealt with it by keeping her head angled toward the window so that when she looked up, she looked out rather than at him—thus allowing him to admire her freely. What he found most intriguing was her very deliberate way of moving, of placing her chin in her hand, each finger resting delicately against her pale cheek, of bringing the soup spoon to her mouth and parting her lips only enough to allow the spoon in, careful not to spill a drop on her red poppy-printed dress, and of holding her head just so, cocked ever so slightly to the side, as she spoke to the waiter, "Yes, that will be all, thank you."

They ended up finishing their lunches and signing their checks at precisely the same time, but Joe let the woman get up first and allowed her several minutes lead time before he rose. However, as luck would have it, she was exiting the ladies' room just as he left the dining room, and the two of them ended up trapped together against a wall of the narrow hallway, waiting for a man in a wheelchair to pass. The woman smiled amiably at Joe. Her eyes were the most extraordinary shade of gray, the same as her straight, chin-length hair. She had evidently applied a fresh coat of lipstick in the ladies' room, and the red of her mouth next to the paleness of her skin and the gray of her eyes and hair gave her a somewhat startling appearance. It was as though she had stepped out of a black-and-white movie, and only her lips and her dress had been colorized.

"I'm sorry. I hope you don't think I'm stalking you," she said.

He returned the smile in effect by brightening his eyes. "Nor I you."

"I don't know why restaurants always insist on seating the loners together. You'd think they'd understand it's far more awkward that way."

"Yes, it's true."

The wheelchair passed through the door, freeing up the way to the lobby.

"Have a nice day," she said.

"You, too."

As he began to worry about getting caught again with her on the stairs up to their respective rooms, she turned and headed across the lobby, then out past the doorman, through the front door. By the time he reached the staircase, the door had closed again, shutting out the image of her slight frame striding into the sunny afternoon, her bright skirt billowing softly in the breeze.

In his dream, she had continued up the stairs with him and down the same corridor, and they had realized that their rooms were side by side. After sharing a laugh over the odd coincidence, they decided they might as well introduce themselves. One thing led to another, and they ended up sitting down together in his room, where, at a certain point in the conversation, the woman noticed that there was a door in the wall dividing his room and hers. Deciding that they would both benefit from a larger room and wouldn't mind the companionship, they set to work on opening the joining door. But before they could get it open, the phone rang.

As he now groggily adjusted his position on the sofa, he observed that there was no such door in his room, only the four white walls and the one door leading to the hallway.

"What do you mean what am I doing here? I'm writing an article for your magazine."

"But you were supposed to fly back this morning."

"No, I wasn't."

"Joe, buddy, come on. Please don't do this to me."

Buddy? He remembered Randy at age twelve, dissolving into a snotty mess of hiccupping sobs because Thomas had thrown his GI Joe in the creek.

"What exactly am I doing to you, Randy?"

"Rick. Look, I gave you this assignment against my better judgment because you promised me it would be different this time."

"Oh, for crying out loud! Get off your high horse. I want to tell you something. The way you run this magazine is an absolute joke. You send me out with no contact list, no research into the area, nothing. It's absurd. And then you can't even bother to check into the details of my flight arrangements before you call me up and harangue me for not returning when I'm supposed to—which, by the way, is tomorrow. Your father would be appalled at the way you treat your writers. The only reason I keep coming to you for assignments rather than going to other magazines is out of fondness for him."

"Do you really think there aren't a thousand and one writers

I'd rather hire? Believe me. All I can say is good luck finding a job elsewhere."

"Oh, go fuck yourself."

As Joe made his way down to the front desk, he replayed the phone conversation in his mind, and the battle's importance mounted with each descending step. These kids had disgustingly little regard for their parents' achievements and no appreciation for the ease of the paths their parents had painstakingly forged for them. He was determined to vindicate not only himself but his friend and Rick's father, Randy Senior, and beyond him, all of the other fathers.

"Good afternoon. What can I do for you, sir?" Chad grinned widely, two charming whirlpools of flesh plunging into his smooth cheeks.

Chad was a member of the hotel's homogeneously handsome and youthful staff (Albert, of course, being the exception). Joe hadn't seen Albert all day, and it now occurred to him that he sort of missed the man's dour, excessively formal pronouncements and the sight of his sagging, bassett hound jowls.

Joe handed over his airline ticket. "I'd like for you to fax this to the number I've written here at the top, please."

"Would you like to fill out a cover page to send with that, sir?"

"No. He'll know who it's from."

"Sure. I'll do that right away, and we can send it up to your room once it's gone through."

"I'd prefer to wait."

"Okeydoke."

Still grinning, Chad slipped through a door behind the desk, leaving Joe with nothing more to do but drum his fingers on the polished wood. Peering over the edge of the desk, he spotted an open *USA Today* and challenged himself to decipher the upside-down lettering. He perused the inverted typescript, finding little of interest. Then, as his gaze shifted to the adjacent page, a name leaped out at him. Rotating the paper for a better view, he was shocked to read an obituary for an actor who, though nearly three decades his junior, had crossed his path multiple times over the years, even playing opposite him in a couple of plays. According to the article, the man had suffered for quite some time from a heart disease that, at six o'clock yesterday evening, finally killed him. *Strange,* Joe thought. It didn't seem so long ago that he had taken a much smitten, teen-aged Emily backstage to meet this very actor. Fully absorbed in the article, he failed to notice Chad returning to the desk.

"The fax is being sent right now, sir. It should just take a second." Joe looked up absently.

"You're Mr. Ascher. Right?"

He nodded, returning the paper to its original position.

"We were just wondering at what time today you were planning to check out?"

"Oh, no. The magazine was confused about my schedule, but we've cleared that up. I'm not leaving until tomorrow. If you look at that ticket I'm faxing, you'll see it's for the first."

"Uh . . . well, today's the first, sir."

Joe felt the energy drain from his body. Could he have possibly gotten the days mixed up? He was absolutely sure that today was the thirty-first.

"Are you certain of that?"

"Um, yes, sir. Would you like to see a calendar?"

"No." Suddenly he recalled the pumpkin soup last night at dinner and the sachet of candy corn on his pillow. Oh, what an idiot.

Under springy, crisp strands of gelled hair, Chad's blue eyes displayed an unbearable look of compassion for his addled, septuagenarian guest.

"Just get the ticket, please," Joe told him. "If it hasn't gone through yet, I'll send it another time."

"Yes, sir. Would you like to keep your room for another night?"

"Get the ticket," he replied firmly.

Chad raised his eyebrows, a gesture of protest masquerading as innocent surprise.

"Yes, sir."

He disappeared once again through the private door and returned momentarily, ticket in hand.

"Here you go. The fax was transmitted successfully, sir."

Joe had to restrain himself to keep from grabbing Chad's rake-like visor of hair.

"Thank you. I'll need the room for at least one more night."

"And would you like me to change your flight arrangements for you, sir?"

"No. I'll do it myself."

"Very well, then. Have a good day."

With a nod, Joe slid the ticket into his pocket and headed slowly back upstairs. It was funny—the fact he'd mixed up the dates seemed inconsequential. What bothered him was the realization that he had sunk to Rick's level. He had had the opportunity to rise above and to commit that ultimate fatherly act, forgiveness, but had declined it in favor of petty jousting. He was a better man than that. So when he opened the door to his room to hear the ring of the phone, he felt a sense of relief. It had to be Rick. Here was a chance to show who he really was, an opportunity to apologize for the mix-up, and also to forgive.

"Hello." He steeled himself.

"Dad?"

"Uh . . . hello?"

"Dad, it's Emily."

"Emily? What are you doing calling me here?"

"Don't act so thrilled."

"How did you get this number?"

"I got it from Rick."

"What?"

"Randy."

There was a nervous cadence to her voice. He wondered what exactly Rick had told her. Down below, he saw someone walking around on the other side of the garden fence.

"Dad, I left two messages on your cell phone. Didn't you get them?"

"Listen, I really can't talk right now, Emily. I'm working here."

He walked over to the window. But by the time he got there, the person had passed out of view.

"I wanted to tell you something."

He released a very audible, frustrated sigh. "What?"

She paused for a moment then said, "Never mind."

"You might as well tell me now that you've got me on the phone."

There was a long pause while he waited for her to begin.

"Forget it," she said finally. "I'll talk to you when you get back."

"Okay. If you like."

"Yeah. Well . . . call me when you get home, I guess."

"Mm-hmm," he said. "I'll do that."

"Sorry to bother you. Bye."

"Good-bye."

As he hung up the phone, he remembered the obituary, and it occurred to him that Emily might have seen it, too. Perhaps this was what she wanted to tell him. It seemed doubtful as they had never been able to discuss the strange relationship that had developed between Emily and that man—nor Joe's own role in unwittingly bringing the two of them together. What news, then, did she have to share? Perhaps she was calling to apologize, though it didn't sound like it.

Shortly before four o'clock, he went back downstairs. Much to his delight, Ingrid was there, standing near the front door, shifting impatiently from one leg to the other and tugging at the sleeves of her oversized blazer. He took her on a tour of the lobby, where like Goldilocks, she insisted on trying out each chair before finding the one that suited her best. She found the leather chair in front of the fireplace so comfortable that it was a struggle to get her out of it, and when he tried to coax her out to the garden for tea, she rolled her eyes and asked him if he'd ever heard of something called polite conversation.

Finally, with the promise of freshly baked madeleines, he got her outside, where it was another beautiful fall afternoon, and they settled in at the same table they had occupied the other day—a cup of tea for him, and for her, a Coke.

"What's this thing?" Ingrid asked.

"That's a Dictaphone," he answered. "I use it for my work."

She pressed the red RECORD button and spoke into the machine.

"Test, test, one, two, three . . ."

The crescendo of Rachmaninoff's *Rhapsody on a Theme of Paganini* swelled from the speakers discreetly nestled in the hedge behind their table. The symphony was part of a loop of classical music that ran continuously on the hotel patio—he knew because he had heard it already a dozen times over the last few days. This time, a minute or so earlier when it had begun, Ingrid had immediately taken notice, claiming that "the chorus," as she called it, sounded exactly like Neil Diamond's "September Morn," one of her mother's favorite songs. And while he would have never made the connection himself, hearing her sing the words along with the piano chords now, he found that, oddly enough, she was right.

She sang into the Dictaphone, "Sep-tem-ber morn . . ."

Tickled to death by her own singing, she howled with laughter. Her mouth was a gaping, purple hole, stained by a piece of candy she'd eaten in the lobby, and it gave her a comically ghoulish appearance.

He looked on, amused. He had forgotten how much pleasure kids could derive from the most mundane activities. At fourteen, Ingrid was on the cusp of losing that forever, but for now, she was having an absolute ball.

Rewinding the tape, Ingrid pressed PLAY, and upon hearing her own voice, erupted in laughter again.

"Woo!" she howled, fanning her hand in front of her face as if attempting to extinguish a fire on her nose. "That's funny. Could I have a worse voice?"

Joe smiled. "So," he said. "Tell me about yourself. How do you spend your time around here?—when you're not reading your way through the school library."

She lowered her mouth to meet the straw in her glass of Coke. And after a long, thoughtful drag, she said, "For one thing, I spend a lot of time at this record store. There's a cool guy who works there, who's a senior. And there's one lady who's, like, much older. She's got kids and everything. And she's really nice. And she always has the coolest earrings. My mom won't let me get my ears pierced until I turn eighteen. Isn't that the most ridiculous thing you've ever heard? I mean, it's my skin and I think I have a right to put holes in it if I choose to—especially if I'm paying for it myself with my allowance. Don't you think?"

"Sounds reasonable."

"Yeah. Well, for now, I spend the money on CDs. But the stupid record store never has anything I want, and I always have to special-order my CDs, which takes *forever*."

He nodded sympathetically.

"It's really lame. Anyway, I can't wait until I can move someplace more interesting."

"I'm sorry. Remind me again. That happens next fall?"

She gave a little, exasperated huff and rolled her eyes. "Well. I mean, frankly, I don't even know now. Because apparently my parents didn't think I was being serious before when I told them I was going to move. So when I said something about it the other day, they were like, *Whoa, whoa, whoa . . . wait a minute. We never said you could do that.* Which is crazy, because it's not like I'm planning on sleeping on the streets or something."

"Where would you stay? Do you know anyone there?"

"No, but I could find a family to take me in. You know—like an exchange student kind of thing."

He smiled. "But think about your parents—how they'd miss you. It would be terrible. And wouldn't you miss them?"

"Yeah. I guess. But it would be worth it. I really need to be around more interesting people." She had wedged the tip of the straw between her two front teeth, and it stuck straight out at him. "Like you."

He was surprised to find how much it touched him to hear her say this, and he began to stammer as he searched for the appropriate response. But before he could get a word out, she was off again.

"Maybe you could even help me get an internship at the magazine. That would be cool. You've got like a super high-powered job there, right? And I'm a really good writer."

"To tell you the truth, I don't really work at a magazine. I write articles now and then for various publications, but I'm actually a playwright."

"Are you serious? That's amazing. I'd love to do something like that. Do you like Shakespeare?"

"Of course."

"I think he's a total genius. I've read *Romeo and Juliet* like five thousand times. Maybe we could write something together. I've got tons of ideas."

"I don't doubt it."

"Why are you smiling like that?" she asked. "Like you're all amused?"

"I am amused."

She folded her arms defensively across her chest. "What do you find so amusing?"

"I . . . Let's see, how do I put this? I think it's wonderful that you're willing to throw yourself so completely and so passionately into something entirely new without any regard for the risks of the unknown."

"What? Is that so strange?"

"I guess not. Not for someone your age."

She raised a suspicious eyebrow. "What's *that* supposed to mean?"

He scratched the side of his face, and his fingers made a scraping sound against the short stubble of his beard.

"Let's take Romeo and Juliet, for example," he told her. "Since you're so big on them. I mean, here's a guy who at the start of the play is desperately in love—so in love that he claims to be unable to even look at another woman. But the very second that he sees Juliet, his love for this woman flies out the window, never to be mentioned again. And within hours—*hours,* mind you—he has proposed marriage to Juliet. She, on the other hand, is a bit more cautious, waiting all the way until the next morning to accept. Then, *one day* later, both of them believe so fervently in the unmatchable perfection of their love that they each choose death over a life without the other."

"Yeah . . . so?"

"So. That is a perfect example of the optimism of youth. I can assure you that had these two lovebirds been ten years older—five even—the story would not have unfolded as it did."

"But it's a great play."

"Absolutely."

"But you're acting like Romeo and Juliet are foolish and naive and immature."

He smiled. "They are. That's what's so wonderful about them. And their premature deaths prevent them from ever becoming otherwise. God forbid Shakespeare had let them both live. No doubt, they would have turned into George and Martha."

"Who are George and Martha?"

"Aha!" he said. "Finally something you haven't read. They're the subject of another play. They're older, and they've been married long enough that their favorite form of amusement is torturing each other. I'll give it to you if you want."

"Sounds awful."

"It's very realistic."

She sighed heavily. "But do you still think it's possible for two people at some point in their lives to have the kind of love that Romeo and Juliet do? I mean, to feel that strongly about each other?"

"Maybe. I certainly don't want to be the voice of doom and gloom here. You've got a lot of wonderful experiences ahead of you."

"Yeah. Whatever."

"What? You don't think your Romeo's out there?"

"I don't know. The guys at my school are dumb. And there's one older guy I kind of like, but we're just friends."

"The one at the record store?"

"Yeah."

"And he's a senior?"

"Yeah."

"So is he leaving to go to college next year?"

"Yeah," she said impatiently.

"And where is he going?"

"He doesn't know. He's doing the applications now. Maybe New York. He has family there."

Joe smiled. "Oh?"

She drew herself up defensively. "I'm not just moving to New York because he is."

"All right." He nodded seriously. "Out of curiosity, though, does he know you're planning to go there?"

"No." She sank back down in her chair. "He wouldn't care anyway. He thinks I'm just some little kid."

He smiled sympathetically and offered her the plate of madeleines. She took one, then after a quick glance at the other things on the table, asked if she could dip it in his tea.

"Sure," he said, passing her the cup.

"He's so funny. You know what he did the other day? His dad's a dentist, right? And he sometimes hangs out in his dad's office and helps and stuff."

As she talked, she carefully dunked the tip of the cookie, then nibbled, then dunked again. He wasn't able to follow the story completely, but the gist of it was that the boy's father had asked him to keep watch for a few minutes over a man who was being fitted for a new appliance, and as the man lay captive in the dentist chair, with pink paste oozing out of the sides of his mouth, the boy took the liberty of lecturing him about the hazards of poor hygiene, illustrating his point with the aid of gory photographs he'd found in one of his dad's medical books. Apparently Ingrid thought this was hilariously funny, and as she tried to tell the story, she kept bursting into such fits of laughter, she had to wipe the tears away with her napkin. Besides the infectiousness of her joy, Joe was touched by the way her eyes gleamed and her voice filled with reverence as she spoke.

"It sounds like you really like this guy," he said as she finished her story.

"Well . . ." She flipped her bangs out of her eyes with one hand, then smiled, and a deep pink blush spread upward from her neck, through her cheeks. "I guess I do." She looked down at her lap, embarrassed. "This probably sounds dumb, but sometimes I think he might be my soul mate."

Joe shrugged. "I suppose he could be."

"Do you really think so?" she asked hopefully.

"I don't know."

"But if he is, how's he ever going to know it? He leaves for college next year, and right now he sees me as some naive little dork."

Joe laughed. "Do *you* think that you're a naive little dork?"

"No," she replied indignantly. "I'm incredibly mature as a

matter of fact. A lot more mature than some of the seniors, that's for sure."

"Well, you've got to prove that to him then."

"How?"

"I'm going to have to think about that."

"Will you?" she asked eagerly. "Will you promise to help me?"

He hesitated. "I'm not sure that I *can* help you."

"Yes, you can. I know you can. I can tell you know so much about this stuff." She gazed at him with wide, expectant eyes.

"I'll try and think about it," he said.

"Oh, thank you! Thank you!" She jumped out of her chair and surprised him by throwing her arms around his neck. "You're the greatest. Seriously. You are."

He patted her back. "Okay. Okay."

After a moment, she finally released her hold and composed herself once again.

"Well, Joe," she said. "Let me know when you're ready, and we'll come up with a plan."

That night, Joe paced around his hotel room in a white terry cloth robe and matching slippers, brushing his teeth. He picked up the clothes he had worn that day and hung each item with care on the wooden hangers printed with the hotel's insignia. Then he sat down and sorted through the mess of miniature tapes scattered across the desk, checking the titles of several before finally replacing the one in the Dictaphone.

We weren't compatible came the voice—his own youthful voice again—from the machine.

He liked the fact that I was a doctor—that people would come to me to find out what was wrong with them. And sometimes that made me uncomfortable. Sometimes I wondered if he didn't love me so much as he wanted to become me. I guess that sounds conceited, but to tell you the truth, it used to make me feel lousy. He was a great guy, and I was completely in love with him. Holy cow, though, did he have a load of hang-ups. About his upbringing, and the fact he'd dropped out of college, yada, yada, yada. Dumb things. But important to him. So the two of us would be out—at a party or something with a group of people—and he'd be telling one of his stories or going off on one of his political rants. And as he was talking, his eyes would wander over to me—you know, the way you kind of look around at different people as you're talking. And I'd always start off nodding and smiling, like I was encouraging him. And then, slowly, while he was talking, I'd start to make this face—not a frown exactly, but a look like maybe I was getting a little worried. And I'd watch him start to get a little nervous. And then I'd say something like, "Are you sure about that?" Or I'd interrupt and say, "Actually, I read an article about this, and I might be wrong, but I think it portrayed the issue a little differently." And I'd do this maybe three or four times—not exactly the same every time, you know, I'd vary it a little to fit the conversation. And by the end of the party, he'd be completely tongue-tied. And a lot of the time, I'd made it all up.

Here, there was a pause.

You know, the funny part is, that was long before I found out he was sleeping around.

Switching off the machine, Joe thought about what the *Times* had written about *Before Swine*, the play that eventually incorporated both this monologue and the one concerning the girl in the purple hat. The *Times* had called it a revelation, an ingenious— almost miraculous—architectural feat. He still remembered portions of the review word for word. "It is a profound mystery how one builds such a thing in less than three hours: an entire three-dimensional world populated by a dozen complex characters—all but one of them female, all played by one man. Most curiously and perhaps most daringly, the fourth wall comes and goes as each character switches between narrating, acting out, and commenting upon his or her scenes. With so little structural support, how does this play stand? I cannot tell you how, but I can tell you that it does—balancing with awe-inspiring beauty on the shoulders of its wildly talented creator and star."

This review had broken everything open, bringing people from far and wide to the tiny off-Broadway theater where *Before Swine* first opened, and finally moving the play to Broadway. But ultimately, everyone had agreed that *Before Swine* was brilliant for the way it accentuated the difficulty—and absurdity—in trying to distinguish villains from victims, despicable characters from lovable ones. The women, all love-interests of one kind or another to the male character, and all simultaneously the subjects and objects of his deceit—chipped away at him, bit by bit, slowly demolishing him. But one by one, he devastated all of them as well. By the end of the play, every character had both endured and inflicted a startling amount of pain. He remembered what a self-righteous jerk he'd been in reality back then, and he marveled at the fact that, still, he'd been able to draw such complex portraits. Why did he now find it all so challenging?

Again he picked up the Dictaphone, this time ejecting the tape and replacing it with another. Once the new tape was in, he listened to make sure that he wasn't about to record over any of the stuff about Ingrid he'd put down earlier.

I told her she shouldn't worry, and assured her once again that we'd figure it out together. "Oh, I'm not worried," she said, her optimism clearly restored. "If it's meant to be, it will happen. I mean look at how Fitzgerald and Hemingway and Stein and Picasso all went abroad and ended up finding each other. Look at how you and I found each other. Maybe he and I, along with some of the other great minds of our day, will meet somewhere and form a group of expats. And you could be part of it, too, if you want."

He stopped the tape then hit the RECORD button and began to speak. "She was so full of dreams, full of life, so innocent and so vulnerable. I couldn't stand the idea that those dreams might ever fade away, and that the life would gradually drain out of her as that wonderful innocence was replaced, bit by bit, with knowledge—not the knowledge which she sought so voraciously from her books and which fed her dreams, but real knowledge, and experience, the kind that snuck up on you when you weren't paying attention until one day, you discovered all at once that you'd not only grown up but that you'd grown a thick, unsightly, and impermeable shell."

He shut off the Dictaphone and leaned back, stretching his arms overhead. He was finally getting some good work done. If this play turned out as well as he hoped, everyone—his daughter included—would be forced to reevaluate him. He thought with satisfaction that for the first time in a long while, as a writer, a father, and a man, he was back on track. And the kind of future that only this afternoon had seemed like an impossibility was suddenly feeling like something that might soon lie within his grasp.

As he sat there, feeling increasingly happy, it occurred to him that there was really no reason why Emily shouldn't accompany him to Williamstown for the premiere. He was sure that once she realized this tribute was really happening and heard reports that this new play he was unveiling was something of a masterpiece, she would be glad to make a weekend of it. They would drive up together, as they used to do years ago, stopping along the way at funny roadside eateries. And over a basket of fried clams, she would tell him all about her job, laughing about the dreary attorneys she worked with. They would talk about Clay—how she thought she might marry him one day, or how she didn't think she ever could, why he made her happy or failed to make her happy . . . and he would listen and offer his advice.

Then he realized she might insist that Clay should come, too. It was hard to imagine how one of their traditional father-daughter outings would unfold with this addition. He couldn't envision Clay sitting through multiple performances of the same play, watching alternately from the audience and the wings; nor could he imagine what sort of contributions the boy might make to the conversation on the drive home as he and Emily exchanged the kind of thoughts they used to in the old days, arguing heatedly and also ardently agreeing, back and forth for hours, over what did and didn't work about the play. He worried Clay's presence might rein her in, and it slowly dawned on him that the two of them—Emily and her boyfriend—were likely to see the play only once. Maybe they would limit the trip to a single night and insist on driving up on their own. It was quite possible that Emily didn't even like road trips anymore. He didn't know. That idea began to sink in and ate away at his exuberance. But before it had the chance to significantly alter his mood, he shoved the thought aside. He still felt pretty sure that she'd come—even if only out of a sense of duty. And he *knew* this was going to be an incredible play, possibly the best he'd ever written. He pushed his chair away from the desk, and standing up, went over to the bed.

Removing the chocolate truffle and the weather report from his pillow and placing them on the bedside table, he stepped out of his slippers. Tomorrow he'd have to figure out what to do about Ingrid and this boy she called her soul mate. He laughed—what a ridiculous notion. Then again, he of all people knew how wonderful it could be to dream.

I N THE LIVING ROOM OF THEIR NEW YORK APART-
ment, Joe stood at the bar—nothing more than a bunch of glasses,
a chilled bottle of wine, and a bucket of ice set up on top of an
antique cabinet which had once held Laura's parents' photo albums
and now held the liquor. As he screwed the cap back on the vodka
bottle, music began to blast from the direction of Emily's room.

Laura turned to him. "See what I mean? She honestly has no
sense of remorse whatsoever. To her this is a vacation."

Joe's childhood friend, Burt Horvath, was down from Boston
for a medical conference. And even though Burt would be accompanying them to a dinner party that evening at Gina Dole's as well
as staying with them for the next six nights, sharing their breakfast
table each morning, and joining them for dinner on all but one of
those evenings, Laura had insisted that it would be terribly inhos-
pitable of them not to sit down with him for an intimate chat before
going out. So the three of them—along with Thomas, who had just
arrived home from basketball practice—were now gathered for a
preparty drink.

"Emily was suspended from school today," Joe explained to Burt. "The principal caught her and another girl smoking pot in the park."

"Oh boy."

"Yes," Laura said with a sigh. "It's been quite a day. Anyway, sweetie," she said, turning back to Thomas. "Finish your story."

Joe wandered over to the armchair next to Burt's and sat down, raising his glass and smiling nostalgically at his friend as his son began to talk. Joe and Burt had grown up on the same block in the Bronx and ridden the bus together every day to school, played jacks and marbles on the pavement, and retreated to one of their homes whenever the tougher kids came out to play kick the can. In an immigrant neighborhood where a sense of community was treasured, the two of them shared the rare impulse to get away the first chance they got, and they spent their time dreaming of the glamorous lives they would live as adults. Now, whenever they were apart, leading their separate lives in their separate cities, Joe still thought of Burt as the old Burt, the kindred spirit. But when they came together and sat face-to-face in the same, small room, and Joe saw Burt's shabby, orthopedically sensible shoes and heard him prattle on about the deck he was adding onto the house and the injustice of the difficult word that trumped his daughter in the district spelling bee, he could not find the old Burt. And he wondered if the old Burt had ever existed or if he had simply seen in him what he wanted to see because he needed a friend. He had tried to speak to Laura about it once, but found it impossible to convey the sense of betrayal and loneliness brought on by his disappointment in Burt's choices. What she heard instead was petty criticism, and what she expressed in response could only be read as disgust. They had sat on the bed in a Boston hotel room for nearly an hour after dining at Burt and Jan's house—he trying to make her see, she lecturing him for being a snob.

He looked at Laura now, curled up on the sofa beside Thomas. With her shoes off and her feet tucked up under her rear, she could almost pass for one of her son's classmates. She wore her customary, minimal touch of makeup and a loose black shift. Even on a muggy, eighty-plus-degree September night such as this one, Joe knew that most of the other women at the dinner party would be wearing tailored suits or form-fitting dresses with cinched waists and shoulder pads, and he felt certain that a few of these women would find Laura's attire inappropriately informal. Sometimes he found this embarrassing, but he always made a point of complimenting her appearance. After years of being told by her mother that she was plain, Laura was exceptionally sensitive about the way she looked. And generally he appreciated the fact that his wife's beauty was her own. Her light hair, still free for the most part of the wiry, silver strands that plagued other women her age, provided a stunning complement to her shockingly white skin. And her figure, though it had lost some of its youthful perfection, still filled him with desire. Just tonight, as he watched her lean over to set a small glass bowl of raw cashews and raisins out on the coffee table, the hint of her well-formed buttock shifting gracefully beneath her dress, he was unable to restrain himself from reaching out and touching her. She tolerated this as she had tolerated so many similar advances, letting his hand fall before she moved on to rearrange the five calla lilies in their vase beside the fireplace.

Though Thomas looked at Burt as he spoke, he obviously sensed his mother's adoring gaze and acknowledged her every now and then with a sideways glance. She had heard the story before. Both of his parents had. Thomas had talked of little else over the last three days. He had wanted so deeply to communicate to his classmates the flaw he'd spotted in the microcosm of their high school world, and to inspire a reaction against the profound injustice of illusory autonomy. But rather than protesting the elections outright, he declared himself a candidate and made the same sort of rah-rah campaign speech as the other candidates—in exactly the three minutes allotted by the school rules—attempting subtly but ingeniously to convey his anarchist message by holding a hand puppet to the microphone throughout his speech.

"When I finished," Thomas explained to Burt, "I thought, *Wow, this is great. They really got it.* You know? Because they were really applauding like crazy. But then this girl—I mean, this is like a pretty smart girl I'm talking about; she makes like straight A's—and anyway, she came up to me and she started going on about how *cute* the puppet was. Right? But I thought, *Oh, she thinks it's cute, but she still got the point.* But then I was like, *Wait, maybe she didn't get it.* So I asked her point-blank. You know, I just said something like, 'Cool, I'm glad you liked it. So you agree with what I'm saying about how we're just a puppet government, and the whole thing is like a total sham?' And she looked at me so blankly and she goes, 'Why's it a total sham?'"

Laura rolled her eyes at Burt. "Can you believe it? And this is the girl who edits the school paper." She turned to Thomas for confirmation. "Right?"

"Yeah. Who edits *my* articles."

"Sounds like she'd fit right in at the *Boston Herald*," Burt said.

Laura laughed.

After pulling Joe away from an important phone call with the director of his current play, Laura had spent twenty minutes talking with Burt about the radical new procedure which he'd been given the green light to start testing at Harvard and which was rapidly generating hope and praise in the medical community for its potential to cure Alzheimer's. Then, upon Thomas's arrival, she had launched right into the issue of the boy's campaign, never in all that time casting so much as a glance in Joe's direction. Now, as Thomas finished the story of his victory, she turned to Joe with an unmistakably self-satisfied look, a look which said, "You don't know these people as I do because you don't share my capacity to care."

"So," Burt said to Thomas, "did the other kids get it?"

"I mean, I think they had some idea that I was sort of challenging the system and stuff, and they were kind of like, *Right on, school politics are dumb,* but *nobody* really had a clue what I was trying to say."

"Christ," Joe said in a tone he thought good-natured enough, "I've never heard anybody grumble so much about winning an election. I hate to think of the state you'd be in if you'd lost."

Burt began to chuckle.

Laura pulled a strand of hair from her cushion and flicked it into the air behind the couch. "Darling, you're missing the whole point."

"Right, Dad. I'll remember that next time you're complaining about a good review because the critic's a moron and missed the point of your play."

Laura clapped her hands together. "Oh, touché!"

Burt began to chuckle again. "Uh-oh. Look out for this one. He doesn't miss a beat."

Joe put up his hands in surrender. "Point taken."

Nobody had anything to say to this, so he shook the ice in his glass. "Anyone care for a refill?"

Burt held up his glass, showing that it was still three-quarters full. "No, thanks. I'm good."

Laura smiled and raised her eyebrows, which meant *No*. Actually, it meant *Of course not. And I wish you wouldn't*.

As Joe made his way back to the bar, Burt turned to Laura. "So what happened exactly with Emily today? She got caught smoking pot?"

"Yes," Laura said. "By the principal."

"At least it wasn't a cop," he replied.

Joe smiled at Laura. "Can you imagine how Barclay and Sandra Davis would react to little Sandy getting arrested?"

Barclay and Sandra Davis, the parents of the other girl, had been present at the meeting in the principal's office as well. Joe and Laura had met them once before when they had gone to their house for dinner along with some friends of Laura's they were visiting in Southampton for the weekend. It was ages ago, and Joe really only remembered a couple of things about that evening. One of those things was the wine—a delicate, deliciously dry Italian white, a Tocai. He'd asked Sandra for the name of the wine and had gone out and bought a case for their hosts the next day as a thank-you for the weekend. But when they opened the first bottle that night at dinner, the wine tasted sickeningly sweet. It turned out that instead of the Italian *Tocai*, he had ignorantly bought the Hungarian dessert wine, *Tokay*. And his hosts pretended to love it, which only made the incident more embarrassing.

"That Barclay Davis is a real number," he said.

"The other girl's father," Laura explained to Burt.

"The moment he sat down next to me in the principal's office, he started looking me up and down with those cold eyes of his, and then he was asking about our place in Litchfield, Connecticut. You should have seen his face when I told him he had it wrong; we were in the Berkshires. He might as well have said he was sorry for us."

"Oh please, Joe."

"I'm not kidding. And you know why, don't you? Because he was thinking Catskills. He was imagining us spending our summers up in some run-down, Jewish enclave. And he felt embarrassed for me. He was literally *embarrassed* for me."

"Honest to God! Do you have any idea how paranoid you sound?"

"I'm not paranoid. There are lots of people who get mixed up between the Berkshires and the Catskills."

He looked to Burt for confirmation, but Burt was smiling uncomfortably at Thomas.

"All of those Hamptons types do," Joe told them all a bit defensively. "This isn't the first time this has happened."

"You know . . ." She shook her head in frustration. "You always think people are thinking about *you*. Barclay was there because his daughter had been picked up by the *principal* doing *drugs* in the *park*." On every word that she emphasized, she stuck out another finger as if tallying up a list.

"Do you really think," she continued, "he gave a damn where your country house was located?"

"If he didn't give a damn, then why did he bring it up?"

"I don't know, Joe." She sighed as if exhausted by his question. "He was probably just making conversation. I can't believe you're thinking about this right now. What you should be thinking about is what we're going to do with our delinquent daughter."

"I have been thinking about that. And it occurred to me that I might be able to get her to do a play with me."

Laura flashed him a look of shock. "A play?"

"Yes. I think she might be getting a little bored."

A hush fell over the room. Thomas and Burt both stared at their feet.

"Well," Laura said, leaning forward and setting her wine glass on the table. "We should probably go. Shouldn't we?"

The moment they walked in the door of Gina's loft, Gina turned from the people she was talking to and held out both arms toward Joe.

"Darling!" she called, coming toward them. "Finally!"

Laura was surprised to find her completely changed. The last time she'd seen her, Gina had gotten pretty hefty. Over the eighteen months it took to finalize her divorce, Laura guessed she had gained at least thirty pounds. And while she knew Gina had been at a fat farm for the last month, she hadn't expected to see such a radical difference. Not only did Gina appear to have lost most of the weight, but with it, she had lost the heavy pall which had begun to burden her features over the last several years. Now, walking toward them, a gauzy, lavender shawl fluttering in her wake and her long, tight, burgundy curls flying every which way, she exuded zephyrean lightness.

"There are so many people I want you to meet," she told Joe as she embraced him. "Come here," she said, taking his hand and starting toward the seating area where most of the people were gathered.

"Gina," Joe said, pulling her back. "This is Burt Horvath."

"Oh, yes! Your nursery school buddy!" She shook Burt's hand. "So nice to meet you. I'm so glad you could come along."

Laura, who had always considered Gina more handsome than beautiful, couldn't stop staring.

"Me, too," Burt said. "Thanks for including me."

"Of course, of course. Oh hi, Laura sweetheart." Grabbing her by her shoulders, she kissed the air next to Laura's cheek. "Don't you look adorable!"

Laura was about to say something about how Gina was the one who ought to be complimented. But before she could put the words together, someone else was coming through the door, and Gina was telling Joe to wait right there while she said hello because she wanted to introduce him to some people.

"Gina is Joe's producer," she told Burt.

"Yes, he told me." He looked around the room. "Do you happen to know where there might be a restroom?" he asked.

"Oh." She pointed down the hall. "Down there, I think. And if it's occupied, there's another one through the bedroom over there."

Burt went off down the hall, and Joe and Laura moved into the room to make way for the people who were coming in behind them.

"Wow, she really went all out, didn't she?" Joe asked, looking over at the table of drinks that had been set up in the corner with a tuxedoed bartender behind it. "Do you want anything?"

She shook her head. They stood there for a moment, looking around at the other people, some of whom she recognized. Joe waved to a couple across the room.

"There's Marty and Ann," he said.

"Joe?"

He looked at her, but his face was still holding the smile he had given to Marty and Ann, and she could see that he was thinking about them or some of the other people in the room.

"Are you honestly planning on putting Emily in a play?"

"I thought it might be a good idea," he said, scanning the room again. "She's expressed some interest in acting lately. And if she were doing something with me, I'd be able to keep my eye on her."

She gave him a hostile look to let him know this was not a casual conversation. "I assume when you say 'doing something with me' you mean something you've written. Or are you planning on being in it, too?"

One of the people who had just come in bumped against her back, and she stepped over to the wall to get out of the way. Joe moved with her.

"I don't know," he said, more attentive now. "I haven't really worked it out completely. It could be someone else's play even."

"What? You mean you're going to convince somebody else to cast not only you but also your daughter, who has never acted before in her entire life?"

"Laura, it was simply an idea."

She turned to the painting beside her and studied it hard.

"What's wrong?" he asked. "Laura . . ."

"I can't believe you would even suggest this," she said, finally turning toward him.

"I don't know why you're getting so angry."

"I find that hard to believe."

"Why would it be so hard for me to get cast in somebody else's play?"

"What?"

"You implied I'd have some difficulty convincing someone to cast me."

"No, I didn't."

"Yes, you did. You said you didn't see how—"

"Oh, for Christ's sake!"

With a look of innocent surprise, he gestured with his hands that he was dropping the issue right then and there.

"I think," Laura continued, "I think the whole idea of her working with you is—it's just plain wrong. Has it occurred to you that you may be part of the problem?"

He looked at her, aghast. "How so?"

"Come on, Joe. We've talked about this a thousand times. I know it's flattering to you, but it's not natural."

Somehow, his wife had gotten this idea in her head that the connection he shared with their daughter was a problem. It was unhealthy, she told him, for a girl to be so starstruck by her own father. To him, it was a wonderful friendship, but to Laura, it was a fixation, an Electra complex, an abnormal attachment.

"Seriously," Laura said, "you have to stop encouraging her."

"How do I *encourage* her? Because I'm nice to her? Because I actually *like* spending time with her?"

She looked away, stung. Then gazing past Joe, she smiled weakly. "And here's Burt."

Laura took Burt in hand and began to introduce him around. *Thank God,* Joe thought, heading for the bar. He really didn't feel like dealing with Burt tonight. Surveying the crowded room, he found a lot of familiar faces. The party was bigger than he'd expected. He knew he would hear from Laura about this later—she hated large gatherings. As he waited for the bartender to make his drink, he watched the other guests, eager to join them.

At dinner, he found himself seated between an avid collector of contemporary art and a woman who was either the founder, or president, or both, of the Santa Fe Opera. He had been looking down the table at Laura when she told him, and was only half listening. He watched Laura laughing with Burt, who was seated beside her. She seemed to be having a nice time despite the size of the party—which he attributed to the fact that she was now sitting down and thus locked within a small group whose parameters set her at ease.

After dessert, still engaged with the woman from Santa Fe, he remained seated while everyone around them began to migrate. The seats in their vicinity did not stay empty for long, however, filling first with a few of Joe's acquaintances who came to sit with him, prompting him to tell this story or that, the telling of which attracted more people until eventually, his audience exceeded the number of available seats.

Joe was telling the story of the time last year when he'd sprained his ankle at the beginning of *Before Swine*'s Broadway run. Because there were no costumes in the one-man show, the believability of each character depended completely on the words and the performance. Each time the lights went up, he would be frozen in a pose befitting whatever persona he'd taken on—lounging in a lawn chair, hunched over a washing machine, standing at a pay phone. This meant that he had to maneuver his way around what had essentially become an obstacle course of props and furniture in the dark. One evening, he tripped and fell over a glass coffee table, landing with a loud crash that sent a ripple of worried gasps through the house. When the spotlight came up on the bed at center stage, he was not on it. Seeing this, the man operating the spot immediately extinguished the light. Joe began to speak his lines in the dark. The light came back on and found him sprawled on the floor beside the glass table at stage right. Making spontaneous adjustments to his monologue, he incorporated his fall into the character's story and joked with the audience about "the drunk light-man." He ad-libbed so successfully that, once he'd sufficiently recovered from the sprain, the fall—this time carefully choreographed—was incorporated into the show.

He was finishing this story, basking in the laughter of his listeners, when he looked up and saw Burt. *Oh, Christ.* It wasn't that he didn't want to give Burt his attention, but he didn't see how he was going to integrate this man into the group that had now formed around him. Was he, he asked himself, a snob as Laura had said? Was he *embarrassed* by his friend's provinciality and, thus, trying to disassociate himself from it?

Joe's empty glass gave him the perfect excuse to extricate himself from the group, and as he rose, he indicated to Burt that he should follow. As they walked together toward the bar, he put his arm around Burt's shoulder.

"Enjoying yourself?"

"Oh, yeah. Sure."

He waited for Burt to say something else. He had thrown the ball into the ring, but Burt wasn't returning it. Removed now from the frenetic energy of the group, Joe realized that he was feeling a bit tipsy.

"Good."

Maybe, Joe thought, letting his arm fall back at his side, *Burt had not wanted to be rescued.* Maybe he had, in fact, been enjoying the chance to drift anonymously through a crowd of somebody else's friends and acquaintances.

"Do you think you can manage the thrill of getting to room with a president tonight?" Joe finally said.

Burt chuckled. "I never mind rooming with Thomas. At least he doesn't snore like Harvey."

Harvey was Burt's son.

"Oh yeah? Does Harvey snore?"

"Does he ever. Sometimes I think he's going to bring the house down."

As they reached the bar, Joe gave a familiar nod to the bartender and asked Burt what he wanted.

People were wandering back in from the dining room now and finding seats around the living room. Burt couldn't seem to get over the number of people Joe knew and kept asking, "And how do you know *him*?" or "How did you meet *her*?" Joe could never tell whether Burt was envious of his life or merely amazed—or even repelled—by its complexity. After a lengthy discussion, which evidently tickled Burt—about a gossip columnist whom everyone detested but invited to their parties anyway—Joe began to tire of his who's-who tour and brought it to an abrupt close.

"And there you have it," he said, rapping his knuckles on the table, "the full house of nuts."

Burt smiled. "What play was it that had that great line? 'I'm from Brazil—where the nuts come from.' Neil Simon, right? Was it *The Odd Couple?*"

"Yes," Joe said with surprise. "Very good."

"I'm not a complete ignoramus."

Joe laughed this off lightly, the alcohol in his system mitigating the sting of guilt. He raised his glass. "It's good to see you, Burt."

Burt dutifully clinked the glass with his own and drank, but his steady, unfocused gaze suggested that he had something else on his mind. Putting down his drink, he exhaled audibly. "I wanted to talk to you about something."

Joe nodded attentively, wishing to convey that he valued whatever Burt had to say and that he did not consider him an ignoramus.

"How are things between you and Laura?"

"Between me and Laura?" He was not prepared for this question. "Good." He shrugged. "Good. Why? Did Laura say something to you?"

Burt averted his eyes.

"What did she say? Did she tell you that I'm *flirtatious* with my daughter?"

"Look, I don't want to intrude."

"Did she say that? Because it's absurd. You've seen us together— and you've seen the way *she* is with Thomas."

"Forget what she said. I want to tell you something."

"Go ahead."

"Remember when, a few years ago, you and I had that conversation about how you sometimes feel like Laura does things to set you off? Like she harbors anger toward you—and feels a constant urge to put you down?"

"I don't remember that."

"All right. Well, I think it's a two-way street."

"What do you mean?"

"It seems like for you to offer Emily a part in a play would be a little—I don't know—cruel really."

"Cruel? Cruel to whom? To Laura?"

"Yes."

Joe laughed at the absurdity of this. "And why is that exactly?"

"Listen. I'm trying to help here."

"I'm listening. Go ahead."

Burt hesitated. "I'm wondering if it may be wrong to give a part to Emily when, in all the years that Laura struggled as an actress, you never lifted a finger to help her."

"Is that what she told you?"

"I don't want to—"

"Is that what she told you? Because it's a lie. I suppose she also told you that's why she quit? Because I never gave her any help?"

"Joe—"

"It's a lie. Let me tell you something. She *hates* acting. She used to vomit before every single audition and every single performance. She *hated* it. If she had ever wanted my help, I would have given it to her in a heartbeat."

"I'm sure—"

"No. This really bothers me. And it bothers me that you would buy the whole thing. Whose friend are you, anyway?"

"I consider myself a friend of both of you."

"Well . . ." He wished he hadn't had so much to drink. The question of whose friend Burt was sounded so pathetically juvenile, he instantly regretted asking it. It seemed the only way to regain control was to put Burt on the defensive. Lacing his words with a sardonicism that teetered between play and hostility, he said, "This is one hell of a way to talk to someone who's putting you up for the week."

Burt hung his head apologetically. "I'm only telling you this because I care about both of you, and I don't want to see things get messed up."

"So you think that I'm the problem?"

"I think—" Burt cut himself short, pausing to select his words carefully. "I think that you can sometimes fail to notice when you do things that are hurtful to others."

"You think I'm the problem."

"I didn't say that."

"No. You didn't have to."

Looking away, disgusted, Joe saw Gina walking toward him with a big smile, and he smiled back.

Burt persisted. "I only say it because I care."

"Yes. You said that."

Gina's arrival luckily precluded further conversation.

"Hello, hello! Please don't get up."

"I was wondering where you were," he said to her as she took a seat beside him and nestled in under his arm, a stray corkscrew curl tickling his nose.

"I had to tend to my guests," she said.

"Great party," he told her, giving her shoulder a squeeze.

Joe asked after a couple of mutual friends she had visited in California on her way home from the fat farm. He made no effort to include Burt in the conversation, hoping that Burt would leave—which he eventually did, politely excusing himself. Once they were alone, he unloaded the whole story of Emily's suspension, beginning with the phone call from the school principal and ending with his own proposal to Laura that he find Emily a part in a play in order to keep her out of trouble.

"I think that's a brilliant idea! Brilliant! I've always said that girl was meant for the stage." She thought for a second, then reached out and grabbed him by the elbows. "She could do that Jeppson play with you."

"That's what I was thinking, myself."

"Or better yet, that new thing you're working on."

"*Prime*?"

"Yes! Let's do it. She'd be perfect!"

"I'm not sure it's a good idea."

She sighed, deflating. "Let me guess. Laura's not behind it."

"No. She isn't—for a number of reasons. She hasn't even read the play yet, but—"

"You know what, Ascher? I'm sorry to interrupt you, but that's really not fair."

"Well." He shrugged his shoulders, caught between an impulse to defend Laura and the desire to hear more.

"Listen. I love Laura. But I am getting really tired of this whole thing she pulls with you where she makes you feel filthy for what you do. You're a great writer and a great actor. If brilliant artists like you didn't have at least a small streak of narcissism, you'd all be shelling peas on some commune or something instead of sharing your brilliance and enhancing the lives of the rest of us. There's nothing wrong with it. And if she felt that she had something brilliant to communicate to the world, you can bet your ass she'd be out there, too."

Joe smiled.

"She's jealous," Gina said. "It's as simple as that. And it makes me mad that she tries to hold you back."

"The irony is that if I ever quit doing it, she'd probably pick up and leave."

"Of course she would. It's what makes you you."

"Yes, but I mean even more than that, it's what gives me value in her eyes."

"Oh, everything gives you value in her eyes. She thinks the world of you. All that talk is just jealousy."

He gave her a dubious look.

"What? You don't think she loves you?"

He hesitated for a moment, trying to figure out how to explain what he meant.

Gina threw her head back. "Oh! Don't be ridiculous. How could anyone not love you?"

He smiled, appreciative but eager to change the subject. "So you think we should do *Prime*?"

"Yes! By all means."

Immediately, she launched into a list of steps they each needed to take to expedite the process and to make it happen the way they wanted—the way *he* wanted. Half listening, he returned mentally to what she'd said about Laura. It was true that Laura made him feel filthy for wanting to act—even for wanting to write, though of course, it wasn't the writing itself that bothered her but the desire to cast it out into the world and parade it around from stage to stage. As much as she pretended not to, she yearned for the attention, herself—and yet she refused to emerge from the safety of the wings. Instead, she found consolation by feeding herself and others the lie of moral superiority. After all, didn't sainthood carry its own breed of stardom?

Gina was squeezing his knee with enthusiasm, telling him some idea she'd had about the play. Her perfume, a mix of orange flowers, sugar, and nutmeg, filled his nostrils. He had not smelled it until this moment. It was probably rising from her skin due to the heat of the room, escaping her pores along with the fine coating of perspiration which now glistened where the candlelight hit her breastbone. The combination of the perfume and the hand on his knee excited him. He had never thought of Gina in a sexual way before, but there was a certain thrill now that accompanied her touch. Wouldn't it be ironic, if he slept with Gina—after all of the crazy suspicions that Laura had harbored over the years? It would serve her right in a way.

"Do you know what I'm saying, though?" Gina said. "About the second act?"

He gave a fervent nod, though he had no idea what she was talking about. "Absolutely."

His glass was empty again, and he wanted to get up and get another drink. But he was afraid that if he did so, Gina would go and talk to somebody else. He was so content sitting here with her. He didn't need any more alcohol anyway. The last drink had relaxed his muscles completely, relieving even the sharp pinch in his lower back.

"Gina," he said.

"What?"

"You look really great."

Laughing, she waved her hand dismissively. "Oh Ascher, cut it out."

"I'm serious."

"No, come on. Really?"

"Yes. You look great."

She smiled, evidently quite pleased. "Thank you."

Laura had been talking to Randy Greenberg for what felt like a life-time. On occasions like this, when Randy drank to excess, he would talk on and on, ad infinitum about absolutely nothing, and whoever he'd chosen as a listener had little choice but to sit and listen. She and Joe referred to the experience as "being trapped in the Greenberg room," and they had both been trapped there countless times.

Finally free, she headed straight for Gina's personal bathroom, where she figured she'd be less likely to find a line. As she'd been to several parties at Gina's apartment and had often made use of this option, the fact that the bedroom door was closed did not deter her. It was only after she had opened the door and found Joe sitting on the edge of the bed that it occurred to her she might have knocked.

He was writing something on a notepad, which he quickly turned facedown in his lap as she entered.

"Oh, hi," he said.

"Hi." She cast a funny, inquisitive glance at the notepad. "What are you doing?"

"Oh," he said, turning the notepad back over as though to show her he had nothing to hide. "I'm playing a little joke."

"Oh." She blinked a couple of times, then told him she was going to use the bathroom. When she came back out, he was gone. But she spotted a piece of the notepaper with a couple of lines scrib-bled in his handwriting propped against a small, needlepoint pil-low in the center of the bed. She tiptoed over to the bed and picked up the note. It said, *If I knew yesterday what I know today, I would have worried a lot more.*

She began to chew on the inside of her lower lip as she stared at the paper. Then she looked at the pillow the note had been sit-ting on, embroidered with the words TODAY IS THE TOMORROW THAT YOU WORRIED ABOUT YESTERDAY.

Okay, she thought. Now it made a little more sense. This was the type of silly word play that Joe reveled in. She read the note again and set it back on top of the pillow. She had to admit that the whole thing made her feel a little uneasy. In other circumstances, she wouldn't have found anything remotely suspicious in Joe leaving a note like this for someone. But something about this particular note rubbed her the wrong way. For one thing, there was a certain intimacy to its location. And she couldn't help wondering if there was a secret coded message there. What might her husband know today that, had he known it yesterday, would have made him worry a lot more?

If the gesture weren't totally innocuous, she could argue, Joe wouldn't have left the note there for her to see. On the other hand, maybe he wanted her to discover it in order to reveal a disturbing truth that he had difficulty divulging another way. Feeling her knees go weak, she sat down on the bed.

Later, at home, Joe and Laura were following the same routine they'd been following now for eighteen years: he, relatively stationary in front of the sink, she, moving about behind him from closet hamper to sink to dresser and back to the closet, each barely conscious of the other except when moving aside to allow passage. They slowly began to return to themselves, to the people they were when they were alone together, divested of the company of others. Dabbing a new hair growth stimulant onto his scalp, Joe looked past his own image at the twice-reflected body of his wife who was standing in front of her own mirror, a full-length pane attached to the inside of the closet door.

As he watched her slip the black dress off over her head, he was struck not only by her beauty but by the notion that her body comprised a map of their life together. Most obvious—but practically invisible to him because he was so accustomed to seeing them— were the cesarean scar from Emily's delivery (she had, of course, refused to be coaxed out the easy way) and the slight sag of her breasts caused by the sustenance they had provided for two children. Beyond these most prominent cynosures, however, lay an infinite number of topographical markers, some of which now jumped out at him for the first time in a long while, and others of which he simply knew to be there, somewhere embedded in or protruding from that flesh, though they were too slight to be seen.

A line of broken capillaries forged a diagonal path across her left, upper thigh. She hated the way it looked and tried never to expose it in public—wearing sarongs and knee-length shorts at the beach where she had once gone without. She claimed their cause to be the wooden chair in which she'd habitually sat during their early years together, reading for hours each day, her right leg crossed in front of her on the seat, the left resting heavily on the chair's angular arm. He'd often wondered then at her choice of roost, but she'd said that the more comfortable furniture lulled her immediately to sleep and was, therefore, unsuitable for getting anything accomplished. On her right leg—on the ankle, exposed by the floor-length mirror—was the scar tissue (still pink after all these years) formed to heal a stingray's angry gash. She had been fortunate, she was told by the owner of a Greek taverna, that the tip of the tail had not broken off inside her skin. He smiled at the memory of this man whom they saw nearly every day that they lived on the island and whose chauvinism drove Laura wild. "You are the man!" he would say to Thomas whenever he bawled over a denied dessert. "Crying is for girls. Girls are weak, but you are the man!"

Laura pulled on her nightgown, concealing her body, then closed the closet and stooped to pick up the dress from the floor. He returned his gaze to his reflected scalp. The idea that he had been excited by Gina's touch now seemed preposterous. The whole inter-action they had had, in fact, now struck him as utterly wrong. Were it not for an excess of alcohol, he would never have let her say what she did about his wife. Somehow, over the course of the party, Laura had transformed in his mind into a nebulous being—more an idea, or a symbol of the enemy, the opponent, the villain, than the woman she actually was. But now that he was back in his apartment—in *their* apartment, *their* bathroom—she was once again his wife.

As he got into bed, Burt's words came back to him. He would not do the play, he decided, and would not cast Emily either. He and Laura would find some other way to keep her occupied and out of trouble. Laura pulled the sheets back and got into bed beside him. She did not look at him. It was late, 2:15 already. He could not tell if she was angry or just lost in her own thoughts and a desire for sleep. She had not said anything about the size of the party, which made him think that she was not angry. She would never admit to feeling irritated he'd spent so long with Gina; she would simply mention that the party had been much bigger than she'd expected—a comment that would not implicate him directly but merely hint that he was somehow responsible for her discomfort. She turned out the light, and he heard her, then saw her as his eyes adjusted—though still only a black form, falling back onto her pillow. He waited for a couple of minutes to see if she would say something, but she didn't.

"I'm worried about Emily," he said.

There was a pause, and he thought she might already be falling asleep.

"Me, too," she said finally.

Afterward, there was only silence and then the rhythmic sound of her breathing.

Winter

EMILY HAD BEEN WAITING AT THE RESTAURANT for about ten minutes, installed with a bottle of San Pellegrino amid the fanciful French fin de siècle decor, when her gaze fell on a face across the room that brought her breathing to an abrupt halt.

For years, she had expected to run into Gina. The city was too small for their paths not to cross, but the sight of her in the flesh was something she wasn't prepared for. Gina sat alone, looking every bit as glamorously disheveled and charmingly neurotic as Emily remembered her, tossing those burgundy-tinged ringlets and making great, sweeping gestures to the waiter. Emily felt a surge of hatred so intense it surprised her a little.

She looked up to find the hostess escorting her mother to the table. Dressed in a black sweater with a plunging neckline, Laura looked unusually elegant.

"Hi," Emily said, standing. "You look nice."

"Sorry I'm late. Have you been here long?"

"Not too long."

Laura leaned across the table and kissed the air on either side of her face. Ordinarily, Emily would have offered her a choice of seats, but tonight she thought it best for her mother to face the wall. If all went well, they could conceivably get through the entire evening without her mother becoming aware of Gina's presence.

"How are you?" Emily asked, once they were settled.

"Great. The new teacher for the program is doing such a fantastic job. I just dropped by, and they're about finished with their play."

Several years ago, Laura had started an after-school girls' theater program, and now that the program was thriving and growing, she was devoting more time and energy to it than ever.

"Did I tell you she's got them scripting a play about themselves?" she asked.

"I don't think so."

"It's been so good for them. They've all come alive over the last month. One of the girls in particular—an unbelievably quiet and serious little thing—has really come out of her shell." She put on her bifocals and looked at the menu. "Do you know what you're having?"

"The vegetable stew, I think."

"That sounds good." Her mother took another look at the menu, then putting it aside, took off her glasses with a laugh. "Can you believe these things?" she said self-consciously.

"They're not so bad."

"I feel like a granny," she said, folding them up. "Anyway, you should see this girl. She's so strong and so lovely, but she's deathly serious about everything. The mother's the same way. She came to one of our mother-daughter circles last Saturday, and both she and her daughter barely opened their mouths the whole time. Still, you could see it meant so much to both of them." She smiled. "It was funny, too. You know I rarely get the chance to spend time with any of the girls' moms. But afterward, a bunch of us got together and laughed about how underappreciated we are. And it's true. You guys never had any idea how much work it was—everything was simply taken care of. I have to admit I felt a little sorry for myself sometimes. But I realize now that freedom of responsibility, that feeling of waking up in the morning with no worries, nothing but excitement for what the day had in store—to be able to give that to your kids—that's a tremendous gift."

Emily smiled uncomfortably, wondering whether she was supposed to thank her. The waiter came to take their orders, and her mother, who hadn't gotten the chance yet to look at the wine list, told him she'd hang on to it for a bit longer. When he left, they delved into the details of the wedding.

"I've been thinking white lilacs would be simple and so pretty," her mother suggested. "Like a picnic on the hillside."

She nodded. "Sure."

"I wonder if they'll be blooming then. I guess it all depends on the weather, which is so unpredictable at that time of year. By the way, did you ever reach your father?"

She stiffened. She'd tried calling him again close to Thanksgiving, first on his cell and then at the hotel. The receptionist told her he'd checked out a few weeks before. Hurt that he'd been back in the city so long without bothering to call, she hadn't tried him since.

"No," she told her mother. "Not yet."

"Hmm. Well . . . I don't know what to tell you."

"Don't worry about it," she said coolly.

"Have you thought of a second choice for someone who could walk you down the aisle?"

"Mom, it's not like he's not going to come to my wedding. Anyway, it's still months away."

"All right. But you might want to have a backup plan."

"I don't need a backup plan."

Putting her bifocals back on, her mother began to peruse the first page of red wines. After a while, she looked up over the tops of the frames. "I saw the most wonderful show at the Whitney today."

"Really?"

"It was a sculpture show. Of course I can't remember the name of the artist right now, but it was very Louise Bourgeois."

"I'll try to go."

With her fingertip, her mother drew a line through the condensation on her water glass. "Sometimes I think maybe I should have been a painter or a sculptor."

Emily had no idea what her mother was talking about. It seemed absurd for her to think that she might have been a painter or a sculptor or anything else other than exactly who she was. When Emily and Thomas were growing up, their mom was always talking about acting—how much she loved it and missed it. But she never did anything about it—never went to any auditions or enrolled in any classes or workshops. Emily and Thomas got the sense that somehow their father was to blame for the fact their mother had given up acting, but that never entirely made sense to them.

"I don't know." Her mother sighed. "I love what I do now. It's only, when I was younger . . . Anyway."

Emily smiled politely and reached into the breadbasket. "Do you ever miss acting?"

Laura rolled her eyes. "God, no." She tore off a piece of baguette and put it in her mouth. "Do you?"

She shook her head. "No."

"Mom?" she said a few seconds later. "Don't you wonder what kind of girl Thomas would have married?"

Laura looked surprised, then taking her butter knife, made a few quick scrapes over the surface of the tablecloth to gather up the breadcrumbs Emily had dropped.

"No. Not really."

"I feel like . . . On the one hand, I can imagine him being with someone serious and pure, someone a lot like him. But then, I sometimes think he would have fallen for a really wild and fun vampy type, who'd shake everything up. You know?"

"Hmm." Her mom began to turn the pages of the wine list. "I'm not sure I understand what you're saying."

"I don't know. I'm just curious what kind of person he'd choose to spend his life with."

Her mom continued to turn the pages. Emily waited, and after a while, her mother finally took off her glasses and called over the waiter.

"I'd like the Château Gloria," her mother told him, handing him the wine list.

"Lovely choice," he said.

When he was gone, her mother looked at her. "How's the case coming?"

"Terrible. I don't want to talk about it."

Laura frowned. "Really?"

"Really."

"Do you think you're going to lose?"

"Mom, I said I don't want to talk about it."

Laura raised her eyebrows. "Okay."

They ate in silence until the waiter returned with the wine.

"Very nice," Laura told him, taking a sip.

He gave an official nod and filled her glass the rest of the way, then turned to Emily.

"Not for me, thanks."

"Come on. Have a taste," her mother pleaded. "It's a very special wine."

Emily looked up at the waiter. "No thanks."

Laura watched him leave. "I don't think a taste is going to kill you."

"No," she said crisply. "It's not going to kill me. But I don't want it."

Laura took a sip of wine and set the glass back down on the table with an irritated sigh.

"Jesus, Mom." She was surprised to feel tears welling up in her eyes.

Her mother softened. "Sweetheart. What's wrong?"

"I don't know." She let her gaze wander for a while. "I'm sorry. I think I'm having premarital jitters."

"Well, that's normal."

Emily sighed. "I don't think so."

"Yes, it is. Absolutely."

"Mom, you're not helping."

"Well, would you rather I say that's totally abnormal and I think you've got serious problems?"

"Is that what you think?"

"No, I just told you what I thought. I will say one thing, though."

"What?"

"I think maybe some of your anxiety has to do with not having told your father yet, and not knowing whether he's going to bother to show up."

"Mom, what is your problem? Of course he's going to show up. Stop bringing your own issues with him into *my* wedding."

"Emily, that's really unfair."

"Maybe you're feeling anxious because you're worried he *will* show up."

Again her mother ran her fingertip along the surface of her water glass. "Is that what your therapist thinks?"

"No, Mom. It's what I think."

"Well, it's not true. I've completely moved on with my life, and I honestly never even think about your father."

"O-kay," Emily said gingerly. "If that's the case, I'm glad for you, I guess."

Her mother picked up her fork, hesitated for a moment, and then placed it back on the table.

"Sweetheart, listen. Of course I hope that your father comes. And I don't mean to sound hostile. It's only that, well, there is a time earlier in one's life when one mistakes a certain tumultuous erraticism for love."

"Tumultuous erraticism?" Emily repeated incredulously. "Mom, you can't tell me you didn't love him. You were with him for *twenty* years!"

"Of course, I absolutely did. But there were things that we put each other and ourselves through which were so completely unnecessary. It was a relief to start over with Earl, to wipe the slate clean of all that nonsense and not let our emotions carry us away. You'll see as you get older. You don't have the energy for all the craziness anymore."

"Clay and I don't have craziness."

"That's good."

"Is it?" As the words came out, Emily regretfully noted the quaver in her voice.

"Sweetheart, what is it?"

She felt her chin tense up, and once more her eyes filled with tears. "I'm afraid it means we don't have enough passion." She pressed her fingers to her cheekbones, trying to stop the flood of emotion. "Or love."

"Sweetheart . . ." Her mother reached across the table, but both of Emily's hands were on her face.

Her mom brushed the pile of breadcrumbs off the table, and sitting back again, took a sip of wine. "Only you can know," she said. "But it seems to me that you have a great relationship. I was watching the two of you at Thanksgiving and thinking how sweet you are with each other." She shook her head. "That sounds too corny. I don't mean it that way. I mean . . . invested. You're both so invested in one another."

Emily discreetly wiped the tears from her cheeks. "What do you mean?"

"Well, for example, when the DVD player broke, and you got into that major argument, you two were so great about apologizing after."

"That was so dumb. Of course we apologized."

"But a lot of couples wouldn't have. They would have let their remarks sit there and fester."

Emily nodded.

"That kind of thing builds up," her mother said.

"I guess so. It's just that Clay's so *nice*. I mean I never thought I'd be marrying a nice guy from Michigan."

"Nice is good. Trust me."

"I know," Emily said, forcing a smile. "You're right."

Later, as her cab pulled away from the restaurant, Emily glanced out the window and noticed Gina walking out. *Thank God* they'd made it through the night without Gina spotting them, and without her mother knowing she was there. Once again, the sight of that woman brought back a flood of memories, and she was filled simultaneously with disgust for her father and with the reminder that she and her mother, regardless of their occasional difficulties, shared an unbreakable bond.

EMILY WAS PLANNING ON EATING WITH HER DAD in the lounge, but he was presently on stage, talking to the director. Having completed the first half of rehearsal, the cast had broken for dinner, everyone scattering to make phone calls and run quick errands. While she waited for her father to come join her, Emily sat alone, picking at the tuna and rye she'd ordered from the deli. As usual, she and her mother were in a fight—this time because she'd failed a math exam, and her mother was threatening to pull her out of the play. Emily wanted to discuss this with her dad as well as get some advice from him about a few of her scenes. Somehow, even though they were working together, he was never around to talk to anymore. She got the sense he was avoiding her and hoped it wasn't because of her performance.

"Hello, little bug," Gina said, wandering into the lounge.

Gina had a whole repertoire of ridiculous names that she gave to the various juveniles in her life. Coming from anyone else, being called by any one of them would have irritated the hell out of Emily.

But Gina was cool enough to pull it off without condescension or corny vulgarity.

"Are you all by yourself?"

"Yeah. I'm waiting for my dad."

Gina sank down beside her. "These couches are so fucking low, I feel like I'm going to tear a ligament in my knee every time I sit down."

Emily smiled. It was because Gina treated her like an equal—swearing in front of her and so on—that she didn't mind those silly pet names.

"What is it?" Gina asked. "You seem kind of down."

"I dunno." She wrapped up the remainder of her sandwich and put it on the floor. "I kind of think maybe I'm really *bad* in this."

"Oh, sweetheart! You're certainly not *bad*. You're terrific! Are you kidding me?"

"Because, like . . . I mean I've never done this before. So if I'm not doing it right, it would be cool if somebody would *talk* to me about it. It's not like I'm going to go, 'What? You don't think I'm the best actress that ever lived? Well, forget it then, I quit!' You know? I mean I can totally take criticism."

"Oh, this is so crazy. You couldn't possibly think you're a bad actress."

Emily shrugged.

"Do you have any idea how often I've heard Bob and Anthony going on and on about how lucky they are to have you in this play, how much you add to it, how *supremely* talented you are?"

"Really?"

"Yes! You'd think they were talking about Marlon Brando. I'm absolutely not kidding."

"But do you think my dad thinks I'm any good?"

"Absolutely! And I'm sure your mom and brother are bowled over. Didn't they come back and see it again last night?"

"They were supposed to, but he wasn't feeling well."

"He's all right now, though?"

"Yeah. He's just got some kind of flu."

"Well—listen, lamb pie, you're a star. You really are."

Putting a hand on Emily's knee, partially for encouragement and partially for her own support, she hoisted herself back off the couch. "Jesus fucking Christ. These things are going to kill me. So," she said, straightening her skirt, "I've got to run. But if I find your father, I'm going to tell him he can't go leaving you here to eat dinner by yourself. That's ridiculous."

"He's just talking to Anthony. I don't mind."

"Well, I mind. I'll see you later. You're a star."

Grinning self-consciously, Emily sank deeper into the cushions. Once Gina was gone, she reveled in the idea of being spoken of like Marlon Brando. It soothed her considerably to hear that Anthony and Bob were that taken with her performance. Also, now that she thought about it, the fact her father hadn't praised her acting probably had more to do with his nerves. After all, he was both the writer and the star. Brando-like or not, she was not the one the audience was watching.

She balled up her sandwich wrapper and chucked it at the wastebasket on the other side of the room.

"Good shot," she said out loud. Then, standing up, she bowed to the water cooler. "Thank you very much."

She moved her father's roast beef sandwich from the couch to the table, where he could easily find it, and wandered off around the corner and down the hall to the wardrobe room. Inside, she found Eric—exactly the person she was looking for. He was standing in the middle of the room with his hands in his pockets, gazing up at the ceiling. The light cut across the dark hairs on the top of his head and bounced off the shiny surface of his scalp. Since he was still very good looking for his thirty-odd years, it surprised her that he didn't attempt to disguise his hair loss better. When she'd seen him on stage in Hartford this last July, she had developed an immediate crush. That, however, was before her father took her backstage to meet him and she discovered that those beautiful, brown curls belonged to a wig. If it were up to her, she would shave his head completely. He had the type of face that could carry that off.

"Hey."

"Oh hi, Emily. How's it going?"

"Good. What are you doing?"

"I've got to do another fitting."

"*Another* one? Jesus fucking Christ." She really had no idea how many fittings he'd already had, but she was feeling punchy.

Eric nodded. "Yeah, well . . . what can you do?"

"Hey, what's all this?" she asked, looking at a rack of costumes that weren't for their show.

"I don't know. Anna brought that in earlier."

Perusing the clothes—western garb with a campy spirit-of-the-frontier flare—she selected a red and black bustier obviously intended for a brothel scene.

"What do you think?" she asked, holding it against her body. "Would this look good on me?"

She didn't have to wait for a reply. She knew from the way she often caught him eyeing her figure that he thought anything would look good on her. It was always exciting to feel his eyes on her body. He clearly assumed in those moments that she was oblivious to his attention, and she would purposely reinforce this illusion by speaking to someone or singing to herself or pretending to read so that he would keep looking. Were he less attractive himself, she might have found it creepy, considering how much older he was. But he happened to be pretty sexy for a middle-aged man. And, frankly, his age only intensified the excitement—particularly since, as a friend of her father's, she knew he would never actually *do* anything. He was her Humbert Humbert—*before* the mother died and everything got so out of hand.

"Maybe," he answered.

She had sort of hoped he would ask her to try it on. Disappointed, she let the hanger drop, dangling the bustier along the floor.

"Hey, Eric. Can I ask you something?"

"Sure."

"What's with the bald head?"

She could see that he was embarrassed. But, what did he think? It wasn't exactly a secret that he had a big, fat bald spot in the middle of his head. Anybody could see it with their own two eyes. She reached over and poked at a tuft of hair above his right ear.

"You've got lots of hair there at least. If worse comes to worst, you can always grow that out and go for the comb-over." She burst out laughing. "Imagine. Oh my God! That's so funny. Wait, seriously. You have to look at yourself in the mirror and imagine that." Dragging him over to the mirror, she continued to laugh.

He smiled at his reflection. "I think that if things ever get that bad, I'll opt for a hat."

"Or, or, or!" She clapped. "Or you could even do that wraparound thing where you take the hair and wind it all the way around your head. Have you seen that? There's a guy at our D'Agostino's that does that. It's so gross. And he, like, never even washes it, I swear."

Still smiling, Eric turned away from the mirror and walked over to his jacket that was hanging over the back of a folding chair. As she watched him rummage around in the pockets, it became clear that he wasn't really looking for anything.

"Whatever," she said. "Don't worry. It doesn't look that bad."

He continued to sift through his pockets.

"Eric, seriously. I was only teasing."

She wanted him to look at her. "Did you lose something?"

"My . . . uh. I think I left my glasses on the stage."

"You want me to go find them?"

"No. I'll get them after the fitting."

As he straightened up, she was relieved to find that he seemed restored to his old self.

She turned back to the mirror and held the bustier up. Then, with a hand on her hip, she spun around and put on her best Mae West.

"Come on over here and fuck me, cowboy."

Eric stared at her without any reaction at all. She felt her cheeks go hot and gave a loud laugh, hoping that he would think it was the laughter that had made her skin turn red. She'd meant it as another one of those silly things they said to each other in their usual flirty way. But the word *fuck* resounded harshly, making it all seem more serious than she intended.

She was relieved to hear Anna coming down the hall, humming, as always, some unrecognizable tune. Emily looked expectantly at the door. She could feel Eric behind her, still staring.

"Watch it, Ascher."

Pretending not to hear him, Emily returned the bustier to the rack. Anna bustled in, panting from the effort it took to carry her own body around, a body as wide as it was tall. Standing absolutely erect, she barely reached Emily's shoulder, though Emily had only seen her reach her full height once, after the director made an off-hand remark about how one of the jackets she'd made looked a little like a burlap bag. Otherwise, Anna could only be found in one of two positions: either stooped over a hemline with a mouth full of pins, or puffing about as was now the case, bent beneath the sheer volume of work that had to be done before the following night's performance. Emily greeted her with enthusiasm and asked about the western clothes, which Anna explained, between labored breathing and heavy, self-pitying sighs, were for a new musical. It was too much. Too, too much. The designer, of course, could say yes to everything because he did not have to deal with the *machinery* of the clothing. But the machinery took time. How was she supposed to make things look right when she had so little time? Then, realizing that time was ticking away even as she complained, Anna shooed Emily out the door so that Eric could finish his fitting before rehearsal started up again.

With twenty minutes left of the dinner break, she decided to go to the fire escape on the floor above. When the weather was still nice, she had gone up there every day, but recently, she hadn't been up so much. She was trying to break her pot habit—or at least cut down on it—because she worried it was affecting her acting. Right now, however, she felt a strong need to go up there. Even though it was raining cats and dogs, there would be a certain peacefulness on the fire escape that she could not find inside.

Pushing open the door, she felt the damp wind against her face and was engulfed by the sounds of the city. To her surprise, the daylight had already vanished completely. Times Square's section of sky stood out with its somewhat less ashen and pinker cast, while the Chrysler and Empire State buildings made the most dramatic impact, searing right through the clouds and illuminating them from within. From where she stood, the wall of brick reaching several stories above the theater protected her from the sheets of falling rain. Leaning against the door, she took a joint from her pocket and lit up. As she inhaled, she watched the water hit the metal stairs, then bounce up and out in different directions.

Watch it, Ascher. Did Eric really think she was coming on to him? He couldn't have thought she really meant she wanted to have sex with him. Could he have? If he did, he didn't seem disgusted by the idea. Nor did he seem to find it completely ridiculous. The way he said "watch it" made it sound as if he might even take her up on the offer.

It would help if she could talk to somebody about the whole thing. The question was, who? Under any other circumstance, Thomas would be the first person she'd consult. But he would have an apoplectic fit over the idea of Eric laying a finger on her. He'd call him a disgusting, dirty, old creep and rant and rave and probably even make her promise to quit the play altogether. That was how he was about her—even more overprotective than their parents— and she had to admit she didn't mind because she knew it was a sign of how deeply he cared. Sometimes it made her feel guilty, though. She knew that he would literally die for her if he had to, and she wasn't sure that she was willing to die for him—or anyone else for that matter. But most of the time, she didn't think too much about it. It was simply the way things were between them, the way they'd always been, and she felt no desire to change it.

Recently, though, her brother had begun to judge her. She got the feeling he thought of her as a promiscuous, pothead loser. He had heard rumors at school that she'd been with a lot of guys, some of them members of his own class, and he said that was embarrassing. She had tried to tell him that she had barely done anything with them and that she would have stuck to one guy if she'd found any of them *remotely* interesting or mature. Furthermore, as for the drugs, at least she wasn't doing coke or heroin or speedballs like some people. But, to this, all he said was that she was hanging out with the wrong kind of girls—and guys, since he had plenty of friends who were both interesting *and* mature.

A thrill shot through her as she continued to puff at the joint. She supposed there was a remote possibility that she and Eric could fool around. It would be pretty cool to lose her virginity, and at least he would know what he was doing—unlike the idiots her age who could barely even find what they were looking for with their *hand*. The more she thought about it, the more excited she got until finally, she realized that she was being absolutely absurd. He may have simply been warning her in a fatherly type of way to watch her tongue. Even though it was obvious that he found her attractive and that he had fun flirting with her, she imagined he considered her far too young to *do* anything with. He probably didn't even mean *watch what you say to <u>me</u>*, but *watch what you say, <u>period</u>*—like, *I understand that this is just a silly joke, but other guys might take you seriously.* And even if he did take her seriously and did, in fact, wish to fuck her, there was, of course, still the issue of her father. It seemed highly unlikely that Eric would jeopardize that friendship by making a move on her.

Laura waited impatiently for Joe and Emily to get home from rehearsal. When they finally arrived fifteen minutes late, she met them in the entrance hall.

"Hi," Emily said uneasily. She'd been swinging her backpack and humming, but immediately stopped short.

Ignoring her, Laura watched Joe prop his wet umbrella outside the front door. He entered a second later, shaking out his coat. Then he, too, stopped abruptly.

"Hello," he said with surprise.

She did not speak—just stood there, glaring at him with hellfire fury.

"What's going on?" he asked, taking a cautious step forward and closing the door.

"Why don't you tell me," she replied.

Emily hurried off.

"I'm really not sure," he said.

"Stop it," she seethed. "Just stop it. I'm sick and tired of being lied to. All those times I asked you, and you swore to me that your work was pure fiction—that you could never even consider having an affair . . . I mean what kind of an idiot do you think I am?"

He closed his eyes and exhaled, then bringing his hand to the bridge of his nose, he gently said her name.

"Of course I am an idiot, I suppose," she went on. "Because I believed you. I wanted so badly to believe you—"

"Laura," he said again. "It's not true."

"Fucking hell, Joe! I know it's true. There's no question that it's true."

"What I meant was . . . it's the first."

She stopped short for a moment, examining him suspiciously. "Come on."

"I swear to you there have never been others. I was going to tell you."

The question of whether or not he was being honest momentarily slowed her down, but then the anger returned, and she went at him again full-force, regaining momentum with each word.

"I don't give a shit! Who cares if the number is one or twenty anyway? You're still cheating on me and lying to me. How do you think that makes me feel? And the fact that it's Gina—my God, Joe! I've known it all along. And for years now, you've been telling me I'm crazy. That you're just friends? That you just work together? Come on! The level of dishonesty is appalling."

He spoke calmly. "I know it probably doesn't matter, but this has only been going on for a couple of months."

"Bullshit!" she yelled. "Bullshit."

She turned away and marched off toward the library.

He followed.

When she reached the desk, she stood with her back to him. Her knuckles pressed into the wood, and her shoulders rose protectively around her lowered head.

He paused, several feet behind her. "Laura," he said.

She refused to turn around.

"In all the years we've been together," he told her softly. "I've never before entertained the notion of an affair. I want you to know that."

She could hear him nervously scratching his chin.

"Of course I've found other women attractive and have had flirtations—even fantasies that I put into my writing at various times, but they were never real. Our relationship always existed on another plane entirely," he began again, a little less surely. "A rare and beautiful thing—and a fragile thing. And I recognized that and took care. And as time went on, it became more rare and more beautiful. But . . ."

He stopped for a moment, and she looked at him. "Honestly," she said with contempt.

He raised his hand. "Please let me finish."

She let out an exasperated sigh and turned her back to him again.

"For the last couple of years," he said, "for whatever reason, things have fallen apart. You no longer make me feel good. I don't know how else to say it—and I don't just mean sexually." He took a deep breath. "You don't make me feel like a good man."

It seemed like a long time after he stopped talking before she could bring herself to turn around again. When she finally did so, she looked him straight in the eye.

"And Gina does?" she asked in a voice that was eerily steady.

"Yes," he answered much less steadily than she. "Actually. She does."

They stood there for a while, staring each other down. She wasn't going to budge, she decided. She had no reason to run and hide. So what if she cried? Let him see it.

Finally, without saying anything else, he walked out, and she let herself crumple into the closest chair.

Emily sat on the couch in Thomas's room, listening to a Pink Floyd CD they'd recently become obsessed with. He sat beside her, doing homework—which she should have been doing, too.

"Hey, Thomas?" she said after a while.

"Yeah?"

"I need to ask you something."

She turned down the music, and he looked up from his textbook.

She bounced her foot nervously. "I guess I kind of wanted to ask you about how to talk to guys."

"What do you want to talk to them about?"

She shrugged.

"Well, basically, most guys are happy for you to talk to them about anything. You can pretty much go 'blah, blah, blah,' and they'll be totally into it because they'll think it's cool that you're even talking to them."

"Really?"

"Yeah. The only thing that can get you into trouble is if you get all self-conscious and weird because then they'll get all self-conscious and weird, and you'll be sitting there staring at each other, both wishing you were somewhere else. But you don't have to worry about that because you never care what people think of you anyway."

"What are you talking about? I care what people think of me."

"No, you don't. Not really. That's why you're so uninhibited."

"What! I *do too* care."

"If you really cared what people thought of you, you wouldn't set Mom off."

"I don't *try* to set her off."

"Don't get so defensive. What I'm talking about is a good thing."

"How can that be a good thing?"

"Look. Either you're the kind of person who's always trying to figure out what everybody else wants from you, or you're the kind of person who doesn't give a shit."

"I give a shit."

"No, you don't. Not really."

"How can you say that?"

"Because it's true. You know exactly who you are, and you're not bending for anyone."

"You're crazy."

"Listen, you probably can't understand this. But the very fact that you're willing to set people off gives you a certain freedom. That's a very good thing. So don't knock it. Okay? And don't change. 'Cause if you do, you'll be sorry. That's all I'm saying. As long as you can piss people off, you're doing all right."

"But you never piss people off."

"That's right, Einstein."

"I don't get it. What's your point?"

"My point is don't be like me."

"Why not?"

"Goddamn, you're slow."

"Stop insulting me. I'm trying to ask your advice about something."

"And I'm trying to give it to you."

"No, you're not. You're talking about all this nutty stuff, and all I want to know is how to talk to guys."

"A mere technicality. It's like you're asking me how to breathe. And I'm saying you're already doing it. Just be yourself. I don't mean that in some corny way. This is very profound what I'm saying. Okay? I'm serious."

She laughed uncomfortably. "Whatever."

After Joe had gathered his things, he walked down the hall to talk to Emily. Her door was open, but she wasn't there. He continued on to Thomas's room. The door was shut.

"Hello," he said, knocking.

"Yeah," Thomas answered.

He opened the door and found his children bunkered down on Thomas's sofa. He had interrupted a serious conversation, undoubtedly about whatever they'd managed to overhear. *At least,* he thought, *they have each other.*

He walked over to the bed and gravely sat down. They both watched him attentively.

"I'm leaving," he said.

"What do you mean?" Emily asked, her expression a mix of panic and befuddlement.

"Your mother and I are having some problems." He could see that they were both totally unprepared for this. "We need some time apart from each other. So I'm going to go away for a little while."

"Where?" Thomas asked.

"I haven't figured that out yet."

Emily's cheeks had turned bright red, and she was frantically combing her hair with her fingers as if to rid it of some undesirable substance.

"Are you still going to do the play?" she asked.

"I don't know."

"How long are you going away for?"

"I'm not sure."

She looked completely forlorn, and he was immediately re-minded of the moonlit night last winter in the Berkshires, when they'd sat outside, bundled together under coats and blankets, drink-ing tea. "Look!" she'd said with girlish excitement, pointing to a bright ball of light on the surface of her tea, "You can see the moon in my cup!" They had talked about the old days then, remember-ing fondly the way they used to look out the window together every night and say goodnight to the moon before he tucked her into bed and read to her.

He stood up slowly and walked over to her, putting his hand on her shoulder. "I'm sorry." He kissed the top of her head. "Remem-ber," he told her. "No matter where we are, or how far apart, we can still hold the same moon in both our cups."

"Oh, Daddy," she said, wrapping her arms around his waist.

He rubbed her back, and then, after a bit, he patted her arms to let her know it was time to release them. As she did so, he turned to Thomas.

"Take care of your mom and your sister."

Thomas nodded. "I will."

Joe reached down and gave his shoulder a big squeeze, then headed back toward the door.

"Daddy," Emily pleaded.

"I'm sorry," he said to both of them. "I'll call you."

Once their dad was gone, Thomas looked over at his sister, who had started to cry. He got up and walked the few steps to the win-dow, where their Camel Lights were hidden behind the radiator cover. He looked out at the raindrops falling on the dramatically lit gargoyles across the street. *Where was their dad going? Did he have a plan? How could this be happening to them?* He'd looked out at this view every day and night for as long as he could remember. But sud-denly everything felt completely unfamiliar. Returning to the sofa, he gave a cigarette to Emily and took one for himself, abandoning any measures to avoid discovery.

Emily's hand was shaking as she brought the cigarette to her mouth. "Mom did seem mad when we got home tonight—but not really worse than other times. I don't understand what's going on."

"It'll be okay," he said, passing the flame. "He'll be back soon."

"How do you know?" she asked urgently.

"Trust me. By tomorrow night, the whole thing will have blown over."

"But what if it hasn't? What if he never comes back?"

"He will," he insisted.

She wrapped her arms around her knees and stared into space as she smoked. He watched her eyes fill with tears again, and he wished like hell that he could run down to the lobby and bring their dad back.

"What kinds of problems do you think they're having?" she asked in a near whisper.

"I don't know. This happens to people," he said reassuringly. "They blow up at each other, and then the next morning they wake up and they're like, *I could never live without you. You're the most important thing in my life.*"

"I don't see Dad saying that," she said.

He sucked on his cigarette, thinking.

"Or Mom," she added.

"Well maybe not those exact words. I'm just saying . . ."

He fell silent again, thinking about their mom and dad. They had always fought with each other, but they'd never had "problems"—not that he knew of anyway, not the kind that made one of them pack up a suitcase and leave the apartment. He rubbed the swollen gland behind his right ear. This damned flu was lasting forever. If only he felt better, he could come up with a better explanation for his sister.

"What if they get divorced?" she said. "Who are we going to live with?"

"They're not getting divorced."

"What if I want to live with Dad, and you decide to live with Mom?"

"This is a stupid conversation."

He reached over and pressed the PLAY button on his stereo, and the dreamy, melancholy tones of Pink Floyd filled the room. He closed his eyes, trying to hear the music.

She was silent for a long time, smoking her cigarette down to the foamy brown filter. Then she went over to the window, opened it up, and tossed the stub out into the rain.

When she returned to the sofa, she said, "You have to promise me that no matter what happens between Mom and Dad, we'll stay together."

"Of course," he said. "I promise."

2007

LAURA SET HER COAT AND PURSE ON THE entrance-hall table and picked a dead leaf off the orchid. There were times when Emily still irritated her beyond belief. She wished she didn't feel that way, but she did—like at dinner tonight when Emily started wondering what kind of girl Thomas would have married.

"Earl?" she called, looking into the living room.

There was no answer. While she was out with Emily, he had gone to dinner with two young guys, an arbitrage team he had met through a colleague and who wanted to manage some money for him. She'd expected him to be back by now. She wandered over to the stereo, where there was already a Miles Davis CD in the player, and pressed PLAY. Then she began straightening the stacks of magazines on the red lacquer table in the corner.

What did it matter what sort of girl Thomas would have chosen? Emily was always wondering and postulating what her brother would do if he were still alive, always asking and providing her own pointless answers to the unanswerable what-ifs. For as long as she could remember, Emily had been like this—getting maddeningly carried away by her own nutty ideas and filling the air with nonsensical musings.

Laura remembered there was a book about nonprofits she had promised to lend to the executive director of her theater program. *Where was that book?* she wondered. As she scanned the shelves for it, she thought again about the mother-daughter workshop they'd run last weekend. It was amazing to her how many of the mothers showed up—and how well they all got along with their girls.

Laura wondered how much she was responsible for the years of strain between herself and her daughter. As far back as she could remember, Emily had seemed to prefer her father, which was strange. Weren't all children supposed to have a natural bond with their mothers from the moment they were born—stronger than any other bond? And now that Joe was all but completely out of the picture, there were still times—like at dinner tonight—when she sensed she was a disappointment to her daughter, and guessed that deep down, Emily might wish that the parent present was Joe rather than herself.

She gave up on finding the book, and turning off the music, went back to her dressing room. While she was brushing her teeth, she decided she'd read until Earl got home. She hated going to sleep without him. In her closet, there was a stack of perfectly folded white flannel nightshirts. She took one off the top, and pulling it on, shuffled into the bedroom. After locating her bifocals next to the phone, she climbed into bed and switched off all the lights but the reading lamp.

She hoped Emily hadn't recognized Gina tonight. It had been quite a shock to see her sitting there at the very moment the hostess asked her name. When she'd sat down, she had moved her chair over in an attempt to block Emily's view, but she still had no way of knowing whether she had succeeded or not. Throughout the dinner, she'd been haunted by the unpleasant awareness that Gina was back there, somewhere behind her, and it had set her on edge. Perhaps that was why she'd been so irritated by some of the things Emily had said. Her daughter seemed so tightly wound these days, overreacting to nearly everything.

Contrary to what she'd said to Emily, it did not make her happy to hear her say, "Clay and I don't have craziness." She knew exactly what Emily meant. And though it was all right for *her* to renounce all of that at her age, to say and honestly mean that she felt fully contented by the even, containable emotions Earl excited in her soul, it saddened her to think that this described the extent of her daughter's experience.

She did not believe that Thomas's death affected anyone more profoundly than herself—for what could be worse than the loss of one's own child? But in some way, she *had* been more fortunate than Emily. At least she had lived a great deal of her life before that crushing blow so significantly narrowed her ability to feel. Emily was only fifteen when her brother died, and Laura had hoped that her youth translated into resilience. She still clung to that hope. But she felt less sure.

She woke up at four in the morning and found that Earl had come home. He had switched off the reading lamp and was sleeping soundly beside her. It took her a while to shake herself awake. She'd been dreaming about Joe, and for a while, she gazed at the ceiling, yearning to return to the exultant head-over-heels, heart-in-throat feeling of her fantasy. She got up and went to the bathroom, but still, the dream clung to her like a cobweb, and as she sat there on the toilet, she had to remind herself of the reality of the situation. Joe had never been right for her, and that feeling she'd had in the dream—though it was something she'd felt with him and hadn't felt before or since—had come and gone throughout their marriage and had always been fleeting. Next to him and his giant ego, the way she felt most often during their time together was small—like a boring housewife, trailing along in his shadow. It used to seem he could soak up all of the energy in a room and take up all of its space— and while that power had made him extremely alluring, it had left nothing for her. He had everything he wanted, *everything*—which made him going elsewhere for pleasure, *more* pleasure, that much more hurtful.

She got back into bed and nestled in against Earl's body. He let out a gentle snore and rolled toward her a little, then fell back into the regular breathing pattern of his sleep. She thought of the way

Emily had described Joe in the fall after she'd last seen him: bloated, red-faced, frail, obviously still drinking. The description had saddened her and made her want to see him again. So much time had passed. She had a new life now, a new husband. She was happy, and it seemed that Joe wasn't—which, in a way, made it easier to forgive him. There were moments when she could see herself calling him, inviting him over to the apartment for dinner, putting everything aside and becoming friends, better friends—or kinder at least—than they'd been before. But then she thought about the wedding, and the idea of seeing him there gave her a pit in her stomach.

Well, it was clear she wasn't going to get back to sleep easily. *Why not get some work done,* she thought, *rather than stare at the ceiling?* Pulling a robe on over her nightshirt, she went into the sitting room and sat down at her computer. The big fund-raiser for her program was only eight weeks away, and she still had an endless number of people to write and call, solicit, thank, and pester. Double-clicking on a file that she and the executive director had made of potential corporate sponsors, she began to run down the list, noting updates and adding the confirmed figures together to determine how far they still had to go. While she was doing this, an uneasy feeling slowly came over her as Emily crept back into her thoughts. She recognized that she'd oversimplified things before; there was plainly more to Emily's turmoil than the fact she'd lost her brother. She recalled how poor her own judgment had been when she was younger—her decision to quit acting, for example, to take charge of her life after her parents died and stop doing things that didn't make her happy. In retrospect, she had been completely confused about what did and didn't make her happy.

One of the things Laura liked about Clay was the way he noticed things about people that often escaped the notice of others. He really paid attention when you talked to him, and frequently continued to think about the conversation long after it ended, bringing it up again later in order to ask a question or add an interesting point. As she watched him with her daughter at Thanksgiving, it was plain that there was a special kind of intensity to the focus he applied whenever Emily entered a room or opened her mouth to speak—or even merely to breathe. He never, however, seemed to demand the same in return—not from Emily, not from anyone. He was very comfortable letting conversations revolve around others, and it was characteristically selfless of him to be cheering Emily on for her dedication to her work regardless of the fact it was depriving him of her company.

Rubbing her eyes, she reluctantly entertained a question that had been nagging her since dinner: had she possibly failed, as her own mother had done, by making her daughter feel wrong to want this kind of attention?

With new resolve, she opened her computer's mail program and clicked NEW, then typed in Clay's e-mail address.

Dear Clay, she wrote, *I'm worried about Emily.*

She sat for a while, trying to figure out what to write next. It was better not to go into specifics, she decided—better to simply leave it at that.

Please call me, she wrote, then typed her name and pressed SEND.

In the morning, she got up and wandered into the breakfast room just before Earl left for the office. He was standing beside the table, briefcase in hand, taking one last glance at the front page along with a last sip of coffee.

"There you are," he said. "You feeling well?"

"Yeah. I had trouble sleeping." She gave him a kiss and took a seat at her regular place, where Lucinda, the housekeeper, had set out fresh-squeezed orange juice and coffee, bran flakes and toast. "How was your dinner?"

"Good," he said, checking himself for crumbs and adjusting his tie. "They were interesting. Smart. Had some good ideas. How was yours?"

"It was all right," she said. "The girls were asking about you yesterday. They wanted to know if you're going to come to the performance."

"Of course. As long as I'm in town."

The one time he had visited her program, she'd worried that Earl, with his business suit and his Waspy manner, might put the kids off. But the girls had instantly responded to his lack of inhibition, and his goofiness not only set them at ease but seemed to amp up that aspect of themselves. Even his clothes were a surprising success. The girls still talked about his "fine" suit and his pink tie with its seemingly abstract design, which if you looked closely, turned out to be dozens of wallowing hippos.

"You should have heard them," Laura said. "'When's Mr. L coming back again? Is he going to come to the show?'" She laughed. "You know, they call me 'Ms. L,' so naturally, you're 'Mr. L.'"

He smiled. "I can live with that."

I should hope so, she thought, considering she had taken his last name—men are so egocentric. And then she caught herself, realizing that this was Earl she was talking about. Joe was on her mind so much, it had her all mixed up.

The phone rang an hour or so later as she was getting dressed for her Pilates class. She already had on a leotard and quickly finished pulling on her leggings before picking up the phone on her dressing table.

"Hi. Laura?"

"Clay?" she said, remembering the e-mail she'd sent last night.

"Yeah. Hi."

"How are you?" She sat down at the dressing table, turning her body so that she didn't have to look at herself in the mirror. "I'm so glad you called."

"What's going on?" he asked, concerned.

"It's nothing too serious," she assured him. "Only that—as you know, Emily and I had dinner last night."

"Right."

"And I thought she seemed a bit—" she hesitated for a moment, searching for the right word "—troubled, I guess you'd say. I didn't mean to alarm you with my e-mail, but I figured you'd be the best person to talk to since you're the one she's closest to."

"Sure."

"So . . . is everything okay?"

"I think so." He sounded a bit confused. "I mean she's definitely been really stressed about this case. Is that what you're talking about?"

"Maybe. I guess that could be all it is. I'm sorry," she said, feeling slightly embarrassed. "I'm probably making too much of it."

"She's been working around the clock. I've honestly barely seen her lately."

"Hmm," Laura said. She didn't like the sound of that, but she didn't think she could ask anything specifically about their relationship without seeming nosy. There was a long pause while he waited for her to say something else.

"I'm sorry," she said again. "Please just—" She broke off.

"Sorry. What?"

He sounded distracted, and she could tell she was about to lose him. She went ahead boldly.

"Emily's lost the two most important men in her life, and I see signs that she's starting to push away."

"Push away?"

"Oh, you know. She . . . how do I explain this?" Laura sighed. "Just don't let her push you away."

"Sure. Don't worry."

She could hear him put his hand over the receiver and tell somebody he was on his way.

"That's all," she said, hoping he'd heard her.

"I'm sorry, Laura. I really have to go. I have a meeting right now. Can I call you later?"

"Of course. Oh, Clay, I'm so happy you two are getting married. Really. I think you're so good for her."

"Thanks. I hope so."

"You are. As a parent, it's so nice to know that your child has found someone who cares about them so much. And it's so nice for me to have someone to talk to as well. Anyway, I don't mean to keep you. Go on to your meeting. Let's have lunch sometime."

"Sure."

After she put the phone down, she turned back to the mirror and began brushing her hair into a ponytail. The mere sound of Clay's voice told her everything was going to be fine. If Emily were beginning to push him away, he would know it, and would have already confronted her about it. She laughed a little at herself for getting so worked up in the wee hours. Her daughter had found the kind of man other women dream of, and he luckily wasn't going anywhere, no matter how crazy Emily could sometimes be.

Emily stood in the office kitchen, inspecting a box of holiday chocolates. She lifted the first tray and found a layer of cocoa-dusted truffles hidden beneath. As she did so, Eric found his way into her thoughts. Ever since she'd read his obituary last month, it kept happening like this—she'd be going about her day as usual when a vague sadness would come over her, and slowly she'd realize it was about him.

"Those ones are good," came a voice from the doorway.

She turned to find her friend Liz entering with a Starbucks cup.

"I shouldn't be eating any of this stuff," Emily said as she popped a truffle in her mouth. "Clay and I are going to Daniel tonight for our anniversary."

"That's so sweet," Liz said, digging a truffle out of the box. "I wish I knew the exact day that Hal and I started dating. I guess it happened so gradually, we never kept track."

"Yeah . . . it was gradual for us, too. There was that whole period when we were like, *No, we're not dating—we're just friends who happen to have sex every now and then.*" She laughed. "But at some point, once we were out of denial, I found this old ticket stub from a movie we'd seen together on December fifteenth, so we chose that as the official starting point. Don't ask me why."

"I should do that, too," Liz said. "Choose a date at random."

It seemed like Liz was always coming up with ways to try to solidify her relationship with Hal, and it made Emily wonder if maybe Hal wasn't as serious about Liz as she pretended.

"Anyway," Emily said, "I'd better get back. I haven't even been by my desk since lunch."

"Uh-oh." Liz shook boogeyman fingers in her face. "Chaos."

Emily laughed, embarrassed. "I know. I'm such a nerd." Licking chocolate off her finger, she headed out the door.

When she got to her desk, there was a yellow Post-it stuck to her computer screen: *Left you a v.m. Call me!!!—Chris.*

She rolled her eyes. She'd taken out her phone at lunch but put it away again as soon as she saw it was him calling. His enthusiasm drove her nuts. Every single thing that happened in the case, including discoveries of minutely trivial bits of information, got reported with the same effervescently urgent tone. When he first started his internship with the office, she tried to be nice and returned his calls as soon as possible, but by now she was past that and took all his messages with a grain of salt.

Still, she picked up the phone and punched in his extension—if for nothing else than to get the call out of the way.

"Emily!" he practically shouted once she'd announced herself, "Hang on. I'll be right there."

Before she could tell him not to bother, he'd already hung up the phone, and within seconds, he appeared in her doorway, beaming.

"Jesus," she said to herself. On her computer screen, a montage played: luminescent jellyfish propelling themselves silently under the sea. With the click of a mouse, she closed the screen saver and began checking her e-mail.

"Guess what?" Chris said, breezing triumphantly into her office.

"What?" she said, scrolling through the messages and finding nothing of much interest.

He was breathless with anticipation. "You're not going to believe this."

"Hmm."

"You know how you were saying yesterday that you feel like that CO might have had it in for Ramon?"

God, he was annoying. "Chris," she said calmly, "it's not a question of me *feeling* like he *might* have. It's an absolute fact. This is what I kept trying to explain yesterday. Ramon had filed a bunch of complaints against him, and he was pissed. He's still pissed. Believe me."

Chris smiled broadly.

"What?" she said impatiently.

"We found a memorandum, prepared by the warden right after the murder."

This caught her interest. "Yeah? What's it say?"

"It says our CO initially reported that *another prisoner*, someone by the name of James Turly, saw Ramon leaving the bathroom approximately half an hour before the body was discovered. But it says absolutely nothing about him seeing Ramon himself."

"Holy shit. You're kidding."

"I'm not."

"Oh my God! That's amazing. That's amazing," she repeated, standing up. "I knew that guy wasn't telling the truth. How'd you find that memorandum?"

"Just going through all the documents."

"Holy shit."

"Do you think the government knows?"

"No way."

Despite the distance, Emily was determined to deliver the news immediately to Ramon, who was being held upstate at Coxsackie while awaiting trial. So she took it upon herself to search down the cheapest car service available and forwarded all calls to her cell. Outside, a mixture of rain and sleet was falling, and it was already getting dark. As she settled into the backseat of the car, she started to call Clay, then decided it was better to wait until she was heading over the bridge, beyond the bounds of Manhattan. Slowly the car maneuvered across town, scooting between double- and triple-parked trucks, and jerking to a halt here and there for pedestrians rushing to get out of the freezing rain. She thought traffic would ease up once they got to the West Side Highway, but it was slow going there, too.

She sat back and listened to the heavy metal music streaming out of the speakers up front. Ordinarily, one of the nice things about a car service—the kind that came with Clay's job, for example—was the absence of offensive talk radio or odd musical selections that often had to be endured while riding in a cab. But this was more like getting a lift from one of your uncle's pals. The car was an old brown station wagon, and the driver—a young heavyset guy with a thick New York accent—was wearing a gray hooded sweatshirt and a Mets hat rather than the traditional black suit and cap. When she got in, he had asked whether she minded leaving the windows open a crack. And for some reason, despite the blustery weather, she'd told him she didn't mind at all. Now she felt she couldn't go back on her word, but the occasional gust of frosty air didn't bother her too much anyway. Nothing could dampen her spirits right now. With amusement, she watched the driver in the rearview mirror. He was one of those people whose mouths inexplicably leak as they talk, and he had to rub his sleeve across his lips every now and then.

"You like this song?" he asked as his eyes met hers.

"Mm-hmm," she lied.

"Pavarotti is the only rock and roll I need," he said very seriously. "Really. I mean that. See, the three tenors . . ."

The car picked up speed, and Emily pitched forward in order to hear him over the whoosh of the air coming through the windows.

"The three tenors—Pavarotti's a lot better than them. And they know that, but they're okay with it. You know?"

"Isn't Pavarotti one of the three tenors?" she asked, trying to figure out what any of this had to do with the heavy metal song playing on the radio.

"Italians are the only ones who can really sing opera," he went on fervently. "I'm not kidding. They know how to live. Just give me a piece of Swiss chard and some Italian bread—I'm set."

Laughing, she nodded at the reflection of his eyes. The dark circles underneath indicated exhaustion, though the pupils darted vigorously between the road and the mirror.

It took them another twenty minutes to make it all the way up the West Side Highway. Finally, once they'd passed through the tollbooth and were zooming up the parkway, she dialed Clay.

"Hi," he said.

"Hi."

"What's up?"

"Well . . ." She winced before she said it. "I can't go to dinner. I have to work."

"Tonight?" he asked, surprised.

"Yeah. There's been an amazing new development. I'll tell you about it later. But I have to talk to Ramon. I'm on my way upstate right now."

There was a long pause. "You know this is the night we were going to Daniel."

"I know. Of course I know."

"Someone else can't go upstate instead?"

"No."

"And you can't do it tomorrow?"

Frustrated, she said, "No, Clay. Come on."

"This sucks," he replied angrily.

"Clay, I have to work. I can't help it. We'll do it tomorrow night."

"We won't get a reservation."

"So we'll go next week."

"Yeah," he said glumly. "Fine."

"I wish you wouldn't be so angry."

"I'm just bummed."

"I understand. I'm sorry."

"Yeah . . . but—" He broke off. "Part of me can't help wondering if you're doing this on purpose."

"What?" she asked, taken aback. "Why would I do this on purpose?"

"I don't know." There was another pause. "Look, Em, if you want to end this, you're not trapped. But I wish you'd come out and say so."

"What in the hell are you talking about?" she asked angrily. "I'm *working*, Clay. This is something I have to do—not something I'm doing *to you*."

"Really?" he said, standing his ground. "It doesn't have anything to do with feeling conflicted about things and trying to avoid me?"

"You're insane."

"I happen to know that you're feeling conflicted about the wedding."

"I am not," she replied defensively.

"Emily . . ." He sighed. "Come on."

"You come on. What's gotten into you?"

"Your mom told me you're having second thoughts."

"What? When did she say that?"

"Listen," he said reluctantly, "I had lunch with her yesterday."

A horrible tingly feeling crept over her. "You had lunch with my mom? Why didn't you tell me?"

"Why didn't you tell me that you're having doubts about the wedding?"

She couldn't believe this. "Because I'm *not*. What did she tell you exactly?"

"That you're having premarital jitters."

"That's ridiculous."

"I'm sorry," Clay said. "I promised her I wouldn't tell you. She was trying to help."

"Help?" she shouted. "How is that helping? What else did she say?"

"She said that you're worried we don't share enough passion or love."

"Jesus Christ. I'm going to strangle her."

There was a long pause.

"That's all you have to say?" he asked.

"No, that is not all I have to say. I can't believe you guys are sneaking around behind my back, having lunch, and talking about me like that. Don't you feel any sense of allegiance to me? *I'm* the one you're supposed to be in love with."

Another lengthy pause.

"Well," he said finally. "I'm the one *you're* supposed to be in love with."

"Clay."

There was no response.

"Clay?"

She looked down at her phone. *Call Ended*, it said.

"Asshole," she muttered.

She sat back and looked out the sleet-streaked window at the passing forest—bare deciduous trees mixed with blocks of evergreens. She couldn't believe her mother. She knew she shouldn't feel so surprised, but she did. Things had been so good between them for the last several years. From the time both male members of the family had made their final, permanent exits, peace had settled in. And now here they were again: a new man was about to join the family, and the peace was quickly slipping away.

She watched the scenery out the window, starting to regret the way she'd spoken to Clay.

"Excuse me," she said to the driver. "I received a call that I'm going to have to go back to the city."

"So you want me to turn around?"

"Yes, I'm sorry. I'm afraid we have to."

"No problem," he said. "It's all the same to me."

She watched as he steered the car off the next exit ramp, then passed through a stoplight and an underpass before looping back around and getting on the highway again. She was afraid to ask how long it would take to get to the city, but from her own calculations, it seemed pretty clear she'd make it to the restaurant without even having to change the reservation time. With relief, she watched the forest whiz past, thinking how close she'd come to missing their anniversary dinner for absolutely no reason at all. After twenty minutes of coasting along like this, she was about to call Clay when the traffic slowed and then came to a dead halt.

"What's going on?" she asked nervously.

"Don't know. Accident maybe."

"Shoot," she said. "I'm really in a hurry. Is there another way we can go?"

"Nope. Not at this point. Later on you can switch to the Deegan, but that's not for a while still."

She chewed her nail, waiting in vain for traffic to pick up speed again, but the minutes continued to tick by as they sat there without moving.

She decided to call the restaurant.

"It's got to be an accident," the driver said, pointing across to the other side of the highway. "See. They're all stopped over there, too. Everybody slowing down to look."

A bright female voice answered the phone, "Good evening. Daniel," with a French emphasis on the last syllable.

"Hi," Emily said. "I was hoping you could help me. My fiancé and I are celebrating a special occasion tonight—an anniversary-type thing. We have a reservation for seven, but I'm stuck in terrible traffic outside the city and was wondering if there would be any chance we could come at eight instead."

"What's the name?" asked the woman.

"Lee."

"Oh." The woman hesitated. "I believe that reservation was canceled."

"I'm sorry," Emily said. "That was a mistake."

"So you'd like to keep the reservation then?"

"Yes, but move it to eight."

"We're very fully booked tonight," the woman replied in a tone that said Emily had no idea what an absurd favor she'd requested. "I can hold your table for you until seven thirty, but that's the latest we could possibly take you."

Emily leaned forward and addressed the driver. "Do you think there's any way we'll make it to midtown by seven thirty?"

He let out a short burst of laughter. "No."

That was all—*No.*

"I'm sorry," Emily told the woman. "I think we'll just have to do it another night then."

"Sure," the woman replied, making her patience palpable across the phone line. "So you'd like to cancel the reservation once again?"

"Yes."

Emily hung up, and tossing her phone into her open bag, buried her head in her hands.

"What in the hell am I doing?" she asked herself out loud.

Thinking she was talking to him, the driver looked at her in the rearview mirror. "Sorry?"

"No," she said. "Nothing."

It was now horribly cold in the car. She pulled her coat more tightly around her body and crossed her legs. All of the optimism and excitement she'd been feeling about the case was gone. She had the sinking feeling that regardless of the news they'd received to-day—no matter what she did, no matter what new evidence she and her team turned up in their favor—it wasn't going to be enough. This boy, this innocent boy, was at the mercy of the state, and the prosecution was going to do everything it could to nail him.

As chilled as she was, she still couldn't bring herself to roll up the windows. She wished that there were a way to make others happy without casting herself into agony. Thomas had excelled at that. For him, pleasing people had come naturally because he was a genuinely good person. As much as she'd tried, she'd been unsuccessful in emulating him. Hers was a sort of false goodness which, more than anything else, created the perfect breeding ground for her own anger and contempt.

In the car next to her, a little boy pressed his nose up against the glass, and she smiled at him. He smiled back and waved. She waved, too. After they'd gone back and forth like this for a minute or so, he jerked his head around and began to talk to the other people in the car. She sat back and closed her eyes, trying to envision her brother lounging casually in the seat beside her.

Do you remember, she began, *when you told me you thought Dad was the loneliest person in the whole world? That he was so fixated on these fantasies of what his life should be? And that's why we always felt like he was only half there—anyway, that's what you said. I'm sure you remember it because you felt it so strongly. And, of course, I didn't agree with you—and really, I'm not sure that I do now. I think he's perfectly content being a selfish and solitary old man. But I know how you can see things about people that I can't see, so you're probably right. You've always been good that way.*

She paused for a moment, thinking.

Here's the thing, though, she told him. *Sometimes I remember what you said about Dad, and . . . I don't know. Maybe if you knew me now, you'd say the same things about me.*

After a few moments, she opened her eyes again. The traffic was still barely moving. Checking the e-mails on her Blackberry—nothing but junk mail, mostly promoting holiday specials—she thought about the Christmas present she'd already gotten for Clay and how much he was going to love it. Thank God next week they'd be on their trip. She'd been a complete jerk lately, but hopefully she could make it up to him.

⌢

Joe took out his cell phone and dialed. He was seated at his usual table in the Jefferson dining room. Over the last few weeks—since he'd moved to the much more affordable Marrisy Motel—he'd continued to come regularly to the Jefferson for meals. The cheerful hotel staff persisted in treating him with the same courteous, accommodating attitude they'd exhibited during his stay, always reserving the same banquette seat for him with its view of the garden—although it was now nearly seven o'clock, and it was dark outside. He normally didn't use his cell phone in restaurants, but he had begun to feel so at home here—and besides, he was tired of eating all of his meals alone. Even at lunchtime, there was nothing to look at. The garden was a pale facsimile of its former self, as were the pastures and woods beyond it. The trees had lost their leaves, perennials had been cut down to the ground, and the rose-bushes were hooded with burlap. The overall effect, heightened by the blur of condensation on the windows, was of an abstract land-scape painted in hues of gray, ocher, and brown. The change of season also meant fewer guests, which was fine in a way but also a little dull, and he often hoped in vain that he would reencounter the captivating woman with the silver hair and the poppy-printed dress.

After several rings, Emily's voice came through sounding vaguely annoyed. "Hello?"

The connection was bad, and in the background, there seemed to be some kind of loud rock music playing.

"Hello?" she said again.

He knew his daughter well enough to deduce from her tone that it was not a good time to talk. Even in the best of circumstances, she could be irritable and impatient when they talked on the phone. He decided to try her some other time and hung up.

He didn't know why he was calling anyway. Thanksgiving had come and gone, and he still hadn't heard from her. He was sure she and Clay had spent the holiday with Laura as usual. He understood that she preferred to spend the important days of the year with people other than himself, and to let her off the hook, he'd always pretended to have plans with friends for Thanksgiving and Christmas and even both of their birthdays. Still, it was unlike her not to call and ask what he was doing, even though they both knew it was only a formality.

As he pushed the last few bites of pot-au-feu around his plate with a piece of baguette, he could feel the woman at the neighboring table staring at him. She'd been doing it off and on throughout his meal while she sat there eating and speaking with her husband, and he found it incredibly annoying. He was about to put the gravy-soaked bread in his mouth when he saw her rise from the table and begin marching toward him with a big, friendly grin. She had a chic, razor-cut hairstyle and walked with a strong, purposeful stride. Her husband, lagging behind and looking somewhat embarrassed, was tall and Nordic-looking and was wearing a pair of trendy athletic shoes that Joe had seen on a lot of the younger men in New York. The two of them were very well preserved for their age, which Joe guessed to be close to his own, and they had a sophisticated but youthful air about them. It occurred to him that they might be people he knew from the city, and he began to rack his brain to try to place them.

"Excuse me," she said in a quiet voice as she arrived beside him. "Are you Joe Ascher?"

"Yes?" he asked, rising from his seat, but making no effort to feign recognition.

"Please don't get up. I'm so sorry to interrupt your meal, but I had to stop by and say hello."

He was standing fully now, and she extended her hand toward him.

"I'm Celine Carlin, and this is my husband, John."

He shook both of their hands.

"I just had to tell you that I was your number one fan." She tilted her head coyly. "Really. I was so completely in love with you—and your plays, of course."

Joe nodded, uncomfortable. "Thank you very much."

"Anyway, the minute I recognized you, I thought I simply had to come and tell you that."

"Thank you."

"Don't let us keep you any longer. I didn't mean to interrupt." She began to retreat toward the door with her sheepishly nodding husband in tow.

"Not at all."

"Good-bye," she said.

"Good-bye."

He sat down and watched them go. Noticing that they didn't speak to each other at all on the way out, he guessed that they were saving their discussion of him until they had left the restaurant. He paid the bill, wiped his mouth with his napkin, and placed it on the banquette. He noticed she hadn't bothered to ask what he was currently working on, which made him wonder whether she no longer cared what he did (after all, she had consistently used the past tense: *I was your number one fan, I was so completely in love with you*) or whether it simply reflected a certainty on her part that he no longer worked at all.

He approached the maître d' stand and saw that it was being manned by Albert. Impulsively, he walked up to him.

"Albert?"

Albert looked up from the reservation book as if it were a list of the recently deceased.

"Yes, Mr. Ascher?"

"Do you recall a woman . . ." He hesitated, trying to figure out how to best describe her. "I was seated across from her at lunch once. She has shoulder-length gray hair."

Albert waited for something more.

"I was wondering," Joe said, "if she's come back at all. I believe she lives in the area."

"I'm not sure that I know whom you mean, sir."

Joe nodded.

"Would you like to leave a message for her in case she comes again?"

"No, thanks. Don't worry about it."

Albert smiled formally. "All right. Thank you, sir."

"Dinner was delicious, by the way."

"I'm glad to hear that, Mr. Ascher. It's always a pleasure to see you, sir."

"Thank you."

As he walked back to the car, he decided that he wouldn't return for another meal at the hotel any time soon. *In fact,* he thought, *especially now that he was staying in a crappy motel, there was absolutely no reason for him to stay in the area at all.* But he was determined not to return home without a play. To those who had something wonderful to give it, New York could be the kindest place in the world. But one did not want to show up there empty-handed. Regardless of residential status, one was always a guest there and one's standing always dependent upon the multitude and worth of one's offerings. Even though he was technically writing the play for Williamstown, there would be plenty of New Yorkers who would travel up to see it, to review it, and if all went well, to bring it back home with them and give it a real life on the New York stage.

When he returned to his motel room that afternoon, he tried to work but ended up staring past the pile of tapes and the computer screen, and through the dirty screen of his room's one small window, out onto the motel parking lot. He had set up a makeshift desk by removing the TV from its stand—a two-foot-square block with phony wood-grain paneling and a drawer containing an untouched copy of the King James Bible. He had dragged the stand over to the window in order to get some natural light. There was no room for a chair at this makeshift desk, but the edge of the mattress made a reasonably comfortable perch. Outside, fluorescent saucer-shaped lamps threw pools of greenish light around the edges of the asphalt lot, and Joe saw that a yellow rubber glove, which had presumably fallen from one of the maids' cleaning carts, now lay like an amputated limb on the sidewalk.

He could see the Indian motel manager through the office window, framed in a square of yellow light. He was sitting behind his desk, arms crossed, nodding and laughing. Joe couldn't tell whether he was watching television or reacting to someone hidden from view. He suspected the former since he never saw another soul in the office at night—only the nice Indian man, alone with his television and his cell phone. He wondered at the series of circumstances that had brought the man to this desolate place out in the middle of nowhere so far from his country, his family and friends, and his past.

Joe liked to break up the pronunciation of the motel's name, calling it the "merry sea." He had vastly preferred the luxury of his previous accommodations to the current assemblage of hideous synthetic wood furnishings and stained, polyester upholstery, preferred the garden and rolling hills to the view of cars parked in an asphalt lot. But the absence of the cheerful Chips and Chads and the eerily omnipresent Albert, each greeting him by name several times a day, was a change that brought tremendous liberation and relief.

What would the woman from dinner this evening think if she saw him now? The seedy motel, the dingy room, the absurd, make-shift writing space, the view of the night manager across the lot, the half-consumed bottle of vodka (though not a cheap brand—there was still a high level of quality in his drink at least) . . . all of these things together added up to form a perfect portrait of defeat. Perhaps his continuing to write would be viewed—by anyone—as the saddest sight of all. He despised the tendency of a bitter and barren public to generate in themselves a sense of superiority simply by passing judgment upon the creations of others.

Admittedly, it would not displease him for people to respond positively to his new work—if only to feel the joy of reminding that public how much more powerful was the creator than the detrac-tor. But he hadn't started writing again to win back his audience. He had begun to write, quite simply, for the Ingrids of the world.

The room felt hot and stuffy. The Indian man had come out of the office and was standing in the tiny strip of grass at the edge of the parking lot. He wore no coat over his thin, button-down shirt, and Joe imagined how sharp the winter air must feel as it pushed its way past the cotton fibers to his skin. The man tilted his head backward and stared for some time up at the sky. Eventually, he raised his arms up overhead, seemingly in order to stretch, though strangely he kept his palms cupped and turned upward. Joe watched him, wondering whether he was engaged in prayer. After a few moments, the man brought his arms back down and examined his hands. Then he returned to the office, and through the window, Joe saw him take up his post behind the desk.

The computer screen glared menacingly, challenging him with its blankness. Glancing down at the Dictaphone and at the multi-tude of tapes scattered across the makeshift desk, he was over-whelmed by a sense of futility. There was nothing here worth transcribing onto the computer. Nothing. What he had before him was a bunch of old, tired material. And what little new material there was—sentimental accounts of conversations between himself and a teenage kid—could not possibly hold the least bit of interest for anyone other than himself.

He closed his computer screen and went over to the dresser to pour himself a glass of vodka. He didn't know how he was going to write this thing. But he knew that he had to find someone to talk to. And not about his work. He could never talk about what he was writing until he had finished. But it would be nice to find someone who could get him out of his own head for a while. It was too bad that the woman with the silver hair and the poppy dress had never shown up again. They'd exchanged only a few sentences, but he had been captivated by her startlingly beautiful gray eyes, and she'd had a way about her—a gentleness that suggested to him she had experienced some sort of difficulty and was kinder for it.

Well, he thought, looking out the window, *it was probably for the best.* He didn't need that sort of distraction. What he needed was quite simply to keep writing. Slowly, he began to sense that the air outside was charged with energy. And as he followed a stream of fluorescence upward from the light pool on the asphalt to its source high above, he suddenly saw the reason for the night manager's odd behavior. There, dancing in the light, were thousands of tiny, glistening flakes of snow.

He sipped his vodka, watching the snow fall, and thought once again about Emily—wondering if he should have at least said hello when he called this evening and let her take it from there. It was all very well to take her judgment and contempt and say to hell with all that. But he blamed himself to some degree for the transformation she'd undergone as she'd entered adulthood. Undoubtedly, over the years, there were certain experiences he should have protected her from. Or if he couldn't have protected her, he could have at least been there more to provide advice and to listen.

Gradually it began to snow harder, and a dusting of white soon coated the surface of the lot and the parked cars. It dawned on him that snow was possibly the clearest visual marker there was for the passage of time. Off the top of his head, the only other thing he could think of that shared this quality was the human aging process.

Day and night were cyclical—as were seasons.

But snow, like human life, built gradually to a certain point, then gradually—or abruptly—melted away.

He started to pace energetically back and forth across the room, stopping briefly at the dresser to top off his drink. He was onto something now, and he was finally feeling that sense of excitement he'd been waiting for for weeks.

1994

In the cab on the way home from the movie, Thomas sat between his sister and his mother, who fought with each other from the moment they got in.

"You never let me do anything," Emily complained.

"Oh puh-leese!" their mother moaned. "Don't be absurd."

He kept his eyes fixed on the black hump that rose out of the floor of the car and forced him to straddle his legs.

After they'd been at it for a while, Emily said, "You're so impossible. Seriously. No wonder Dad left."

Their mother turned and looked out her window. Emily soon did the same, and nobody said anything else for the rest of the ride.

Their father had been gone now for about five weeks. It was strange to be the only male in the family. He'd never noticed before how much his mother and his sister got on each other's nerves. And yet he'd also never noticed how similar they were. They were both maddeningly stubborn—neither tended to apologize or admit that she was wrong—and they shared a prideful way of masking their emotions that could make them seem cold and distant at times.

But he had also seen them both completely unhinged, crying—sometimes even sobbing—while going on at length to him about their feelings: what had made them upset, or how they weren't even sure why they were upset, how they felt one way and then at the same time also another way, and it was so hard to explain but did he see what they meant? (He always said yes even if he didn't.) And it was probably because of this or that, didn't he think so? (Again yes.) So really what they had to do was probably x, y, and z—that was all. They were so glad he understood, and so relieved he'd helped them figure the whole thing out.

He imagined that when his father had been around, they had gone to him with their troubles. Or perhaps, his father's absence had simply tipped them over an edge—a certain point where, unbeknownst to him, they had been teetering precariously for years. He didn't have an answer for the change. He just knew that he was now the person to whom his mother and his sister came to unburden themselves. And he also knew that he was tired.

When they got home, Emily followed him down the hall toward their rooms.

"What are you doing?" she asked casually.

"I need to go to the bathroom," he lied.

"Then what?"

"Then I'm not sure," he said impatiently. "Maybe I'll climb Mount Everest. I've always wanted to do that."

Clearly stung by the rejection, she continued past him to her own room.

"Don't get on the phone," her mother called after her. "I'm expecting a call from Dr. Herschfeldt."

Thomas rubbed his fingers over the bump behind his ear. A lymph node, the doctor had told him, could be swollen for *any number* of reasons—the cause could easily be nothing more than an infection from picking one of his zits at some point. He wished his mother would calm down about the goddamned thing.

Emily's door slammed shut. *Christ,* he thought, *enough drama.* He'd always thought his dad was the dramatic one in the family, but he was apparently wrong about that.

Emily marched over to the desk, where she had a phone number written at the top of an old *Times* crossword puzzle. This would be only the second call she'd made to her father since he'd been away, and the first since he'd been in Florida. The other time, a few weeks back, he'd still been living at Gina's New York apartment. Gina had answered the phone, and Emily had attempted to disguise her voice, asking for her father in a very low, womanly tone. But Gina still knew it was her, and tried to draw her into a friendly chat, asking questions about her school and her acting class and her friends as if nothing had happened. Not knowing what else to do, Emily curtly answered a couple of the questions, then asked again for her father. But when he finally came on the line, she found that talking to her dad felt at least as awkward as talking to Gina—maybe even more so. About a week later, he had called and left a message for all three of them on the answering machine in the kitchen, saying he was in Florida and giving them his number. But she was pretty sure nobody had used it. She and her mother and Thomas had discussed the message briefly, wondering—without conclusion—what he was doing in Florida and if it meant he'd left Gina. They'd heard about the play's disastrous reviews and the early closing. As to whether the affair had ended as well, she hadn't heard anything—not even from Eric, the one person she'd stayed in touch with after dropping out of the cast.

The phone rang several times before her father picked up. "Hello," he said gruffly.

She'd noticed the last time that he had a very theatrical way of speaking, but she couldn't tell if this was something new, or if it was only the way he sounded on the phone. Or maybe this was how he always was.

"Hi, Daddy. How are you?"

"Well, hello there! How goes it in the wilds of Manhattan?"

"Not so great."

"Oh?"

"We went to the movies this afternoon—"

"Yeah? What did you see?"

"Whatever—it doesn't matter. But after, I ran into Sophie and Kate, and they were going to Tower Records, so I told Mom I was going with them, and she goes, 'No you're not.' And I was like,

'What do you mean no you're not? That's totally crazy. Why not?'
And she's just like, 'Because you're not.'"

"Hmm," her father said.

"Can you believe that? I mean she won't even let me have a life.
I have no life. I'm not kidding."

"Well, maybe she didn't like the idea of you wandering the
streets for hours on end."

"Dad, I wasn't going to wander the streets! I was going to a
music store."

"Maybe she didn't trust that you were actually going to go to
the music store."

"Well, that's her problem. She has no faith in me. It's ridiculous. I'm not three, you know. I have to be able to hang out with
my friends. Recently it's been like a total lockdown. I'm practically
not even allowed to leave the house."

There was a short pause, during which she chewed nervously
on her hair. Then her father said, "How's your mom doing?"

"How's she *doing*? She's a total asshole. Haven't you been listening to anything I've been saying?"

"How's your brother?"

She held up her hands as if motioning to someone else in the
room—*can you believe this?*

"Fine," she said with a huff.

"Well . . . give everyone my best."

"Great," she scoffed. "Thanks a lot, Dad. You've been really
supportive. Really glad we got to talk."

"All right," he said. "I love you."

"I love you, too," she mumbled.

Joe let the receiver fall back into its cradle and turned to Gina, who
was watching him behind her Jackie O sunglasses. Standing in her
bathing suit and sarong at the wainscoted counter that separated
the kitchen from the living room, she was applying another coat of
sunscreen to her arms. A breeze blew through the screen door, and
a cloud of coconut oil wafted over and settled around his chair.

"Emily?" Gina asked.

She'd ambled in from the porch when she heard the phone ring.

Gina could spend all day on the porch, reading and drinking and playing Scrabble. The house—a stunning little cottage right on the beach—belonged to a friend of hers who wasn't using it for a couple of weeks and was thrilled to provide the perfect getaway spot for Gina's burgeoning romance.

"Yes." He nodded. "Emily."

When she finished with the sunscreen, she came up behind him and wrapped her arms around his neck, leaning down so that he could feel her hair and her breath against his cheek.

Instinctively, he turned the legal pad in his lap facedown.

"I was thinking we could go to the crab place tonight," she said. "What do you think?"

"Great."

She kissed his cheek. "I'll leave you alone. I know you're working."

"No, I'm getting up."

He stood up from the chair and stretched, then followed her out the screen door onto the porch. There was a garden of tropical plants that wrapped around the house, and the moisture from the sprinklers that had recently shut off was visibly rising from the giant green leaves, drawn into the air by the blazing afternoon sun. Beyond this steamy strip of jungle, the sea sparkled invitingly. She pulled a teak chaise out of the shade and after covering the cushion with a towel, lay down on her belly. He lingered for a moment, taking in the view, then started down the steps.

She lifted her head.

"I'll be back in an hour or so," he told her.

"Want company?"

"No, I'd better go on my own—I've got a scene that keeps giving me trouble. Maybe if I walk for a bit . . ."

"Sure," she said, and lay back down.

The steps led to a path of narrow wood planks, which meandered through the tropical plants then arched tidily over a grassy dune before giving way to the open expanse of the beach. As he stepped off the last plank, he felt a familiar sense of release. He walked down to the shore, his feet sinking into the sand, and his mind—no longer confined to the house—began to expand and make room for thoughts he hadn't been able to accommodate inside.

How his heart had leaped with happiness at the sound of his daughter's voice. And yet the experience had been painful, too—imagining all of them there in the apartment without him: Emily stretched out on her bed with the phone, her feet tapping restlessly against the headboard; Laura and Thomas perhaps sitting together in the library, listening to NPR or poring over garden catalogs; all of them going to movies and meals and parties together, talking and laughing and fighting and sharing in each other's daily ups and downs. He felt terrible about his conversation with Emily. Countless times in the past she had come to him with complaints about her mother, and he had always been there for her, offering his support, advice, and consolation. But today, he simply couldn't give any of it. He understood, of course, why Emily was upset with Laura. However, to even say that much—that he understood—was a disloyalty to his wife he felt himself unwilling to assume.

He'd been thinking about Laura a great deal lately. This morning, he'd been walking with Gina along this same stretch of beach and had seen a group of kids playing in the ocean, reminding him of a scene long ago in Cancun: Laura was sitting under a thatch *palapa*, watching Emily and Thomas clown around in the surf. The children were jumping up and down and splashing each other, and with a look that was both happy and confounded, Laura said, "Look at them. That's so wonderful—how they play like that." From the way she said it, he instantly grasped (and strangely for the first time) that she had never, even as a child, really known how to play.

The memory had filled him with tenderness and remorse. Laura's seriousness was one of the things that first attracted him to her. He had never before met someone who viewed everything—even something as banal as a card game—as an opportunity to so keenly judge her entire self, assessing where her weaknesses lay and immediately setting to work on them. He was fascinated by this, and he admired her vigor. But there was something sad about it, too—the girl who didn't know how to play. To say that her parents had been reserved would be the understatement of the century.

Dour and strict, they believed that children should be rarely seen and never heard. Their constant fear that she might embarrass them—or herself—continued to inhibit her to this day. From the start of their relationship, Joe had taken immense pleasure in providing her with a different perspective on things, helping her laugh off some of her mistakes and making sure she had her share of pure pointless fun. At some crucial juncture, however (and he wasn't sure when it had occurred), he'd switched from being the one who led her out of the darkness to the one who led her into it. He hated the feeling that everything was his fault, and his resentment toward her had grown along with the oppressiveness of his new role. But as he watched the kids on the beach this morning, his point of view had shifted, and he was struck by the realization that he'd let her down.

Still, he could not deny that in some ways it had been wonderful being away from her and being with Gina. At first, while he and Gina were still in New York, living at Gina's apartment, it had been difficult. Nagged by the guilt of what he was doing, and constantly terrified he was going to run into Laura—as well as anxious about the horrendous state of *Prime* and the awful reviews it was getting—he'd been unable to enjoy the fact that he and Gina were finally together. When they arrived in Florida, however, that all changed. The natural beauty of the place, the cottage, and the balmy weather infused each day with a honeymoon feel. And for the first week or so, they reveled in their various discoveries: tidal pools filled with brilliantly colored anemones; charming restaurants that served fresh seafood and wonderfully dry martinis; sunsets and starry skies enjoyed on their own front porch; and the other kind of discoveries—equally as magical—of one another. Sexually, Gina was constantly surprising him with her willingness to do things and let things be done to her he hadn't experienced in many years (or never at all, as was the case in a couple of instances). He also liked the way she lolled about in such a leisurely way. She was so unconcerned with anything other than what the two of them were doing in each particular moment, she'd almost managed to convince him there was nothing happening outside of their own small, happy world.

But as the days wore on, Joe began noticing that he would often go to bed early instead of having a nightcap on the porch, or would insist on working when Gina wanted to drive into town or go for a dip in the ocean, or would even pretend to be asleep when he felt her reaching for him in the night. He was sick to death of stone crab claws and sand in his sheets and the constant rustle of palms. He was getting restless, yearning for home.

Dr. Herschfeldt didn't call until seven at night. Laura had tried him twice from the movie theater, and the second time, she'd left their home number with his nurse. So after they got home, there was nothing to do but wait. She was a nervous wreck by the time he phoned.

"Hello," she said, picking up on the first ring.

"Hello, Laura. Marty Herschfeldt. I'm sorry it took me so long, but I do have Thomas's test results."

She drew a deep breath. "Okay."

"Would you like to get Thomas on the phone?"

"Um. I don't know. What do you think?"

"I usually do with patients his age. I could also see you both in the office tomorrow morning if you'd prefer."

Her head started to spin. If the test results were negative, wouldn't he say so straight out?

"Just a minute," she said.

She called down the hall for Thomas and told him to pick up the phone.

"He's getting on," she told the doctor. "It'll be just a second."

"How was your Thanksgiving?" he asked.

"It was good. Thank you. And yours?"

"Hello?" Thomas's voice broke in.

"Hi, Thomas. I was telling your mother that I have your test results, and I thought you might like to be part of this discussion."

"Yeah, sure."

"Well," Dr. Herschfeldt continued, "the test for gland fever came back negative, but there were some things that turned up in the CBC. Your platelets are low, and you have a very high white count."

"What does that mean exactly?" Laura asked.

"It's not totally clear yet. What I'd like to do is send you to Sloan-Kettering for further testing. There's an oncologist-hematologist there by the name of Dr. Browning—an excellent doctor whom I've worked with for years—and he'll be able to give us a much better idea of what's going on."

"Are we talking about cancer?" Laura asked with alarm.

"I really can't say until he's had further testing. Dr. Browning will probably want to do a CT scan and a surgical biopsy of the node as well as a possible bone marrow aspiration and biopsy—all of which might sound a little scary to you, but they're all very standard and painless tests. Thomas, you might get a little sedative for the bone marrow biopsy, but really none of these tests are a big deal. And I know you'll like Dr. Browning. He can explain everything to you better than I can, but in the meantime, do you have any questions for me?"

"I don't think so," he answered calmly.

"There's really no cause for either of you to be worried yet. I really want to make that clear. Don't jump to any conclusions before Dr. Browning has done his tests."

"Of course," Laura said, hoping that Thomas couldn't hear the doubt in her voice.

"I'm away from my desk right now," the doctor told her. "But if you'll call my office in the morning, the receptionist can give you Dr. Browning's number. And I'll call him as well to let him know I'm sending you over."

"Thank you," she said.

After they said good-bye to the doctor, Laura stayed on the phone. "Thomas?" she said.

"Uh-huh?"

"You're going to be fine."

"Yeah."

As soon as she hung up, she got up from the desk and walked back to his room. Through the crack in the door, she could see him sitting on the couch next to his phone.

"Can I come in?"

"Sure."

She stepped into the doorway. "Are you okay?"

"Yeah, Mom."

She could tell that he thought she was hovering. "All right, I'm sorry. I just wanted to check."

Forcing a smile, she withdrew and walked back down the hall. If it was nothing, then why were his platelets low and his white count high? She should have asked the doctor that. She wanted to call him back, but it was late, and he'd already told her she wasn't supposed to worry. She needed to talk to someone. For a moment she considered calling Joe. Then she decided it would be better to wait until they'd gotten all the tests back from Dr. Browning. If there was nothing to report, she'd be relieved she hadn't dragged Joe into it. And if there was a diagnosis she needed to discuss with her husband—well, she'd call him then.

INGRID!" JOE CALLED.

She was tramping down the hill, toward the garden, her rabbit backpack flopping around behind her open parka. The snow, which came up to her knees, blanketed everything around her and sparkled in the midday sun.

He had asked her to meet him in the garden so that they could enjoy the first snowfall together. On the phone, she was distant at first. *Where had he been? Why hadn't he called? It had been ages since she'd heard from him.* But after a while, she agreed to meet him.

A breeze stirred through the garden, making all the boughs creak and sending mounds of snow cascading down onto the snow-covered earth. And then, as the snow settled and quiet descended over the garden and the surrounding hills, the only thing he could hear was the swish-swish of Ingrid's legs trudging through the snow.

"Good God," he said, meeting her at the gate and letting her in. "Couldn't you have simply come through the lobby?"

"I like it better this way."

"Mmm." He nodded. "Living more deliberately."

"No. I just didn't feel like dealing with those snoots at the front desk."

As she pulled the wool cap off her head, he examined her face, trying to figure out whether she looked any older than the last time he'd seen her. Sadly, he decided she did. The difference was barely perceptible, but it was there, and he chastised himself for getting so caught up in his own business that he'd managed to miss part of this magical process.

Her cheeks were red from the cold, and her eyes shone brightly. "I'm glad you finally called. I have tons of stuff to tell you. Where on earth have you been?"

"It's a long story, and not very interesting. I'd much rather hear what you've been up to. Should we go inside and have some tea?"

She looked reluctantly toward the French doors leading into the hotel. "I dunno," she said. "I can only stay for a few minutes."

"What do you mean?" he asked.

"Don't get upset with *me*! You're the one who totally disappeared."

"I was working," he said. "And it was going very badly."

He could see from her expression that she wasn't terribly sympathetic to this excuse.

"But that's all changed," he added quickly. "Listen. I realized something when I was watching the snow fall." He hesitated for a moment. "Are you sure you can't stay for a quick cup of tea?"

"No," she said. "Let's just hang out in the garden. Do you need to sit down?"

"No," he said, slightly offended. "I'm more worried about you getting cold."

"I'm fine."

"Good. Well . . . here's what I wanted to say. If you were looking at a picture book or watching a silent film, and you slowly saw snow building up, what would that tell you?"

She looked at him blankly.

"Time!" he said excitedly. "Time is passing. You wouldn't have to be told. You'd see it. It's obvious. Right?"

She gave a vague nod.

"That's what I see when I see you."

He waited for the comprehension to spread across her face.

"What do you mean?" she asked.

"What I mean is, you're in such a hurry to grow up. Stop rushing. Time is passing every minute, every second. You don't need to move away from home three years early. You don't need to find your soul mate right now—"

"But that's what I've been wanting to tell you! He made me a ring."

"Your senior?"

She nodded. "Want to see?"

"Sure," he said, trying to adjust his mind around this new development.

She held up her right hand and started to pull off the bright pink mitten. Then hesitating, she said, "You're going to think it's kind of weird. But you have to understand, it's a little punk rock 'cause at the record store everybody's really into that."

"Come on. I'm not completely out of touch."

She pulled off her mitten with a flourish and held her hand up for him to see. "Ta-dah!"

He leaned down to get a closer look. In the center of a very crudely molded silver band, there was something irregular and bone-colored.

"You know how I told you he helps his dad sometimes? Well, he had nothing to do on Saturday, so he used the machine his dad uses to make dental appliances, and he made this."

"Is that a tooth?" he asked with disgust.

"Yeah. He said he knew I'd think it was funny. And you have to admit it *is* pretty funny."

He grimaced.

"Oh whatever," she said, putting her mitten back on with an annoyed look. "It's the thought that counts. I mean you're not even getting the point here. He made me a ring!"

"I think that's terrific," he said, trying to sound enthusiastic.

"And it's all because of you!"

"It is?" he asked with surprise.

"Of course. If it hadn't been for you, I wouldn't have had the guts to start talking to him like we're on the same level. I even told him about how I'm moving to New York, and he said he'd put me on the phone with his aunt up there and see if she could help me find a place to live."

"He did?"

"Yeah, I didn't even ask him to. He volunteered—said she's a piano teacher and knows tons of families. So we're calling her this afternoon, which is why I've only got a couple of minutes."

She was beaming with excitement, and it made him feel tremendous that he could have been responsible in any way for this happiness. But he could tell from the way she was starting to bounce around on her feet that she was getting impatient.

"Go ahead. I don't want to keep you," he said. "I'm so glad that everything's working out."

She smiled. "Me, too."

"What's his name by the way?"

"Jake."

"Well, good luck."

"Thanks."

He walked her to the gate, and they said good-bye. He watched her tread back over the tracks she'd made a few minutes before, and when she got to the top of the hill she turned around and waved. He waved back and watched her disappear over the crest.

The sun had reached its noontime high, and the ice that had formed along the arch over the gate was beginning to drip. There was so much he wanted to tell her. And yet there was so little to actually say. *Enjoy it,* he thought—that was the one thing he'd like to tell her. *Enjoy it.*

1994

Thomas picked up the last present left under the Christmas tree. According to family custom, everyone was in charge of handing out his or her own gifts, and he had purposefully kept this one back until all of the others had been opened.

"Who's that for?" Emily asked as he crossed back to the area in front of the fire.

"It's for Dad." And as he watched a look of pleasant surprise spread across his father's face, he knew that he had done the right thing in saving this gift until last. His mother hadn't gotten any presents for his father this year. Neither had Emily.

"It's nothing major," he said, handing the package over.

"Oh." His dad feigned disappointment. "I thought maybe it was a Picasso."

Emily gave an irritated snort.

Their mom smiled cordially as she played with the gold chain at her neck—a gift from their father. "Or that Rembrandt you like." She was trying really hard for their sake, but in a way it only made things more awkward. He and Emily exchanged a quick look.

Their dad let out a forced laugh. "Yeah. What's wrong? The Met wouldn't sell it to you?"

Thomas smiled weakly. He'd been standing for too long, and he was starting to get nauseous again. He walked over to the couch and casually sat down—though not casually enough. Out of the corner of his eye, he could sense his mother's focus honing in on him. He refrained from lying down and settled back into the cushion as his father unwrapped the gift.

It was a watch for jogging that had a stopwatch on it and a nylon Velcro strap. He had run out and gotten it at the last minute yesterday afternoon from the Sharper Image around the corner.

His dad beamed, holding it up for everyone to admire as if he'd unwrapped his favorite Rembrandt after all.

"Wow," his mom said. "That's great."

His dad read the writing on the box that held the watch. "There's even a light on it for running at night. It's terrific. Thanks."

"Sure." His head was throbbing between his eyes in that way it always did right before the nausea escalated to the point where he had to run for the bathroom.

His dad turned to Emily, who was sitting the same way she had been all day, with her arms crossed over her chest and a scowl on her face.

"You feel up for a jog tonight?" he asked.

"No," she said curtly.

"Maybe tomorrow."

Ignoring him, she stood up. "Thanks for the books, Mom, and the shirts. They're really cool."

"I'm glad you like them, sweetie."

Emily turned to Thomas. "And thanks for all the computer stuff."

She didn't say anything about the enormous VHS collection of classic black-and-white movies their father had given her.

As his sister walked out of the room, Thomas stood up quickly. In trying not to draw attention to himself, he had waited too long. Stepping over a mound of paper, he took a few swift strides to the other side of the desk and vomited into the wastebasket. His mother was right behind him with a roll of paper towels.

"Sorry," he said.

"Don't worry about it." She placed her hand gently on his upper back. "This is an easy cleanup. Stay here as long as you need to."

"I'm done," he said, taking a paper towel and wiping his mouth.

"Do you want to go to the bathroom, or do you want to lie down?"

"I'll lie down."

She picked up the wastebasket. "I'll go get you some more water."

"I'll get it," his dad said, leaping to his feet and taking the wastebasket from her.

"Do you want juice, too?" she asked.

"No."

"Anything else?" his dad asked, leaning down in front of him. "I'd be glad to get anything you need."

"No thanks."

As Joe walked out of the room, he noted the stupidity of his question. Of course there wasn't anything else. If there were, Laura would have already thought of it. Since he'd been back, he had marveled at her ability to know what their son needed before he needed it. She seemed to be functioning with a sixth sense, and beyond that, she was functioning more efficiently and gracefully than he'd imagined anyone could under such circumstances. She was the woman whose son might be dying, and she was stronger than he'd ever seen her. In the two weeks since he'd been home, Laura had been constantly at Thomas's side, ready to adjust his pillows, bring him a fortifying soup or cooling calorie-laden juice, or, when he couldn't get those down, a glass of water. When his soaring body temperature made his surroundings feel arctic or uncomfortably warm, she was there with a blanket or a cool washcloth and a vigilant eye on the thermometer. She accompanied him to every treatment and was an endless source of entertainment, reading to him from the paper, sharing her favorite of the current week's *New Yorker* cartoons, and playing shows that she'd taped for him on television or movies she'd picked up from the video store. They were the very picture of har-

mony, cloistered together in whatever space best suited Thomas's
state of health. Though not necessarily physically removed from
the rest of the world, there was something about their unity that
set them apart. Even in the hospital, Laura stood as a protective
barrier between the medical professionals and her son. She was
neither hostile nor suspicious, yet it was obvious from the way the
doctors and nurses spoke to her that they understood her role. Beneath the heavy sadness and anxiety there was something else, a
brightness—he would even call it a glow—that seemed to come from
a new sense of purpose and importance. It occurred to him that she
seemed to know exactly who she was for the first time in her life,
and it was an exciting thing to witness. Then again, he speculated,
setting the wastebasket in the kitchen sink and turning on the faucet, perhaps he was only seeing her differently because he'd been
gone and because for a couple of months he thought he'd lost her
forever.

The time he'd spent with Gina in Florida seemed light-years
away. He wondered what she was doing for Christmas and imagined she was probably alone. As he poured a glass of Evian for
Thomas, he realized he should have asked Laura if there was anything *she* wanted. She had Thomas covered, but at least he could
take care of her. He poured a second glass for her and returned to
the living room. Thomas was lying on his side, eyes closed, facing
into the couch with a cushion between his knees. Laura, having organized all of the gifts into neat individual piles by the door, was
stuffing Christmas paper into a garbage bag. Joe set the water down
on the table and wrapped his arms around her.

"I'll do that," he said gently. "You sit down and relax. Why
don't I get you a glass of wine or something?"

"No thanks." She smiled, but her look was firm. "I've got it
under control."

Thomas woke up to the sound of the front door slamming, followed
by his father's voice. "Where's she going?"

His mother was sitting at the desk, talking on the phone. She
cupped her hand over the receiver and sighed. "I don't know. I
don't have time to worry about her right now."

She went back to the phone conversation, talking very cheerfully to whoever was on the other end—evidently some friend of hers who had called to wish them all a Merry Christmas. "Yes," she said, looking at his father. "He's right here."

In the chair beside him, his dad looked back at her and shook his head emphatically *no*.

Rolling her eyes in annoyance, she continued in the same cheerful tone. "Oh, that's so sweet of you, but he's helping Thomas with something right now. I'll tell him you said hello. He'll be really sorry he missed your call."

Unable to find a comfortable position, Thomas shifted restlessly on the couch. He was sick of sitting in here, but he didn't know where else to go. There was no place in the apartment that seemed inviting anymore. By now, the mere thought of any of his usual spots called up vivid memories of excruciating physical discomfort. And besides that, while he was in here, listening to his mom on the phone, he felt safe. He knew that as appealing as solitude seemed at the moment, once he got off by himself, he'd start having those horrible thoughts again, imagining that he could feel his lymph nodes and his organs, even his blood, all slowly giving way to the invading cells. The doctors insisted his physical exhaustion was a normal reaction to the chemo, but he was still terrified by his own weakness.

He reached over to the coffee table and picked up the book he'd gotten as a Christmas present from his mother, *Dirr's Trees and Shrubs*. As he settled back into the couch with it, his mother's voice shifted to a normal tone.

"Look at the section on maples," she told him quickly, then uncupping her hand from the phone, went back to her conversation.

Scanning the table of contents for the Latin name, *Acer*, he wished his sister hadn't left. Lately, especially since their father had been home, she'd been spending more and more time away from the apartment, and it bummed him out. Not only did he miss having her around, but he was worried about what kind of trouble she might be getting into. She seemed dark and broody these days, and treated him as if he were a parent she had to hide things from, avoiding his questions about who she was hanging out with and where.

He felt guilty that since he'd been sick, she'd gotten even less attention than usual from their mother. Though, as always, Emily didn't seem to care. He could also see that there was a certain advantage to her position. There was something suffocating about the enthusiasm his mother showed for everything he did. She was so deeply invested in him, it was as if she shared ownership in all of his accomplishments, his choices, even his interests. It had occurred to him the other day that if he were to die right now, he would die his mother's son, absent of his own individual identity.

As his mother got off the phone, he noticed his father struggle to tear himself away from the article he was reading, lowering the paper and turning his head toward her while his eyes still lingered on the page.

"Did you see the thing about the sugar maples like the ones we've got up in the woods?" she asked.

"Jeez, Mom. Give me a second, will you? I've barely had a chance to open the book."

She looked a little stunned. "Oh . . . sorry."

Setting the paper down, his dad asked. "How's Johanna?"

"Fine," she answered curtly.

"I didn't mean to put you in a difficult spot, but I couldn't talk to her right now."

"All you had to do was say 'Hello, Merry Christmas. I hope we get to see you soon.' I don't think that's asking too much considering that she got us an appointment with Dr. Bergen."

"You're right," he said. "I'm sorry."

She stood up, straightened a few papers, and then started for the door.

"I'll call her tomorrow," he added as she passed his chair on her way out.

"That would be great," she called from the hall.

Thomas heard her footsteps retreating toward the kitchen. From behind his book, he watched his father, who was still gazing expectantly into the hallway.

"So, Dad, you really think that watch will be good for jogging?"

"Yeah," his father said, turning back. "Fantastic."

"Maybe I could start running with you sometimes—you know, when the doctors say so."

His father smiled a faraway smile and nodded. "Mm-hmm."

In the kitchen, Laura got out the turkey that was left over from last night, and set it on the counter. Joe had insisted on doing the turkey his way—soaking it in salt water and cooking it upside down. The end result was delicious and exceptionally juicy, but it meant that all of the time she'd spent going through recipe books and locating the right seasonings had gone completely to waste. And she didn't have time to waste these days. She had so much reading to do, and then there were those endless hours at the hospital, sitting with Thomas while he underwent his treatments. She'd have to remember to find the article on vitamin D that she'd mentioned to Dr. Bergen. It surprised her that he'd expressed such interest—she'd been so sure he would dismiss it that she almost hadn't mentioned it. And now there was a possibility that from the research she'd done on her own, she'd discovered something that could help Thomas in some way.

She picked off a piece of dark meat and put it in her mouth. She was dying for a cigarette.

"There you are," said Joe, entering through the door behind her. "Having a snack?"

"Would you like some?"

"No thanks."

He stood beside her, leaning against the counter. It made her nervous when he hung around like this—like he was waiting for her to bring up any of the various things they'd agreed not to talk about. She hadn't made any decision about the marriage yet; it was still too early, and there was too much else going on. They just had to get through the next few months in one piece. She'd explained that to him, and he'd consented—the most important thing was for their home to feel stable right now. Joe moved in behind her and placed his hands on her shoulders. "Today was so nice. You have no idea how wonderful it feels to look around the room and see you and Thomas and Emily."

"Don't," she said. "Please don't."

He dropped his hands from her shoulders and slowly moved away.

The more he talked, the less she believed what he was saying. His first day home, he'd gone on about how he'd had an epiphany in Florida—how he knew as soon as he got there that he'd made a terrible mistake. He'd begged forgiveness, said that she was his entire life. She wanted to believe all of that was true. But she had a strong feeling if his son weren't sick, he wouldn't be here.

Eating another piece of turkey, she replaced the tinfoil over the bird and returned it to the refrigerator.

"I'm so tired," she said. "All I want is to go to sleep."

"Go ahead."

"I can't. I've got tons of reading to do."

"Let me do some of it."

"No, I need to know all of this stuff—I want to know it."

"I'll take notes for you."

She sighed. He was trying to help, and she appreciated it in a way—he was making much more of an effort than he had in years—but she'd gotten so used to doing everything herself, it was a nuisance to have him in the middle of everything again. Besides, she liked the rapport she'd developed with Dr. Bergen and the other doctors, and she wasn't about to give that up.

"I'll get a second wind in a minute," she said. "I think I just needed to eat something."

He stepped back farther still, leaning against the counter.

She hesitated, then looked at him deviously, then hesitated again.

"What?" he asked, intrigued.

"Should we have a smoke?"

He thought about it for a moment, his eyes wandering the room. "No," he said finally. Sternly. "We can't. We're doing so well."

She scooped the turkey scraps into her hand with a dishrag and flung them into the sink.

"You're right."

Carefully, she folded the dishrag and draped it over the oven handle. Then she walked out of the room, leaving him standing against the counter.

Extricating herself from the telephone cord and from Eric's arm, Emily rolled out of his bed. She found it profoundly irritating that he should be talking to his mother, even though it *was* Christmas and she knew that everyone, even people his age, made a point of talking to their mothers on Christmas. It was all over the TV in those stupid phone ads—parents and children of all ages reaching out to touch someone and wish each other happy holidays. But there was something about the idea of Eric talking to his mother that seemed wrong. It was not the timing. She didn't think so anyway. They had finished; and his mother had called him, not the other way around, which would have been *really* weird—a postcoital call to mom.

She picked up his burgundy bath towel off the floor and threw it over the armchair by the bed. Then sitting down on it, she lit a cigarette. She tried to imagine how his mother would react to the news that he was screwing a fifteen-year-old girl. Statutory rape. That's what it was, technically. Though if anyone was doing the raping, it was most definitely her. He had been at his apartment at four o'clock as she'd instructed, waiting for her like an obedient little puppy. He was smitten with her. That was obvious. Not that it was a one-way street by any means. She found him attractive enough, and besides ridding her of her loathsome virginity, he provided a much-needed distraction from the exceptionally vivid, waking nightmare that had seized her home.

"Love you, too. Bye, Mom." Reaching across the bed, he hung up the phone. "Sorry about that. You shouldn't smoke."

"Oh, please." She blew a big puff at him.

"At least come over here and share it with me. It'll do half the damage that way."

With exaggerated weariness, she rose and dragged herself over to the bed. As soon as she lay down, he took the cigarette from her and stamped it out in the ashtray.

"Why did you do that?"

"I was just trying to get you over here."

"Jerk."

He ran his hand down her side, starting at her breast and continuing down over her hip. An onslaught of hormones had recently caused her body to swell into a voluptuous shape she still had trouble recognizing as her own. She pushed his hand away.

"What?" he asked.

"It makes me feel fat when you put your hand there."

"Where?"

"On my stomach and my hips. I know I need to lose some weight."

"You don't need to lose any weight. You're beautiful. Perfect, in fact."

"Whatever," she said, picking up a roach and a lighter from the bedside table. The words *Viva Las Vegas* glittered in gold script against the neon green plastic of the lighter. "Classy," she said, lighting the joint. "Did your mom give you this?"

"No. I don't know where I picked that up, to tell you the truth. I must've nabbed it from somebody."

"Mmm." She held the pot in her lungs, forcing her voice into a much lower register. "Along with those bumps on your dick."

"I told you, they're hair follicles or something. A lot of guys have those."

She laughed uproariously.

"What's so funny?"

He took the joint from her and inhaled. When, after several seconds, she hadn't stopped laughing, he looked annoyed.

"I'm imagining what it would look like if it started sprouting all this hair."

"Well, let's hope that doesn't happen."

"Oh-ho, it would be so gross!"

She broke into another round of uncontrollable laughter. Eventually, he joined in, but she could tell that he didn't really think it was funny. He wanted to laugh with her, so he was pretending to be stoned. She considered calling him on it but decided to let it go since it was more fun laughing with him than laughing alone. They both stretched out the laughter for as long as they could, passing the joint back and forth to refuel. When it finally ended, they looked at one another, each expecting the other to say something.

"So . . . ," she ventured, "I guess I should go."

"You just got here."

"Like an hour ago."

"Stay. Let's talk for a bit."

"Okay."

"How was your family Christmas?"

"Oh, it was fabulous. You know, with my brother lying on the sofa, getting up to vomit every now and then, and everyone acting all phony baloney like we're on *Leave It to Beaver* or something. It was a real barrel of laughs."

"How's he doing?"

"What do you mean how's he doing? He's got fucking lymphoma."

"Is the chemo starting to work?"

"No. They say they can't tell yet, but . . . it sure doesn't seem like it to me."

"I'm sorry. I know it must be hard for you."

"Whatever. I mean it is what it is." Sitting up perkily, she said, "Hey, guess what? I had a great idea today."

"Yeah?"

"You know how his hair's falling out?"

Eric nodded.

"I was thinking I could save it and make you a toupee." Clapping her hands together, she uttered a high, shrill laugh. "Oh my God! I'm like hair-obsessed."

Manically, she kept laughing. He reached over and gently took her hand in his. The surprise of this gesture stopped her short, and the smile on her face slowly faded to reveal a brief flicker of terror before she composed herself again.

"Hey," she said. "Do you remember when we first met?"

"At your audition?"

"No, no. The first time. In Hartford."

"Hartford?"

"Yeah. The summer before last. My dad brought me backstage to meet you."

He sat up, interested. "Your dad? I forgot—did he like it?"

"I don't know," she said irritably. "Anyway, you want to know something really funny?"

"What?"

"When I saw you in that play, I thought that wig was your real hair."

"Really?"

"Yeah. And when I saw you backstage, I was so bummed. I was, like, totally devastated."

"Well . . . I apologize."

"I should really go," she said.

She could feel him watching her as she got up, and she hurried to get her clothes on quickly so that he would have less time to see her naked body. Once she was dressed, she sat back down on the bed.

"I'm sorry. I wish I could stay longer."

"Don't worry about it."

"What are you going to do after I leave?"

"I'm not sure."

She nuzzled her nose into his neck. "Are you going to be sad without me?"

He laughed. "That tickles."

"Are you?"

"I'll manage."

She sat up and began to pout, then changed her mind and said sincerely, "I'm glad you stayed in town."

"Good. Me, too."

As she rose from the bed, he gave her a playful whack on the behind.

"Hey!" she scolded.

"Hey."

She turned away quickly in an attempt to capture the moment before it faded. Between now and the next time they saw each other (whether that was tomorrow, or the following week, or never, she hadn't decided), this was the way she wished him to look when she encountered him in her mind: content but not besotted.

As she walked home, the cold inhibited her breath and made it feel thick and cottony when it reached her lungs. She thought about all that hair she'd pulled out of the bathtub drain this morning. She'd come close to losing it then, sitting there on the edge of the tub. She couldn't cry—hadn't been able to since she'd heard the diagnosis. Her mother had shed enough tears for both of them, but she had not been able to squeeze out a single one. As the days and weeks wore on, she could feel the pressure mounting inside, but it felt more like a need to vomit than to cry; the fistful of hair this morning had induced such nausea that she'd felt sure it was all finally about to come up. There was something so revolting about the sight of those long black strands, knitted together and holding the evenly pocked impression of the drain. They had sprouted from her brother's head, masses of cells, bound together and ready to lengthen indefinitely until cut or broken. She didn't tend to think of hair as a part of one's body, didn't really even consider it an organic substance, preferring to classify it with the pleasantly scented and packaged chemical products one bought in order to treat it. As she sat on the edge of the tub, it was as if she were looking at hair for the very first time, and it scared the hell out of her.

Now, as she walked up Fifth Avenue, angry tears clouded her vision. She thought back to the day, last summer, when she and her father had driven up to Hartford. She remembered how, in her excitement, she had doused herself with so much perfume, it had taken her and her father a full half hour to get it off. But there her father's attentiveness had ended. By the time they got backstage, he seemed to have completely forgotten why they were there. He was distracted by all of the people gathered there, and failed to introduce her to his pal Eric—forcing her to take the initiative and stammer through an embarrassing self-introduction. And then, *then*, after she'd reached the devastating realization that Eric was not in real life a dashing Brit, but instead a balding American phony, her father offered her no consolation, in fact did not even bother to ask why she was so quiet all the way home. The following year, the episode had apparently slipped his mind altogether when he failed to warn her she would be working with Eric if she signed on to the cast of his play. She had simply shown up for the audition, and there he'd been. Well, she thought, her father's self-consumed oblivion had cost him after all. If only he could see her and Eric now. That would certainly teach him to pay more attention to what went on outside of his own big head.

From his table, set for one, in the room that doubled as the Jefferson's bar and tearoom, Joe watched a new girl (Julia, her name tag said) glide across the brown tapestry rug to attend to one of the guests. She had the same fresh-faced beauty as the rest of the hotel staff and sported a deliciously broad smile, which she shared liberally with her customers. What stood out about her, aside from an exceptionally dark tan, was the way she moved, drifting from table to table as if propelled not by the muscle and bone of human legs, but by the gentle force of a summer breeze, her upper body curved forward like a yacht sail. He turned and gazed out the window at the garden, where, in the waning afternoon light, the planter boxes and pots now acted as pedestals for formations of snow and ice.

Once again, he had been unable to resist the allure of this splendid hotel. Especially today, the thought of spending the afternoon alone in his room at the Marrisy proved unbearably depressing. Though, to be honest, he had generally taken an odd pleasure in the small punishments of his new home: the dismal motel decor;

the mildew on the shower curtain; the smell that rose from the drain every time he turned on the sink; the impossibility of restraining the thermostat from either cooking him or flash-freezing him; and the misery of making his way a mere ten feet to his car, which donned a shiny new coat of ice every morning. The first snowfall, a dazzling production that swaddled both town and countryside in a magical white cloak, had been deceptively gentle. It was followed by an all-out arctic assault, which blew sheets of ice against the motel windows and frequently installed a snowy blockade on the other side of his door. His appetite for winter had subsided around the time he began having to tape towels to the borders of each pane and call the manager if he wished to exit his room. Still, in many ways, he preferred these various forms of discomfort to the sybaritic circus he'd enjoyed at the outset of his trip. Being at the Jefferson tended to spotlight the deep rift between the hotel's splendor and his true state of mind.

Julia placed another vodka and tonic on the table before him. "Anything else, sir?"

"Thank you, no. Just this for now. Where's Albert, by the way?"

"He's off today," she told him with a polite smile as she removed his empty glass, making a quick wipe with the napkin before balling it up in her hand.

Behind him, the fire crackled in the fireplace. Around the corner, a man called out, "Marvelous! Me either! Ha! Ha!" The rest of the conversation was lost amid the general buzz of the tearoom, which had filled to capacity. Joe pulled out his Dictaphone and set it on the table.

Julia soon returned from the kitchen to attend to a couple with two teenage sons. Apparently immune to her luminous smile, the boys stared sullenly at her while she answered their parents' questions. Joe found himself hating the boys for their solipsistic blindness. How could they remain so indifferent in the midst of people who wanted nothing more than to provide them with pleasure? He supposed it inevitable that all children lack that vision. Justice would be served once they had children of their own. He, certainly, had been paid back many times over for the misery he had inflicted on his own parents. To have lost a child—that was one thing. He did not consider that punishment, for there is nothing one can do in one's youth to deserve punishment that severe. However, to have the surviving child cast judgment upon his every move—that struck him as just. To listen to Emily's condescending and condemning tone could, at times, send him into a tailspin of contrition, awakening a longing to see his parents again, if only to finally express his gratitude.

He still hadn't heard from her. Two months had now passed since the last time they spoke. He figured the silence was bound to end eventually, and he wondered if there was any chance that today would be the day. *I should call*, he thought. But he really didn't feel like talking to anyone. He hadn't even been able to bring himself to call his home answering machine since November. *Later*, he decided, then ordered another drink.

After waiting nearly an hour for Ingrid to materialize, he was beginning to lose patience. Just before he gave up, she appeared in the doorway, looking remarkably different from the last time he'd seen her. Her hair was pulled back into a tight knot, and she wore a simple brown dress. Stomping her feet to shake the snow from her shoes, she scanned the tables until she spotted him. She started toward him, walking in a more erect, less childlike way.

"Hey, Joe," she said, stepping up a little more somberly than usual alongside his table.

"Hello." He smiled. "I'm so glad you could join me. I know you probably have a lot to do today."

"Not really." She shrugged, dropping her coat on the floor and settling into the chair opposite him. "I'm not celebrating Christmas."

"Really? Why not?"

"I'm a Buddhist."

"Are you?" he said with a degree of surprise. "I wasn't aware of that."

She nodded.

"How long have you been a Buddhist?" he asked.

"I don't know," she said vaguely, looking around the room. "For like—a week maybe."

"I see."

She folded her hands in her lap and stared at them.

"I haven't seen you in a while," he said.

"Yeah, no kidding."

"Well . . ." He started to make an excuse for his absence, then decided against it. "What else have you been up to?" he asked. "Any progress on your New York accommodations?"

"I decided I'm not going."

"Oh? Why not?"

She shrugged. "It was a dumb idea."

He nodded. "And what about your senior?"

"Jake?" She sighed. "It turns out he has a girlfriend."

"Really? But he made you that ring—"

"I know. He said he likes me a lot, but only as a little sister or something. It was really humiliating. I mean I totally spilled my guts to him, and then he turns around and tells me he has a girl-friend."

"I'm sorry."

"It doesn't really matter that much." She chewed on her nail. Then, dropping her hand over the arm of the chair, she said, "I've realized something really important."

"What's that?"

"All desire is meaningless."

He couldn't help but smile at this statement.

"It's not funny, Joe. I'm totally serious."

"I'm sorry."

It occurred to him that she had not only lost interest in college and her senior, but possibly in him as well. She'd still shown up to-day, but she lacked that starry-eyed quality he'd found so charm-ing, and he got the feeling she didn't really want to be there.

"Tell me," he said encouragingly. "I'd like to hear about this realization."

She spent some more time chewing her nail, evidently trying to decide whether or not to indulge his curiosity. "Okay," she said finally. "Well . . . I was walking past the diner the other day, and I saw this woman through the window. She was by herself, and she was all dressed up with her hair done and everything like she'd gone to some really important meeting. And as I passed her, I noticed that she looked absolutely miserable—like she'd just suffered the very worst disappointment of her life. I started imagining all the things that could have happened to her: she could have lost her job, or maybe the guy she liked was supposed to meet her and never showed up. And all of a sudden, I realized that none of those things meant *anything* to me. There was all of this stuff that was so unbelievably important to her, that she wanted so badly. And it meant nothing to me. And of course, there was all this stuff that I really wanted—like New York and Jake or whatever—and it all meant nothing to her. So it occurred to me that the things themselves have no value whatsoever. We just give them value. You know?"

He reached across the table and gave her shoulder a consoling squeeze. "Listen," he said. "I know you really liked this guy. But you'll find someone you like even better. And you'll go to New York in a few years."

She shook her head emphatically, shrugging his hand away. "No, but you don't understand. I was totally able to see everything I wanted from this woman's point of view, and it honestly all seemed so stupid."

"Come on. Desire is not meaningless. It's what makes each of us who we are."

"Why do you have to argue with me about this? You're not even listening to anything I'm saying."

"I am listening," he said defensively.

She rolled her eyes. "Whatever."

He flagged down the waitress and requested that she bring them a pot of tea.

"Even Buddhist monks drink tea," he told Ingrid as Julia walked away.

Ignoring him, Ingrid stared silently at the floor, and he wondered if she might be about to cry.

"Look, I'm sorry," he said. "But I think everything probably worked out for the best. Think of your poor parents. They must be so happy you've decided to stay."

"My *parents?*" Ingrid asked.

"Yes. I don't care how annoying they might be at times; they would do anything in the world for you."

"What are you talking about?"

"Trust me. When you have your own kids, you'll understand."

"Whatever." She sneered. "You actually think things worked out for the best with Jake?"

"Maybe. Who knows?"

"I don't care anyway." She sighed. "I told you it's all meaningless."

He watched her for a moment. "I can tell from the way you're looking at me right now that you blame me in some way for this."

She raised her eyebrows in surprise. "What? I'm just sad."

"I understand that. And it's hard for me to see you so distraught."

"Why?"

"Why? It simply is." He shifted his position, catching a glimpse of his reflection in the window as he did so. "For one thing, I suppose I do feel somewhat responsible," he said, running his hand through his hair.

"That's dumb."

"It's not dumb. You said yourself that you would have never had the guts to pursue Jake if it hadn't been for me."

She rolled her eyes. "Oh my God! Why does this have to be about you? I already told you it's not your fault."

"Believe me, I certainly don't need to make this about me. I've got my own share of shit to deal with at the moment. Serious, grown-up shit that you couldn't possibly begin to wrap your head around."

He could see that she was taken aback by this. "I'd like to help you sort this stuff out," he added quickly. "I really would. But you're making it pretty difficult."

"Difficult?" She shook her head. "You're nuts."

"See? You say you're not angry with me, but you are."

"Oh my God! What is your problem? I am *not* angry with you. I'm *sad*. I'm not allowed to feel sad?"

He threw up his hands. "I give up. I don't know what you want from me."

"All I want is somebody to talk to. I don't expect you to solve all my problems for me. I only want you to listen."

"Well . . . ," he said with a sigh, "I really don't think I've done such a lousy job."

She grabbed her head with both hands as if trying to keep it from exploding. "Oh, just forget it!"

For a long time, they sat in silence. Then, finally, the tea arrived. He poured some for Ingrid and for himself. And when he'd finished, he raised his cup.

"Merry Christmas," he said.

Morosely, Ingrid picked up her cup and tapped it against his. The china made a brittle, clinking sound. She took a sip of tea and set the cup back on its saucer.

"Hey," she said, brooding. "D'you want to hear something I read the other day? It's by Vincent van Gogh."

"Sure."

"He said, 'One may have a blazing hearth in one's soul, and yet no one ever come to sit by it.' Isn't that the most tragic thing you've ever heard?"

He considered this for a moment.

"It's certainly sad to think that a talent of that magnitude can go utterly unappreciated for so long."

The look she gave him was withering. "Joe, I'm not talking about *art*! I mean, what if I never find anyone who *really* understands me? What if nobody falls in love with me? Ever. In my whole life. It's possible, you know."

"I'm sorry," he said gently. "I misunderstood. And you're right, that is possible. But by the same token, you might just as easily say that a person may be surrounded throughout his life by blazing hearths but, because of his own stupidity, wander eternally in search of warmth and light."

"*Wander eternally*? God," she sneered. "You sound like you're, like, ninety million years old."

Unlike the lighthearted way she'd made fun of him in the past, this time there was a chilling cruelty to her tone.

Without trying to hide his injury or surprise, he said, "Is that so?"

"Yeah," she replied flatly. "That's so."

Taken aback, he waited for her to apologize.

She gave an insolent shrug. "I've got to go."

"Where are you going?" he asked.

"Wherever."

"Wherever?"

"Yeah. You know. I've got stuff to do."

"What kind of stuff?"

"Just stuff. What do you care?"

He examined her closely, trying to find the old Ingrid. "I care."

He saw one of the overhead lights reflected in the surface of her tea, and—perhaps because of the vodka—he found it exquisitely beautiful.

"Look," he said hopefully, pointing it out to her. "I can see the moon in your cup."

Rolling her eyes, she stood up. "I'll see you later."

She started to walk away.

"Wait!" he called after her.

She stopped and turned, annoyed. "What?"

"Come back. I'll order us some madeleines. I promise I can cheer you up."

She gave him an exasperated look. "I told you I've got stuff to do."

"Fine," he said, and he watched her go.

He looked around, searching for the waitress. She was helping a stooped old woman with a walker to the door. One of her hands rested ever so gently on the woman's back, and the other she extended in front of her to show the way. As they walked, one slow-motion step at a time, they carried on a conversation. He wondered what she might be saying to that old woman, who, in her fur stole and red pillbox hat adorned with a sprig of holly, resembled an artifact from another era. There was nothing so abhorrent to him as the idea of depending upon the kindness of strangers to execute a task so basic as crossing a room, a horror compounded by the strangers' doting smiles and sing-song voices revealing that, no matter what you say or do, they find you absolutely adorable. He prayed he would die before he reached that moment.

"Are you a doctor?" Julia asked once he had put in a request for another vodka.

"What makes you think that?"

"I don't know. The tape recorder, I guess." With her eyes, she indicated the Dictaphone sitting on the table before him. "My brother-in-law's a radiologist, and he uses one of those things. Plus, you kind of look like a doctor."

He hoped that by this, she meant he looked intelligent, distinguished, or wealthy.

"It's so funny to see somebody working," she said. "I forget that for some people, this is another ordinary day." Then, as if to explain that she didn't find him freakish, she added, "My husband's Jewish, too. Though he celebrates Christmas for the kids—does the whole Santa bit even."

He gave her a smile and nodded, sending a clear signal that he preferred to be left alone.

"Let me go get your drink," she said.

He felt a bit guilty when she returned, and asked how old her children were.

"Two and four," she said. "Can I get you anything else?" It was her turn now to cut the conversation short.

"No thank you," he said.

As he drank his vodka, he remembered how he and Laura had helped the kids set out brandy and cookies for Santa every Christmas Eve and how, as the kids got older, they'd had to take increasingly greater measures to convince them of Santa's existence.

He was flattered by the notion that Julia had mistaken him for a doctor. There was something noble about an aging doctor—he supposed because a doctor could only improve with age and the steady accumulation of knowledge and experience. He recalled how arrogantly he used to behave toward Burt Horvath, intoxicated by his own sense of superiority. Why, he asked himself now, had Burt allowed him to carry on like that? Never once reminding him that his own work could not possibly be exceeded in importance. He wondered what the figure had grown to by now—that number of people who literally owed their lives to his friend.

Outside, the light retreated, pulling with it the definition of branches from the thickets and shadows from the snow. He watched the garden and the landscape beyond disappear gradually as he finished his drink. Then, while Julia was busy taking someone else's order, he paid the check and slipped out.

Joe gave a nod to the doorman, who wished him a merry Christmas and opened the door to a gust of sharp, fresh air. He was careful as he picked a path across the frozen lot. The slush had hardened in the absence of the sun, and danger resided in slick, black patches of ice on the asphalt. Cautiously, he followed a pair of crystallized footprints that led roughly toward his car, the treads of a previous pedestrian's boot soles crunching under each step. The wood smoke, which had thickened the air inside into an overly rich gravy, now gave a pleasantly light accent to the chill rushing through his nostrils and down his throat.

As he sank into the driver's seat of his car, he remembered how the very last year that he and Laura bothered to go through the Santa routine at all, the kids had set out a Polaroid camera and a note on top of the mantel, next to the cookies and brandy. *If you're real*, they wrote, *we need you to prove it.*

The place reeked of Sex Wax. Emily thought that was what they called it—the stuff people put on snow skis to make them go fast. She could see a guy in the back applying it to ski after ski, his khaki shorts and Billabong T-shirt exposing the muscular body of an active outdoorsman as he worked. All the guys who worked in the shop had the same build, sported the same ski-bum togs, and approached each customer with the same roll-with-the-punches "it's all good" attitude.

"Isn't there another option?" Clay asked the guy who was helping her, the only dark-haired man in the place and a little older than the rest.

"Yeah. She could do nothing. But she probably won't be able to ski tomorrow."

Clay looked at her, his face full of concern.

"What do you think?"

She looked at her throbbing toe. By now, it was about 30 percent bigger than normal, and the black streaks under the nail seemed to be slowly expanding like bleeding lines of ink. She could feel the guy shifting his gaze between her and Clay as he thumbed his goatee.

"Well . . . ," she said, "you really want to ski tomorrow, right?"

"Yeah, of course. But this is totally up to you. I want you to do what you think is best for your toe."

"I'm not crazy about the idea of going to the hospital," Emily said.

"Nah." The guy waved his hand dismissively. "No need to go to the hospital. We can do it right here."

She eyed him nervously. "Who can do it right here? You?"

"Yeah. Me, Zach, whoever. We've all done it a bunch of times. Zach," he called to the guy waxing skis in the back. "Tell this girl how easy it would be for one of us to drill her nail."

"Piece a cake," Zach called back over the hum of his machine. "I'd say I do it for people three to five times a week. Haven't lost a single toe yet."

She smiled uneasily.

Clay knelt down beside her. "Em, if you're not into it, we can wait and see how it is in the morning and make a decision then."

"Yeah. But then we might not be able to ski."

"That doesn't matter."

She looked up at the guy who was helping them. "You'll sterilize the drill, right?"

"Oh, no. We let everyone's blood cake up on there." He winked. "Makes us feel like we're livin' on the edge."

She didn't appreciate the humor. "All right. Which one of you has done it the most?"

"Probably Zach."

"I'd like for him to do it then."

"Zach, man, you got another victim here."

The machine whirred to a stop. In the absence of its muffling hum, the voices and other sounds within the shop acquired a metallic sharpness. Zach casually walked over, picking up a drill, a bottle of rubbing alcohol, and a small, red towel on the way.

"You sure you're cool with this, Em?" Clay asked.

Without glancing at him, she nodded. The goateed man stepped aside, giving Zach his stool.

"Hi," Emily said.

Zach wasn't a particularly good-looking guy, but there was something sexy about him.

He took a seat before her. "How's it going?"

"I've had better Christmases."

He smiled, his chapped lips and crow's feet testifying to the amount of time he'd spent in the sun, wind, and cold.

"Don't worry. We'll get you all fixed up."

She watched him unscrew the cap from the rubbing alcohol and dip the drill bit into the bottle's plastic mouth. Clay put his hand on her shoulder and gave it a reassuring squeeze. This was all his fault. All of it. If she hadn't been so worried about him having a good time, she would have come down as soon as her boots started to hurt instead of letting her toe ram into the lining all afternoon. She would have much preferred to sit at the bottom of the mountain, reading by the fire—as she could be doing tomorrow if she hadn't agreed to this crazy procedure.

Zach positioned the tip of the drill bit on the center of her toenail. "Ready?"

She nodded. Nobody could accuse her of being a spoilsport, that was for sure. She was certainly holding up her end of the deal.

The drill started, and she winced, preparing herself for the pain. She tried to distract herself by making a list of all the things she hated about skiing. Vermont in the dead of winter was her idea of hell. Equally as bad as the single-digit temperature was the tedium of waiting on line—both for the lifts and for lunch. And who could possibly enjoy their meal when they were being knocked about by people in fluorescent snowsuits, clunking their way between tables in half-buckled boots, pushing and shoving their kids onto the bench to hold a spot until they returned with the food? There was something about skiing that brought out the worst in humanity. No doubt, it was the very misery of it all.

She felt a keen pressure in her toe from the drill, but still no sharp pain. As she waited, the anticipation made her feel queasy. She couldn't look, but she knew that Clay was watching. And she hoped he was racked by guilt at the sight of the drill boring into her nail. Right when she started to think she might faint, the drill stopped.

"Okeydoke," Zach said. "All done."

She opened her eyes to find him holding the red towel around her toe. "What do you mean? That's it?"

"Yup. That's it." He grinned. "Like I told you, piece a cake."

She smiled back at him and felt her pulse quicken as they locked eyes for a brief second.

"Did it hurt?" Clay asked.

Annoyed at having to answer the question negatively, she shrugged. "Not that bad."

"Thank God. It looked awful." He turned to Zach. "Thanks, man. You did a great job."

As if he would know the difference. Zach showed her how to hold the towel so that it soaked up the blood without stopping up the hole, then he and Clay went over to the register to settle the bill. She wished that the towel were white so that she could tell whether it was clean. Also, a white towel would show the blood a lot better, and she didn't think that Clay was able to see enough blood.

By the time they left the shop, the pressure in her toe had already decreased considerably. There was no chance, Zach said, that she wouldn't be able to ski tomorrow. He and the guy with the goatee would be there starting at seven the next morning, ready, whenever she showed up, to get her into a better-fitting pair of boots free of charge.

"All I can say," Emily told Clay once they were in the car heading back to the condo, "is you damn well better hold up your end of this deal."

"Of course I'm going to."

"It's not like we're only going to go to a couple of lessons, and that's it. Once we've learned how to dance, we're going to go out and do it. And you're not wearing jeans, you know. People get totally dressed up at these swing-dancing clubs."

"Hey. Listen, I'm going whole hog. As soon as we get back to the city, I'm getting a full-on baby blue tuxedo with a ruffled shirt. I'm even wearing it to the lessons."

She laughed. "You don't have to go that far."

"Oh, you wait. I think I might even get a pair of those shoes with the three-inch heels."

"Yeah. Let me tell you, nothing's going to compare with having to wear those fucking boots and getting my toenail drilled by some dude in a ski shop."

"I'm really sorry about that, Em. You've been such a good sport." Reaching over and pulling her head to him, he kissed her hair. "Thank you."

"Sure. Keep your eyes on the road, please."

"My eyes are completely on the road."

"I don't want to end up in a ditch."

Releasing her head, he moved his hands into the ten o'clock/ two o'clock, driver's ed position and thrust his chin forward in a display of unswerving focus.

"Is this good?"

"Yes. That's good."

She tried to imagine swing-dancing with him and wasn't pleased with the picture that came to mind. Even if he upheld his end of the bargain and went through with the lessons, she knew he wouldn't enjoy it. He would only be doing it for her. She wished she were with someone more fun, someone less conservative and more adventurous.

"It's nice those guys are giving us your boots free of charge tomorrow," Clay said.

"You're kidding."

"No."

"*Clay,* they gave me a pair of boots that made my toe swell up so much, they had to *drill a hole* in it! *And* they made me pay for them. *And* they charged us for drilling the hole!"

"Em, I don't think it's their fault that that happened to your toe. You know, people have problems with their ski boots. And, as they said, if you'd stopped skiing as soon as they started hurting—"

"Oh, right!" She snickered contemptuously.

"What?"

"That would have gone over really well. Me wrecking the whole ski day by going down after the first hour."

"What are you talking about? Obviously I would have been happy to stop skiing if I'd known that you were so uncomfortable."

"Yeah, whatever."

"Emily, I feel like you're trying to blame this whole thing on me, and I don't think it's fair. I don't know what I could have done differently when you didn't even let me know you were in pain. I'm not a sadist."

She nodded. "Yeah, I know."

"Listen. We won't ski tomorrow if you don't want to. How's that?"

"No, I'll ski."

"Don't do it for me. I don't want to go up there with you and have you be miserable."

"I said I'll go."

They pulled into their assigned parking spot outside the condo.

"I don't know what to do." Clay sighed. "You seem determined not to let me make you happy."

"I'm happy. Don't worry about it."

She gathered up her things and hopped out of the car before he could utter another word.

"Do you have the key?" she asked as he got out.

"Yeah." He dug around in the pockets of his parka. "You know, I don't really appreciate the way you're talking to me right now." He held up the key.

"Let's go," she said. "It's freezing."

Inside, the string of lights on the miniature tree they'd bought twinkled in the corner. Emily dropped her stuff on the floor and kept going, limping slightly.

"Are we going to do Christmas now?" he called after her.

"Yeah, but I want to change out of these wet clothes. Aren't you going to change?"

"No. I don't think so."

She stared at him, waiting for an explanation or a change of mind, but got neither.

He followed her into the bedroom. "Just tell me. What do you want me to wear?"

"I don't care. Whatever you want."

She pulled off her ski pants and sat down on the bed, the tight long-underwear bottoms making her legs look disproportionately tiny under the many layers she still wore on top.

Softening, she added, "I mean, I just thought since it's Christmas . . ."

"No, you're right. I understand."

"Don't be mad at me."

"I'm not."

"Promise?"

"Promise."

Passing her on his way to the closet, he rubbed the top of her head. "I love you."

She smiled. Charged by contact with his sweater sleeve, several wisps of hair danced above her scalp. "Me, too," she said.

He dressed, as usual, more quickly than she and left the room before her. While she finished getting ready, she thought about Zach and the way he had so brazenly bored the drill into her toe without ever asking whether he was hurting her. Then she thought about Clay, asking what she wanted him to wear, and it made her skin crawl.

By the time she came out of the bedroom, he had already made a fire in the fireplace. She wandered into the kitchen and found him sitting on the counter beside the stove.

"I feel so much better," she said.

"Good." He hopped down from the counter and picked up the pot of water, which had started to boil. "I'm making you some hot chocolate."

"Mmm. Thank you."

She walked back into the living room and pulled her cell phone out of her parka. About a week ago, she'd finally phoned her father and left a message on his answering machine asking him to call her back. Since then, as the days had passed by and she hadn't heard from him, she'd figured he was waiting until Christmas. But so far the only person she'd heard from today was her mother, calling from St. Barts. Her phone showed no new voice-mail messages. She dialed her home number, but the voice-mail there was empty, too. She put the phone away and examined the Christmas tree on the table.

"Gosh," she called out, holding the tip of a tiny branch between her fingers. "This really looks kind of pathetic. Don't you think?"

"Why?" came the response from the kitchen. She could hear the bang of metal against metal as he returned the pot to the stove.

"I don't know," she said, picking off a couple of needles and putting them to her nose. "It's so . . . small. And then with these two sad little presents underneath . . ."

She wandered back to the kitchen doorway and watched him rummage through the drawers.

"Jeez, look at this," he said, more to himself than to her as he pulled out a long spoon with a piece of turquoise embedded in the handle.

"Are there any candles in there?" she asked.

He gave the cup a good stir, licking the spoon as he handed it to her. "I don't know."

As he walked out, she began to rummage through the kitchen cabinets and drawers.

"Em?" Clay called out after a while.

"Okay. I give up."

He had turned out the lights so that the room was lit only by the tree lights and the fire.

"Oh, this is nice." She sat down beside him, bathed in the glow of the leaping flames. "I guess we don't need candles after all."

"See," he said. "Our tree doesn't look so sad."

"Well . . ."

"What?" he said, annoyed.

"Clay, I don't understand why you're taking this so personally."

"Well, I don't understand what's so wrong with our tree."

"I didn't mean to make a big deal out of it. I just think it looks a little sad. That's all."

He turned away.

She leaned over and kissed his cheek. "Thank you for making my hot chocolate." She took a sip and set the cup down on the cof-fee table with an apologetic smile. "It's really good."

He looked at her and smiled. With his finger, he drew a line across his upper lip. "You have a mustache," he said.

"I do?" She wiped her mouth. "Did I get it?"

"Not quite."

Leaning toward her, he spoke in an intimate tone. "Come here."

They began to kiss, chastely at first, and then gradually less so. After a bit, he slid his hand suggestively up her pant leg. She tensed up a little at first, then released as he began to massage her. But as soon as he began fumbling with the button on her pants, she pulled back.

"Let's open our presents."

He closed his eyes, dropping his chin to his chest and released an exasperated sigh.

"What?" she asked.

"You really have no idea why I might feel frustrated at the moment?"

"Clay, I happen to have a *hole* in my foot. So excuse me if I'm not exactly in the mood."

He shook his head. "No. This has been going on for a while now—ever since we decided to get married. You never want to be with me anymore."

"That's not true."

He gave her a look—*Get real.*

"Well," she said. "Maybe we shouldn't get married."

He stared at her, stunned. "Tell me you didn't mean that."

"I don't know."

"You don't know? That's . . . well." He pulled away from her. "That is really great. What do you propose then? That we break up?"

"Don't be like that."

"Like what?"

"All angry and defensive."

"Oh, I'm sorry. How am I supposed to be when you're telling me you don't want to get married?"

"That's not what I said."

"No? What *did* you say?"

"I said *maybe* we shouldn't get married. You know, I was just throwing it out there as a possibility."

Yanking a pillow off the sofa and pushing it into his face, he let out a muffled scream. After a few seconds, he released the pillow. His cheeks were red, and the hairs of his eyebrows all pointed downward as if he'd surfaced from a dive. "Why are you doing this? What could possibly be making you even think this way?"

"Um . . ." She hesitated. "I guess I just wonder if we have enough in common."

"Jesus Christ!"

"What? It's just a question. Don't you feel like it's important to address these questions now? I mean it's better than asking them later. Right?"

He leaned forward, elbows on his knees. Slowly, he stood up and started to walk away.

"Where are you going?"

He kept walking, and she heard the bedroom door slam shut.

She stayed on the couch for about ten or fifteen minutes. Then she put on her boots and her parka, and grabbing the car keys, walked out the door, making sure she slammed it loud enough for him to hear it in the bedroom. All the way into town, Christmas decorations adorned the snowy lawns, giving off so much colorful light that the constellations overhead looked like the effort of a poor neighbor. Her toe throbbed every time she pressed the brake pedal. If she weren't able to ski tomorrow, it would serve Clay right. Though, in some strange way, she'd gotten off on the pain and on having her toenail drilled. Today could have been a great day if only she'd admitted she didn't want to keep skiing. "You're so lucky," Thomas always used to tell her, "because you're not afraid to piss people off." But she never pissed people off anymore. Not in the same direct way that she used to.

When she got to the ski shop, it was closed, but she could still see Zach, the guy who'd drilled her toe, walking around in the back. She pounded on the door, and he looked over. Pointing to his watch, he mouthed the word *closed,* then turned away and began stacking skis against the wall. She pounded again, and after a while he came over.

"Oh, hey," he said as he opened the door. "What's up?"

"I need to talk to you."

He stepped back and let her inside. "How's your toe?"

"It's fine. But I want to tell you something. The fact that you charged us for those boots and for drilling my toe is a total joke."

He gave her a look that was both surprised and amused, and

thumbed the black plastic disk he was holding. "O . . . kay," he said slowly.

"I want a refund," she said.

"Well, there's nothing I can do about that. You'll have to take it up with the manager, Dan, and he won't be back till noon tomorrow."

"I thought you said you were opening at seven."

"Yeah," he replied patiently. "But Chris won't be in till noon."

"That sucks," she said, taking off her hat.

He shrugged. "Sorry."

She continued to stand there for a moment, feeling frustrated that she'd driven all the way into town only to be told to come back the next day.

"Okay," she said finally, turning back to the door and putting her hat on again. "That was a waste. Well . . . Merry Christmas."

"Do you want a whiskey or something?"

She looked at him, trying to figure out if he was serious. He had a wry smile on his face that threw her. "I don't drink," she said.

"Hot chocolate?"

She thought for a moment. "All right. Thanks." She wandered over to the bench where she'd tried on her boots that morning and took a seat.

"Okay," he said. "Let me get some clothes on."

"Oh. You don't have it here?"

"No. There's a bar right across the street."

"Oh," she said again. "You mean go there?"

"Yeah." He was looking at her like she must be really dim. "Is that okay?"

She nodded. "Sure. I guess. I just thought you had it here."

He disappeared into the back for a few minutes, and while she waited for him, she wondered whether this was a weird thing to do to Clay. *Why?* she thought. It was only a hot chocolate. He was the one who'd walked out of the room and left her sitting alone in front of the fire on Christmas Eve—*and* the one who'd gone to lunch with her mom.

When Zach returned, he was wearing sweatpants and a fleece.

His blond hair, which had been hanging down in tangles around his ears, was pulled back into a ponytail.

"Ready to roll?" he asked.

The bar was mobbed—mostly college kids and local ski bums, like Zach, whose weathered skin and raccoon eyes gave them away. Zach slipped away as soon as they walked in, telling her to stay by the door. Within minutes, he'd somehow managed to get them a wooden booth, and by the time they sat down, had already ordered her hot chocolate and a whiskey for himself. Van Morrison blasted from the speakers, and a few people danced, but mostly they just stood around, crowding against the tables and the bar.

"So," Zach said, settling into the booth and pulling his fleece off over his head. "Where are you from?"

"New York."

"Thought so," he said.

"Why?"

He shrugged casually. "This your first time skiing?"

"No. I did it a few times as a kid."

"You ever powder ski?"

"No. I don't think so."

"Oh, man. Don't let the ice up there today put you off. We're supposed to get about thirty inches day after tomorrow. Then you'll get the good stuff. It's a whole different thing. Like floating or flying."

"Yeah?"

He nodded. His lips were cracked and peeling, but he had a wide, infectious smile and beautiful green eyes.

"I don't know." She laughed. "I don't think I'll ever float or fly on skis unless it's going over a bump I didn't see coming."

"Don't say never until you've tried powder. I'm telling you, it's an entirely different sport. Closer to paragliding than what you know as skiing. That's what I do in the summer—paraglide." He raised his hand in the air and made it glide. "Whoosh . . . like a bird. All over the world. Germany, Nepal, Kenya. Meet the coolest people that way, too. And in the winter, I do powder—backpack, helicopter, all that. Mostly here. Although last year I went to Chile."

"You helicopter ski?"

"Yeah. I got a buddy who's a pilot."

"Aren't you afraid?" she asked.

"Of what?"

"I don't know. Crashes, avalanches—all those things you read about."

He shrugged.

She remembered how, way back, when she was a teenager, she'd had that same kind of daredevil spirit. It wasn't that she'd believed herself to be invincible in those days; she simply hadn't thought about it.

A waitress brought their drinks.

"Cheers," Emily said, holding up her mug of hot chocolate.

"Cheers."

His eyes locked onto hers as he clinked his glass against her mug. Smiling, she looked down quickly at her hot chocolate, blowing on it to cool it down. She felt her cheeks turn red.

"Tell me about paragliding," she said. "Is that when you jump out of a plane, or is that the thing that looks like you're hanging from a kite?"

"Kite? No, I think you're talking about hang gliding. In paragliding, you use a wing that looks more like a parachute, but you go off a mountain instead of a plane."

"Oh, wait. I think I saw some people doing it today. They had their parachutes all laid out on the snow."

"Yeah," he said, smiling. "That's it."

The bar was hot. She'd already stripped off her sweater and was still steaming in her tank top. She wished she'd ordered a seltzer instead.

"Cool." She nodded. "And you travel all over the world doing that? Isn't that expensive?"

"No, you can always find cheap flights."

"And where do you stay?"

"Wherever. You camp, or you meet people and stay with them."

"How do you meet people when you're traveling like that? I mean I'm guessing from the sound of it, you're going to a lot of places where people don't speak English. Is there always someone in the group who knows the language or something?"

"No. But you kind of make do—gesturing and whatever. When you're dropping out of the sky, people are usually pretty stoked to meet you. They want you to come to their houses and show your wings to their families and everything. It's like having a golden ticket."

She felt so provincial all of a sudden, and she couldn't help wondering somewhat guiltily whether earlier, when he'd guessed where she was from, he was thinking about those New Yorkers who mistake the city they live in for the center of the world.

He was a real raconteur. His descriptions of people and places were amazingly vivid, and he had several artful ways of holding her attention, gesticulating wildly at times to bring things to life, and then becoming totally still, staring into her eyes and speaking so quietly that she had to lean in to hear him. He also used her name often: *I'd lost everything, I didn't know where my friends were, and I had absolutely no idea where I was. And do you know something, Emily? I was scared shitless . . . At that moment, Emily, you're not going to believe what happened . . . And Emily, it probably sounds ridiculous, but that hut was the most beautiful thing I'd ever laid eyes on.*

After a while, he paused, sitting back and drinking his whiskey, his arm draped along the back of the booth.

She leaned on her elbows, as if pulled forward. "Do people ever paraglide together? You know, like, two people on the same wing?"

"Tandem." He nodded. "All the time. You thinking about trying it?"

"Maybe. It sounds pretty amazing. But I don't think I could go on my own. I might pass out or something."

He laughed. "You won't pass out."

He shook the ice in his glass and gestured to a waitress across the room: *one more.*

"I'll take one, too," she said impulsively.

With no reaction at all, he held up two fingers to the waitress, who nodded.

"It's a real rush," he said. "Like the best sex you ever had."

"Yeah?" She smiled and felt her cheeks go red again. She was wondering when he was going to ask about Clay, and wondering what she was going to tell him.

"Yeah. When I took my girlfriend for the first time, I said if that was how she felt, she'd better not share it with me."

At the mention of his girlfriend, her stomach did a little flip.

"Where is your girlfriend?" she asked as casually as possible.

"She always spends Christmas with her mom in Montpelier. That's where I'm from, too. We went to high school together."

"Huh," she said. She was thinking about the type of feverish sexuality she'd had back in high school, how everything was new, everything had that dangerous free-fall feel—the kind of rush he'd been describing all evening. She imagined that he and this high school girlfriend of his still had that—fucking relentlessly. She used to fuck Eric several times a day; nothing could stop her. She even fucked him when she had strep. Now she knew why he hadn't asked about Clay.

"Anyway," he said. "I could take you anytime. It's better in the summer, but it doesn't matter."

He reached under the table and put his hand on her leg. The placement was too high to be an innocent gesture. Delighted by the feel of his touch, she also found it unsettling. It was obvious now that he wasn't fazed by the fact they were both attached to other people.

"Excuse me," she said after a moment. "I'll be right back."

She slipped out of the booth and made her way through the crowd of bodies to the line of women standing outside the ladies' room.

She was fourth in line. One of the other women, a college-age girl in a cowboy hat and braids and a tie-dyed T-shirt, smiled at her, then turned back to face the door which they were all waiting to swing open. Emily leaned against the wall. *Sometimes,* she thought, *you have to break out of your old patterns to find what makes you happy.* She could go back home, or she could go with Zach—unleash herself, find that part of herself that she'd lost, and that she would do well to find again.

Since November, Eric's death had been floating somewhere around the outer edges of her consciousness, a dull gray thing that she mainly managed to avoid. But as she stood in line, it finally came at her head-on. His obituary hadn't listed any names as "survived by," though that didn't necessarily mean Eric had died alone.

She wondered if he'd ever told anyone about her. It seemed un-likely because of the age difference. Quite possibly, he had carried the secret of their relationship to the grave. As she'd gotten older (she was close now to the age he'd been at the time of their affair), she wondered about what the relationship had meant to him. For her, in addition to being her first foray into adult sexuality, it had been a way of rebelling against convention and feeling brazenly empowered during a time when she otherwise felt anything but. And when, after Thomas died, Eric ceased to serve a purpose, she disposed of him and thought nothing of it, assuming that his age insulated him from any pain she could possibly inflict. She would have been much gentler with a boy half his years because she mis-takenly equated experience with resilience. Now, after years of her own experience, she knew that it worked the other way around. With each relationship, she grew increasingly vulnerable to heart-break.

Suddenly, she wanted to be with Clay more than she'd ever wanted to be with anyone in her life. For some time now, a nega-tive force had been building between them, threatening to drive them apart, and all at once, she understood *she* was that force. Her parka and her sweater were both back at the table, but she didn't care. She walked straight out of the bar and down the street to the rental car.

Speeding back over the snowy roads as fast as safety would al-low, she thought about the William Carlos Williams poem that had originally united them.

This Is Just to Say

I have eaten
the plums
that were in
the icebox

and which
you were probably
saving
for breakfast

Forgive me
they were delicious
so sweet
and so cold

Years ago, when she'd first read it to him, Clay had marveled at these words—at the deceptive simplicity and the odd earth-bound romanticism. She didn't need to travel halfway around the world and throw herself ecstatically off the side of a mountain, dropping down thousands of feet into a group of awestuck and awesome strangers. What she needed was right here in this unassuming little poem. And, inside their condo, she had a first edition of Williams's collected works wrapped for him beneath the tree.

When she got there, Clay was sitting in front of the fire, his hunched shoulders visible over the back of the couch. She saw him as soon as she entered, but even when the wind pulled the door shut with a startling bang, he didn't turn around.

"Sorry I acted like a jerk," she said.

Still he didn't turn.

Good, she thought. He wouldn't see that she was missing her coat. She unlaced her boots, and ignoring the spot of dried blood on her sock, walked over to the couch. He glanced at her briefly, then stared at the ground.

"I really feel awful," she began nervously. "Not just about today. I've been a nightmare lately. I can't believe the things I've said, the way I've acted. It's completely wrong."

He looked at her, then down again. She'd never seen him so grave.

"I'm so sorry," she whispered.

"How's your toe?" he asked.

"Better."

He smiled slightly. "That's good."

Relieved, she sat down beside him. She opened his palm and traced her finger over the outline of his hand. He stared at the fire. She thought of her brother once again and how he used to tell her she was lucky because she wasn't afraid of pissing people off.

"The one thing is," she said boldly, "I really don't want to ski tomorrow."

He nodded. "Yeah, I know. You made that pretty obvious."

"I'm sorry. It's not my thing."

He laughed. "No, I don't think it is."

She smiled appreciatively—she hadn't expected it to be that easy.

"What do you want to do instead?" he asked.

"I don't know. We'll figure out something. Should we open our presents now?"

He looked away. "No. We can't. I burned them."

"You're joking. Right?"

"No, unfortunately I'm not," he said. "I'm sorry. I was really angry."

She gazed into the leaping flames. There was a pile of black char in the fireplace beneath the burning logs.

"Did you open yours?" she asked.

"No."

"It was a really good present."

"Don't tell me what it was. I don't want to know."

"You idiot," she said.

But she was happy—elated even—to find that he could do something so rash.

1995

EMILY SAT WEDGED ON THE SEAT CUSHION OF Thomas's bedroom window, toying with the idea of going to visit her brother. In the old days, he often sat here with her, his back and head resting against the same molded wood panel as her feet and vice versa so that their bodies formed a wide W against the glass. They used to share cigarettes, passing them back and forth below the open window so that their mother wouldn't catch them. One time they'd gotten caught, and Thomas had fully taken the blame. But of course it hadn't worked. Their mother was always convinced that she was the instigator.

More than a week had passed since Emily had last been to the hospital. She was the only member of her family who had not basically lived there over the past eighteen days. Of course, she had school and homework and acting class as excuses, but the truth was that she frequently blew all of that off anyway, and Thomas knew it. The real reason she didn't visit was that, no matter how much her parents insisted it would help him to simply show up and shoot the breeze with him every now and then, she couldn't stomach it.

Whenever she had gone, the sight of him lying helpless in that bed, hooked up to machines, surrounded by all of those dying people, had made her want to tear the place up and scream and yell at every one of those doctors. They were the ones who were killing him. Why couldn't anyone see that? If they would let him go home, maybe he would have a chance. The place was like some horrible prison camp where everyone had been lulled into a twisted reverence for their captors. And for her to sit by his bedside and smile sympathetically while he slowly wasted away made her feel like an accessory to his murder.

But now that his body had started responding to the chemo and the doctors were letting him go home, she had to face the fact that beneath all of that anger and blame, it was her own cowardliness that had kept her away. And though he was leaving the hospital the following day, she finally decided to take advantage of this last opportunity to show her brother that she cared and that she was not neglecting him.

As she walked east toward the hospital, she perspired through her shirt and sweater even as she exhaled visible white wisps of breath through her nose. Brought on either by nerves, lack of sleep, the profusion of alcohol and drugs in her system from the night before, or a combination of all three, the perspiration seemed to ease up after she passed the entrance to the hospital and began to approach the East River, far enough from the busy, police-populated avenue to smoke a joint. Intending at first only to take a couple of puffs, she ended up smoking it down to a nub, one side of her arguing that it would bum Thomas out if he could tell she was stoned, the other insisting that the visit would be a lot more pleasant for both of them if she did something to keep from losing it as soon as she saw him.

While she smoked, she thought about Eric, wondering why he hadn't called. She supposed it was pretty lame to be his age and to date someone who was still in high school. All their rendezvous had to be conducted on the sly, without the knowledge of her parents or his peers. If he could only hang on a little longer until she got another play, she'd be financially independent and could quit school and move into her own place. Then they wouldn't have to worry about her parents, and he could simply lie to his friends about her age. She could pass for young twenties, she thought—or at least nineteen, which wasn't so very young. It would be so great to be able to go out to dinner together, either alone or with his friends, and there would no longer be that seedy feeling of having to get up and leave his apartment as soon as they'd finished having sex. They could spend the entire night together whenever they wanted, reading poetry, practicing scenes, watching movies. It would be such a relief to leave her high school life behind. She was sick to death of hanging out with her girlfriends, spending Friday and Saturday nights doing drugs in people's living rooms and going out to stupid clubs where everyone stood around looking at each other because it was too loud to talk and nobody wanted to dance. Maybe she'd move in with Eric. On the other hand, he could be sort of standoffish when they spent more than an hour or so together, and she got the feeling he was the kind of person who needed his space.

The second she entered Thomas's room and saw the weird, alien look that his face had taken on in the absence of fat and hair and sun and whatever else he was missing that every healthy teenage boy had, she was glad she'd smoked the whole joint.

"Hey," she said cheerfully, walking over to his bed. "How's it going?"

Miraculously, their parents weren't there for once.

"Good."

He studied her. "Are you stoned?"

She pulled a green plastic chair over to the bed and sat down. "Sorry I haven't been here in a while. I've been super, super, super busy. Oh, *dah*-ling," she said, imitating the absurdly exaggerated, eastern seaboard accent of one of their parents' friends, "you can't imagine what all I've been up to."

"Cut it out. I can tell you're stoned."

"No, I'm not," she said.

"Whatever. What have you been doing? You look terrible."

"You're one to talk." She meant this as a joke, but it fell flat, and she wished she hadn't said it.

"What have you been up to?" he asked again.

She shrugged. "Nothing. You know, stuff. Is that new?" she asked, indicating a framed poster of *The Scream* by Edvard Munch hanging over a table in the corner.

"No."

"*Really* cheerful. Did you pick it out yourself?"

He ignored this question and examined her face closely. "What kind of stuff?"

"*Stuff.* Jeez. Why are you being such a hard-ass?"

He watched silently as she crossed her legs and began bobbing her foot up and down. She seemed so nervous. He wondered if she was always like this these days, or if it was simply from being here with him.

"So," she said, "let's just hang out and have a nice chat."

"I'm worried about you."

"Ha ha ha!" She burst out laughing. "Why would you be worried about me?"

"That's what I want you to tell me."

She shook her head to get her bangs out of her eyes. "There's nothing to tell."

"Mom says you're practically flunking out of school."

The conversation was quickly degenerating, and Thomas could feel himself slipping into the role of the disapproving older sibling, which he regretted.

Emily sighed heavily. "You care too much about what Mom says. Don't listen to her."

"Well," he said, trying to sound a little less harsh, "is it true?"

"Who cares about school? It's totally artificial. You learn much more in the real world. I can read, you know. Anything I'm interested in, I can learn on my own. Who cares about, like, the exact date that General Sherman marched into Savannah or whatever?"

"You still need a high school degree," he urged gently.

"For what? I can get plenty of jobs acting right now. Why do I need a degree? It's not like I want to go to med school or anything. I have a new plan, by the way. I'm going to move out and get my own place."

She took a cigarette out of her bag.

"You can't smoke in here."

She rolled her eyes and striking a match, lit up.

"I really wish you wouldn't smoke in here."

She exhaled a cloud of smoke, then put the cigarette out on the bottom of her seat. Looking around for a wastebasket, she asked, "Did you hear what I said? About the apartment?"

"Yeah. I don't understand why you would do that."

She found a blue plastic bin underneath the bedside table, but realizing that Thomas might be able to smell the singed tobacco from his bed, she decided to hold on to the cigarette and dispose of it later in the toilet.

"What do you mean? It'll be really cool." She sat back down in the green chair. "Think about it. I'll have my *own* apartment! And you can come live with me if you want. Wouldn't that be amazing? We would have the best time."

He looked at her as though she was speaking utter nonsense, and it took some of the wind out of her sails.

"I mean of course I have to get another play first and make some more money."

"You know," he began after a long pause. "You're really making things hard for Mom and Dad."

"Well, fuck them. They're making things hard for me, too."

"How?"

"*How?* How aren't they? They're impossible. Did you know a few months ago, Mom actually told Dad not to spend time with me? I mean she's such a fucking psycho, she honestly thought I was, like, in love with him or something—which I'm *obviously* not. But now you're sick, she's apparently changed her mind, and he's acting all buddy buddy as if he never went along with the whole thing in the first place. I swear I hate them both right now."

He smiled. "You know what you have to do? You have to pretend they're strangers."

She gave him a look to let him know she thought he was out of his mind.

"I'm serious," he insisted. "I mean, you think they're driving *you* crazy. I've got them sitting here around the clock."

He could see that she was amused by this, and it made him happy. It was a relief to feel that they were united again.

"Listen. There was this one day," he told her. "The doctor came in and was trying to just do one of his, you know, routine whatevers, and Mom was being all holier than thou, like trying to get a gold star from him for all of the time she was putting in, and Dad was telling some dumb story, dropping all of these names to try to impress him."

She smiled knowingly.

He continued, "I mean, they were just competing like crazy for this guy's attention and sort of using him to make these little jabs at each other. It was awful. I swear to God, I wanted to kill them. And then, all of a sudden, it was like I left my body or something, and I kind of watched the whole thing like it had nothing to do with me. It was so amazing. They were just, like, these two people—like strangers."

Emily was looking at him once again as if he'd lost his mind. He wanted to explain it better, but he didn't know how. He wanted to tell her how at that moment, he had suddenly seen all of their parents' flaws and needs and vulnerabilities and how he'd been overcome right then with this intense affection for both of them. Not just affection, but deep . . . love, really, is what it was.

But he didn't know how to tell her that.

"I think your medication has made you insane," she said.

"Fine." He shrugged. "Whatever. Don't listen to me. I'm trying to impart to you the wisdom of a dying man."

"Shut up. You're not dying. You're coming home." She stood up, and throwing her hands up over her head, yelled, "Woohoo!"

"Shhh!" Embarrassed, he glanced toward the door.

"What? Who cares?" She yelled again, "Woohoo!"

"C'mon," she said, turning her back to him and leaning down. "One last piggyback."

Feigning reluctance, he climbed onto her back as he had done a few times when he had been too weak to walk.

"Ugh," she moaned, "I think you gained some weight."

He pulled on her ponytail. "Giddy up!"

Laughing, she began loping around the room. After a couple of laps, she stopped, panting. "Shit," she said, "this is exhausting."

She felt Thomas's arms tighten around her neck, and she

thought at first that he was readjusting his position. But when he kept holding her, squeezing her shoulders and her neck with his arms, she realized he was giving her a hug. A lump formed in her throat, and she felt like she might snap right in two. She wanted to hug him back, but he was behind her. So she grabbed one of his ankles instead. As she pressed the bone between her fingers and her palm, the combination of being able to carry her older brother on her back and his clinging to her so fondly incited such rage and pain that without being fully conscious of what she was doing, she backed into the yellow flowered wall.

"Ow!" he yelled, more surprised than hurt as his body slammed against the wall.

Emily stepped forward. But instead of staying there, she backed up into the wall again.

"Ow!"

This time it hurt.

She knocked him into the wall three times. On the last time, she let go of his legs, and he dropped to the ground, landing on his feet. As she turned toward him, she tucked her head to try to keep him from seeing that she was crying. Then she came at him like a wrestler, plunging her head into the side of his midsection and grabbing him around the waist. He wrapped his arms around her and felt her body shaking. He held her like that for a while until eventually, the shaking stopped.

When she finally pulled away, her face was blotchy and swollen and smeared with tears. She didn't look at him. "Well," she said, wiping her nose with her wrist on her way over to the chair for her purse. "I'm going to go."

"Sure."

She turned and looked over his shoulder at the Munch poster, which was directly behind him now. "Man," she said with a sniff. "That really is ugly."

"See you tomorrow," he told her.

She let her eyes meet his and gave a sheepish little wave. "See you tomorrow."

T HIS LOOKS GOOD," AMANDA REMARKED, RUN-
ning her exquisite, pale gray eyes over the special menu the
hotel had made up for the last evening of the year. *What a magnificent
coincidence,* Joe thought, to have been seated across from this woman
once again, the two of them absurdly intruding on each other's solitude for the second time. He had felt apprehensive as he approached
her table, but her consent to share it with him had immediately put
him at ease. She, on the other hand—Amanda Ritter—seemed a
bit anxious still. The way that her upper arms flexed and released
told him that she was tugging at something—the napkin, he presumed, or the skirt of her dress—underneath the table as she read
the menu.

"Yes, it really does," he replied. "It looks like we don't even
have any decisions to make, except for the wine. Should we order a
bottle?"

"Sure. Why don't you choose?" She picked up the encyclope-
dic, leather-bound list from her plate and passed it to him. "I know
nothing about wine."

"Red or white?"

"Red, I think, don't you? To go with the rabbit."

"Or we could start off with white and still have red with the rabbit."

"That's true." She laughed. "I hadn't thought of that. The wine's up to you. Really. You choose."

He set the wine list down. "I don't need to look at this. I know exactly what we'll have. And with two bottles, if you get tired of me, you can always banish me back to my table with whichever one you like least."

She laughed again. "Yes, and we can resume the pretense we're both so involved in our own meals that neither of us is aware of the other."

He was surprised by her highly educated way of speaking. Even though she looked quite sophisticated, he had not fully expected her to sound so.

"I'm glad that you agreed to my remedy of that awkward situation."

"Oh, well." She smiled at her plate, embarrassed. "I'm glad you came up with one."

"So if you don't mind my asking, what brings you here tonight? Are you staying at the hotel?"

"No." She shook her head. "No, no, no. I could hardly afford that. No, I live in Shelby, about an hour away. You're staying here, I presume."

"No. I was, but unfortunately my pockets aren't quite that deep either. I've moved to more reasonable accommodations."

"Do you have work in the area?"

"I suppose you could say that."

"May I ask what you do?"

"I'm a playwright."

"Oh, how interesting."

"And you?"

"I teach psychology at the university."

"Aha. And does that mean you're a therapist then?"

"No, I really devote myself to teaching now, though I have practiced in the past."

"My daughter's completely hooked on psychoanalysis."

"Is she?"

"Yes. Her doctor seems to have done a real number on her."

"How so?" Propping her chin up with her hand, she gazed at him with interest. She seemed to be gradually growing less nervous as they talked.

"Well, let's see . . . Other than the fact that my daughter no longer has any respect for me and generally finds fault with everything I do?"

"And you hold her doctor responsible for that?"

"I'd like to."

She laughed. "I have a son who feels the same way about me. Maybe worse."

"I doubt it."

"You have no idea."

Though she smiled as she said this, there was a change in her gaze as if behind her eyes, a shade had been pulled or the lights dimmed.

"This is such a lovely room," she said, looking around. "Isn't it?"

He nodded and surveyed the familiar assemblage of dark wood and creamy linens which provided a background for the faces, flickering candles, and fishbowls of white lilies, all doubled by the dancing reflections on the floor-to-ceiling glass windowpanes. He tried to catch the eye of one of the waiters so that he could order the wine, but they were all busy with other tables.

"I suppose it might seem a little strange to you that I'm here by myself on New Year's Eve," Amanda said.

"Wouldn't that be hypocritical of me?"

"No. Because you don't live here, and I assume you don't know anyone. Whereas I'm alone by choice."

"True. Nonetheless, I don't think you're strange. I'd say more mysterious."

"Oh. I like that. I'm not sure I've ever been considered mysterious before."

"That's a shame. Everyone needs to feel a little mysterious once in a while."

"Well, perhaps. But, as a professor, I'm surrounded by these kids, and they're evolving all the time, and after a few short years, I see them off, neither they nor I having any idea what's to become of them. You want to talk about mystery . . . Next to all of that, I feel pretty boring. I suppose I like it that way, though. I like the stability of my life. And at the same time, I find it comforting to be surrounded by impermanence. That's one of the reasons I like to come here—all of these transient people, each on the way to or from somewhere, something, someone." She laughed. "I suppose you're one of those people."

"I still regard you as deeply mysterious."

"Oh, stop it. Now you're flattering me. Where do you live, by the way?"

"New York."

"I used to live there."

"Not enough impermanence for you?"

She looked contemplative.

He slid his hand forward on the tablecloth. "I was joking."

"Oh, I know," she said. "Ah. Here we go."

Joe looked up to find Albert arriving. It was the first time he had seen him in weeks, and Joe smiled at him as if he were welcoming back an old friend. Albert, however, remained as dour as ever. Greeting both Joe and Amanda with customary formality, he immediately moved on to the business of wine selection, and after nodding politely in response to Joe's choices, took his leave with a "very well, sir," and a slight bow.

"He's a real character, isn't he?" Amanda remarked as soon as Albert was out of earshot.

Joe leaned forward and gestured for her to do the same so that he could let her in on a little secret. Grinning, he said quietly, "He has a sign in his car window—with a cartoon character on it—that says DO NOT TICKLE DRIVER."

"You're kidding!" She laughed.

With this information, Joe realized, she could reduce Albert to a comic-tragic caricature—a sad old fool. This was, of course, exactly what he had intended, to give her something to laugh at. But now that she was laughing, he regretted it.

"A homemade sign?" she asked quietly.

Sitting back, he shook his head in a way that suggested the subject wasn't a very interesting one after all. "No. Store-bought."

"Isn't that funny? DON'T TICKLE DRIVER. I never would have guessed it of him."

"He might have been borrowing someone else's car. I really don't know."

"What a riot, though."

"Mmm. Is it a long drive to get here from where you live?"

"About an hour."

"That's right. You told me that."

He noticed that the stones on her ears were the same shade of red as her lips.

"I like your earrings," he remarked. "I've always been partial to rubies."

She touched her fingertips to her earlobes, and seeming embarrassed, said, "They're not real."

"I wouldn't have known."

Embarrassed again, she smiled. "No, I guess not."

During the silence that ensued, she began once again to knead the napkin in her lap, and he felt concerned that his presence disturbed her.

"Listen," he said. "It was very presumptuous of me to ask to join you, and you've been very gracious about it. But I think that I should return to my own table now."

"Oh, sure." She seemed genuinely surprised. "I didn't think it presumptuous at all. But, of course, if you'd like to go . . ."

"It's not that I'm not enjoying your company, but it's occurred to me that you did come here alone by choice. And if you don't want to dine with a friend, I can only imagine how you feel about dining with a complete stranger."

"No, it's not like that. Really. Please feel free to go, but don't do it on my account. I'm very happy to have you here."

"Do you promise you'd let me know if you weren't?"

"Yes, I would."

"Then I'll stay."

Albert brought the wine and oversaw the delivery of their first course: butternut squash custard topped with asparagus tips, which, as he explained, signified "the passage of winter and augury of spring."

As they ate, they talked about the beauty of the area, and Amanda gave him a rundown of the sights she'd seen and explorations she'd made over the seven years she'd been teaching at the university. After a few more thematic courses—a salad of bitter greens sprinkled with sesame "seeds of change," a "river of time" (thyme-infused consommé), and rabbit accompanied by a timbale of black-eyed peas for luck in the new year—and a few glasses of wine, she loosened up considerably, recounting funny, little anecdotes with unchecked enthusiasm. Even her hair, which had looked a little stiff at the start of the evening, had begun to loosen, and a few silver strands fell over her ears, giving her a softer, more natural appearance.

At a certain point, when Joe was returning from a visit to the men's room, he saw her sitting opposite his empty seat, and his heart soared. As he resituated himself at the table, he could tell from the intent look about her eyes that there was something she wanted to say. She waited until he was fully settled, then leaned a little farther toward him and in a lowered voice began, "Joe."

It was the first time she had spoken his name, and it gave him a thrill. He then realized that nobody had called him by his first name in months.

"I know that I've been acting a little—well, I don't know—funny."

"No—"

She cut him off. "Please. Let me explain. I think it's what you were picking up on when you thought I wanted you to go back to your table." She pulled a strand of hair out of her eyes. "And it's only that—well, I know who you are."

A steel vice clamped itself around his rib cage and began to press in on his lungs.

"As soon as you introduced yourself, you know—I recognized the name, of course. And then, when you said you were a playwright—"

"Oh." The vice released slightly.

"I really like your work."

He nodded, still afraid that she might know Laura or any number of other people who knew him or knew of him and might have unfavorable things to say.

"I didn't feel comfortable saying anything at first because—I'm not sure quite how to put it." She thought for a moment, her gray eyes widening and searching. "I guess there's a certain shyness I've got—an embarrassment really—about knowing your work since it feels that I know you so intimately. And yet I really don't know you at all."

His chest expanded with relief.

"It seems premature or something. Does that make any sense?"

"I think so. I've never heard anyone put it that way before, but it's an interesting idea."

She laughed. "It's unfair, really. Since you know absolutely nothing of me."

"We'll have to even the score then."

"What do you want to know?"

"Everything."

"You'll have to be more specific."

"To begin with, why do you come here alone? You never really answered that."

"Oh . . ." She sighed. "I don't think I like people very much."

"Neither do I."

"Really? But if you don't like people, how can you write about them?"

"I thought I was asking the questions."

"You're right. I'm sorry."

"If *you* don't like people, how can you be a psychologist?"

"I can tolerate them—even like them—from a distance."

"And yet you've let me sit here."

"Because I'll never see you again."

"How do you know?"

"I should say, because I never have to see you again."

"That is true. In fact, it's precisely the reason I came over. So here we are, two incurable misanthropes, united by mutual mistrust."

She threw her head back and let out a laugh of pure delight, the paper-thin skin of her neck stretched into a translucent, white band. "We do sound ridiculous. Don't we?"

He swirled the wine around in his glass, watching the burgundy liquid wash the sides then settle back into a dark pool. "Rather than continue questioning you in this silly way, I'd prefer to let you tell me whatever you like."

She smiled. "Now that you've loosened my tongue . . . The wine is fabulous, by the way."

"I'm glad you like it."

"Let's see." She set her interlaced fingers on the table in a business-like manner. "I grew up in New Jersey—" She broke off. "You're going to know far more about me than I know about you."

"We can settle that later."

Nodding, she began again. "So I grew up in New Jersey, went to college at Mount Holyoke, and afterward moved to the city, where I met my husband, a stockbroker. We lived on the Upper West Side. He worked. I stayed at home with our son, and then when he went off to boarding school, I went back and got my doctorate at Columbia. My husband was not fully supportive of that, and we had a hard time for a while before we finally decided to get a divorce. It was relatively amicable, though, and our son split his vacations between the two of us. It was hard for him, but he really seemed reasonably well adjusted to the whole situation, and . . . um, well, he went off to college. Hampshire. And that was fine for the first couple of years. You know, he did the whole ultraliberal, antigovernment, anticorporate, protest-everything-and-everyone college thing, but he continued to get good grades, and even though I didn't agree with most of what he had to say, we talked a lot whenever he was home."

"Um . . ." She sighed. "And then something cracked. He dropped out of school and joined a commune in rural Massachusetts. He wouldn't speak to his father or me. In fact, for a while, neither of us even knew where he was. And then the letters started coming—fanatical, rage-filled letters in which he accused us both of being wretched human beings and leading despicable lives. His father, according to him, was a greedy, capitalist pig who cared about nothing but money—which, whatever his father's problems, was neither true nor fair. The man was passionate about his work, but it was the work that interested him, not the money itself, and it wasn't his only interest by any means. He was a wonderful father, really. It was so painful for both of us to read those letters and then, later, to have him repeat the same, awful things to our face when we visited the commune to try to figure out what was going on. His criticism of me was equally heavy. I was a big phony, he said, a narcissistic nightmare who worked as a psychologist in order to seem, in the eyes of the world, like a person who cared for others. I understand that after our little discussion, that may not sound too off base. But I was a completely different person then. Quite the opposite of a misanthrope, I assure you."

She paused for a second and took a sip of her wine.

"And so what was it?" Joe asked. "Was he into drugs or something?"

"At first, we thought that the group he was involved with was a cult, but it wasn't. It was just a group of kids, and they were all very nice. The only one who seemed to have any real hostility was Kyle—that's his name, our son. We did think maybe he was on drugs, but that, too, proved to be wishful thinking. There was nothing obvious that we could blame for his behavior. Anyway, soon he stopped writing, and we heard that he'd broken away from the group. Again, for a while, we had no idea where he was. Then we found out that he was living on the street in Boston. Begging. Imagine. For years, I'd seen kids like that on the streets in New York, sitting out on the sidewalk with their cardboard signs and their paper cups. I know you've seen them. And I always thought, whenever I passed one of these kids, *My God, what sort of horrendous things must they have suffered at home to be driven to this? The parents—wherever the hell they are—ought to be locked up.* And suddenly, there I was. I *was* one of those parents, and I can tell you, there was nothing remotely bad about that boy's home life. He had two parents who thought the world of him and offered him every advantage a child could wish for . . . I have spent years trying to figure out what I—or we—did wrong, and I simply can't."

A waiter arrived with their desserts, followed immediately by Albert, who announced, as the waiter set the plates in front of them, "individual, champagne-strawberry soufflés served with house-made, chocolate fortune cookies."

Nodding to the waiter to pour them some more wine, Albert hurried off to present the next set of soufflés to another table.

"This looks good," Amanda said once the waiter had left.

"It does. Though I don't know how much more I can eat."

"No kidding. I wasn't prepared for this much food."

Joe dipped the spoon into his soufflé. "Mmm," he moaned. "Very good."

Amanda nodded, and as she swallowed, an amused smile spread across her face. "You know, it's funny. This reminds me of a time when I was in college, and I took a film class. We were watching Godard's *Breathless*. And as the opening titles came up, they were, of course, in French. So, up came the name of the film, and it said, *Au Bout de Souffle*. And there were a couple of southern debutante types in the class from, I don't know, Atlanta or something. And one of them said in a very loud voice with her heavy, Georgia accent, 'About a *soufflé*?!'"

The two of them erupted in laughter, causing people at the neighboring tables to cast curious glances in their direction. When she finally caught her breath, Amanda sighed, dabbing underneath her eyes with a napkin.

"We all died."

"And was she serious?"

"Oh, yes!"

"That's brilliant."

"Isn't it? I loved it."

"Oh . . . boy." Stretching, Joe held his arms out in front of him. "What do you think about moving to the bar? I'm feeling the need to spread out a little after this feast, and it's a lot more comfortable there."

"Sure, but we have to open our fortune cookies first."

Joe picked his up. "Should we open them at the same time?"

"No. You first."

He cracked open the cookie and drew out a slip of white paper.

"'You will live a long and happy life.' This is a dud. Let's see what yours says."

"I think that's a good one. Here, I'll take it, and you can have mine."

"I'm not taking yours until I know what it says."

She broke the cookie in half, pulling the folded fortune from one side. "'You will travel far and see many great things.' I think this was meant for one of hotel guests. You're right. These are terrible. Should we move to the bar?"

As they got up, he motioned to Albert that they were moving to the next room, and Albert responded with a nod so solemn it would have been a perfectly suitable indication to pallbearers to begin lowering a coffin into the grave.

"Lord, I wonder what his fortune would say."

Amanda giggled. He found it hard to believe that she could be the subject of anyone's hatred and was eager to know more about what had happened with her son. Once they were settled on a couch in a quiet corner of the bar, he asked her to resume her story.

"Oh, you don't really want to hear about that. We all have our own tragedies."

"I would like to hear the rest—if you don't mind talking about it."

"I don't mind. But . . . I don't really even remember where I was."

"Your son was on the street, begging."

She crossed one leg over the other and picked up a book of matches. "Right."

Her skirt had opened slightly over her crossed knees, and Joe noticed that she had beautiful, thin, and surprisingly muscular legs.

She fiddled with the matchbook. "Ultimately, after hundreds of attempts to get him off the street, his father and I realized that we had to give up. And that's when I decided to leave my job and leave New York and start over."

"Here?"

She nodded. "I knew I didn't want to practice anymore—not for a while anyway—but I didn't have the luxury to stop working either. I felt that if I taught, I could get to know other kids and . . . this might sound really crazy, but I felt that it was important to work with undergraduates in order to spend time with students who were the same age and in the same stage of life as my son was at the time that he snapped. I think I hoped, rather, I *know* I hoped I would encounter other kids like him. I wanted to believe that there was a widespread phenomenon that had not yet been identified, something we did not yet understand about this moment in history, our society, our country, the world at large that was creating this devastating effect on our young people as they were hitting adulthood. I had this idea that if I could see enough of these kids, get to know them, I could get to the root of the problem. But, as it turns out, there was—or is—no such phenomenon. At least not as far as I've been able to tell."

She fell silent. Her facial muscles worked involuntarily, revealing the pain caused by this conclusion. She took a sip of her drink, then, as if remembering that Joe was there, looked over at him and smiled politely. He reciprocated with a look of compassion.

"Where is your son now?"

"I don't know. But he knows where I am, and he knows where his father is. And I have to believe that deep down he knows we care. When he's ready, if he's ever ready, he can find us. Until that moment—"

She was interrupted by the commotion that broke out by the bar area and quickly spread through the rest of the room, then into the lobby and dining room. People cheered and blew on the paper horns and kazoos that had been put on all the tables in preparation for this moment and had, until now, served as inanimate decoration. Over the sound system came the first, familiar chords of "Auld Lang Syne," which were immediately joined by voices of all tones, timbres, talents, and lacks thereof. He and Amanda looked at each other, both struck shy by the sudden outburst of extroverted merriment.

"Happy New Year," he said, holding his glass out. She picked up her drink, but instead of simply reaching her hand forward, leaned her entire upper body toward him and planted a kiss on his lips at the same time that their glasses met. Utterly astonished but pleased, he didn't know quite how to react, and grinned like a delirious fool.

Driving back to the motel, her lights shining in his rearview mirror, all that he thought about was whether he would be able to perform. Even though Amanda seemed like a forgiving down-to-earth sort, he couldn't help but worry about her expectations. For one, it seemed conceivable that part of his attraction for her lay in the impression she had gathered of him from his work, specifically from those plays in which his own virility played such a large role. For another, he had tried to debunk any notions she might entertain about a celebrity lifestyle, but still he wondered how she would react when confronted with the duct-taped windows, the soiled chartreuse bedspreads, and the cracked toilet seat to which she would soon be exposed. A two-hour drive home by herself on the icy highway might seem like a preferable close to the evening. Even he was not entirely thrilled with the idea of waking up to the start of a new year in that setting.

In the end, he wasn't sure that he didn't *want* her to cut the evening short. Back in the hotel bar, when he proposed that they retire to his room, he had been completely overcome with sexual desire and was single-mindedly focused on getting her alone as quickly as possible in a place where they could explore each other beyond the few, rather chaste kisses they had exchanged on the bar's velvet sofa. However, now that he'd had a chance to cool down a little, he doubted whether the sex would be worth the amount of time they would inevitably have to spend in further conversation both before and after. He enjoyed talking to her, but there was a limit to what he wanted to know about her life or wanted her to know about his.

Meeting her at her car, he considered telling her that he'd changed his mind. Instead, he opened the door and offered his hand, which she took, leaning upon it as she stepped gracefully out onto the asphalt.

"Thank you."

He waited while she locked the car, then guided her, his hand on her elbow, across the icy lot. When they reached his door, she stopped and looked at him, hesitating before speaking.

"Maybe I should go home."

He had not expected this to happen before she'd even stepped foot in the room.

"Would you mind if I just used your powder room first? It's a long drive."

"I'm not sure you could really call it a powder room. It's not very elegant." He opened the door and flicked the light on. "It's over there."

"Thanks."

She walked across the carpet, and he noted the absence of irritating creaks that cried out from the floor whenever he crossed the room, her shoes instead issuing a nice soft sound as they pressed against the pile. She closed the bathroom door, and he went to the closet to put away his coat, creaking all the way there, then back to the desk, where he rearranged his books while he waited for her to come out again. When she emerged, she took a few steps forward and surprised him by sitting down on the edge of the bed nearest the bathroom.

"I never got to ask you any questions, I was so busy talking about myself." She laughed. "I'm sorry about that."

"Don't be. I enjoyed it."

"I don't want you to think that I wasn't interested in what you had to say. I'm really not so self-absorbed usually. In fact, I normally don't speak about myself at all. I'm a pretty good interrogator—to the point of being a bit intrusive, I'm afraid. My reputation at the university is being the one everyone else comes to when they need to unload. Pretty predictable for a shrink, I guess. Anyway, none of them know about my son. You probably find that hard to believe since I launched into it with you so readily."

She paused for a moment but did not look to him for an answer.

"I suppose I'm trying to apologize for kissing you." She looked up, her face twitching slightly from embarrassment.

He smiled. "Would you like to have a drink? I have some vodka here, and there's an ice machine outside. The only other thing I can offer is tap water."

"Vodka would be nice."

"I'll go fill the bucket."

He picked up the plastic bucket and carried it outside to the ice machine under the stairs. When he returned, he saw that she had taken off her coat and was sitting beside it, a little farther back now on the bed so that her feet dangled off the floor. He poured the drinks, apologizing for the lack of mixers. Then, handing her a glass and keeping one for himself, he sat down on the second bed. She pivoted to face him so that their positioning felt more natural, the aisle between the beds giving approximately the same separation a table would ordinarily provide.

"I had a son, also."

"Yes?"

"Yes. He died of lymphoma."

"I'm very sorry."

"As you said before, we all have our tragedies."

"I didn't mean to belittle them. The loss of a child is . . . well . . . I can't begin to imagine how painful that's been for you. At least my son is alive." Dropping her gaze, she fell silent, then added, "As far as I know."

He stood up and sat down again beside her. She closed her eyes, surrendering, and he kissed her long and hard. Gradually gravity pulled them horizontal, and when after a while their mouths parted, Amanda laughed. "We're still holding our glasses."

"Here." Joe took hers from her and set them both on the night-stand, then lay back down beside her.

"I'm sorry," she said.

"Why?"

"My mind is still on what we were talking about."

"That's all right."

She propped herself up on her elbow. "I don't know how to say this exactly, but . . . please don't take this the wrong way. I've some-times wished that my son had died—from a disease, maybe—something that didn't implicate me. That probably sounds horribly selfish." She shook her head. "I don't know why I'm telling you this. I think I've had too much to drink."

"There is nothing that happens to a child that doesn't impli-cate the parent in some way."

"But you couldn't possibly feel responsible for what happened to your son. For God's sake, he had cancer."

"Well . . ." He hesitated, trying to decide whether or not to plunge into the complexities of this issue.

"My son didn't actually die of lymphoma."

She shook her head, confused.

"He did have lymphoma. But . . . Well, I made a mistake, which I'd rather not go into. But both my wife and my daughter blamed this incident, this mistake of mine—me, really—for his death. They still blame me for it to this day. And I don't know if . . . Well, perhaps he would have died anyway, from the lymphoma. But I also know that what I did was incredibly stupid—more than stupid . . ."

He had thought that Amanda would absorb this information without emotion, making a clinical examination of what she learned and offering the same type of detached assessment she had given of her own life. But it seemed that she was now observing him with suspicion—as if his divulgence had thrown into doubt everything that she thought she knew and understood about him.

"This thing I did was far more innocent than either of them think," he assured her.

She gave him a smile that was at once cool and sympathetic, and he realized that he was being paranoid to think that she was eyeing him with anything more than the dispassionate interest of a psychologist. He decided to stop talking and wait for her to deliver a response.

"You seem as if you're posing a question," she told him, "but I'm not sure what it is."

He smiled, somewhat embarrassed. "I'm not either."

"Are you wondering why you never told them the truth?"

"No." He shook his head dismissively. "There would have been no point to that. All of them—including my son—were going to believe what they believed."

"I see."

"No," he began again. "I guess what I still can't understand is this. If I was fully aware that by doing this thing, I was potentially throwing away everything that meant anything to me . . . then, why did I do it?"

"Maybe it was preferable to give everything away than have it taken away, easier to accept the blame than to live with unanswerable questions like why your son was dying."

"No," he said angrily. "You don't understand. I *never* thought I would be endangering his life."

"I'm not blaming you for your son's death."

He rubbed his eyes wearily. "I didn't mean to sound so defensive." Lying back down on the bed, he said, "I've spent the last several years dwelling on all the things I could have done differently."

He noticed with disgust an area on the ceiling stained yellow and brown from a leak. The paint there was starting to peel away and dangle down.

"My daughter is a very unhappy person," he went on. "Very cynical, very bitter."

"And that's your fault?"

"I don't know."

He could feel Amanda leaning closer to him. His desire for her had pushed out any anxiety about his performance, and he was beginning to feel impatient with the delay. Reaching out, he pulled her down beside him.

"It's a good thing the perpetuation of the human race depends on people under forty. Once you get older, there's too much to talk about to ever get anywhere."

"That's fairly blunt of you." She smiled coyly. "Are you suggesting that I came here in order to sleep with you?"

"Who's suggesting sleep? I'm being far blunter than that."

Nose to nose, they laughed and began kissing again.

In the morning, Joe woke to a sound that he first registered as rain, then eventually, as he gradually gained consciousness, recognized to be the shower. Stretching his leg out across the bed, he came across a patch of moisture on the bottom sheet and was pleasantly reminded of the past night's activities. He smiled at the absurdity of the nervousness he'd felt beforehand. Not only had he performed— and really, if he had to rate himself, he'd done a top-notch job— but he was surprised to find that he had actually sort of fallen for this woman. Even as he drifted off to sleep, there had been some feeling that perhaps in the morning, he would regret some element of the evening—if not the entire thing—and would want nothing more than to have her disappear, leaving behind only the relieving assurance that he'd never have to see her again. He found, however, that the sound of the running water and the knowledge that it was she, standing naked under the not so well calibrated head of his diminutive motel shower, filled him with a soothing sense of well-being. The fact that she felt comfortable enough upon waking to get up and make herself at home in his bathroom rather than self-consciously throwing on her clothes and either sneaking out or waking him with an awkward good-bye made him like her even more. He assumed the fact that she was still there meant that she, too, harbored no regrets about the previous evening, and he guessed that she might be easily persuaded to turn this into more than a onetime event.

Rolling over, he looked out the window. The light was dim and wintry. The sun either had not yet risen or was hiding behind a thick blanket of clouds. Glancing over at the clock, he saw that it was already after ten. It had been a while since he'd been able to sleep so late. He stretched his arms and legs outward, luxuriating in his slothfulness. Again, his leg hit the area where moisture had been soaked up by the poly-cotton blend, and it occurred to him that too many hours had passed now to account for the spot still being wet. Wide awake now, he pulled back the pile of sheet, blanket, and bedspread under which they'd slept and revealed the wet bottom sheet to the light. It was exactly as he feared. In the bathroom, he heard the shower shut off and wondered if this was the reason she had gotten up to shower instead of dressing immediately for a quick departure. Possibly, she hadn't noticed or had, like he, groggily misinterpreted the wetness. Both seemed unlikely.

Cheerfully, she stepped out of the bathroom.

"Good morning."

She had one of the skimpy motel towels wrapped around her torso like a strapless dress and was combing her wet hair out with his comb. It was the first time he had seen her standing in the light without her clothes on, and he was struck by the loveliness of her long, bare limbs.

"I hope you don't mind that I'm using your comb."

"No," he answered, thinking with relief, *She does not know.* "That's fine."

"How did you sleep?"

"Very well. And you?"

"Perfectly." She stood, looking at him, the comb held midstroke. It seemed for a moment as if she wanted to say something. Then she started combing again and walked back into the bathroom. His heart sank. *She knows.* He debated whether he should address the wet spot, perhaps make an apology, but then decided it was better to ignore it. There was nothing he could do to change matters. There was no point even in feeling embarrassed. She would dress; they would say a polite good-bye; and he would never. have to see her again. Once more, he picked up the covers and looked at the spot in order to assure himself that he had not made a mistake. He hadn't.

After a few minutes, Amanda reappeared, fully dressed in last night's outfit. He guessed she had taken her clothes in with her so as not to parade naked before him in broad daylight. This sudden self-consciousness on her part lessened to some degree the regret he felt regarding her imminent exit, restoring a lack of intimacy and reminding him that they were virtual strangers who, only hours before, held no significance to each other whatsoever.

"I don't suppose you have a hair dryer," she said, obviously aware that it was an absurd question since he had so little hair to dry.

"No."

She let out a melodic laugh, and immediately, a touch of the former intimacy was restored. He couldn't help but smile in response.

"Oh, well. It probably won't kill me to go out for breakfast with wet hair. I used to never dry it when I was younger, and somehow I managed to survive."

He found it curious the way she talked of going out to breakfast as if it were something that had already been planned, and he tried to think back through the sweet murmurings they'd exchanged before drifting off to sleep, then realized that she might have a prestanding appointment with someone else. She walked over to the bed and sat down directly (though protected by the intervention of sheet, blanket, and bedspread) atop the source of his shame, a choice which could be taken to mean that she did not know, or conversely, that she did know and wished either to pretend that she didn't or to show she did not care. He was soon startled out of this line of thinking by the sensation of her lips on his, and he let his displeasure dissolve into the electric soap-scented air.

"Starving," she murmured, kissing his neck. "I'm starving. Let's go get some breakfast."

"You want me to come to breakfast with you? I thought this was a one-night stand."

"Even on a one-night stand, a girl's entitled to be taken to breakfast."

"I thought you were a liberated woman."

"You're right. I'll take you to breakfast."

"I was only kidding. It would be my pleasure to take you to breakfast."

She gave him another kiss. "Then get up, lazybones."

While he dressed, she lounged on the bed and watched him, occasionally making eye contact in the mirror.

"Where should we go?" she asked. "I feel like going someplace different."

"Not the hotel, in other words."

"Do you know any good places?"

"Not really," he said. "Do you?"

"No. But we could do some exploring. There's bound to be a good breakfast spot on Main Street. Some place with eggs Benedict. That's what I want. Or an omelet. What do you want?"

"I don't know. Isn't there something special you're supposed to have on New Year's Day?"

"Black-eyed peas, but we had them last night."

"That doesn't count," he said. "You have to have them on the first."

"Oh. Do you think they'd be hard to find?"

"Not on New Year's Day."

"Really?" she asked. "I'm not so sure that custom is as widespread as you think. I've never had black-eyed peas on New Year's Day."

"Well, neither have I, but I imagine other people do."

She laughed. "That's ridiculous logic."

"Is it?"

"Yes, but I'm willing to go with it."

He tucked his shirt into his pants and turned around. There was something irritating about the sight of her with her wet hair and last night's clothing, lying there so contentedly on his bed.

"Are you ready?" she asked.

"Sure."

Evidently, she'd detected the shift in his demeanor, and she gave him a questioning look.

"Let's go." He pulled his coat off the metal clothing rod in the corner and crossed to the desk for his keys.

"What's wrong?" she asked, slowly rising from the bed.

"Nothing."

He held her coat out for her, and she took it.

"If you don't want to go to breakfast, I understand."

He leaned back against the desk. "Listen. I think you're wonderful—"

"Don't worry about it." She pulled her coat on, looking very officious. "I agree. It's better to leave things the way they are."

He was relieved to find her so accommodating. But at the same time, he no longer felt sure he wanted her to go.

"Thank you for your hospitality." She held out her hand. "I had a lovely time."

He shook her hand. "Me, too."

He walked with her the short distance to the door and held it for her after she opened it.

"Good luck with everything," she said.

"You, too."

"Good-bye."

"Good-bye."

He watched her walk across the pavement and get into her car, then he shut the door against the chilly, January morning.

1995

JOE HAD FELT SOME TREPIDATION WHEN LAURA suggested that he and Thomas go up to the Berkshires together. The two of them rarely spent any time one on one, and his son's quiet manner tended to unsettle him when they were alone. After coming precariously close to death, Thomas was doing considerably better. His body had finally started responding to the chemotherapy; his white blood cell count was way down from its high of 18 to an optimistic 9; and the doctors had switched his medication so that he was no longer suffering from so many side effects. This radical improvement afforded Laura a much-needed respite from the near ceaseless vigil she had kept up over the last hundred-plus days and nights. And it was only now, after getting a little rest, that she began to realize the full extent of her exhaustion. So a plan was hatched for a father-son excursion. In the men's absence, Laura and Emily were going to sleep late, order pizza, watch bad TV, and if they felt up to it, go to Bergdorf's for what Laura liked to call a "poodle day," meaning manicures, pedicures, haircuts, and a little shopping. Ordinarily, Emily did not go in for this sort of thing. Nor, for that matter, did Laura. But after the doom and gloom of the past several months, they both seemed to be looking forward to some feminine frivolity.

Joe felt mixed about the fact that Emily had chosen to stay in the city with her mother. On the one hand, he found it encouraging that Laura was reaching out to her. Since his return from Florida, he had been trying to spend as much time as possible with Emily—especially to counterbalance Laura's limitless attention to Thomas. But Emily had been so openly hostile, he'd hardly had a chance.

He suspected that a large part of her decision to stay in the city with her mother this weekend was an effort to protest his behavior— not only his affair with Gina but his neglect for some months prior to his departure. Laura had helped him comprehend that a crucial step to Emily gaining maturity was to separate from him and shift her idolatrous gaze farther afield. And so he'd agreed to keep his distance, though it had been extremely difficult to do, especially while they were working together on the play. It had pained him to see the incomprehension and disappointment with which she'd re-acted to his rebuffs. And now that he was back from Florida, she was repaying him in spades.

Still, he hoped that the outcome of the weekend would be good. There was a chance that Laura would make some strides over the next couple of days toward connecting with their daughter. He was happy she was making the effort at least. More than anything, Emily needed someone to talk to. His only worry was that this mother-daughter weekend was simply setting up both mother and daughter for disappointment. As intent as Laura was on her vision of it, he himself had great difficulty imagining the two of them lounging around in bed with pizza, laughing and gossiping over simultaneous pedicures, and so on. It seemed to him like some fiction-fueled fantasy that Laura had in her head of the way mothers and daughters were meant to interact rather than even a far-fetched version of their reality.

During the drive up, he gradually let go of his worries about the two of them and began to focus his anxiety on his son. As usual, Thomas wore a pink baseball cap, which appeared to have once been red, though Joe couldn't remember it ever looking different than it did now. Ever since the chemo began to expunge Thomas's straight, dark locks, the cap had become a fairly constant appendage. Beyond masking his baldness and, to a lesser extent, his lack of eyebrows, it made the ghostly pallor of his face and the dark circles underneath the eyes look a little less scary. It could not, however, hide the boniness of Thomas's frame. No matter how much clothing he wore or what position his body took, the excess of protruding angles and the slackness of insufficient strength betrayed his stoicism and spoke loudly of sickness and discomfort. Simply to look at him often turned Joe's stomach. The desire to make things right, combined with the impossibility of doing so, proved overwhelming to him, and he thanked God—or whatever force was responsible—for giving Laura the strength to do what he could not.

Frantically, he tried to remember the list of reminders Laura had orally given that morning: to make sure Thomas took his medication, to not let him exert himself too much . . . To take his temperature? Was that one? He didn't know if the house even had a thermometer.

"I'm going to swing by Rite Aid on the way. So, be thinking if there's anything you need."

"Nah. I don't need anything."

"You sure?"

"Yeah. Why are we going to Rite Aid? It's, like, thirty miles out of the way."

"For a thermometer."

"I have one."

"You do?"

"Yeah."

"Where is it?"

"In my bag."

"You sure?"

"Yes. Dad, don't be so nervous."

"I'm not nervous."

"Whatever."

"Don't whatever me."

He immediately regretted the remark and tried to think of
something funny to say. He wanted for Thomas to say something,
so that he could say "whatever" to him and they could both laugh.
But Thomas just fiddled with a piece of thread he'd pulled off his
sweatshirt and stared out the window. He turned on the radio, and
they listened to the news. Eventually, Thomas said "meat head" to
a quote the news lady gave from the Speaker of the House. There
was no way Joe could say "whatever" to that. So he remained quiet
until the weather report, then asked Thomas what kind of music
he wanted to listen to.

"Your stuff's good."

"My stuff?"

"Yeah, you know. Classical."

"You sure?"

"How come you keep asking if I'm sure about everything?"

"I thought you might rather listen to something else."

"No. I like classical."

There was a Chopin tape already in the cassette player, and he
simply had to turn the knob to make it play. The gorgeously timed
swells and pauses of Chopin's Nocturnes had an instant, relaxing
effect on him and, he thought, on Thomas as well. He was surprised and touched to hear his son say he liked his music. He knew
that Emily considered him a dinosaur for listening exclusively to
classical and had assumed Thomas felt the same way. It was a
revelation to discover there was at least this one area where their
tastes overlapped, and he chose to take it as a portent of further
pleasant discoveries to be made over the course of the next couple
of days.

When they arrived at the house, it was late afternoon, and the
sun painted the fields and the aluminum siding of the neighbor's
tool shed with gold and lavender. A herd of dairy cows poked
around in the frosty patches of dead weeds up on the hill.

"Home sweet home," Thomas said, reluctantly stepping aside
for Joe to take his bag for him.

"Yep."

"Maybe we can go for a walk."

Joe hoisted the bag to his shoulder and slammed the trunk.

"I don't know. Your mom made me promise not to let you exert yourself."

"Dad, c'mon. I can *walk* at least. Even in the hospital, I had to walk down the hall a few times a day."

"Let's see how you're feeling tomorrow."

"Sure. Whatever."

Joe smiled, realizing he'd missed the perfect chance to use the word himself when Thomas told him he'd had to walk at the hospital. He carried the bags in, and Thomas followed, both of them cursing the disgusting crunch of dormant ladybugs beneath their soles as they entered the dark house.

"Home sweet home," Joe quoted with a note of sarcasm.

After he delivered Thomas's bag to him and deposited his own on the threshold of his and Laura's bedroom, Thomas tried to help him clean up the house. Thwarted, he retreated to his bedroom with a book on forest ecology, leaving Joe to pull the slipcovers off the furniture, sweep up the insects from the floor, open the curtains, raise the blinds, and put away the groceries. The food consisted of chips, nuts, olives, and a number of more substantial dishes already prepared and neatly packed by the neighborhood gourmet market for customers who wished to limit their cooking to a douse of dressing and a couple of minutes spent standing in front of the microwave.

As he was unloading containers of vitello tonnato, haricot verts, duck à l'orange, and cannelloni from a brown paper sack, he glanced out at the garden. Despite Laura's and Thomas's efforts to educate him, the only plant that he could successfully identify on a regular basis was the rosemary bush, which used to sit on the sill above the kitchen sink in their apartment, its roots confined to a ceramic pot, its branches stretching toward the little bit of sun that filtered between the brick of one building and the stone of the next. In time, the strain of city life had forced the rosemary into early retirement. Relocated among other herbs, vegetables, and fruits, it luxuriated in the boundless, black soil and long days of full sun shining down upon Laura's Berkshire garden and grew into a strong and beautifully showy plant. The sight of this transformation weighed upon his conscience, causing him to wonder whether he was depriving his wife of the ability to flourish in the same way. It was no secret that she would have preferred to move out of the city years ago. Initially there were thoughts of moving to Greece, then more realistically to Massachusetts. But her plans were dissolved each time by his inability to embrace them until finally, she settled for weekends away—and a few long stretches during the summer. When he saw the passion and obsessiveness with which she pored over seed catalogs and horticultural books, he felt cruel for keeping her cooped up in the city and sometimes went so far as to consider relocating to the Berkshires. But however deprived she felt in Manhattan, it was nothing compared to the slow death he knew he would suffer in the country. The bustling high-paced energy of the city was his lifeblood. Without it, he would waste away. This was what he told himself, anyway—a more noble explanation than the myopic ambition that *did* make him feel truly, profoundly, that to turn his head from the city for even a second was tantamount to suicide.

The unsoundness of this way of thinking had become increasingly obvious to him lately, thanks to a new perspective gained in part from stepping away for a little while—from his city, his family, and his work—and in part from confronting the crisis of Thomas's illness. No joy born of satisfying the whims of any producer, critic, or audience could ever come close to the joy he felt in making his wife and children happy. And no displeasure was as difficult to bear as watching one of them suffer. The fact that they had accepted him back made him that much more appreciative of them and that much more determined to place their happiness above all else. He was not unaware, however, of the tenuousness of his position. There was a palpable undercurrent of resentment and suspicion, and he knew it was quite possible that the hatchet could still fall.

Having tucked all of the groceries away in the cabinets and refrigerator, he wandered into the living room and punched his home number into the phone. Laura answered with her usual air of surprise, as though the last thing she ever expected was to receive a telephone call.

"I wanted to let you know we're here," he told her.

"Good. Thanks."

"Thomas is in his room, reading."

"Mmm."

"How are things there?"

"Fine."

"You know, I had a thought just now. What do you think about taking a trip to Greece once Thomas is well?"

"With the kids?"

"Sure, with. Or without. It's up to you."

"Hmm. We'll see."

He heard the rip of paper on the other end of the phone. "What are you doing?"

"Going through the mail."

"Oh. Where's Emily?"

"Out."

"I thought you guys were going to do something."

"Yeah . . . well."

He wanted to ask what had happened but was afraid of what the answer might be. "I'll let you get back to your mail," he said.

"Have a good time."

"You, too."

She made a little grunt in response to this.

"I love you," he said.

"Mmm. Bye."

He hung up the phone, wishing he hadn't called, and sat down in the armchair. The house was remarkably still. Getting up again to put some music on, he called out toward the stairs.

"Thomas?"

He turned on the stereo, loaded some CDs into the player, then called again.

"Thomas?"

The music began to play, and still there was no answer. Getting nervous, he walked down the hall and mounted the stairs. At the top, he turned left. Thomas's door was open. He stopped on the threshold.

"Thomas?"

He stepped into the room but found no sign of Thomas. Remembering the boy's desire to go for a walk, he looked out the window, but there was nothing to see except darkness. Panicked now, he ran down the stairs and out the back door. The dim light of a new moon separated the fields from the forest and the treetops from the sky but otherwise did little to articulate the vast expanse of space before him. He made out a black vertical line on the hillside and thought it might be moving.

"Thomas!"

The line did not answer. Most likely it was only a tree trunk, its limbs lost in the lack of light. What if Thomas had collapsed somewhere and was lying by the creek or up on the hill or in the woods? If he were unconscious, it would be impossible to find him.

"Thomas!" he yelled more urgently. Even if he located a flashlight, its battery would probably be dead, and who knew if there were any replacements. Coyotes were afraid of humans, he reminded himself. But if the human were lying on the ground, weak and possibly unconscious? He strode briskly toward the field, which rose gradually to his left into a forest-capped hill. To the right stretched more forest, and within it, the creek.

"Thomas!"

His heart was racing as fast as his mind. Thomas had always loved the view from the hill. What was there to see now, though? He wished he had some idea of what time the boy had set out. The creek seemed more reasonable. "The creek, the creek," he muttered under his breath, and veered off to the right. He tripped over an exposed root, cursed it, and kept going.

"Dad!"

He stopped. Had he actually heard that?

"Thomas?" he yelled.

"Dad! I'm right here."

He turned around, toward the house, and there stood Thomas, silhouetted in the doorway. The sight brought on a mixture of confusion and relief, which then began to gather bits of anger at its edges. Once he got close enough to the house to make out Thomas's features, the anger fell away in another flood of relief.

"Where in the hell have you been?" he asked the boy.

"Upstairs," Thomas answered casually.

"You weren't in your room."

"I was in Emily's room."

"Didn't you hear me calling?" he said sternly.

"I had on headphones."

"What were you doing in Emily's room with headphones on?"

"I was listening to music. Is that a crime?"

"No, but . . ." Sighing, he patted Thomas on the shoulder and stepped past him into the room. "Jesus Christ. You know, you got me a little worried there."

"Sorry. Where'd you think I went?"

"I had no idea."

Instinctively, he crossed to the liquor cabinet, then reconsidered and sat down. One of the concessions he'd voluntarily made since his return was to try and drink less. He could have a couple of glasses of wine with dinner, but that was it.

Thomas locked the door to the outside and settled into the couch beside him. The energy generated by their reunion dissipated, leaving an awkward denouement during which they sat quietly listening to the music he'd put on earlier, both of them embarrassed by the false alarm set off by a flimsy set of headphones.

"Dad, is this Wagner?" Thomas asked after a while.

"Yes." He raised his eyebrows, genuinely impressed. "How did you know?"

"I can't believe you're listening to *Wagner*." He pronounced the name with distaste.

"Why not? I thought you liked my music. Is that why you were listening to headphones?"

"No, you can't hear it up there. *Dad*, the guy is a notorious anti-Semite."

"Yes. And he also happened to be an incredibly talented composer."

"Yeah, but . . ."

"But what? Are you going to dismiss the man's music because of his beliefs?"

"Sure. I mean I wouldn't *listen* to him."

"Really? Even if you immensely enjoyed his music?"

"Yeah. I wouldn't."

"Say you had a friend who you thought was a really great guy, but he made truly terrible art. Would you dismiss him as a person?"

"Of course not."

"Well, it's the same thing."

"No. It's not the same thing at all. We're talking about *character* here. We're talking about anti-Semitism, for God's sake. I mean, Dad, by listening to him, you're like totally turning your back on your people."

Joe chuckled. "My people?"

"Yeah, you are."

"I'm assuming that by 'my people,' you mean the Jews. First of all, may I remind you that my mother was Catholic, and that I am not Jewish. Second, I am not and have never been a religious man and do not consider anyone outside of my immediate family 'my people.' Now, beyond all of that, I have to tell you that you are being absurdly naive. All humans are flawed. All of us. So if you're going to utterly reject anyone who fails to live up to your ideals, you might as well crawl into a hole right now and forsake the entire lot of us."

"I can't believe you. This whole thing about you not being Jewish is so ridiculous and self-loathing. I don't understand why you can't accept who you are and who Grandpa was instead of constantly trying to be somebody else. And it doesn't only affect you either. By denying your affiliation with Judaism, you're only perpetuating the entire cycle of prejudice and shame. You're like practically an Uncle Tom or something."

"Thomas . . ." He smiled. "*Uncle* Thomas . . ."

Thomas rolled his eyes. "Dad, please."

"Don't you see that by lumping me into a group of people with whom I share nothing but a partial bloodline, you are exercising incredible prejudice yourself? I would appreciate your treating me as an individual rather than reducing me to an ethnic stereotype."

"Dad, I'm not. I'm just saying, I think it's kind of weird the way you're so embarrassed by being Jewish. Or half-Jewish. What-ever."

"And what gives you the impression that I'm embarrassed?"

"Because you're always trying to get into all these stupid Waspy clubs, and you're like horrified if somebody thinks we have a house in the Catskills instead of the Berkshires, and you have this whole thing about Mom's family and stuff."

"What whole thing about Mom's family? You know, your mother is so convinced that nobody could possibly find her appealing in her own right, that she makes up all kinds of reasons to explain anyone's interest in her."

"*Do you* find her appealing?" Thomas asked.

"Of course I do. I've been married to the woman for twenty years, for Christ's sake."

Thomas eyed him skeptically.

"You mean because of the thing with Gina?" he asked.

Thomas adjusted the pillow behind his head. "Yeah, I guess." He picked up the pillow again and gave it a few, plumping whacks, then shoved it down behind his lower back. "No. I understand why you had to leave."

"You do?"

"Yeah."

He studied his son, looking for further explanation of this surprising divulgence. After finally settling into position, Thomas returned his gaze, and it was apparent from his expression that he needed something he hoped Joe could give him.

"But, Dad?" he said solemnly. "You didn't just come back because you thought I was going to die. Did you?"

"No."

"Truthfully?"

"No. I came back because . . . I came back."

Uncomfortable with the turn the conversation had taken, Joe stood up. "Hungry?"

Thomas shrugged. "Sure."

As he made his way between the coffee table and the section of couch where Thomas was sitting, Thomas stuck his hand out and touched his pant leg. Surprised, he looked down to find his son staring up at him with wide, hopeful eyes.

"I'm glad you're back, Dad."

He nodded stiffly. "All right," he said, rubbing his hands together. "I'm going to get dinner together." Starting toward the kitchen, he called over his shoulder, "You hang out here and listen to Wagner."

"Actually . . ." Thomas looked at his watch. "How long do you think it'll be until dinner?"

"I don't know. Half an hour?"

Thomas scooted to the edge of the couch and began shoving his feet back into his sneakers. "Can we wait to eat until 7:45? I want to drive up the road and see if I can catch the last half of *Fresh Air*."

This was a ritual that Thomas and Laura had. Because they couldn't receive the station that carried their favorite radio show up here, they would drive up to the top of a nearby hill each evening and listen in the car.

Joe shook his head. "No. Come on. We just got up here. I don't want to get back in the car again."

"You don't have to come. I'll go by myself."

"No. That's ridiculous. I'm not letting you do that."

"Dad, are you serious? Why not?"

"Because—it's dark out, and you're tired."

"I am not tired!"

"Well, I'm tired. And I don't want you going out on your own."

Thomas sat back, throwing his hands up in surrender. "Whatever. I mean, I think that's really lame. But . . ."

"C'mon. Sit back and relax, listen to Wagner. You might find that you like him."

"No, *uh-uh*. I'm *at least* going to change the CD."

"Fine. Put on whatever you want."

"I'm going up to Emily's room. She's got all the good music."

"Tell me what you want, and I'll go get it."

"Jesus. I don't know. I'd have to look through them."

"Then I'll bring down a bunch, and you can look through them down here."

Thomas stretched out, resigned to his inactivity. Meanwhile, Joe headed up to Emily's room, where he grabbed as many CDs as he could from her dresser.

Thumping his way back down the stairs with an armful of

plastic-cased albums, he called out, "What kind of nerds are you kids?" He rounded the corner, adding, "This stuff's all from my generation. Don't you listen to anything current?"

"Sometimes."

He unloaded the CDs into his son's lap. Thomas shuffled through them, and selecting one, offered it up to him. "*Blood on the Tracks.*"

"Hmm," Joe replied. "Interesting choice. A Jew who changed his name from Zimmerman to Dylan."

"Okay, Dad. You've made your point."

"I'm not making any point. I'm just saying . . . Hey"—he shrugged exaggeratedly—"whatever."

Thoroughly enjoying himself now, Joe did a little dance as he made his way over to the stereo cabinet. "*Hava nagila, Hava,*" he sang, "*. . . nagila, Hava nagila ve nis'mecha!*"

As much as he may have wanted to, Thomas could not keep himself from laughing at this ridiculous performance. Joe, delighted that he had managed to amuse his son, sang with even greater fervor, snapping his fingers over his head. "Hava nagila, Hava nagila, Hava nagila ve nis'mecha!"

"C'mon," Thomas pleaded, putting his hands over his ears. "Put the CD in, and go make dinner." But when Joe looked at him, he was smiling, and the smile reminded Joe of the little boy squeezes Thomas used to give, yelling "Da-deeee!" at the top of his lungs as he gripped his father's knees with unbridled affection.

Joe continued loudly humming the rest of the song while he loaded the *Blood on the Tracks* CD into the player. And when he was done, he once again made Thomas laugh out loud as he danced his way out of the room.

Once he was in the kitchen, he selected containers of chicken, vegetables, and risotto from the refrigerator and transferred them to the microwave, then set about making a salad. From the other room, the music blared.

"I was standin' on the side of the *road*," he sang, emulating Dylan's distinctive croon, "Rain fallin' on my *shoes*. Heading out for the *East Coast*. Lord knows I've paid some *dues* gettin' *thruuuuuu* . . .

Tangled up in *blue!*" Exuberantly, he tossed the wet greens in the salad spinner and gave them a spin. "We'll meet again some *day* on the *avenuuuuue . . . Tangled* up in *blue!*"

He wondered whether he should have gone ahead and driven the boy up the road to listen to the radio show. It was kind of silly of him, he knew, but it had irked him that Thomas wanted to carry on this ritual during their weekend together. He'd read the boy's desire to do so as a wish that his mother were there instead of him, but he could see now that this probably wasn't the case. What a pleasant surprise it had been to hear Thomas say he understood why Joe had left with Gina. It was remarkable really, especially because it was the first time in his life that he'd ever heard Thomas reveal anything but blind devotion to his mother. And in this one, short statement, he felt the door creak open onto a whole new world of possibility. If his son understood his departure, who knew what else he understood, and accepted, about him. This was potentially the beginning of an entirely new phase in their relationship—a phase in which they might begin to speak to each other as two sympathetic and respectfully objective adults.

The microwave beeped to let him know that its contents were ready. Belting out the last lines of the song, he removed the food and dished it out onto two plates. "Point of *vyuuuuu . . . Tangled* up in *bluuuuue!*" The harmonica howled out its final verse as he drizzled the dressing over the salad with a flourish.

"Dinner's ready," he called. Tossing the empty containers in the garbage, he grabbed a bottle of Chianti off the shelf and took a corkscrew from the drawer. But when he inserted the metal spike into the cork, the cork split in two, and only part of it lifted out. He fiddled with the remaining bit of cork for a while, trying to puncture and retrieve it without letting it crumble. After he'd been at it for some time, it occurred to him that Thomas hadn't come in yet.

"Thomas?" he called out.

There was no answer.

He walked into the living room and found Thomas where he'd left him, stretched out on the couch.

"Thomas?" he said again.

The boy's eyes fluttered open.

"Dinner's ready," he said. "Do you think you could eat something?"

"Sure."

He went back into the kitchen, and by the time he got the cork completely out of the bottle and sat down to pour a glass, Thomas had shuffled in and seated himself at the table.

"Mmm. This looks good."

"Well, I wish I could take credit, but . . ."

"You bought it."

"That's right. I did buy it. And there's no cheese or bacon on anything," he added proudly, showing that he had kept Thomas's cancer diet in mind while shopping. "Do you want some wine?"

"No thanks."

They ate for a while without speaking, the clacking of their cutlery accompanied by Dylan's guitar.

"You know," Joe began, breaking the silence, "I introduced your sister to this music a long time ago because I thought she'd really get into the poetry of his lyrics. And she did."

"Huh."

Another bout of silence ensued.

"How do you think your sister's doing these days?"

"I don't know. Why don't you ask her?"

He couldn't tell whether there was an intended barb in this comment. "Well, I'd like to. But Emily isn't really talking to me much lately."

"C'mon, Dad. Get real. The fact of the matter is, you really hurt people's feelings, the way you keep dropping out. You can't blame this on Emily."

"Dropping out?"

Joe decided to push his luck and say something which, until this evening, he wouldn't have dared say. "Look. It's not the way you guys think. To tell you the honest truth, your mother decided some time ago that it would be best for your sister if—"

Thomas shook his head, annoyed. "I know. Emily told me. That has nothing to do with it. I'm talking about how everything has to be on your schedule. It's like all about what suits you. And whenever you don't feel like dealing with people, you just tune out or disappear."

Joe scowled, smarting from this unexpected attack.

"I mean, whatever." Thomas shrugged. "I'm just saying . . ."

"It sounds like what you're saying is that you're all furious with me."

"No . . ."

"No? Well, that's a pretty ugly picture you're painting of me there. From the sound of it, I don't see how any of you can stand to live with me."

"Dad, don't get all defensive. I'm saying this because I think it's important that you know what kind of effect you have."

He stared at his plate, refusing to look at Thomas. "Well, you got your message across loud and clear."

"Dad, c'mon. Please don't be like that."

As Joe shoveled food into his mouth, he could feel Thomas watching him, presumably waiting for him to recover from the sting to his pride and acknowledge that he understood what Thomas was saying. But as it eventually became clear to the boy that this wasn't going to happen, he started eating again, too.

When Joe finished, he got up, took his plates to the sink, where he deposited them loudly, and returned.

"Finished?"

"Yeah."

He took his son's plates and banged them down on top of the other two, then turned on the faucet and began to rinse and transfer all items to the dishwasher. He could feel Thomas watching him.

"Why are you so mad?"

Without pausing or looking up, Joe replied evenly, "I'm not mad."

Thomas let him continue for a few more minutes. Then, when the dishwasher was loaded, and Joe was wiping down the sink, he spoke, his voice soft and low so that Joe had to turn off the faucet to hear him. "I know you don't like criticism. I mean, who does? But, I've gotta say, Dad, you've always taken it especially badly."

"No. What I take badly is this condemning, self-righteousness with which you and your mother view everyone."

"Let's leave Mom out of this. That's between you guys, and I don't want to get into this whole thing of who's done what to the other. But I really don't think I'm being self-righteous or condemning or whatever."

"Well, you're entitled to your opinion."

"You should thank me, Dad. Because nobody else is going to say this stuff to you."

"I should thank you? That's not self-righteous?"

"No. That's the truth. I mean you can do what you want. It's up to you whether you choose to participate or not."

"I'm not participating? What am I doing right now? I'm spending the whole weekend with you."

"Yeah, fine. But you ask me how Emily's doing, and then you're like, 'Oh, well, I would be hanging out with her, but she's not really talking to me, and your mother blah, blah, blah . . . '"

Joe squeezed the water out of the dishrag and hung it over the faucet. With a heavy sigh, he dried his hands on his pants.

"Even though it seems like the last thing in the world your sister wants right now, I will try to spend more time with her. Would that satisfy you?"

"Dad, it's not about satisfying me—"

"Knock it off. I get it," he said, swiping his hand through the air as he walked out of the room.

Joe went to his bedroom and lay down on the bed until he heard the stairs creak under Thomas's sock-clad feet. Relocating to the empty living room, he built a fire and sat beside it, nursing his second and final glass of wine and squirming his way through a disastrous play that his friendship with the writer obligated him to read. As he neared the finish of the 140-page manuscript (if only the man had limited himself to a one-act), his attention was again drawn to the staircase and then to the figure of his son, who wordlessly crossed the room, flopped down on the sofa, and stretched out to take a nap.

"How you feeling?"

Eyes closed, Thomas answered softly, "So-so."

"Can I get you something?"

"Nah."

"Do you want me to put the music back on?"

"No. I like the sound of the fire."

Uneager to return to his reading, Joe let his gaze linger on Thomas's inactive body. The positioning of the cushion under the boy's head had caused the pink cap to pull away from his skull, exposing the pale dome of his naked scalp. The absence of a hair-line or a hat bill, as well as eyebrows, threw off the proportions of his face, making the eyes, the nose, and the mouth all seem to oc-cupy a small and oddly low portion of the skull. When the children were younger, their physical slightness made their vulnerability obvious. And that, combined with their newness, would have made any person a fool to believe that nothing would attempt to sneak in and prey upon them. From the moment the hospital entrusted their two-day-old son to their care, he and Laura became warriors, vigilantly looking out for the smallest sign of harm, and ready at any moment to leap to the newborn child's defense. But as the years passed, and first Thomas, then Emily passed safely through in-fancy and toddlerhood, they slowly let down their guards. By the time the children reached adolescence, he and Laura had both grown just short of complacent. They did, of course, hear stories of people losing grown children to accidents or disease, but like news of third-world starvation or the death and destruction of distant wars, these stories reconfirmed the strength of the hand they'd been dealt and increased their own sense of security, comfort, and good luck.

Soon, the purring of Thomas's nasal passages signaled that he was fast asleep. Joe decided that tomorrow afternoon, he would drive him up the road to listen to the radio show. The brash ring of the phone broke the silence, and he rushed to get it before it could wake Thomas.

"Ascher!"

His heart sank at the sound of Gina's voice. Apparently, through some fairly ingenious sleuth work, she had discovered his location and *happened*, she said, to be up at her country house as well.

"Gina," he said softly, "can I call you back?"

"No. You absolutely cannot."

"Well, I'm going to have to."

"Fine. I'm coming over."

"Please don't."

"Then you come over here."

"You're being unreasonable. I promise we'll get together soon, but I need to call you back."

"No. No, no, no, no, no. I know that's not going to happen. If you hang up this phone, I'm coming straight over."

He looked over at Thomas and saw that he was still sleeping soundly. To let Gina show up there would be an invitation for disaster. But he also knew that what he had to say needed to be said in person. She undoubtedly believed that the only reason he had returned to his wife was to help tend to their sick son—a belief planted and perpetuated by his own cowardly white lies. It was now imperative that he tell her the truth and sever any hopes she held of a future together with him. He did care a great deal for her. She was highly intelligent, amusing, and physically attractive in her own quirky way. But perhaps most important, she was passionate about theater, and particularly passionate about his work—and him.

"Fine," he relented. "I'll be there in twenty minutes."

Hanging up, he treaded softly across the room, observing the peacefulness of the scene before him: the boy slumbering on the sofa beside the crackling fire, the warm glow adding some color to his cheeks. Joe tiptoed past, confident that if Thomas woke in his absence, the boy would simply trudge off to bed under the assumption that he had already done the same.

When he arrived at Gina's, she had abandoned the hard line she'd taken on the phone for a gentler, more genial approach.

"Darling," she said with a sigh.

She called everyone *darling*, but over the last year, the tone with which she addressed him imbued the term with an increasingly intimate and possessive quality.

"Hello." He loaded the word with rigidity, letting her know right off the bat that his presence there did not translate as surrender.

She led him into her living room and offered him a drink. Owing to the difficulty of the conversation he was facing, he felt he deserved a vodka, and she poured out two generous drams from a bottle she kept in the freezer.

"To us," she said, as they had both done so often in recent months.

With a set jaw and an uninviting smile, he clinked his glass against hers and sat down. On the table was a pile of manuscripts, capped by one that lay prostrate, a pair of bifocals resting in the crotch of its seam.

"How's Thomas doing?"

"He's . . . ah, he's all right. The chemo seems to be working finally. So that's a relief. But, you know, it's still touch and go."

"Right. Well, let's hope it keeps working. That's encouraging news."

"Yes."

"And Emily?"

"Good. She's good."

Gina nodded. "Have you been writing?"

"No. I haven't had a lot of time."

"Well, listen. I talked to Ralph, and he loves the idea of bringing *The Morning Men* to Chicago, but he wants you to do it. He says he wouldn't care if Malkovich was begging to do it, he only wants to put it on if he's got you."

"Hmm. He'd be much better off with Malkovich."

"Oh, stop it."

"I need to stay at home."

"Well . . . sure. But in six months or so . . ."

"No, Gina."

The room fell horribly silent. There was no doubt that she understood his subtext. He had read hers immediately. In six months, when your son is well—or dead—and you're able to leave again, permanently . . . He had delivered the bomb. But her expression of hopeful anticipation told him that it had not detonated yet. She looked at him with pleading eyes, waiting for him to retract and defuse it. And as the silence grew heavier and more difficult to bear, he wished he could. All around, he saw evidence of a single life waiting to be turned into two: papers ready to be cast aside for more companionable company, the blanket strewn across the sofa, the half-eaten bowl of candy surrounded by empty wrappers, and the remote control—all of which had gone unused and forgotten whenever he'd been there. Where once he had marveled at Gina's self-sufficiency (before, after, and even during her short marriage)— especially pronounced in the way that she would drive up to the country, week after week, year after year, to spend her weekends alone—he now saw a void yearning to be filled. He had been allowed behind the curtain and made privy to her bouts of loneliness and depression, had witnessed the relief and welcome with which she accepted his company and the excitement brought on by sharing her space, her time, her body and soul. It was equally as wretched to be the one to rob her of all of this as it had been gratifying to be the one to bestow it, and he struggled to find a way to remove himself from that position without giving up all that was required in return.

"I'm sorry," he finally said, unable to find better words.

"Ascher," she answered evenly. "Don't be a fool."

Meeting her stare, he held firm.

With a hiss of deep aggravation, she stood up and began to pace the room.

"You know, I can see how she's got you guilted into this. It doesn't take a rocket scientist to figure out how she could turn this whole thing to her advantage. And I'm not saying that you should leave now. I absolutely understand that you need to be there. But to go right back into the same situation you've been in for years . . . You can't do that. I've seen how she tries to hold you back, and it's ridiculous. It's more than ridiculous. It's disgustingly mean and selfish. She's a horribly jealous, unhappy person, and she's determined to make you suffer!"

"Gina—"

"No, really. And completely aside from the way *I* feel about you, it's not fair to *you*. You deserve more than that. And I'm not saying this in some self-interested way. How do you think things are going to change? Once Thomas is well, and things are back to normal, do you really think anything's going to be different?"

She stood there, one hand on her hip, and stared him down. When she failed to get an answer, she began again. "Seriously. Think about that. Because once you've made your decision, that's it. I'm not going to sit around waiting for you to realize you've made a mistake. So you'd better be damned sure about what you want."

"I understand," he said quietly.

"And?"

"And I'm sure."

She paused for a long time, looking down at the floor. Eventually, she raised her eyes. "You're not going to be happy."

"That's a risk I'm willing to take."

She shrugged, the muscles of her face fighting to suppress a show of emotion. "What can I say? It's your decision."

He stood up and took a step toward her. "I'm sorry. I wish I could. I don't want to hurt you."

Again, she shrugged.

"Should I stay for a little while?"

"For what?" she asked, the hostility back in her voice.

"I don't know. I guess I'll go."

She nodded, clearly intending to remain where she stood. He didn't feel that she wanted him to come to her, but he felt strange simply walking out. He hesitated there for several seconds, trying to decide what to do next, then finally made up his mind to leave.

On the drive home, he conducted a mental debate with his conscience, arguing that he had made a grave error, then thinking that he should be congratulated for the strength of his resolve. It consoled him to consider how Thomas would have applauded his decision, and he wondered if things might have unfolded differently had it not been for the conversation they'd shared earlier that evening. He played Yo-Yo Ma's recording of Bach's Cello Suite number one, and the motion of the music seemed to propel the car along the dark country roads, pulling him around each curve with exhilarating centripetal force.

Lulled by the rhythm of the music and the meandering road, he almost did not recognize where he was when he rounded a bend and was met with the sight of the hill that stood between him and his house. Backlit by an unearthly cloud of blazing scarlet and amber, it sat there like the mother ship, emitting a glowing welcome to the line of wailing police cars, ambulances, and fire trucks streaming toward it from the opposite direction.

ON THE FLOOR OF HER WALK-IN CLOSET, LAURA was kneeling beside her suitcase, unpacking the summer clothes she'd taken with her to St. Barts for Christmas. She couldn't believe the vacation was over already. Normally, when she and Earl traveled, they took plenty of time to relax. But on this trip, even though they were at the beach, it seemed like she was in constant motion—taking tennis lessons, and snorkeling, and shopping in town—and whenever she did finally settle down on a chaise with a book, instead of reading or gazing at the sea, she found herself anxiously scribbling notes to herself on the back cover about things she needed to do for the wedding.

The doorbell rang.

She balled up the pile of garments she was holding in her arms and tossed them in the hamper as she rose to her feet. There was a definite purpose to Emily's visit; she just didn't know what it was. The anxiety in her daughter's voice had been audible over the phone this morning: "Hi, Mom, are you busy? Clay and I got back last night, and I was wondering if you wanted to get together—maybe go shopping or something." *Shopping.* As if it were something Emily did on a regular basis. Since they hung up, she'd been trying not to think too hard about all of the possible reasons Emily might need to see her, though she suspected that as usual, Joe had done something to upset Emily—perhaps she had finally reached him, and he had refused to come to the wedding after all.

In her haste, she knocked a basket of potpourri off her underwear shelf, scattering its contents all over the floor. Stepping carefully and cursing under her breath, she went to open the door.

Emily was holding the bottle of Chateau Lafite that she and Earl had given them as an engagement present.

"What's this?" she asked, stepping back to let Emily in.

"I thought you and Earl should enjoy it together," Emily said, breezing past and setting the bottle down on the red lacquer entrance-hall table. She didn't volunteer an explanation, and Laura decided not to press her. But it was all beginning to make sense now—the anxiety in Emily's voice, the sudden need to see her. Laura watched her fiddle with the ski pass dangling from the zipper of her black parka. As was ordinarily the case when she wasn't working, Emily was wearing jeans and sneakers, looking like she was about to head off on a hike.

"So," Emily said. "Where should we go?"

She seemed a little tired but not too upset. She certainly didn't look like she'd been crying. Laura wondered whether it had been her decision or Clay's. She assumed it had been hers.

"It's up to you," Laura said. "Have you eaten?"

"Yeah. I just had a huge brunch."

Out with friends, she thought, *trying to keep busy, keep her mind off the breakup.* She was going to have to try to keep things peppy, make sure she didn't get Emily down.

"Let's just start walking," Emily said.

"Great! Let me grab my coat."

They walked down Madison, and Laura kept the conversation light, telling her about the trip to St. Barts—the magnificent hotel perched on a cliff right over the water; the strange dance-music playing everywhere.

"It's got this crazy techno-beat." She smiled unsurely. "I guess that's what you'd call it. Really dance-clubby. And every now and then, these jungle sounds chime in." She laughed. "The first night, Earl thought there were monkeys outside the restaurant."

"That's funny," Emily said.

She seemed distracted, and Laura wished she could do a better job of holding her attention. She could only imagine how Emily was feeling right now. She and Clay had been together for over four years. It was going to be very strange to be single again. Most of her friends seemed to be pairing off, and it wouldn't be long, she imagined, before they started having children. Emily and Clay had already started talking about children themselves. Now who knew what was going to happen? She hoped against hope that there was still a chance they'd get back together.

In the store window they were passing, there was a bright red three-quarter-length wool coat on the mannequin, and Laura stopped to admire it.

"That's cute. Don't you think?" she asked cheerfully.

"M-hmm." Emily nodded.

"It's sort of Holly Golightly," Laura said. "Old-fashioned but still very young."

"You should try it on."

"Oh, not for me. I meant for you."

"Mom, I would never wear that."

"Why not? It's adorable."

"It's not my style."

She gave Emily a disappointed look. The way her daughter dressed always made her feel guilty somehow. She was so pretty and young. Why not take advantage of it?

"What?" Emily said. "Why don't *you* try it if you like it so much?"

"No, I'm too old for it. And the color's much too bright for me."

Emily turned away from the window with a shrug, and they began walking again.

After a while, Laura said, "So what's going on with the case? Earl said you told him it's over."

"Yeah, it is basically. We proved to the prosecutors that their main eyewitness testimony was perjured, and they dropped the case."

"That's terrific!"

"Yep."

"Emily, good for you! See? I knew you could do it."

For some reason, Emily seemed annoyed by this.

"Well, it wasn't me, Mom. It was a bunch of us, and it was mostly luck."

"Come on. Don't sell yourself short."

"I'm really not."

"Okay," she said, backing off.

"I've got to go upstate later to visit Ramon."

"Today?"

"Yeah. I'm not looking forward to it at all."

She didn't understand what this meant, but she got the feeling Emily wasn't in the mood to talk about it. So she left the matter alone, and they walked on for several blocks without either one uttering a word. She was surprised to find the avenue teeming with shoppers and decided that most of them must be tourists, still in town for the holidays. Since today was New Year's Day, they would probably be leaving in the next day or so, passing returning New Yorkers on the bridges, in the tunnels, or in the air as they made their way back to their various homes.

Emily broke the silence. "Listen," she said. "I need to talk to you about something."

Laura looked at her, prepared for the news she'd been waiting for.

Emily exhaled nervously. "I know you think that Clay's really great, and that he could make me happy for the rest of my life."

"Yes," she said sadly. "I really do."

"Well, it happens that I do, too, Mom. But I feel like you don't trust me to recognize that on my own."

She went over Emily's words again, trying to understand. "You mean you haven't broken off the engagement?"

"No," Emily replied irritably.

"Oh." She smiled. "I'm so glad. I thought when you brought back the wine—"

"I brought back the wine because I don't drink, and I need you to respect that."

She was surprised by her daughter's tone. "I understand," she said with a nod. "I'm sorry."

"I feel like you don't trust me to make the right decisions for myself. You know? Why do you have to have your hands in my business all the time?"

"I apologize," she said. "I didn't mean to be disrespectful by giving you the wine."

"It's not only that. There are lots of other things. Like why in the hell are you e-mailing and calling my fiancé and taking him out to lunch to talk about me behind my back?"

Laura kept walking, trying to figure out how to respond. This was exactly why she hadn't wanted Emily to know about her conversations with Clay—because Emily took everything wrong and viewed everything she did with suspicion. Eventually they reached the crosswalk and had to stop for passing traffic. She turned to Emily.

"I did talk to Clay a couple of times. But I think there's a real difference between talking to him because I'm concerned about you and talking about you behind your back."

"You didn't talk to him because you're concerned about me. If you were concerned about me, you would have talked to *me*. I've been so furious with him ever since he told me—so mad he'd betray me like that. But it wasn't his fault. You put him in that position. You could have ruined my relationship."

"What?" She looked at her daughter in disbelief. "That's ludicrous."

"No, Mom, it really isn't. You do all these things under the guise of doing them for me. But you're not doing it for me. You're doing it for you. I don't know why you're doing it for you. But if you really had my best interest at heart, you wouldn't tell my fiancé that I'm having premarital jitters. I mean seriously, Mom. Think about it."

Laura fought back her frustration. "Sweetheart . . . ," she tried. "I wish you wouldn't be so suspicious and angry all the time. This is such an amazing point in your life. You're about to get married, and Clay's so great . . ."

Emily rolled her eyes. "Here we go again—*Clay's so great*. And excuse me, but I'm not suspicious and angry."

"Why do you have a problem with my saying that Clay's great?"

"Because I'm great, too, Mom. What about me? Why do you always have to act like it's such a miracle that anybody could possibly like me?"

"Emily—"

"For as long as I can remember, you've taken some weird pleasure in putting me down. Like when I decided to go to law school and you were like: *What are you doing? You're a dreamer. You like poetry and acting* . . . As if I'm some kind of airhead who could never possibly make it through law school."

Laura kept walking, and there was a clip in her step now. She couldn't say what she was thinking: *I didn't want you to give up acting because you were so good at it.* Emily wouldn't believe it anyway.

Finally, she said, "I only want you to be happy."

Emily kept up the pace beside her. "I'd be much happier if you left me alone and let me make my own decisions."

Laura slowed, crossing her arms defensively. "Fine," she said. "I'll stay out of your life completely if that's what you want."

"Mom," Emily said a little more softly. "Of course I don't want you to stay out of my life completely. I'm just saying that what happens between me and Clay is between me and Clay. And I can't have you working behind my back to keep us together or tear us apart."

Gazing blindly at the various window displays, Laura continued to walk along. "It makes me sad you could ever think I'd try to tear your relationship apart or take pleasure in putting you down in any way."

"Well . . . ," Emily replied after a moment. "It makes me sad, too."

Abruptly, Laura stopped walking. "What do you want to do?" she asked. "I'm getting the feeling you don't really want to shop."

Emily stopped a few feet farther down the sidewalk, then turning, took a couple of steps back toward her again. "I should probably go home."

"All right."

Emily shifted awkwardly and looked around as if she wasn't quite sure what to do next. Finally she said, "I'll talk to you soon."

"Okay," Laura replied stiffly. "Happy New Year."

"Happy New Year."

Emily forced a smile, and with a wave, she turned on her heel and walked off.

Laura watched her head up the avenue, her sneakers pressing into the pavement with each gracefully determined stride. As she watched, she was reminded of how she used to try and try to keep Emily from tripping over her own shoes; the child had always been in such a hurry, and Laura would cringe at every fall, mortified by her clumsiness. Observing the way Emily walked now and knowing that she was in no way responsible for the change, it dawned on her that her children's mistakes and failures had always been their own, rather than the mistakes and failures of herself as a mother. Likewise their triumphs.

Her daughter's voice resounded in her head: *You do all these things under the guise of doing them for me. But you're not doing it for me. You're doing it for you.* What could Emily have possibly thought she was getting out of her conversations with Clay? It certainly hadn't been pleasant or easy to repeat her daughter's words to him and to see his reaction—although he was very nice about not shooting the messenger. He understood she had their best interest in mind, and he seemed grateful for that. Unlike Emily. *All these things*—as if this were simply one of many affronts. It was hard to have a child who thought of you this way. She longed for the days when she could turn to Thomas—or Joe—somebody who knew her and Emily, who knew their history, and knew how Emily always put a negative spin on everything she did. But both of those men were gone now.

Tourists swarmed over the crosswalk, ignoring the DON'T WALK sign and the honking horns. Preferring to wait, she stopped at the curb. *I probably shouldn't have reached out to Clay,* she thought, watching some pedestrians scamper out of a truck's path. She could see now how that was probably the wrong choice.

After going through the usual clearance procedures required of all prison visitors—including getting hand-wanded because the metal detector was broken as usual—Emily was escorted to the visiting room. She followed the guard down the hall, with its fluorescent tube lights and speckled linoleum floor, feeling her insides constrict in anticipation. There was something about visiting someone in prison that reminded her of visiting a hospital. While she'd been out in the world, going about her daily routines, the person she was about to see had been suffering in a way that she could never fully know—and because of this, there was the unease of not knowing exactly what state she would find him in. She passed through a seemingly endless corridor of padlocked, solid steel doors, and she reminded herself this was the last time she'd have to come to Coxsackie. For a while, at any rate. It was of course possible that at some point in the future, another case would require her to return, but this was certainly her last time to see Ramon here.

James Turly—Ramon's fellow inmate at Rikers Island Prison, and the person who had reported to the corrections officer that he'd seen Ramon leaving the scene of the crime—had confessed. What Emily had told her mother earlier that day was true: the case had basically solved itself. Unlike Ramon, who had no history of real violence, James Turly, a forty-five-year-old Caucasian male, was a twice-convicted murderer. As soon as it became clear that the corrections officer had not, in fact, seen Ramon leaving the bathroom himself, but was merely parroting Turly's claim, the prosecution dropped all charges against Ramon. And with very little effort, a confession was extracted: after a heated argument over twenty dollars the victim had purportedly stolen from Turly that morning, Turly had stabbed him in the neck with a shiv formed from the handle of a metal cup.

So the case was over, but Emily was still dreading the visit. The guard slowed in front of her and began to fish out of his pocket the long chain of keys hooked to his belt loop. She stopped and waited while he opened the door to the visiting room.

When she entered, Ramon was already seated as usual at the table in the middle of the room, lounging casually in his blue inmate's chair.

"Hi," she said.

"Hey."

He looked her up and down with his deep-set brown eyes. Over the last several months as they'd gotten to know each other, he'd stopped ignoring her whenever she entered the room. It was obvious that today, however, what had his attention was her outfit. She'd always worn her work clothes when she'd come to visit him—conservative skirts and suits—and she could tell he was surprised to see her in jeans and a sweatshirt.

"The office is closed," she explained, looking down at her clothes. "I'm still technically on vacation."

He nodded, and Emily thought she detected a brightness about him that wasn't ordinarily there. She pulled out the plastic chair opposite him, and took a seat.

"So," she said, "how are you feeling? You must be happy about getting out of here."

"Yeah."

"They tell me it's happening tomorrow."

"Yeah," he said again.

"What are you going to do?" she asked.

He narrowed his eyes. "What do you mean?"

"Well, do you have any plans? Like, where are you going to live?"

"I'll probably move in with my cousin."

Emily nodded. "Where does your cousin live? Red Hook?"

"Yeah."

"How old is he?—*he*?" she asked.

"Yeah. Twenty-two."

She nodded. "And have you thought at all about what you're going to do? Finish high school?"

"Man," he said, shaking his head, with the faintest hint of a smile. "Still with all the questions. Same as always. I thought we were done with that."

She smiled. "I'm sorry. Listen," she told him, "that organization we talked about before can really help you. They do counseling, job training, everything. If you run into problems with your housing or anything, they can help with that, too. I really want you to promise me you'll hook up with them as soon as you get out of here."

He nodded.

"It's going to be hard. Getting out after all this time is great. But it's hard, too."

"I know," he said.

She smiled. "I know you know."

"Yeah."

"There's another thing." She hesitated for a moment then said, "I have some bad news."

Putting his palms together, he brought them to his mouth so that his fingertips rested under his nose. He closed his eyes and waited.

"I went to the shelter," she told him. "And your dog, Moses. He died."

His eyes popped open.

"I'm so sorry," she said.

"You went to the shelter?" he asked. "In Red Hook?"

"Yes."

"To look for my dog?"

She was about to explain that she'd meant no harm, when he burst into laugher. His laugh was loud and raucous as if this were the funniest thing he'd ever heard. She couldn't understand why he was laughing so hard, and gave him a questioning look. But he just kept laughing and laughing.

And then he stopped. He was silent for a while, staring at the floor. Then he put his hand over his mouth and started to cry. He wasn't crying as hard as he'd been laughing. But there were tears in his eyes, and his chest heaved a little. For the first time ever, she could see—really see—that the person before her was only nineteen years old.

She felt terrible. "I'm so sorry," she whispered.

After a while, he wiped the tears away with the back of his hand. Then with a big sniff, he shook his head. "Nah—it's okay," he told her. "Dogs die."

He tapped his heart two times with his fist, then held out his hand. It was clear to her now that he wasn't crying about his dog. She grasped his hand firmly. What she had done was nothing. It had been so easy—too easy for someone else not to have done it. But nobody else had.

"You've got my number," she reminded him as they said goodbye. "Call me."

"I will."

But she knew he wouldn't call unless he got into trouble. Before turning to go, she took in his face one last time: the deep-set eyes, the hard lines cut into his forehead, and the fleshiness of his cheeks that for a brief moment today, when he was crying, looked like baby fat.

↬

Lying fully clothed on top of his motel bed, Joe reached over to the ice bucket beside him, fished the last handful of shrunken ice cubes out of the water, and dropped them into his glass. He lifted the bottle and poured, noting that it felt remarkably heavy for being nearly empty. Suspecting that the liquor company might have reduced the weight of the contents and increased the thickness of the glass, he looked at the label. It took him a while to make out the print, but the number confirmed that there was no less liquor in the bottles than before—assuming the number could be trusted. He shifted the bottle from hand to hand then set it back on the table. All but the two glasses he and Amanda drank last night had been consumed in this one sitting. And still, he was waiting for the horrible electric buzz to leave his system and grant him a little peace.

Today was the start of a new year—the ideal opportunity to turn over a new leaf. He was at the beginning of something great. No pressure. Don't put the pressure on. This was not punishment. He had already been absolved. His son had cancer, for God's sake. And as for his daughter—well . . . there was a part of him that had come to believe the version of himself that others saw and the version of his story that they told. But nobody knew the full story.

He stood up, and taking the ice bucket with him, left the room. In order to avoid booby-trapping himself, he walked a couple of doors down before emptying the bucket at the curb. When he finished, he stood there for a while, enjoying the cold air, which after hours spent in a cramped and heated room, brought a welcome cleansing. He looked up at the lone star above, twinkling vigilantly amid the clouds, then wondered if those clouds would bring more snow.

Equipped with Cheez-Its and ice, he returned to the room. And after washing the entire pack of greasy, fluorescent orange crackers down with a drink, he sat down at his makeshift desk, picked up the phone, and dialed information. It was a shot in the dark that he would get anywhere, which was probably the only reason he tried. But, low and behold, when he punched in the number of the university, a real live operator picked up the line.

"Yes," he said, "I'm trying to reach a faculty member by the name of Amanda Ritter. She's in the psychology department."

"One moment, please." There was a lengthy pause that lowered his hopes considerably, and then, "Extension 201. I'll connect you."

As he expected, Amanda did not answer. But there was a voice-mail announcement, which gave another number for "urgent" calls. He scribbled down the number and debated calling it. Finally, sure that she would not answer this one either, he dialed.

"Hello?" She picked up on the second ring. He was as surprised to hear her voice as if it had been she who called him.

"Amanda?"

"Yes?"

"Joe."

When she did not immediately respond, he added, "Ascher."

"Yes, I know. How are you?"

Her voice sounded hollow and remote.

"Good. I take it you got home safely."

"Yes."

"I'm glad."

"Did I give you my phone number?"

"No. I called the university. Amazingly enough, there's an operator on duty at this time."

As he said this, he became aware that he was slurring his words, but hoped it was slight enough that she didn't notice.

"It's a twenty-four-hour service," she replied.

"Uh-huh. It's very convenient."

"Mmm."

He could hear from the questioning tone of her voice that she was wondering if he had a reason for calling.

"Well, I thought I'd call and make sure you got home safely."

"Thank you."

"I had a very nice time last night."

"Yes. So did I."

"Good. You know, I went into town for lunch and asked at the diner if they had black-eyed peas. And I think the waitress thought I was out of my mind."

"Really?"

"Yes. Needless to say, they didn't have them. You were right. I'm not sure the waitress had ever heard of them, frankly. She asked if I wanted potato salad instead."

Joe waited for some sign of amusement but did not receive even a polite laugh.

"My son died of pneumonia," he told her.

"Excuse me?"

"I thought you may have been wondering . . . I told you last night that he didn't actually die of lymphoma."

"Yes. I remember."

It was clear from her tone that she didn't understand why he was telling her this now. He assumed she was no longer interested in the specifics, but he had to tell her anyway.

"It was a freak accident. Something—a bird's nest, they think— was in the chimney. A spark from the fire in the fireplace came up and caught it, and the whole house burned down. Because of the smoke and his weakened condition, his lungs filled with fluid. I should have been there with him when it happened, but . . . I wasn't."

There was a silence on the other end.

"Who would ever guess?" he said. "A bird's nest."

"I'm sorry."

"Anyway." He realized there was nowhere left for them to go on this particular topic. "I was thinking we might meet at the hotel sometime for a drink or dinner."

Again silence.

"Or somewhere else if you'd like. I could come there."

"I don't think so, Joe. I'm sorry. It seems to me it would be better to leave things as they are. I hope you understand."

"Absolutely. Well . . . I wish you the best."

"Thank you. You, too."

He hung up. Across the parking lot, the window of the motel office hung like a bright yellow picture on a wall of black sky. Through it, he could see the Indian manager sitting behind the front desk, apparently watching TV. He should have realized as soon as she told him she was a psychologist that it would end this way. She had drawn a red herring across her trail by complimenting his work and by divulging in such an open, confessional manner, the story of her son. It sickened him now to think how he had offered up his own son in return, tossing Thomas before her like common barter. Whatever she thought of him, whatever he had said or done to transform her admiration into disrespect, he was well rid of her. The only thing that bothered him was that Thomas still rested there in her mind, tainted by a wrongful proximity to that angry fuck-up who slept on the streets.

He poured the remainder of the vodka into a glass and drained it. Then, feeling exhausted, he laid his head down on the desk. *Let's drink a cup o'kindness yet* . . . the words came to him as if they were drifting up from the sandy bottom. What were those words, and where did they come from? Oh, yes . . . *Let's drink a cup o'kindness yet for auld lang syne, and you can pay for your pint cup, and I can pay for mine.*

Who was there now? Who was left to share a cup of kindness with him? *Ingrid*. He laughed bitterly.

And yet he had to admit that her kindness was what he wanted most right now. A simple acknowledgment that he wasn't so monstrous after all. Perhaps if he explained everything, if he told her the truth . . . He was flawed, but he wasn't a monster. He could still help her.

He pulled the cell phone out of his pocket. It felt tiny in his hand, the buttons even tinier, and he struggled clumsily to punch in the right number with his thumb. As he fumbled with the phone, it slipped, and bouncing onto the floor, rolled under the TV stand that served as his desk. Carefully, he lowered himself down to the ground and onto his stomach, then stretched his arm out, groping around for the phone.

From somewhere back near the wall, he heard a muffled voice. "Hello?"

His fingertips finally made contact with the device. "Hello?" the voice said again as he finally managed to get the phone in his grasp.

"Hello?" he said, bringing it to his ear.

"Dad?"

"Emily? Is that you?"

"Yeah?" She sounded tired and confused, but not irritated. "Is everything okay?"

"Yes."

There was a long silence while he searched for the right words. His head was pounding, and he wasn't thinking well.

Finally, Emily's voice broke in again. "Dad, it's two a.m. Can I call you tomorrow?"

"Your brother—listen, I need to tell you. Thomas. He had pneumonia. It was a bird—a nest."

"You're drunk."

"No, but you don't . . . you don't understand. You don't know."

"Dad," she said impatiently.

"Listen to me. Okay? Listen. It wasn't what you think."

"Dad, please. Let's talk in the morning."

"Don't be so difficult."

"Difficult? You've been back for months, and you haven't called me once. And now you phone me up drunk in the middle of the night—"

He interrupted her. "I knew you'd be like this. That's why I didn't call."

"Like what?" she asked angrily.

"You think what happened to your brother—that I'm some horrible monster."

"I'm not going to have this conversation right now."

"Yes. Now," he insisted.

"I'm hanging up. We can talk in the morning when you're sober."

"No, wait. Emily. Just wait."

But she was gone.

He shouldn't have mentioned the pneumonia and the bird—all of which she already knew. He should have cut straight to the chase. Frustrated, he dialed again. The phone rang four times, then went to voice mail.

He dropped the phone and lay down on the floor, defeated.

Closing his eyes, he began immediately to drift off. *We two have paddled in the stream from morning until noon, but oceans lie between us now since days of auld lang syne. So take my hand, my trusty friend, and give a hand o'thine. And we'll take a right good drink together for auld lang syne. For auld lang syne . . .*

When he opened his eyes again several hours later, morning was beginning to break. He had been dreaming, and the image of a pumping heart—fist-sized and deep, dark red, gushing blood with every thunderous beat—was seared on his brain. He stood up and, feeling unsteady, collapsed onto the bed. His head was throbbing, and his mouth was sour and cottony. Slowly, he got to his feet again. *I'm fine,* he told himself, *I know what I'm doing.* He got his jacket from the closet, stopped in front of the mirror to smooth his hair down, then, opening the door, walked out.

⌒

The lights of a police car flashed across Ingrid's face: red, blue, red, blue, red . . .

He said we were going to the beach for ice cream cones. And I didn't believe him. But he really wasn't joking. He drove me all the way to the beach. And there was a playground there, and there was a man selling ice cream out of one of those little trucks.

We were the only people there. I mean it was totally . . . deserted. And he got us both ice cream cones. At first I wasn't going to have one because I'm a Buddhist and everything. But he bought one for me anyway. And we hung out on the playground while we ate the ice cream, playing on the slide and the swings and stuff like I used to do with my dad. Then I went off and started climbing on this jungle gym, and I yelled for him to look at me. And that was when I realized he was gone.

We had driven over the same bridge on the way there. He'd pointed out the window at the water, way down below as we were going over it, and he'd said, "Imagine what it would feel like to fall from something this high."

⌒

When the cab driver pulled up to the Marrisy Motel, Emily was sure one of them had made a mistake. Convinced that her father was too much of a snob to stay in this fleabag motel, she told the driver to wait while she ran inside and asked.

In the office she found an Indian man pacing back and forth behind the desk and talking on a cell phone. While she waited for him to hang up, she flipped through a brochure on a river outfitting company. Eventually he smiled warmly and asked if she would like a room.

"No," she replied. "I think that I'm in the wrong place. Is there possibly another inn—not a motel, but something . . . I don't know. Is there another place with a similar name?"

Puzzled, he said, "I don't think so."

"Hmm. Well . . . I don't know if my father was staying here, but . . . Joe Ascher? He had a heart attack the other night."

His eyes brightened with recognition. "Yes, yes," he nodded, evidently proud to provide a piece for her puzzle. "They found him outside. On the sidewalk."

"Oh." She took this in, wondering who *they* were. "Well, I need to pack up his things and check out for him."

He kept nodding enthusiastically. "You want to pay?"

She was a bit surprised that he didn't express any concern for her father, even if only to be polite.

"Sure. Let me go pay the driver first. I can call for another cab later, right? When I'm ready to leave?"

"Of course."

She resented having to handle her father and his affairs all alone. Her mother had spoken at length to the people at the hospital and made a number of requests on her ex-husband's behalf. And Clay had offered to drop everything and come with her. But she was the only living person on the planet who had any real responsibility toward her father, and unless something drastic happened either to her or to him, that was how it would remain.

And if he died—what then? She would have to arrange for the body to be transported back to New York, have to organize the funeral, make the calls to his friends and colleagues, select the music, prepare a eulogy to give at the service . . . He had looked so pitifully small and feeble today asleep on the bed. Despite his fairly average physical size and the bloating around his face from the drinking, he appeared so shrunken and helpless as he lay there in that enormous railed-in bed, eyes closed, hooked up to bags of medication and surrounded by machines. What was he thinking, hiding out here in this fleabag motel in the middle of nowhere? He might have at least called to let her know that he wasn't feeling well.

Before she walked out of the office, she told the Indian man, "He had a quadruple bypass, by the way." But the man either didn't hear her correctly or didn't hold much affection for her father, because he smiled broadly and nodded, then reminded her to return the key to him before she left.

"Believe me," she told him, "I'm not taking it as a memento."

Already the idea of entering her father's hotel room and going through his things made her somewhat uncomfortable. So she was particularly taken aback when she spotted the DO NOT DISTURB sign on his door. He had obviously left the room with the expectation and intention that nobody—not even an anonymous housekeeper—would enter in his absence. To open the door would be to disregard his wishes. She was also beginning to feel anxious about what she might find. Who knew, really, what he was up to here?

As she was debating whether or not to enter, she noticed that there was something oddly familiar about the sign. Made from what appeared to be homemade paper flecked with bits of woody fiber, it was not weatherproof. Nor was it remotely typical of anything she had ever seen on the door of any other motel room. Removing the sign from the knob, she turned it over and examined the back: PLEASE MAKE UP MY ROOM. At once, she was struck with the recollection of placing the same sign on her own door that very morning, and she realized that her father must have taken the sign with him when he checked out of the Jefferson. With a little laugh to herself, she folded the sign into her purse. This was her father as she had always known him—vain and proud and concerned with appearances to the point of absurdity. If she knew him at all, she knew that he was just the kind of man to distinguish himself from his fellow motel guests by hanging out a sign from the most expensive place in town.

Emboldened, she inserted her key in the knob and opened the door. The space seemed reasonably tidy, and at least upon first sight, did not reveal anything that caused her instant embarrassment or dismay. The beds were both made, and her father's clothing hung neatly from a bar in an alcove adjacent to the bathroom.

Again, she experienced a moment of humor as she detected, amid the folds of clothing, the fancy, mahogany hangers with the gold goose insignia of the Jefferson Inn. Unlike the DO NOT DISTURB sign—which he'd clearly taken for show rather than for any practical purpose—the hangers, she knew, had been stolen not for their gold insignia but for the elegant curve of the wood. Even if her father was staying in the crappiest of accommodations, he was not going to walk out into the world each day with a wrinkled jacket.

She, on the other hand, did not care how his jackets looked. And so she folded them, two or three at a time, into the suitcase. It felt strange to be packing somebody else's clothes, and it reminded her of her mother packing up Thomas's room, a lengthy process that began a day or so after the funeral and stretched on for many weeks. She could still see her mother sitting on the edge of Thomas's bed, her shoulders hunched with grief, her face hidden by the hair hanging limply from her bowed head. Her hands, usually clenched around each other or moving agitatedly about, rested in her lap with such uncharacteristic surrender that Emily would have thought she was sleeping if it weren't for the iron erectness of her spine. It was unclear now whether her mother had sat there day after day, her body frozen in a single posture, or whether this was a passing moment captured like a photograph. Whatever the case, her mother did manage eventually to move off of the bed and divide the entire lot of her son's possessions into different piles, then boxes, according to each item's designated fate. At the time, Emily could not fathom her mother's desire to take on such a project. She herself found it too difficult even to set foot in that room. Over the years, however, she had come to envy her mother's experience, holding it responsible for that sense of closure which continued to elude her father and herself.

As she shoved the last pair of trousers into the bag, something gold sitting on top of the dresser caught her eye. Looking more closely, she saw that it was an earring—a sparkling red gem on a post. Whether it belonged to a hooker, a serious love-interest, or a casual acquaintance of her father's she had no idea. And since she certainly wasn't going to ask, she supposed she'd never know.

Next, she noticed the empty liter of vodka standing in the waste-basket. Disappointed but not surprised, she pressed on. The desk her father had made out of a TV stand was messier than she first real-ized, and among a number of food wrappers and old newspapers, she was intrigued to find a pile of Dictaphone tapes. Earlier that day, when she'd found the Dictaphone among his things at the hospital, and placed it beside him on the bed, she'd merely thought of it as a comforting object he liked to have on him at all times—something of a security blanket or even an affectation. It hadn't occurred to her he'd actually used it lately. But since her father had always filled a number of tapes with oral ramblings before organizing his ideas into a play, the discovery of all these tapes on his desk implied that he might be working again. She stood there for a moment, trying to register what this meant. It was possible she had misjudged him.

She gathered up potato chip bags and candy wrappers, and tossed them into the wastebasket. "Jesus," she said out loud. "No wonder the man had a heart attack."

Suddenly, she was stopped short by the sight of a tattered, old snapshot propped up against the base of the desk lamp. Picking it up, she saw that she was about half her current age, teetering on the brink between childhood and adulthood. The photograph per-fectly captured the optimism and giddy anticipation with which she faced her future, making her vividly remember how old and sophisticated she'd felt at the time and how eager she'd been to put her girlhood behind her. It was amusing to see how young and un-sophisticated she actually looked, dressed in an outrageously over-sized men's blazer with a plush, bunny rabbit backpack slung over her shoulder—a sure indication that whether she was aware of it or not, part of her still clung desperately to her girlhood. Beside her stood Thomas in his faded red baseball cap and underneath it, a full head of healthy hair. His arm was thrown casually around her shoulder, and he was bending toward her, his head resting affectionately on top of her own.

She wanted to believe that the presence of the snapshot on her father's desk was proof that he shared with her a certain nostalgia for those years and a wish to rekindle the closeness they'd once shared. However, the fact that a telephone sat a matter of inches from that propped-up photo kept her from getting carried away. Over the last several months, they'd both made very little effort at contact. As a lump formed in her throat and her eyes began to sting, she warned herself to keep a safe distance.

You have to pretend they're strangers, she could hear her brother say. Trying to keep her mind on the task at hand, she tucked the picture into the dictionary. But as she stacked the dictionary together with the other books, she was interrupted by a strange, high-pitched wail, which she was startled to realize came from her own mouth. The sound of it—and the accompanying recognition that she was buckling under Thomas's weight—crushed any last bit of resolve to steel herself against the memory of that awful day she'd smashed him against the hospital wall. All afternoon today, she had been struggling not to remember as she waited to see her father, inhaling the disinfectants and cleaning fluids that didn't quite mask the smells of illness, death, and decay, and watching other patients' red-eyed family members, huddled together outside the elevators or standing individually in a corner or behind a column as they silently sobbed. Her father, when she had finally seen him, had had a giant blue tube shoved down his throat, connecting him to a machine that breathed for him.

Taking a seat at her father's makeshift desk, she could feel the tightening ache of an oncoming meltdown. Slowly reaching into her purse for her phone, she managed to keep it together until she heard Clay's voice.

"Emily?"

She responded with a mournful yelp, which once again surprised her by its foreignness. It was not a sound she thought herself capable of making.

"Emily?" he repeated nervously.

Sniffling and snorting, she managed a pathetic "uh-huh."

"What's happened? Are you okay?"

The panic in his voice made her step away from herself for a moment. "I'm fine," she sniffed. "Nothing happened."

"What's wrong? Is your dad all right?"

Now that he sounded calmer, her own emotions started to run rampant once again.

"Em? What's going on?"

She couldn't speak.

"I wish you'd talk to me. You're freaking me out. Did anything happen?"

"I'm such a mess," she finally blurted out between sobs.

"What are you talking about? Why are you a mess?"

"Because I am. I'm a mess. Please don't leave me," she pleaded.

"Emily, I'm not leaving."

She started to cry again. "Thomas never even got to have a serious girlfriend. And I get to have you. You know? I mean it's so unfair."

"Well . . ."

"And," she wailed, "and I was so awful to him."

"No. Shh. C'mon, Em. I know that's not true."

"Yes, it is. I was completely awful. I was so goddamned screwed-up and awful, and he was never anything but nice and sweet and . . . wonderful. It's not fair. It's not fair that I'm the one who gets to be happy."

"Well, don't worry. You don't really seem all that happy."

She smiled through her tears.

"I promise we won't be too happy together," he went on. "I'll make sure that you get your share of misery."

"I'm sorry," he said when she didn't laugh.

"Clay?"

"Yeah?"

"I'm scared my dad's going to die."

"What did the doctors say?"

"They said he's going to be fine."

"Well, then he's probably going to be fine."

She told him about the machine that was breathing for him and the way the nurses came in every few minutes to check the equipment and change his tubes, putting on special plastic gloves that they threw away and replaced with new ones every time they touched anything. She explained how her father looked like a zombie, and how she had sat with him all afternoon, talking to him without knowing whether he was even able to hear her.

"Emily," Clay said. "He'll be okay."

"Yeah. I know. You're right."

She was relieved to feel herself finally regaining control.

"Well, I should go. I have to finish packing up his stupid hotel room."

"Are you sure *you're* okay?"

"Yeah. I'm fine. Thanks." She paused, then added, "I love you."

"Love you, too."

After she hung up, she pulled the photograph out of the dictionary and looked at it one more time. This adolescent girl—though self-consciously hiding behind overly long and limp brown bangs—showed an openness and exuberance that seemed at such odds with the way Emily thought about herself, it made her feel like she was looking at a painting in which the artist had taken the liberty of lightening and brightening his subject for a more pleasing affect. And though she'd been an actress at the time, she knew what she saw in the picture was something that could not be acted. About a year or so after that photograph was taken, however—some time shortly after her brother's death—she had entered the biggest acting job of her life. In attempting to emulate Thomas, she had discarded herself somewhere along the wayside.

And yet she had to acknowledge that some good had come of it as well. In many cases—possibly even most cases—by making the choices she felt her brother would have made, she had made the right choices. God only knew where she would be now had she continued hurtling at breakneck speed down the same crazy road she had started on around the time she hit adolescence. She thanked

Thomas's spirit for guiding her down a path that had led not only to a sensible and meaningful career but, most important, led her to Clay.

She wanted desperately at that moment to pick up the phone and call her brother.

"Hey, guess what?" she would tell him. "I finally got my own place."

Twelve weeks had passed since Thomas's death, and the apartment where he'd grown up was slowly letting go of him. Clothing and other possessions had been sent off to Goodwill, and the family was gradually growing used to not hearing his voice and his footsteps. Only rarely now would they catch themselves expecting him at a certain time or mentioning him in the present tense.

The apartment was extremely quiet, like a door had slammed closed, shutting out all the noise of the period just before he died. During that time, when he was in the hospital with pneumonia, Laura and Joe were fighting all the time—as were Laura and Emily, and Emily and Joe. But these days, none of them ever raised their voices above a polite conversational volume.

At the moment, Emily sat alone in the living room, curled up on the window seat, studying for her math final.

Laura was in the library, trying to remember where she'd left her keys. Joe would be back any minute. She scanned the desktop, and not finding them there, hurried into the living room.

"Hey," Emily said.

"You haven't seen my keys, have you?" she asked, reaching her hand down between the cushions of the couch.

"No. I don't think so."

Laura noticed something on the floor behind the couch and stooped down to pick it up.

"Found them?" Emily asked.

"No. It's a piece of pretzel."

Emily smiled disdainfully. "God, it's like Hansel and Gretel or something. And he's always got crumbs and stuff on his face, too."

"I know." Laura sighed.

"What's the deal?"

"Stress, I guess."

"He'd better stop soon. It's making him fat."

Laura looked around the room, still trying to locate her keys. "Well—"

"Are you going out?" Emily asked.

"Yeah. I'm going to run get my hair cut."

"I can let you back in. I'll be here."

"You will?"

"Yeah. I've really got to study hard for this."

Laura went over and sat down on the window cushion beside her. "I thought your teachers had all said they were going to cut you some slack on the finals. Didn't they even say you could take them late if you needed to?"

"Yeah, but I'd rather get it out of the way. And besides, I don't really feel like I need the extra time."

"Okay. I just don't want you to push yourself too hard."

Emily nodded. "I won't."

She rubbed Emily's back, and Emily smiled.

Then she got up, and as she crossed the room, Emily called after her. "Oh, by the way, there're some phone messages by the door."

"Thanks."

Walking through the front hall, she thought about how drastically Emily's behavior had changed. She'd become so responsible— and so compliant. It was hard to see her taking everything so seriously all of a sudden. In some strange way, she'd feel relieved if Emily went out all night tonight and smoked pot with her friends.

Finding the phone messages on the entry-hall table, she shuffled quickly through them before throwing them away. Her friend Sarah had called for the third time this week. She was sure it was about the invitation she'd sent for the birthday dinner for Earl Gleason. She didn't even know who Earl Gleason was. Presumably, Sarah was only trying to get her out of the house. It would probably be good for her to see some friends, just as she knew it would be good for Emily, but she couldn't face it right now. First, she wanted to get everything cleared up at home: finalize the divorce, figure out where she and Emily were going to live. She didn't want to stay here, and she knew Joe would be happy to keep the apartment. She opened the drawer of the hall table, and there were her keys. The housekeeper must have put them away. As she took them out, she noticed a tiny blue rubber band in the back of the drawer. It was one of Thomas's from when he wore braces, way back when he was thirteen. She'd been finding the little blue circles here and there for years now. She leaned on the hall table for support. She was constantly getting ambushed these days.

She heard the key turn in the door. *Shit.*

"Hi," Joe said, stepping in.

He was carrying a shopping bag from a men's clothing store, and she wondered what on earth he'd been doing all afternoon. Surely he couldn't be concerned with updating his summer wardrobe.

She opened her purse and dug through it. "I'm on my way to the hairdresser."

"Oh."

She started for the door, and he moved out of her way.

"Some more insurance forms came today," he said. "Medical stuff."

She nodded. "Go ahead and put them on my desk."

He looked tired, and Emily was right—he was starting to put on weight. Quite a lot of weight in fact, probably ten or fifteen pounds. Strange she hadn't noticed before.

He held the door for her, and she went out and rang for the elevator. She waited a moment, then turned back to him.

"Emily has to study tonight," she said. "So I'm just going to pick up some dinner on my way home. What are you going to do?"

She could sense him trying to read her.

"I guess I'll go out," he said.

For a moment, she felt sorry for him and considered inviting him to join them. And then, remembering that he was the one who'd done this to them, she held firm. They waited in silence until the elevator came. Then she got in and heard him shut the door.

Joe went back to Thomas's room, where he'd been sleeping for the last few weeks. The room had been stripped of most of Thomas's belongings. The only item remaining that strongly bore his personality was a coat rack he'd made in a woodworking class out of a bunch of birch he'd hauled back from the country. Joe hung his shopping bag on one of the hooked branches and wandered off in search of Emily.

"Hello," he said when he finally found her in the window seat of the living room. "Which one's tomorrow?"

"Math," she answered without looking up from her textbook.

He sat against the arm of the sofa and waited in vain for her to give him her attention, then got up and wandered off to the kitchen. Pulling out the Arts section from its place under the fruit bowl, he sat down at the counter and began to thumb through the movie listings. But the sheer volume of information and choices—titles, times, locations, etc.—soon proved overwhelming, and he figured it would be much easier to walk to the nearest theater and see what was playing.

At one point on the way over, a uniformed nanny pulled up alongside him with a baby carriage. He peered down into the silent wonderland—a sleeping infant surrounded by white cashmere. He thought about Emily as he had left her just now, with her nose in her textbook. In some ways, it didn't feel like such a long time ago that he was still reading to her. He remembered so clearly coming up with elaborate explanations for the parts of her storybooks that she didn't—and he didn't want her to—understand. *Don't go into Mr. McGregor's garden, mother rabbit said.* So went the classic tale. *Your father had an accident there, and Mrs. McGregor put him into a pie.* He was constantly amazed by how violent most children's books really were. "Mrs. McGregor was angry," Joe told his kids, "because Peter's father kept eating her blueberries. So, to teach him a lesson, she plunged his head into a blueberry pie. It took all the bunny neighbors a full day to lick all the pie off of Peter's father and get him all clean again." Emily, in particular, loved the licking part and would laugh and laugh whenever he told it.

And then there was the dog in Greece, who had followed them to the beach every day. They'd never learned his actual name, but Laura, inspired by the dog's obscenely spectacular endowment, had laughingly come up with Zeus. On their last day, the dog was lying dead in the road—hit by a car. Joe told the kids that Zeus was basking in the sun. "Bask," Emily repeated over and over—fixating on it as if somehow she knew there was something mysterious there to figure out. Afterward, back in New York, he'd sometimes catch her lying in a patch of sunlight pouring through the living room window—calling out cheerfully, "Daddy, look! I'm basking in the sun!"

Even in those days, he'd known it wouldn't always be so easy. But whatever inkling he'd had then of how helpless he would feel when he could no longer shelter his kids—and how painful that would be—he could have never foreseen the kind of pain he'd felt a few weeks ago on that hillside as he watched his daughter scatter her brother's ashes.

When he got to the theater, he discovered that none of the movies would start for at least another hour. He could go have dinner alone, he supposed. But he wasn't hungry. And home was off-limits until Laura and Emily ate. He certainly didn't feel like walking. After an upsetting meeting with Anthony, the director of his last play, he'd walked around all afternoon, finally going into a store and buying himself a belt to have something to do.

Ultimately, he went into one of the movies that was already playing, even though it was halfway over, and with a bag of popcorn, settled into the dark.

Lying on the bed after dinner, surrounded by her math books and notes, Emily stared up at the poster of Buddha hanging on the wall above her dresser. There was no passion or excitement in his face.

Nor was there any sign of yearning or pain. He looked only serene—beautifully, unshakably serene. She pushed herself up off the pillows and crossed her legs. Then, letting her hands rest lightly on her knees, she closed her eyes. She breathed in slowly through her mouth, then slowly let the air pass back out through her nose. Again, she breathed in, and again she let the air out. She began to imagine that she was sitting on a hill somewhere in Asia, and the wind was rustling through a copse of fifteen-foot-tall, feathery bamboo. She breathed in and breathed out, trying to concentrate on her breath. She wore flowing, saffron robes, and behind her, instead of her headboard, there was a path leading up to the door of her monastery. She had founded it, and within only two years, it had become the most famous monastery in the world. People covered tremendous distances in order to come see it and to be in her presence. She returned to the sound of her breath, inhaling and exhaling, inhaling and exhaling, in and out, and in and out.

As she sat there, meditating in front of the monastery, she sensed that she was not alone. Continuing to sit and breathe without opening her eyes, she began to feel that there was something familiar about the presence of the other. And then, all of a sudden, without looking, she knew that it was her father. Hearing of her enlightenment, he had traveled for months, first by plane, and then boat, and then train, and finally by foot, over mountains and through jungles. He had been ill prepared for such a journey, but he had refused to back down. The one thing he knew was that he had to see her, whatever the risks.

After several minutes, she raised her right hand to let him know that he was forgiven. Thanking her, he began to cry. But she gave him no more acknowledgment. She was busy breathing in and breathing out.

Realizing she had completely lost track of her breath, she opened her eyes and sighed. At this rate, it did not look likely that she would find enlightenment any time soon—certainly not soon enough to become the youngest enlightened person on the planet. *There's a chance,* she thought, *a real chance that I'll never rise above the person I am now, and never discover my true self. Or,* she thought with horror, *what if I've* already *discovered my true self?*

She inspected the pink polish on her toenails, assessing the need for a new coat.

"Emily?"

It was her father.

"Emily?" he repeated, opening the door.

She pretended to be too absorbed in her math notes to notice. She could feel him waiting for her and could hear him crunching on something—peanuts probably.

"What?" she asked, annoyed.

"How's it going?"

"How's *what* going?"

"You know. *It*. Stuff. Whatever. How are things going?"

He walked over to the bed, and she remembered a train she'd had when she was little that had magnetic buttons on the front and back of each car. If you tried putting it together backward, the magnets would repel one another, pushing the cars apart with the same forcefulness she was feeling right now.

"Dad, I'm in the middle of studying," she said as he sat down at the end of her bed. He looked exhausted, and she could see even from there that the peanuts had left a coating of salt on his upper lip.

"Well, you can go back to it after I leave. I just wanted to stop in and say hi."

"You've got salt on your mouth," she said with disgust.

He rubbed his mouth with the back of his hand, then continued to sit there, looking around the room while she willed him to leave.

"Listen," he said, "we've got to talk about something."

She folded her arms across her chest. "What?"

He began looking around again, and she could tell he was nervous.

"I heard something today which—well, if it's true, I find disturbing."

What if somehow he had found out about what she'd done to Thomas in the hospital? She realized he might think she was as morally corrupt as him—which infuriated her. She was *nothing* like her father.

"What?" she said.

"Rumor has it that you and Eric Pascal are . . . involved. Is this true?"

"No," she said icily. "That's the dumbest thing I've ever heard."

He nodded, looking simultaneously relieved and doubtful. Then he unexpectedly reached out and put his hand on her bare ankle. His hand felt strong and warm. She curled her toes, hoping that he didn't notice she was wearing nail polish—which he'd always detested.

"I know you're really angry with me," he said, "and you have every right to be. But I would hope that if anything . . . major came up, we could still talk about it."

For months she had been wishing that her father would catch wind of her affair and step in to rescue her from the adult world she had accidentally ventured into. But by now, it was basically over. She picked up her notes and raised them until he couldn't see her face. "If you're done, I'd like to get back to studying, please."

"Sure."

He got up slowly.

Peering over her papers, she watched him walk out of the room and close the door. Her eyes traveled back to the poster of Buddha. *If I can find enlightenment,* she thought, *I'll never need to talk to Dad again.*

JOE WOKE WITH A START AND, IN HIS GROGGY stupor, was unable to recall where he was. As he tried to sit up, a sharp bolt of pain in his chest concisely answered his question and forced him to surrender to the hospital bed. Stranded on this island in the middle of the room, he lay there in the darkness, listening for some sign of what had woken him. He'd thought he heard a loud crack, which his dreaming mind had attributed to a breaking chair. But now that he determined his location, he was mystified by the true source of the sound. The room was very quiet aside from the pumping and hissing of a machine sitting to the right of the bed, casting a dim orange glow on the floor and wall. Beyond the door, the daytime hustle and bustle of the hallway had been replaced by a late-night calm. It seemed that nobody and nothing stirred, and he felt as though he were the only one awake on the entire floor. After listening for a while and hearing nothing out of the ordinary, he decided that the loud crack had sounded only in his dream. His throat burned from the giant tube lodged inside, and he longed for some water or some ice cubes to soothe it. He seemed to remember Emily feeding him ice cubes earlier that day. But knowing that was impossible, he wondered whether he could have dreamed her entire visit. Had she been there at all?

Lulled by the *husk-ahh . . . , husk-ahh . . .* of the machine, he was beginning to drift off once again when his ears were met by a snore. Wide awake now, he listened and again heard the long, congested throttle, which filled him instantly with dismay. He distinctly remembered Emily telling him that Laura had gotten him a private room. So if he had a roommate, he could reasonably conclude that he had imagined Emily's visit. Though he had not dwelled on it, he realized now that the visit had given him a great deal of comfort and that somewhere in the back of his mind, he had been looking forward to her return the next day. The notion that instead he might be stuck in a strange place, surrounded by strangers, with a heart condition that had pulled him startlingly close to death and, he presumed, continued to pose some threat to his life, was terrifying. The fact that he remembered Emily and Ingrid both being there did not bode well. He wished that he were back in New York. Even trapped inside of a hospital, he would be able to feel the city's energy; it could penetrate any windowpane and reach the darkest, dreariest depths of any building. He yearned for the sight of the city's multiple, soaring towers, each speckled throughout the night with office lights and kitchen lights, work lights, party lights, and flickering, blue television lights. There was nothing for him here in the middle of the night.

He ran his hands over the area of blanket on either side of him, searching for the Dictaphone. Eventually, he found it, and because it was by now almost an extension of his own body, he needed no light to guide his finger to the right button.

He said we were going to the beach for ice cream cones. And I didn't believe him. But he really wasn't joking . . .

He could hear the exhaustion in his voice, and he wondered if he had felt anything, any signal from his body as he was speaking—a pain in his chest or in his left arm. He had remembered what was on the tape, but he couldn't remember making it. According to one of the hospital workers, a couple of motel guests had found him outside on the sidewalk. But he had no idea why he'd gone outside.

He wondered what he had at this point. Or rather, he knew what he had—he just didn't know whether it amounted to anything. He had hours of conversations between Joe and Ingrid as well as monologues in which Joe, as both the writer of the play and its main character, reflects alternately upon the girl and the play and his relationship to each. He had recorded lengthy musings on what it meant to him to create and to be a father, and how by giving life, one also—no matter how innocently—unlocks the door to suffering and death. He had also kept a record of every meal he'd eaten at the hotel, originally for the purpose of the *Contact* article and then later as the work of Joe, who was also writing a travel piece for a magazine called *Contact*. He had included other elements of his trip as well. The hotel, the motel, Albert and Julia and the Indian motel manager, the snow and ice, the moldy shower curtain and the cracked windowpane, even the embarrassing inability to control his own bladder—all of this was on tape. He had not included Amanda, though he thought now that he could use her, too. There was a tape he had made years ago of his own children when they were very young. He had discovered it one day in his hotel room among the other tapes, and he had been toying with the idea of incorporating it into the play as well. If he were able to do that, and if he were also able to talk about those children and what had happened to them—and to him—since the day that tape was made, he suspected he might have something interesting. Maybe even great. But he didn't think he wanted to do that.

Imagine what it would feel like to fall from something this high.

As Ingrid's monologue ended and he switched off the machine, he heard the sounds of fabric brushing fabric and of weight shifting in a chair. He had forgotten about the roommate and was now perplexed to find that the man was across the room, evidently in a chair rather than in the neighboring bed. As Joe moved his head to look in the direction of the noise, he saw a dark form move in the corner, condensing and lengthening as the figure seemed to lean down and sit back up. Then a tiny light switched on, and he saw a book opening and then resting in the lap of either a female or an extremely small male.

Emily? he thought hopefully.

"I'm sorry." The voice was female, but not Emily's.

His heart sank.

"I dropped my book."

That explained the loud crack, at least.

"I'm Cindy," the woman continued. "The night nurse. I hope this light doesn't bother you. My grandson got it for me."

He thought she sounded too young to have a grandson. He wondered if Cindy would be gone by the time he woke up in the morning or if he'd get to see what she looked like. She stopped talking to him and returned to her book, and for several minutes, he stared at the ceiling, listening to her turn the pages and thinking back on Emily's visit. She *must* have been to see him. He now remembered something about Laura getting him a private night nurse along with the room. Who else would have told him that? He also thought Emily might have announced that she and Clay were engaged, but he wasn't sure. He wondered if he would have grandchildren. He would like that. There was something so beautiful about children. They were so . . . what was it exactly? Young. Maybe that was all it was.

His mind wandered back again to his writing: *Imagine what it would feel like to fall from something this high.*

It was a wonderful thing to be with someone who truly believed you had all the answers—the right answers, born of strength and goodness. At a certain point, he'd almost managed to believe it himself. He wondered now whether that was really so delusional. Of course he'd never had all the answers, but he'd had enough strength and goodness in him to supply what his children needed— for a while anyway, while the questions remained relatively simple. And yes, perhaps he'd allowed them to get carried away at times, forgetting that he was only a regular run-of-the-mill guy, with plenty of flaws, just like anyone else's dad. But all children needed heroes. And so what if he'd done that not just for them but for himself, too—for the sheer joy of the way it felt.

He noticed that Cindy's pages had stopped turning, and he

guessed that she might have drifted off to sleep again. Too tired to open his eyes and look over, he lay there listening for the sound of her breath over the pump and hiss of the machines. It was a bizarre sensation to share a sleeping space with an absolute stranger. And yet, at the same time, there was something about it that felt completely natural. In sleep, one was neither alone nor with anyone, simultaneously solitary and united with every other sleeping soul.

As he slipped into slumber, he thought about his family, scattered as they were across the map, but all joined in sleep. Even Thomas was there, sleeping soundly on his hillside. Each night, the barriers between them fell away, and they all came together. *How magnificent*, he thought. *Absolutely magnificent*. And with that, he fell asleep.

When Emily came the next morning, Joe was propped up on pillows with his eyes closed, still connected to a machine by the big blue tube coming out of his mouth, and to sacks of liquid by small clear IV tubes.

He heard a soft knock on the open door and raised his eyes.

"Dad?" Emily said quietly. "Hi." She set down a duffle and a paper shopping bag on the floor, then straightening back up, walked toward him, smiling. "How are you feeling today?"

He raised a trembling hand and began to smooth down the white wisps of hair on his head. The ends of his sheets were bunched up around his calves, and his hospital gown had somehow gotten pulled forward so that it exposed his upper chest and the beginning of his bandaging.

Emily pulled the covers back down over his feet and tucked them in along the bed's baseboard.

"You seem much better, Dad," she told him, speaking a little too loudly as one might do to someone who either was deaf or could not understand English. Carefully, she reached out and took the hanging fabric of his gown's neck in her hands.

He closed his eyes—*she's here*.

"Here," she said, covering him up. She retied the gown behind his neck, then coming around to face him again, noticed the Dictaphone in his lap.

"I can come back," she told him, "if you're working."

No, he thought with panic. *Don't go.*

She stepped over to the door where she'd put down her things. "I brought you your books and tapes."

She carried the shopping bag back to the bed and set it beside him.

He pulled it closer and looked up at her with deep appreciation. But with the tube in his mouth, he could tell that she was unable to read his look.

"I got them from your motel room," she said brightly. "I figured there was no point in paying for an empty room, so I checked out for you."

She stood beside his bed, fiddling with the ring on her finger, and smiled calmly. "I assume you'll be going back home once they let you out of here?"

Yes, he wanted to say. *Definitely yes.*

"I'm sorry," she said. "I promise I didn't listen to any of them."

She seemed afraid of him, which he found surprising, and it made him wonder.

She handed him copies of the *New York Times* and the *Wall Street Journal*. "Here. I got you these."

He picked up the papers, but lacking the strength to hold them, immediately dropped them onto the bed.

She went back over to the door. "I was thinking I could shave your face for you if you'd like," she said, unzipping the duffle she'd brought in. "Would you like that?"

He wasn't sure how he felt about it, but the nurses were likely to have a conniption fit. They'd been coming in with less and less frequency, however, and since nobody was there to stop her, he figured the decision was up to Emily. Evidently, she chose to go ahead with it, and he watched her dig through the bag and gather everything that she needed—a razor, shaving cream, toning lotion—all items he recognized as his own. After a couple of minutes, she came back and took a seat on the bed beside him. She squirted a mound of shaving cream into her hand and spread it over his cheeks, his chin, his upper lip. Then she picked up the razor and carefully ran it upward from the right side of his jaw to his cheekbone.

"I've never done this before," she said. "I hope I'm not hurting you."

She swished the razor around in a bowl of water beside the bed and made another careful upward stroke. "It's kind of fun actually."

After that, she worked quietly for a while, biting her lip in concentration. When she was close to finishing, she said, "You've got around four months to get your strength back so you can walk me down the aisle." She paused for a moment, looking calmly into his eyes, then went on with her shaving. "Clay and I are getting married in May. We're doing it on the property. In the Berkshires."

He'd always assumed that whenever, if ever, Emily told him she was getting married, he'd feel all sorts of conflicting emotions. But right now, he only felt pleased—that she'd found someone, that she wanted him there, and that the Berkshires remained for her a place of joy.

She wiped his face with a towel. "There," she said. "That looks much better. I didn't do the area around your mouth because I didn't want to cut you. But I can do that after they take the tube out."

She poured some toner on her hands and patted his face. "I have no idea if this is what I'm supposed to do with this stuff." She laughed. "You can make fun of me later. I'm sure you will."

The toner stung, but the sound of her laugh and the feel of her hands patting his cheeks took him back a couple of decades.

He thrust his hand into the sack of tapes she'd given him and began to rummage through it.

"Do you want me to leave you alone for a bit?" she asked, standing up.

He tried to shake his head, and though the muscles didn't seem to move at all, the effort caused him enormous pain. Wincing, he patted the bed. She sat down again and watched while he pulled one tape after another out of the bag, looked at each one, and then dropped it back in.

"Can I help you?" she asked.

Ignoring her, he continued to sort through the bag. He eventually found what he was looking for, and ejecting the tape in the player, replaced it with the one in his hand. Emily watched as he searched out the PLAY button with his forefinger. The tremor in his hand made the finger dance as it hovered above the machine before landing with force on the correct key.

His voice, youthful and vibrant, came out of the tape player . . . *with a daisy on it—a real one.*

He switched off the machine, and after holding up his hand to tell her to wait, he hit the FAST-FORWARD button.

When the cassette started rolling again, all that could be heard was the churning of the tape, and then the unmistakable, nasal pitch of a very young Thomas cut in. Emily looked startled.

Ladies and gentlemen! he called out, full of his own importance, *May I introduce to you the most magnificent magician of all time . . . Myself, the amazing Thomas Moorefield Ascher!*

Emily smiled.

Joe had no idea where Thomas had come up with the name Moorefield, his actual middle name being Joseph, after himself. Following this announcement, there was a round of applause from his parents.

And, Thomas continued, *may I also present the supremely talented dancer—*

Here, he was interrupted by his little sister. *No! I'm not a dancer!* she whispered loudly.

Some incomprehensible, hushed dialogue ensued between the two of them before Thomas resumed his role as master of ceremonies. *And may I also present my sister, Aurora Ascher, the supremely talented trapeze artist!* Then, in his normal, kid's voice, he added, *Even though we don't have a trapeze.*

Well, if you're such a great magician, then why don't you make one? came her snappy retort.

Touché! said Joe from somewhere inside the time warp of the machine.

Joe felt Emily glance up at him, but he kept his eyes on the Dictaphone.

Nobody spoke for a little while, and there was a lot of banging around while Thomas set up his act. In the background, the crickets chirped. An owl contributed a haunting solo.

Hey, Thomas said, *I hear an owl.*

Well, I hear a bird, Emily added proudly.

It's an owl, said Thomas.

No, Emily insisted. *It's a bird.*

At this point, Laura's voice broke in. *An owl is a bird, sweetheart.*

Oh.

After this, Thomas began his banging around again, and Joe asked him if he wanted some help. Thomas said he didn't, and they all waited silently for him to start his act. Again, the crickets took center stage. Then, as if she'd been thinking about it for a while, Emily said very quietly, *Hey, Dad? What does* powerful *mean exactly?*

Abruptly, the machine shut off.

Emily looked up at him again. He could tell immediately that the tears in his eyes caught her off-guard and that she didn't know quite how to respond.

"That's it?" she asked.

He continued to stare at her. She seemed annoyed.

"How can that be it? You didn't flip it over or something, Dad?"

He'd expected the tape to please her, and was disappointed by her reaction. Several times he'd imagined playing it for her and had imagined how delighted she'd be to discover that he'd made this recording and had held on to it for all these years.

"Jesus . . ." Emily said. "I don't know why you even played that for me." Angry tears welled up in her eyes. "I mean, what was the point of that? Gosh," she said, catching a tear with the back of her hand as it rolled down her cheek. "I don't know why I'm getting so emotional about it. I mean it's really no big deal."

She tried to laugh it off, but the tears kept coming. She took a couple of deep breaths.

He reached out and grabbed her hand. She seemed surprised and embarrassed, and turned her face toward the wall so that he couldn't see it. But she didn't pull away.

Even thinking the very worst of him—that he had left Thomas sleeping in front of the fire to go fuck Gina—she was still here.

After a moment, she stood up and got a tissue, then sat back down. At some point, when he had his voice back and the moment was right, he would tell her what really happened that night in the Berkshires. But for now, all of it—even that—seemed insignificant. He reached his hand out again, and she took it.

Spring

L AURA STOOD FOR A FEW SECONDS WITH THE ME-
tal tip of her sunglasses in her mouth, comparing the vase of
flowers before her to the others to make sure that there was suffi-
cient uniformity to the arrangements. Feeling satisfied that there
was, she picked up more narcissus from the sofa, where she had
laid them on a sheet of brown paper. She and Emily had decided to
use only white flowers that bloomed in the area at this time of year:
lilacs, hyacinths, narcissus, and tulips. And that, combined with the
fact that she was arranging the flowers herself, gave her a sense of
connection to the earth she hadn't felt for a very long time.

The flowers had taken over the entire hotel suite. She'd used
every hard surface she could find in the sitting room, including the
top of the television and the minibar, for the twenty-odd square
glass vases, each of which by now held a nearly completed bouquet.
In the adjoining bedroom sat several buckets of additional flowers.

Outside, stretching over the hotel's lawn, which was just beginning to turn green, and over the regal hemlocks that rimmed the
lake, the sky remained cloudless. She had been watching the

weather channel like a fanatic for the last twenty-four hours since she'd arrived at the hotel, and so far, everything looked good. The outside temperature right now was seventy-two degrees, and the forecast for the next few days was warmer still. Even the ground at 42 Chatham Lane—normally a brown quagmire at this time of year—had held firm beneath the sharp points of Emily's heels today as the two of them had traversed the hillside to make sure the bride wasn't likely to suffer an embarrassing wipeout during either the rehearsal tonight or the actual event tomorrow.

She was relieved to see how contented her daughter seemed as they went about their business that morning, showing the wedding planner where they wanted the tables to be placed and discussing a few last-minute changes with the caterer. She was pleased, too, to observe the genuine gush of enthusiasm from both Emily and Clay as they opened the first box of programs together and admired the freshly embossed pages. Privately, she thought the William Carlos Williams poem they had selected, with its exceedingly realistic portrayal of the often selfish and tenderly cruel give-and-take of marriage, was an odd choice for the frontispiece. But it struck her as she watched them how attuned they were to each other and what a contrast they provided to the poem in their mutual generosity and desire to please. It was interesting to watch the younger generation put to work tools honed from their parents' mistakes. Having witnessed their share of bad marriages and divorces, these kids were wiser, more cautious—and, for better or worse, more cynical. And yet there was also a certain optimism which stemmed from the conviction that having seen their parents fail and having learned from those failures, they could not possibly fall prey to them, themselves.

Opening the window to let some fresh air into the oppressively fragrant room, she remembered how angry she'd gotten at Joe on the night before their own wedding. He had made a beautiful toast—so beautiful, in fact, that people couldn't stop talking about it. And even though the toast had been about her, it had felt at the time like an effort to hijack the evening for the purpose of his own grandeur. It was unsettling to think back on incidents like their rehearsal dinner now. Surprisingly, this was not so much because the old unpleasant feelings resurfaced, but because they often didn't.

The years of distance allowed her to understand something about her ex-husband that she had failed to understand before: his public persona was not simply a mask he wore for attention; on the contrary, it was as authentic and fundamentally Joe as Joe got.

Back then, she had needed to possess him, to feel that the truest part of him belonged exclusively to her rather than being something she shared with countless strangers. It would have been too painful to acknowledge that she and he simply existed on different planes: she in a miniscule, private world into which she would admit only him—if only he would come—and he in a much bigger world she could not enter without losing all sense of her self.

She was actually looking forward to the party tonight, and even her anxiety about seeing her ex-husband had a faraway, low-volume quality that kept it from infringing on the pleasure she was getting from arranging the flowers. She was so glad that she'd added the narcissus to her order at the last minute. The perky, sharp edges of their petals as well as their size made them a nice accent to the larger, heavier blooms. As she began to insert the last bunch of cut narcissus into the arrangements, a knock came at the door, and there was Earl in his business suit, standing with a duffle bag over his shoulder and a big, happy grin on his face.

"My God," he said, taking in the room.

"You made it!" Dropping the flowers, she leaped up and flung her arms around him. "What took you so long?"

He gave her a hug. "Traffic."

"I feel like I haven't seen you in *ages*." She held on for a little longer before letting him in.

He searched for a place to set down his bag. "This place looks like a floral shop."

"Here." She led him between the vases into the bedroom. "Put your stuff in here. I'll be done in two minutes, and then I'll get all this stuff out of your way."

"My God," he said. "I'm glad you hired a caterer at least."

She leaned against the doorway and smiled, adjusting the glasses on her head.

"You did, didn't you?" he asked, totally deadpan except for the glint in his eye.

She laughed. "Only because I couldn't find a decent hotel room with a kitchen in it."

Laughing, he set his bag down on the bed.

"Where's your briefcase?" she asked.

"I didn't bring it."

She raised her eyebrows in pleasant surprise. "Really?"

"I'm at your beck and call."

While she finished the flower arrangements and Earl unpacked, they called back and forth between the rooms, filling each other in on the various events of the day. He told her briefly about a pharmaceutical company he was excited about, and she brought him up to date on which friends and relatives she knew had arrived and whom she'd already run into in the lobby. After the two of them had relayed what each felt to be their most significant news, there was a period of silence, and she wondered what Emily was doing. Her daughter had said something earlier about taking a nap, but Laura doubted she'd be able to sleep. She remembered how nervous she'd been before her own weddings. Before the first, her mother had her so worked up over the idea that she might trip on her train or miss a cue for a vow or accidentally insult one of the guests, she could barely see straight. By the time she and Earl were married, she no longer cared whether or not she made a mistake during the ceremony. But, having been through one marriage, she felt tremendous trepidation standing at the threshold of a second. With these memories, the placement of each flower began to take on a type of superstitious significance, as if by the care she took, she could ensure that everything would go smoothly for Emily—not only tomorrow, but for all the years that would follow.

Please, she thought, closing her eyes for a moment and wishing for her daughter as she had wished for herself over birthday candles year after year, *please let them find happiness in each other.*

As it happened, Clay's parents and older brother were the first guests to arrive at the rehearsal, and Joe followed immediately after, pulling up alongside their car as they were getting out. While the Lees made their way up toward the tent, where Laura and Earl were standing, she watched Joe smooth down his hair in the rearview mirror, and then emerge finally into the daylight, where she could see, even from there, that he looked much the same. For the last year or so, Emily had been going on about how old and feeble he seemed—and he did look older of course, but not nearly so much as she'd expected. He'd hung his jacket on a hanger in the back of the car, and she watched him take it out and put it on, checking his reflection in the window. Then Clay's mother, father, and brother were standing in front of her, and she had to pull her attention away from him and say hello.

Luckily, she and Earl had met them before, at an engagement party for Emily and Clay. They weren't a wildly exciting bunch, but they were very nice. Over the mother's shoulder, she saw Joe stride toward them, up the gentle slope from the road—the familiar brisk gait, the same upright stance. Her heart was racing as she looked up and met his gaze.

"Hello," he said, smiling warmly at her and then Earl.

"Hi." She returned his smile, then turned back to the Lees, hoping she didn't look as nervous as she felt. "This is Emily's father," she said. "Joe Ascher."

Earl took over, introducing each of them and allowing her a moment to compose herself as they all shook hands. Finally, after saying hello to everyone else, Joe stepped toward her, and she leaned in, touching his shoulder and kissing the air beside his cheek. Her face brushed against his briefly, and she noticed that his skin felt soft, the way hers had started to lately, like an overripe apricot.

"How are you?" he asked.

"Good. It's nice to see you."

With everybody standing there, watching them, it was impossible to say anything else. So they engaged in small talk with the rest of the group until Clay and Emily arrived, and the rehearsal began.

Later that evening, during cocktails at the restaurant, she and Joe finally got a moment alone together. She had gone back to the kitchen to let the manager know they'd be ready to sit down in forty minutes or so, and as she came back out through the swinging double doors, Joe was standing right there.

"Hi," she said. "Can I get you something?"

"No." He raised his glass to show her he had his drink. "I'm fine. Thank you."

It looked like seltzer, and she hoped it was.

"Well, the rehearsal went pretty smoothly," he said. "Don't you think?"

"Yes. Thank God the weather's cooperating."

"Yes, thank God." He looked around at the crowded room with its chic bamboo paneled walls. "This seems like a nice place. How'd you find it?"

"Oh, I don't know. Somebody recommended it, I think, when we were looking. You know everything up here now is new."

He nodded.

"The food's great," Laura said. "We've eaten here a couple of times."

He nodded again.

"Are you going to make a toast?" she asked.

"I thought I would. Are you?"

"I don't know. Maybe tomorrow."

He looked concerned. "Should I wait until tomorrow?"

"No, no," she reassured him. "Tonight's really the night for it, and I'm sure you've got something perfect prepared."

"I haven't really. I was up all night trying. I'm hoping it will come together at the last minute."

"I'm sure it will."

There was a pause, and they both watched the other guests for a moment.

"Where are you—," she began at the very same moment he started to speak.

"Who's the—I'm sorry. What?"

"Oh, no. I was just going to ask where you're staying."

"At home."

She gave him a surprised look. "So you're driving?"

"Yes. I wasn't in the mood for a hotel."

She nodded understandingly. "I was sorry to hear about your heart attack."

"Thank you. And thank you, by the way, for the arrangements you made at the hospital. I should have written a note. I meant to—"

"Don't be silly," she said. "How are you doing now?"

"Good, I suppose. I'm slowly learning to live with the new rules. And I've perfected the fine arts of grilling, poaching, and steaming."

She laughed. "Well, you look great."

"Thank you. So do you."

She looked away. "What was it you were going to ask?"

"Oh. I was wondering who that young woman is. The maid of honor."

"Liz. You didn't meet her? I'll introduce you. Come on."

Laura started to step forward, but he stopped her. "No, I met her earlier—at the rehearsal."

"Oh," she said, confused, then realizing what he meant, explained, "she and Emily work together."

"I see."

He smiled at her tenderly as if to say it was nice to see her again. She was struck by the recollection of what it had been like to be married to this man: she had wanted him to soar—and to feel the rush of gliding on the strength of his wings—at the same time, fearing the intoxication of flight would cause him to forget her and leave her behind. And so she'd fought against herself, trying simultaneously to launch him and ground him.

"Are you working on anything at the moment?" she asked.

"Yes—in a way."

She waited for him to elaborate, but he switched the subject back to her.

"I hear you're doing wonderful things with the organization you started."

She smiled modestly. "It's very fulfilling work."

"I would imagine so. I've always thought you'd be great at running a business or an organization of your own."

"Really?" It was surprising to hear him say this, and she wondered what particular talents or skills he had noticed to make him draw such a conclusion—especially since she herself had only become aware of them in the last few years.

"Of course," he said with total conviction. "I always used to tell you that."

"You did? I don't remember."

It would have made such a difference, she thought. She considered saying as much, then realized perhaps she was wrong. He had failed to save her from herself. But who wouldn't have?

Just then, Earl came up and put his hand on her elbow.

"I'm sorry," he told Joe before turning back to her. "The bartender wants to know if he can open the red wine you're using for dinner."

"He's already out of the other?"

"Apparently."

"Excuse me," she said to Joe. "I've got to go deal with this."

In fact, she could have very easily sent the answer back with Earl, but she was happy for the chance to slip away. The conversation with Joe had gone on long enough.

After she told the bartender to go ahead and open the dinner wine, she pulled Earl through the closed doors, into the dining room, where all of the tables were set and ready.

"Hold me," she said.

And he did.

Emily and Clay walked down the stone path of the restaurant's front lawn. She turned and waved to her mother and Ella Greenberg, who were still standing together on the restaurant steps.

"See you in the lobby at nine a.m.!" Laura called.

If it hadn't been for her mother stepping in and explaining to Ella that Emily really needed to go so that she could get some sleep, Ella might have blabbered on all night about what wonderful times they all used to have up here when they visited, picnicking in the fields and—when Emily, Thomas, and Randy Junior were still young—catching frogs in the creek and chasing chipmunks along the old tumbled-down stone walls.

Earlier, Emily had watched Randy Junior, aka Rick Renzwig, working the room with his usual, remarkable smoothness. Her father had pointed him out while they were standing together in line for the buffet, referring to him rather hilariously as "the artist formerly known as Randy Greenberg." She was surprised to find her father in such good spirits, so much so that at a particular moment during the rehearsal, she had leaned in close—ostensibly to whisper something about the judge, but really so that she could sniff his breath. She had been relieved not to detect any trace of alcohol then and relieved to observe as the night wore on that he shunned the limitless flow of wine and champagne in favor of mineral water.

It was remarkable how drastically his appearance had changed since he'd stopped drinking. He was thinner—a little on the gaunt side even, for someone his age—and the redness in his face had faded to a rosy pink. But, more important, since his heart attack, he was more pleasant to be around. She still, of course, had difficulty communicating with him. And there were frequent signs that he remained as narcissistic as ever. Tonight, for example, she noticed that he wore a small bronze medal pinned to the lapel of his jacket, which she knew to be an award he'd received years ago for his writing or possibly his acting. It had annoyed but also amused her to think that as he was getting dressed that afternoon, alone in his apartment, he had actually had the impulse to dig up this small treasure and decorate himself with it. It seemed so childishly transparent, this little gesture—this need to bring to her rehearsal dinner some proof of his importance for everyone to see. What had annoyed her more, however, was the scene he had caused while the family photographs were being taken. For some reason—she guessed in order to make himself the center of attention—he had disappeared so that everyone had to wait, standing in their places for about ten minutes while the photographer went in search of him. Then, once he finally showed up, he refused to be in any photographs with Earl. Though after much coaxing, he finally relented, it made her furious that he'd felt justified in allowing his need for the limelight and his jealousy of his ex-wife's spouse to intrude upon everyone else's enjoyment of the evening—particularly hers.

Seeing her parents together tonight had brought up a mixture of strange and conflicting sensations. In a way, the reunion felt like the most natural thing in the world. But there were times, too, when she would glance up and find them either eyeing each other warily across the room or speaking politely to one another, looking so incongruous, side by side, that it was impossible to conceive they'd ever felt strongly enough toward one another to get married—and to stay married for twenty years. She wished that after all the time that had passed since they'd last seen each other, they could have made a bit more of an effort tonight. It would have been so easy for her mother, seeing that her father was feeling left out, to introduce him around to several of the guests he didn't know. By the same token, her father might have dropped his guard and approached her mother—and Earl—with less suspicion and less obvious distaste.

She was tired of dealing with her family, tired of dealing with everyone else's faults and foibles, including Clay's mother's bossiness and Ella's teary-eyed sentimentalism. Even her mother had commanded a good share of attention earlier that morning with her silly attack of nerves about the weather and other things—like how well Emily would be able to negotiate the hillside in her heels. In fact, the only person who she could honestly say had behaved completely admirably over the last couple of days was—thank God—the man who was now walking beside her and to whom she would soon give a solemn vow to share the rest of her life.

As they arrived at their Honda, they heard a couple drunkenly call out, "Good luck!" from somewhere in the darkness. Laughing, they realized the voices belonged to one of Clay's friends from college and Emily's maid of honor.

"Did those two hook up?" Emily whispered across the roof of the car.

"Who knows?"

"Thanks!" Clay yelled back before climbing into the car and slamming the door shut.

"Ahhhh," Emily sighed, dropping into the passenger seat. "Tell me again why we didn't elope."

"Because we're cowards," he said, backing the car out of the lot.

She watched the headlights pull white clouds of mist out of the darkness as the car weaved its way through the forest. Driving around here on foggy nights always made her feel like she was in one of those old film noirs where somebody was waiting for the car at the shipping docks or the warehouse or the mansion—with a gun. Unaware of this, the main characters drove on in silence, their headlights forming a golden sphere in the fog around their car.

"What was the deal with my dad creating that major drama in the middle of the photo session?"

"What about my mom?" Clay asked. "The entire day, she's done nothing but come to me with one thing after another that she's freaking out about. I swear to God, we're two seconds away from starting the rehearsal, and she's going on and on about having to climb the hill. I really think she half believed I was going to say, 'Oh, wait. You know what, Mom? Don't worry about it. We'll move the ceremony.'"

"Why does he always have to make himself the center of attention?"

"Did you hear what I said?"

"Yes. But, did you hear what I said? I mean he's so crazy, don't you think? I honestly think my dad's a little bit crazy."

"Well . . . consider this. Tomorrow we'll be on a plane."

"Thank God." She leaned down and began undoing the tiny buckles on the straps of her shoes. "Hey," she said, excited. "Let's go see if they finished putting up the tent."

"I thought you wanted to go to sleep."

She was turned around now, fishing a pair of sneakers out of the backseat.

"I changed my mind."

When they arrived at the property, the tent was up, and the crew who'd made such a racket throughout the rehearsal had all gone home. Clay held back one of the weatherproofed, canvas flaps that served as a door, and she entered.

"Wow," she said. "This looks pretty good."

She crossed to the opposite side of the tent and opened those flaps as well. Since the property was at a lower elevation than the restaurant, there was no fog. And once they'd tied up most of the flaps, the land, bright with moonlight, was visible all around them.

"They even laid the dance floor down," Clay remarked.

It was a rhetorical statement as Emily was now standing in the center of the dance floor, bouncing up and down on the balls of her feet to test the springiness of the wood.

"Want to practice?" Clay asked, joining her on the floor.

"*Again?*" she moaned.

He took her hands and began spinning her around. Laughing, she began to cooperate, the rubber soles of her sneakers squeaking along and tripping her up every now and then.

"Come on, twinkle toes," Clay laughed as she crashed into him, "show me what you've got!"

She fell against his chest, panting and laughing. "I can't do this anymore! I'm going to sprain my ankle. Let's take a break."

He let her lead him outside.

"What's this?" she asked, pointing to a champagne bottle and a sack of short, clear plastic cups sitting on the ground outside the tent.

"Oh." He leaned down and picked up the bottle. "The guys brought this to the rehearsal. I guess they left it. There's still some in here. Want to try it?"

"Sure."

He drew a couple of cups out of the bag and split the remainder of the champagne between them.

Emily took her cup from him and tapped it against his. "Cheers."

"Cheers."

"Woohoo!" she yelled after swallowing a mouthful.

"Watch it," he teased, wrapping his arm around her waist. "You're probably going to have to build up a tolerance for that stuff."

"I can't believe we're really getting married," she said, grabbing him in a tight hug.

"I know," he whispered.

They held each other for a while. From the direction of the creek, there came a low rhythmic murmur.

"The bullfrogs trump!" Emily whispered in his ear then laughed.

He gave her a perplexed look. "What's that mean?"

"It's something we used to say when we were little. I think it's from Emerson or Thoreau or somebody like that."

She looked up at the moon. "I want to walk up to the top of the hill."

"Really?" he asked. "Now?"

"Yeah. After tomorrow, it will always be the place where we got married. Right now it's not."

He nodded. "Do you want me to come with you?"

"No. I'll be back in a few minutes," she said, wandering off.

On the hillside, the moonlight spangled silver threads along individual branches. But mostly, it was the apple blossoms that were visible, standing out like white blankets of snow in the dark. There was a path that had been mowed for people to use today and tomorrow, but she decided not to take it. Walking slowly through the thick new meadow, she was reminded of the silly walking meditations she used to do on the property, and it made her smile at her own naiveté. She was reminded, too, of a night sometime well before she met Clay when she had been up late, studying for several days straight with the television on in the background for company. She thought it must have been during second-year finals, but she couldn't remember for sure now. She only remembered the crushing loneliness she'd felt at the time. In the middle of the night, she'd driven up here by herself—the full three hours—so that she could sit up on this hillside, under the trees for a while.

It was a relief to know that there would be no more nights like that.

When she reached the grove of apple trees, she sat down on the ground. The grass, which had felt so prickly earlier that day, now lay flat and smooth after being trodden by several dozen pairs of shoes. She tried to imagine what the scene would look like from this spot tomorrow, with all of those people standing around, staring at her and Clay and the judge. Later, the big-band strains of a trumpet and a stand-up bass would drift up from the tent. And the people, milling about the lawn in colorful dresses and dark suits, would look like ants from up here.

The wind blew down a shower of pollen-laced petals, and she sneezed.

"Here," she said, wiping her nose and pouring a little champagne out of her cup onto the ground. "Cheers."

It still felt a little strange to be drinking after abstaining for thirteen years.

"I've decided it's all right," she said out loud, feeling the need to explain herself to Thomas. "I've decided I'm not dead."

As she heard the last word come out of her mouth, she laughed, shocked.

"What I meant to say was, 'I'm not Dad.'"

～

> For my young poet,
>
> You are so young, so much before all beginning, and I would like to beg you . . . as well as I can, to have patience with everything unresolved in your heart and to try to love the questions themselves as if they were locked rooms or books written in a very foreign language. Don't search for the answers, which could not be given to you now, because you would not be able to live them. And the point is, to live everything. Live the questions now. Perhaps then, someday far in the future, you will gradually, without even noticing it, live your way into the answer.
> —R.M.R.
>
> Love, Dad

Joe sat at his desk, still dressed in his new, lightweight wool suit. He'd only been home for an hour, but he was very happy with his decision not to stay in a hotel.

There was a moment tonight, during the screening of Emily's bridesmaids' video, when he and Laura had locked eyes. She'd smiled at him briefly before turning back to the screen, and he thought he'd detected an element of pity in her smile. Was it brought on by the simple fact that he was alone? Or was the look a reflection of something more sinister? A judgment passed on the state of his health? Or of his career?

He resented that nobody ever bothered to consider he might be alone by choice. The promise of something new and unexpected, so alluring to him when he was younger, now put him off. He was too old and too tired for the little discoveries made while building a relationship from scratch. Some of the discoveries were sure to be delightful, but he lacked the tolerance for those that weren't.

Laura looked surprisingly beautiful. That stunned quality she used to have was now gone. He hoped that it wasn't his absence that had allowed her to soften. But tonight he didn't wish to dwell on the past. He was doing pretty well, all things considered. It was certainly odd to be back on the old property for the rehearsal and afterward, at the restaurant, to be confronted by so many familiar faces. But he was not as unnerved by it as he had expected to be. Amazingly enough, even his body's call for a drink remained relatively quiet—more an occasional whisper than the constant, deafening scream that plagued him shortly after he left the hospital.

He had admittedly felt a little awkward talking to Burt and Jan Horvath in the beginning, especially once it became clear that they saw Laura and Earl fairly regularly and that Jan was to be seated next to Earl during dinner. But as the evening progressed and everyone began to loosen up, things became easier. At a certain point, watching Burt stoop with difficulty to pick up a cocktail napkin that had fluttered off the table when he lifted his glass, all of the old affection came flooding back, and Joe found himself overwhelmed by gratitude for this one constant in his life. It was amazing to realize that having been through a marriage, a divorce, the births of two children and the death of one, a heart attack, and now his daughter's marriage, there still remained by his side the same human being with whom he began shooting marbles on a Bronx sidewalk when their pasts consisted of six short years. He tried not to chastise himself too much for letting the friendship slip away after his divorce. He looked forward to seeing Burt and Jan again tomorrow and to learning more about their travels. Burt, as it turned out, had retired three years ago, and the two of them had been adventurously exploring the world ever since. It was possible that he might even join them on a future expedition.

He pulled the white handkerchief out of his pocket and unfolded it. Finding a mix of flesh-colored makeup, black mascara, and bright orange lipstick on the once pristine cloth, he balled it up and threw it in the wastebasket beneath the desk. Clay's mother— a redhead with feet so tiny it was hard to believe they supported the rest of her body—had teetered as fast as her little hoofs could carry her over to the bride and groom as soon as the rehearsal ended, leaving everyone else to eat her dust. Being the one man who was not helping a wife, mother, or bridesmaid negotiate the rough terrain, Joe soon found himself standing directly behind her while she hugged and kissed her way between the bride and groom in a manner that was, at best, vaguely intrusive, and at worst, revoltingly self-centered. Then, when he thought she was going to finally step aside and clear the way for him and the rest of the group, she grabbed his forearm with both of her plump, manicured hands, and began to cry. Drawing the crisp, white handkerchief out of his breast pocket, he reluctantly pulled the woman toward him so that everyone else could proceed past them into the vans that were waiting to take them to the restaurant.

"Wasn't that gorgeous?" she sniveled, taking his handkerchief and dabbing with it at her rouged cheeks. "He's my baby, you know."

"Yes, I know." He looked around for her husband—an exceptionally nice and soft-spoken Korean man who resembled Clay in both appearance and manner—but didn't see him anywhere.

"I suppose it's different for fathers," she went on. "Also, you gave Emily up at such a young age, this is probably peanuts for you."

He nodded, then realized he wasn't quite sure what she was saying. "I'm sorry?"

"Well, because of the divorce, I mean. Wasn't Emily still very young?"

"Fifteen," he answered sharply.

"Oh, I guess I'm confused. Somehow I thought that Emily had grown up with Earl."

"Earl?"

"I'm sorry," she said, then used one of his least favorite expressions. "My bad. Please don't take that the wrong way. I don't even know which way is up right now. They just seem so close, I thought . . . Well . . ."

Noticing that she was about to miss out on a seat in the first van, she shoved his handkerchief back into his hand and mumbled something about "helping out"—though whether she was thanking him or simply informing him of her duty to take the next available seat, he couldn't tell.

For the next hour, he couldn't help wondering what it was that could have possibly given her the impression that Emily and Earl were so close. He watched them together, and while they were certainly polite with one another—even friendly—they hardly seemed *close*. The possibility did not escape him that, perchance, Clay's mother had pettily concocted her little "misunderstanding" as a reprimand for failing her baby's sweetheart. He felt like a paranoid lunatic. And yet he was also unable to shake the notion that he had been discussed among the various people in the midst of whom he stood, as the problematic relative—the difficult father, the impossible ex-spouse.

He was still gripped by this idea when the photographer came over and told him everyone else was already in place for the family photo.

"Dad," Emily called, as he rounded the corner of the building. "Come on. Get over here."

"That's okay," he replied. "Why don't you do this one with Earl."

As soon as the words escaped his lips, he knew he'd made a mistake. A hush fell over the lineup, and all eyes shifted about uncomfortably.

"Dad, what are you talking about? Come on."

Earl started to step away. "Joe, you stand here. I'll sit this one out."

"No." Emily grabbed Earl's arm. "You stay. We're all going to be in it together."

Mortified, Joe walked over to the assemblage of relatives, looking to the photographer for some indication of where to stand. She placed him between Uncle Pat and Laura, who kept her eyes focused straight ahead as he took his position beside her.

Looking at his computer once again, he reread the passage that he'd transcribed from Rilke. There was something about it that didn't feel right. Not only was the poet quoted in nauseating abundance by every writer, toastmaster, or speaker searching for the right note of subdued sentimentality for, say, a commencement address or a wedding ceremony, but the words also seemed to refer too heavily to a time in his relationship with his daughter when she was a child and both needed and wanted his guidance.

He looked across the room at the blinking light on his answering machine, which he had been avoiding ever since he'd returned home that evening. He suspected that it was a message from his friend at Williamstown, and he dreaded hearing what the man had to say. Reminding himself that the dread was always worse than the actual, dreaded event, he pushed himself out of his chair and shuffled in his socks across the rug to the machine.

"Friday. Five. Fifty. Two. p. m.," said the mechanized voice.

"Oh, hi, Joe. It's Robert. Got your message, and ah . . . Well, we should talk about it. Of course it would be nice to have a new play to put on. But it's not essential. And ah . . . I understand. If you don't have one, you don't have one. So let's figure out what to do instead. I've got some ideas. But I want to hear yours, too. So let's talk next week. I'm away this weekend. But ah . . . Don't worry. It'll be good. Have a good weekend. Talk soon."

The machine beeped.

Worried that he might have missed something in the message, he played it again.

He'd heard right; he didn't have to write a play.

He didn't have to write a play! *This is the end of it then,* he thought as he crossed back to his desk. Ingrid would not exist. Nor would Joe—at least not the version of himself he had created this time around.

With a tinge of nostalgia, he thought back to the day in the Jefferson garden when he'd first come up with the character of Ingrid. There had been that girl—an actual, living and breathing girl—whom he'd caught peering in at him through the bushes and whom Albert had shooed away. He'd only seen her eyes, but it was such a funny, wonderful moment. And he'd hoped to catch a glimpse of her again—to get a chance to see what she looked like and to talk to her about herself and what it was that brought her there. Regrettably, however, he never saw her again. The play wasn't really about her anyway, of course. Still, he felt a certain sadness that both she and the character had now slipped away into the past.

Sitting down once again, he moved the Rilke book aside and erased what he had written.

Dear Emily, he wrote. He could barely type fast enough to keep up with the words as they poured out of his head.

Dear Emily,

Do you remember that night, so many years ago, when we sat together outside under the full moon, and you noticed that the moon was shining in your cup and also in mine? I was thinking today about that night and how we said that no matter where we were and how far apart, we could always hold the same moon in each of our cups.

I realize it might seem absurd to you that I'm hearkening back to this now. But I want you to know that I'm not so unfeeling, nor myopic, as I may sometimes seem. There is much about my behavior of the last several years that I deeply regret, one of the most significant things being that I have managed in my stupidity to make us near-strangers to each other when we used to be, I think, great friends. This letter is not intended as a substitute for the time and effort required to gain back your trust and your friendship; I'm not sure that those blessings even lie within the realm of possibility anymore. But the horrible thought occurred to me when I was in the hospital that you may not know—and might never know unless I tell you—how much I value the times we've shared or how often I revisit those conversations we used to have.

This evening, as I watched you and Clay together at the wedding rehearsal, I was reminded of the quote you once recited to me by Vincent van Gogh, "One may have a blazing hearth in one's soul, and yet no one ever come to sit by it." Well, Emily, I can honestly say to you that I always knew your hearth would never lack for company. But I must admit that I doubted whether you would ever allow yourself to settle beside that of another. I could see in your face tonight that you have found the warmth and the light for which some people search their entire lives, and for that I am truly happy.

Love, Dad

Laura watched the last groomsman and bridesmaid pass by on their way toward the central apple tree, where the other members of the wedding party were already lined up on either side of Clay and the female judge. With the exception of the bride, everyone who was playing a role in the ceremony was dressed in shades of beige, and Laura admired the way they all looked against the pale pink blossoms in the light of the setting sun. As the man and woman who had just passed took their place in the lineup and the cellist switched to the lively Bach piece that Clay and Emily had chosen to accompany the flower girl, Laura began to get butterflies. Squeezing Earl's hand, she turned to look back over her shoulder—and past the several dozen guests assembled behind her—at her daughter.

Luminous in her simple cream-colored silk gown, Emily was leaning down to urge the flower girl forward. With intense concentration, the child started up the short stretch of hill, carefully placing one foot directly in front of the other as if she were on a high wire. Once the girl had made it halfway to her destination without any problems, Emily turned to her father.

"Dad?" she said quietly.

"Yes?"

He was watching the flower girl with great amusement.

"Thank you."

"I don't think she's got any petals left," he said. "Look. She's miming. How cute."

Emily touched his shoulder to direct his attention away from the child.

"I read your note."

"Oh. Already?" he asked.

She gave him a perplexed look. "Well, yes. It was in my bag."

Shifting restlessly from one foot to another, he mumbled something about thinking she wouldn't get it until she was on the plane.

She ran her hand down his arm and squeezed his palm. "Thank you, Dad."

"Sure," he said, motioning toward her feet. "C'mon. Put your shoes back on. That little girl's already halfway there."

Steadying herself on his arm, she flipped a creamy satin pump over with her right big toe and stepped into it.

The cellist drew out the last few notes to give the flower girl time to take her place. Then she raised her bow to signal them.

Joe checked again to see that Emily had her shoes on.

"That's our cue. You ready?"

"I think so," she said.

"Then here we go. Break a leg."

She smiled nervously. "You, too."

Though they moved slowly to the accompaniment of the cello, the distance was short, and they covered it in little time. When they arrived beneath the apple branches, Joe shook Clay's hand and gave Emily a kiss on the cheek just the way they had rehearsed it the day before. Then, having finished his part, he went to stand with the rest of the guests.

After everyone had finally stopped moving and the cellist had finished playing, there was a brief moment of stillness during which Emily looked around, taking in the judge in front of her, Clay at her side, and behind them, all of the people she and Clay had gathered to witness this occasion. Above, the branches swayed in the breeze, and she felt as if she could sense a few last buds pushing open.

The sun and the moon, which had each circled the crest of this westward-facing hill almost five thousand times in the last thirteen years, were now traveling together. The sun, a brilliant red fireball on the verge of dipping down below the horizon, had begun to tint the sky and the clouds in shades of pink and violet that were growing more unnaturally vivid by the second. And against this changing backdrop, the moon seemed to hang like a giant pearl suspended over the heads of everyone there—the friends, the acquaintances, and the beautiful strangers.

ACKNOWLEDGMENTS

First and foremost, to Dorian Karchmar, an exceptional agent and invaluable partner: my deepest thanks for the insights and enthusiasm brought to each draft over the past two years. Enormous thanks as well to my editor, Helen Atsma, for her passion and expert guidance, to Dan Farley for publishing me, and to my wonderful copy editor, Vicki Haire, and to Jennifer Rudolph Walsh for her faith in me and this book. I am also grateful to the following people for their help: Daniel Alitowski, Claudia Ballard, Carin Besser, Caroline Cheng, Molly Doyle, Robert Glick, Adam Schear, Jonathan Marc Sherman, Alice Truax, Joanne Wiles, Andy Young, and Harris Yulin. Lastly, for their support, I owe loads of gratitude to my family: my mother, my father, my sister—and of course, my husband, who encouraged me to write this novel, then provided inspiration, advice, and loving patience throughout the process.

DISCUSSION QUESTIONS

1. What were your first impressions of Emily and her family? How did your opinions of them shift as you learned about their shared history? What are the most striking differences in the way they each experienced Thomas's death?

2. Did anyone do anything "wrong" during the therapy session with Dr. Shepherd, or was the impasse between Emily and Joe already simply too great? What does Joe really mean when he blurts out, "I didn't do anything"?

3. Joe and Laura's marriage was on rocky ground even before Joe's affair and the events surrounding Thomas's death. Why were they growing apart? Did their difficulties seem insurmountable?

4. Emily and Thomas have a complicated—though loving—relationship. How does the dynamic between them compare to your own experience of siblings? Could you understand Emily's

need to act out during Thomas's illness? Could her parents have done more for her during that period?

5. How does Earl handle his role as a stepfather and second husband? Does Laura respond to him differently from the way she responded to Joe? Do the two men have any traits in common?

6. What does Ramon's case represent to Emily? What makes her well suited to her job as his attorney?

7. Clay and Emily experience a turning point in their relationship on their holiday ski trip. What is the source of their fights? Were you rooting for them to work things out? How do their personalities complement each other?

8. What memories does Ingrid stir in Joe? In turn, what does she need from him? Did learning the truth about who Ingrid really is surprise you?

9. What are Joe's motivations in taking Thomas on a trip to the country? How are Laura and Emily affected not just by Thomas's death but by the way he died? Do the circumstances that led to Thomas's pneumonia warrant blame?

10. What does *The Embers* reveal about trust and authentic love? What enables the Ascher family to grieve and to feel hope again? Has your family experienced a similar loss that was never fully addressed?